William Sloane Kennedy

John G. Whittier, the Poet of Freedom

William Sloane Kennedy

John G. Whittier, the Poet of Freedom

ISBN/EAN: 9783743422889

Manufactured in Europe, USA, Canada, Australia, Japa

Cover: Foto ©Andreas Hilbeck / pixelio.de

Manufactured and distributed by brebook publishing software (www.brebook.com)

William Sloane Kennedy

John G. Whittier, the Poet of Freedom

JOHN G. WHITTIER

The Poet of Freedom

BY

WILLIAM SLOANE KENNEDY

<hr>

" He that knows anything worth communicating and does not communicate it, let him be hanged by the neck."—TALMUD.

<hr>

PRINTED IN THE UNITED STATES

New York

FUNK & WAGNALLS COMPANY

LONDON AND TORONTO

1892

PREFACE.

WHILE the manuscript of this volume was lying in the safe of the publishers, I made a little Whittier itinerary along the storied Essex coast,—a voyage through Whittier ballad-land, bringing before my eyes the very scenes of the poems in the study of the sources of which in the libraries I had made such delightful and exciting discoveries. After adventures manifold and pleasant I found myself on the top of Powow Hill, that rises just above our poet's old home in Amesbury. From this coigne of vantage the eye takes in, in one swift *coup d'œil*, a mighty spread of landscape and sea, beginning with conical Agamenticus, violet-dim and far, in Maine, resting for a moment on the Isles of Shoals, Little Boar's Head, Great Boar's Head, and Salisbury Beach, traveling along the tumbled sand dunes of the Ipswich coast, catching over the blue sea-floor the white sparkle of the houses of Cape Ann, fetching a compass over Danvers and Haverhill, to finally rest on the far range of the Pawtuckaway Hills. This is Essex County with its winding roads, old shingled barns, huge stranded rocks, sea estuaries, clean quiet little sea towns and rugged honest folk,—the Attica of Massachusetts. What the view from Powow Hill is to the traveler I hope this book will be to the indoor reader of Whittier's ballads. I have done my best to show that Flood Ireson was justly tarred and feathered, that John Brown did stoop to kiss the slave child, that Barbara Frietchie did wave that historic flag in the face of the Confederate troops, that at

Lucknow both loud and sweet " the pipes of rescue blew," that Whittier's story of the wreck of the " Palatine " is true to the letter, and that the romantic story of Harriet Livermore is truth stranger than fiction. If, however, you observe with curious interest how very often the poet slips in minor matters of historical accuracy in his rhymed poems, you may ponder the words of Ruskin where he tells us that " a lovely legend is all the more precious when it has *no* foundation." Cincinnatus or any other man might have plowed a field fifty times over and it would have signified little to us ;. but if no Cincinnatus existed at all, and yet the Roman people, to express their conviction that tilling the soil is a noble occupation, invented a Cincinnatus out of hand and enshrined him for all time in their literature,—" this precious coinage out of the brain and conscience of a mighty people " we had better take to heart most diligently.

The full story of the part Whittier played in the anti-slavery movement is here set down for the first time in book form. Many interesting and unexpected things plowed up during my researches into such subjects as the mobbings in which Whittier was a sufferer, the burning of Pennsylvania Hall in Philadelphia, the estrangement of years which Garrison's narrow intolerance produced between himself and Whittier, with the subsequent reconciliation of the two, and the story of the rise and fall of the Liberty Party, the lineal predecessor of the party that saved the Union.

Belmont, Mass.

CONTENTS.

JOHN G. WHITTIER.

CHAPTER I.

ON THE FARM.

In July, 1867, Bayard Taylor wrote to his friend, Edmund Clarence Stedman, from Friedrichroda in the Thüringian forest: "How delighted I am with Whittier's success! Fields writes that his 'Tent' has already sold twenty thousand copies. Here is a man who has waited twenty-five years to be generally appreciated. I remember when his name was never mentioned without a sneer, except by the small Abolition clique. In England, too, they are now beginning to read him for the first time." [1]

These statements of Whittier's friend are true in the main, but need to be somewhat qualified and annotated. It will hardly do to say that Whittier was not generally appreciated previous to 1866–67, when we remember that an edition of his collected works had been reviewed with high praise by Edwin P. Whipple as early as 1848; that in 1857 he had helped to establish the "Atlantic Monthly," and that in the

[1] Life and Letters of Bayard Taylor, ii. 479.

same year the little two-volume blue and gold edition of his poems was published by Ticknor & Fields, and had a tolerably large circulation throughout the country. And it is further to be noted that his " Kansas Emigrants " song had been sung from Massachusetts Bay to the Missouri River by the pioneer settlers of the debated ground ; that the maturest creations of his art had been published (such ballads as " Maud Muller," " Barbara Frietchie," " Skipper Ireson," " Mabel Martin," " Telling the Bees," and " The Pipes at Lucknow ") ; and that at least two of his war poems—" Ein' Feste Burg " and " Song of the Negro Boatmen "—had been sung in the Northern armies.

Still, it is a fact that the publication in 1866–67 of " Snow-Bound " and " The Tent on the Beach," with its included ballads, greatly increased the poet's fame. For thirty-five years he had been chiefly known as the bard of a despised cause. But the war had come and gone, the slaves had been freed, and in any case the people of the whole country would have turned with reverence to the pages of the poet of freedom ; but his idyl " Snow-Bound," and his beautiful ballads, lifted him into the rank of a national poet, and he has since been greeted as such on both sides of the sea.

There is fitness in the title " Poet of Freedom " as applied to John G. Whittier; for the master-passion of his soul is hatred of tyranny. When there is no brother-man, heart-broken and in chains, to rescue, no inhumanity to arraign in words of withering scorn, then he finds a little leisure to write ballads and songs. I find by actual

count that in more than a third of his poems freedom
is either the main theme or is alluded to in passing.
In love of liberty and the singleness of aim with which
he has devoted his life to its defense Whittier re-
sembles John Brown. In both, the moral idea flames
out with volcanic power. Both were sinewed by out-
door life. But John Brown was a mechanism of steel
and iron ; the soul of Whittier may be likened to the
frail plant *Dictamnus* set in a porcelain vase,—a plant
which on a hot day is surrounded by an inflammable
gas that ignites with a sudden flash when a flame is
applied to it.

In the later poetical work of Whittier—that produced after the Civil War—purely literary topics
naturally predominate, although at irregular intervals the old lyre of freedom is taken up, either to
chant a pæan for some triumph of human rights at
home or abroad or to strike the minor chords over
the passing away of a comrade of the old anti-
slavery days. Indeed, for several years before the
war broke out, he had been engaged in purely literary
work (Songs of Labor and folk ballads). So it is
evident that the lines of his intellectual development
were not altogether determined by national or
political events, nor were precisely coincident with
these, but that his growth followed the common law
of men and nations,—first the age of manly energy,
self-assertion, and moral strife ; then an epoch of
peace, in which the ideal arts, after long slumber,
suddenly crystallize into shapes of beauty.

Although the lives of poets are seldom rich in
dramatic events, they are often ennobled by rare
friendships and set in an interesting environment. In

the case of Whittier, extreme dislike of publicity has
not availed to conceal his personal adventures in the
anti-slavery crusade, nor to keep enthusiastic friends
from printing descriptions of his personal appearance
and ways. After all, his life has been a semi-public
one, and I feel sure our dear friend will forgive me
for just weaving into a connected narrative such
matters as may permissibly be known of his outward
life.

The rugged and hilly old county of Essex, Massachusetts, may be called the cradle of American
poets ; for in its town of Haverhill, by the Merrimack, the poet Whittier was born (December 17,
1807 [1]), and in the neighboring town of Newbury
lived the immediate ancestors of Longfellow and
Lowell. The old farm-house, the birthplace of
Whittier, is only five miles from the ancestral estate
of the Longfellows. Three miles to the southeast
lies the town of Haverhill. The Whittier farm is at
the junction of the main road to Haverhill and a
cross-road to Plaistow. It is so situated, in a de-
pression between surrounding hills, that no other
house is visible from it in any direction. The whole
locality reminds one of the " Knobs " of Kentucky,
being made up of gently rounded hills set close
together. In the Great West they call such rough
land as this "sassy country." On the road to Haver-

---

[1] Some one having raised a doubt as to the exact date of his
blrth, Mr. Whittier humorously said, " I cannot say positively from
my personal knowledge when I was born, but my mother told me
it was on the 17th of December, 1807, and she was a very truthful
woman."

hill you pass, on the left, Kenoza lake,—so christened by Whittier,—filled with purest water, and terraced by thick-wooded slopes. A little farther on, the road skirts the base of a high hill crowned by a castellated stone dwelling, from which one catches glimpses, far off, of blue Monadnock and many New England towns, sparkling white on the slopes of azure hills.

Past Haverhill winds the placid Merrimack, now made classic by the genius of Whittier. Born amid the snows and springs of the White Mountains ; taking tribute of many crystal streams as it flows south; its mountain brawling hushed by a plunge through the deeps of beautiful Winnepesaukee ; sliding through the grassy meadows of Concord studded with elms ; fretting and chafing among the rapids of Suncook and Hookset ; turning successively the wheels of the huge mills of Manchester, Nashua, Lowell, and Lawrence ; passing by Haverhill, New-bury, Amesbury, the mouth of the winding and narrow Powow, the silver Quasycung, and the bough-hung Artichoke, and at its mouth separating .the towns of Newburyport and Salisbury,—it finally falls into the sea at Ipswich Bay.

It is about seventeen miles from Haverhill, down the river, to Newburyport ; and about half way down lies Amesbury, at the junction of the Powow with the main stream. Amesbury was the home of Whittier for twenty-five years ; and he still owns his house there, and keeps in it a study, with a few books and pictures and an open fire, as a place of retreat, and for the sake of many precious memories. A horse-railroad connects Amesbury with Newbury-

port, the birthplace of William Lloyd Garrison. As
you go down, you look across at the wide and far-
reaching salt meadows of Hampton, emerald green
in summer, and purple and brown in autumn. About
half way from Amesbury to the sea, your horse-car
trundles across Deer Island,—wild, rugged, and
picturesque, its huge one-handed pines griping the
weather-stained granite with knotty fingers, their
branches the resting-place of hawks and crows,
eagles and herons. The only house on the island is
the home of Whittier's friend, Harriet Prescott Spofford.

Off the mouth of the river, Plum Island lies " like
a whale aground." Off to the northeast are discernible the Isles of Shoals, whose fair Calypso (Celia
Thaxter) is said to have been introduced to the world
of letters by Whittier. On the rocks of Appledore
he has often sat, of an evening, to watch the gold-
lamps kindled in the lighthouses of Portsmouth and
White Island. Indeed, this whole sea-region—Hampton beaches, Rivermouth Rocks, Plum Island, the
Isles of Shoals—has been sung by Whittier in his
classic ballads. He is familiar with almost every
acre of this part of Essex County. Some lines he
wrote in 1885, for the 250th anniversary of the settlement of Newbury, would apply to half a dozen other
neighboring towns as well. He said : " Although I
can hardly call myself a son of the ancient town, my
grandmother, Sarah Greenleaf, of blessed memory,
was its daughter, and I may therefore claim to be its
grandson. All my life I have lived in sight of its
green hills and in hearing of its Sabbath bells. Its
history and legends are familiar to me. I seem to

have known all its old worthies, whose descendants have helped to people a continent, and who have carried the name and memories of their birthplace to the Mexican Gulf and across the Rocky Mountains to the shores of the Pacific."

When, in early boyhood, Whittier first read the poetry of Burns, and learned from it where to look for true poetic material,—namely, in the common heart and the common life,—he found a store of legends ready to his hand, in the homes of the inhabitants of the Merrimack Valley, just as Burns had found them on the banks of the Ayr. Burns tells us that, when he was a boy, his imagination was greatly stimulated by the talk of an old woman who resided in the family. She had the largest collection in the country of tales and songs concerning devils, ghosts, fairies, brownies, witches, warlocks, spunkies, kelpies, elf-candles, dead-lights, wraiths, apparitions, cantrips, giants, enchanted towers, dragons, and other trumpery. So Whittier grew up in an atmosphere thick with legends of the marvelous,—stories of headless men walking about with their heads under their arms; traditions of second-sight; of witches innumerable and their wicked deeds; of haunted mills kept running o' nights by ghostly millers; of phantom ships and spectral armies; of singing witch-grass at the spring " where withered hags refresh at ease their broom-stick nags "; and of wizards skilled in calling birds out of trees, hiving the swarming bees, and by a potent spell making the dry logs and frosted branches of winter green with summer bloom. I shall speak, farther on, of the pretty superstition of

telling the bees of the death of a member of the
family. The belief in fairies was by no means extinct
in the Whittier neighborhood. The poet has several
folk-lore incidents about them in his prose and
verse.

One cannot open any early book published in
Newbury without coming across queer legends and
superstitions. In the Reminiscences of Mrs. Sarah
Emery, we are told that her aunt, Ruth Little, had a
heifer that one day kicked over the milk-pail, whereupon she declared that the animal was bewitched by
a poor woman who lived near. So off she rushes to
the house, gets her sharp shears, and, cutting off some
hairs from the heifer's tail, burns them. In a few
days it was learned that the suspected woman had
badly burned her hand on the warming-pan. Aunt
Ruth stoutly maintained that the burning of the heifer's hair and that of the woman's hand were cause
and effect, and, in her mind at least, no doubt
remained as to the woman's character.

Of a certain extremely thin and gaunt spinster,
reported witch, it was mysteriously whispered to Mr.
Whittier by one of the pall-bearers at her funeral
that her coffin was so heavy that four stout men could
barely lift it.

Mr. Whittier tells of a stout, red-nosed farmer
whom he used to meet occasionally in boyhood, who,
having emigrated to Ohio, and taken a certain widow
to wife, became gradually convinced that the warn-
ings he had received from her neighbors were true,
and that his wife was a witch. He grew so hypo-
chondriacal over this idea that, unable any longer to
endure her society, he ran away and came back to

New England, but was followed, captured, and taken back to Ohio by the too-fond wife.

Near the home of the mother of our poet, in Somersworth, New Hampshire, there dwelt a quiet old Quaker, named Bantum, who exercised, in all simplicity and sobriety, the art of magic and conjury. His help was sought by lovers of both sexes and by persons in search of stolen goods. He would receive them all kindly, put on his huge iron-rimmed spectacles, open his conjuring-book—a great clasped volume in blackletter—and give the required answers without money and without price.

I am indebted to a friend for calling my attention to an incident related of Daniel Webster's early life, which is explained by the above anecdote. When Prof. Francis Lieber visited Webster in 1845, Webster told him that, when he was a lad in New Hampshire, a friend of his father's seriously advised him (Daniel) to become a sorcerer, as they needed one to recover stolen cattle, children, etc.

Mr. Whittier tells some amusing stories of old Aunt Morse who lived at Rocks Village near Amesbury. He says that one of his earliest recollections is of this reputed witch, who was accused of preventing the coming of the butter in the churn, snuffing out candles at huskings and quilting parties, and even of more serious injuries. One night, he says, there was a husking at Rocks Village, and about the middle of the evening a big black bug came buzzing into the room and kept bumping against the faces of the merry huskers. At last it was knocked down with a stick; and about the same time Aunt Morse, who was at home, fell downstairs and got covered with bruises. But the huskers stoutly affirmed that the black bug was Aunt Morse, and that the places where she was bruised were where she had been struck by the stick. A certain old Captain Peaslee who lived near her covered his house and barns all over with horseshoes to ward off her evil influence. She at last became so annoyed by this silent persecution that she went to a justice of the peace and took oath that she was a Christian woman and no witch.[1] But it seems that her undeserved reputation followed her even into the grave, as the following story by our poet—not included in his collected works—will show:

"After the death of Aunt Morse no will was found, though it was understood before her decease that such a document was in the hands of Squire S., one of her neighbors. One cold winter evening, some weeks after her departure, Squire S. sat in his parlor, looking over his papers, when, hearing some one cough in a familiar way, he looked up, and saw before him a little crooked old woman, in an oil-nut colored woolen frock, blue and white tow and linen apron, and striped blanket, leaning her sharp, pinched face on one hand, while the other supported a short black tobacco pipe, at which she was puffing in the most vehement and spiteful manner conceivable.

"The squire was a man of some nerve; but his first thought was to attempt an escape, from which he was deterred only by the consideration that any effort to that effect would necessarily bring him nearer to his unwelcome visitor.

"'Aunt Morse,' he said at length, 'for the Lord's sake, get

---

[1] For this story I am indebted to an article in "Harper's Magazine," February, 1883, by George M. White. Mr. White has, however, got "Morse" somehow changed into "Mose." I here take pleasure in acknowledging my obligations to the same writer for several other interesting anecdotes, published in the periodical just mentioned.

right back to the burying-ground !   What on earth are you here for ? '

" The apparition took her pipe deliberately from her mouth, and informed him that she came to see justice done with her will ; and that nobody need think of cheating her, dead or alive.   Concluding her remark with a shrill emphasis, she replaced her pipe, and puffed away with renewed vigor.   Upon the squire's promising to obey her request, she refilled her pipe, which she asked him to light, and then took her departure."

The first of the Whittiers to come to America was Thomas Whittier,[1] of whom two noteworthy incidents are recorded,—first, that he brought with him a hive of bees ; and, second, that he declined to make use of the garrison house of Haverhill as a defense against the Indians, preferring to rely on kind treatment of them and on faith in the Lord.   John Greenleaf Whittier's paternal grandmother was of the Greenleaf family, of Newbury, highly respected for integrity of character and religiousness of life.   It is recorded of Prof. Simon Greenleaf, professor of law at Harvard College, 1833–1845, that he was one of the most spiritually-minded of men, and very benevolent and kind-hearted.   He published some dozen works. His son married a sister of the poet Longfellow.   One of the English Greenleafs took part with the Roundheads in all the wars of the English Revolution ; while in this country the old records tell of a Captain Stephen Greenleaf, of Newbury, who, in pursuing a party of Indians up the Merrimack in 1695, got shot

---

[1] The word Whittier is a corruption of white-tawier, the verb "to taw" meaning to dress the lighter skins of goats and kids, and then whiten them for the glover's use.

in the wrist and side, and lost, in consequence, the use of his left hand. The moose-skin coat he wore is still preserved. It is believed that the Greenleafs are of Huguenot descent, and that their name has been translated from the French Feuillevert.

Whittier's father and mother were both of Quaker stock, and were themselves, also, it is needless to say, members of the Society of Friends. On his mother's side the poet is descended from the Quaker Husseys of Somersworth and Hampton, New Hampshire, and from those who were among the founders of Nantucket. Through his mother he is also descended from the Rev. Stephen Batchelder of Hampton, New Hampshire, the eccentric parson, noted for his philoprogenitiveness and for his wonderful black eyes, bequeathed by him not only to Whittier, but also to other descendants of his,—Daniel Webster, Caleb Cushing, Col. William Batchelder Greene, and William Pitt Fessenden. Stephen Batchelder also gave to all those just mentioned their massive features and swarthy, Oriental complexions. At the time of Daniel Webster's subservient Southern tour, Garrison suggested that his complexion might have caused him to be arrested as a runaway slave and sold to pay his jail fees.

He was nicknamed " Black Dan " ; and of his father, Captain Webster, it was humorously said that burnt powder could not change his complexion in battle. "The Bachiler eye" is dark and deep-set under heavy eye-brows, inscrutable in depth, now shooting out sudden gleams of lightning, and now suffused with the lambent fire of tender emotion. Webster was known in the village of Fryeburg as " All-eyes " ; one speaks of his eye as being as black as death and as heavy as a lion's ; Carlyle, as in all his portraits, gives one or two Velasquez-strokes, and behold the thing done once and forever ! Describing Webster, he speaks of "the dull black eyes under the precipice of brows, like dull anthracite furnaces, needing only to be *blown.*" The poet Whittier's glance has not ordinarily anything of that *indignation* which Carlyle noticed in Webster, though beyond a doubt, when he is aroused by injustice, or by oppression of man by his fellow-man, his face is capable of expressing (in a momentary flash) the fierce scorn and righteous wrath of the prophet.

This expression is caught in a well-known portrait of him taken during the anti-slavery days. Having once seen him, one can well understand what he himself once related,—how that when some rough fellows threatened him, as he came out of an anti-slavery meeting, he turned and faced them, and so holding their eyes went out.

The family life of the Whittiers on the old farm was made delightful, notwithstanding the hard work, by the perpetual cheerfulness, humor, and wit, and calm and trustful piety of all its members. The cheeriness of atmosphere is insisted on with emphasis by all acquaintances of the family. They were not poor for farmers in those days, although they had to stretch the strap pretty hard, and " pull the devil by the tail " pretty vigorously, in order to make both ends meet. The farm (bought for $600, borrowed money) yielded nearly every article of food consumed, as well as the flax and wool spun and woven by the diligent mother into cloth for their home-made clothes. Yet the finances of the household did not permit the owning of rich robes and furs, and there were no ulsters in those days, and warm flannels were little worn, so that our young poet says he often suffered bitterly from the cold, especially in those long drives to the Friends' Meeting-House eight miles away, in Amesbury. The reading matter of the family consisted of a few religious books, the almanac, and a local weekly newspaper. In Whittier's boyhood the whipping-post and stocks were still to be seen at Newburyport, and he was one day shown in Salem the tree on which the witches were hanged. People were mostly their own doctors then. If a tooth was to be pulled, you must go either to a physician or to a horse-doctor. I have been told of a horse-doctor down East who, when the trembling victim, seated in a chair, was ruefully eying his rude instruments of torture, always used to say consolingly: " Don't ye be scared now. If I break your jah, I 'll give ye my oxen!" The Whittiers were very hospitable, and the little farm-house was always sought by Friends in their travels to and from the annual meetings and conventions. It is recorded that as many as sixteen were entertained at one time. Other guests less welcome, but not the less uniformly provided for, were the " old stragglers," as they called them, whose visits were so regular that their orbits could be accurately calculated. Speechless beggars; *quasi*-lame beggars; bearded herb-doctors; peddlers with wild hairy faces peeping from under enormous packs; an old Edie Ochiltree, who was poet, parson, doctor, and mendicant in one; a drunkard-parson; horse-thief beggars; fierce and well-bodied gaberlunzies, who ordered their

cider and meat with terrifying gestures and looks
(when the "men-folks" were absent); Italian wan-
derers; Scotch strollers; and many a withered bel-
dame of the gipsy fraternity,—they were all sure of
a nice free farmer's luncheon at Quaker Whycher's;
for very rarely would the too kind-hearted mother turn
one away, and, if she did, was sure afterwards to be
smitten with remorse. In Mrs. Emery's recollections
of life in Newbury we get a glimpse of the same old
stragglers. She tells us, for example, of an old lame
peddler named Urin, who used to stump into her
father's house, usually at dusk, with his bag and
basket, and, dropping into the nearest chair, declare
he was "e'en a'most dead" he was so lame and tired.
Then, without stopping to take breath, he would reel
off, "Tree fell on me when I was a boy, killed my
brother and me jest like him, here's books, pins,
needles, black sewing-silk all colors, tapes, varses,
almanacks, and sarmons, here's varses on the pirate
that was hung on Boston Common, the 'lection sar-
mon when the guv'ner took the chair, 'Whittington's
Cat,' 'Pilgrim's Progress,'" etc.

Of course in a back-farm neighborhood on the
Merrimack there was no hint in those early days of
the colonial magnificence of old Salem and Boston,
or even of Newburyport; no old-family balls, rich
foreign dresses, gay knee-buckled gallants, East India
punch-bowls, mahogany furniture, or stately equi-
pages or costly libraries. And especially in a Quaker
family was everything of the plainest and severest.
Carpets were unknown As a substitute the floors
were from time to time scrubbed or strewn with fresh
white sand. They must have had stout nerves in those

days to endure the gritting and grating of sand under their feet. When the old Holmes manse was being torn down in Cambridge, I remember noticing that the foot-deep spaces between the joists underneath the floor of one upstairs room were completely filled with white sand that had for generations sifted through the cracks. It is to be understood that the great kitchen fireplace formed the magnet of the farm-house, and around it on winter evenings clustered all the poetry of the young people's life. Here the nuts were cracked, the cider was drunk, the axe-handle whittled out, stockings knit and stories told; and not a boy or a man but was familiar with the mysteries of green back-log, dry back-stick, fore-stick, split-wood, cat-stick, and kindling-chips; and, particularly in prosaic Quaker Whittier's house, to understand how successfully to build the kitchen fire was considered of vastly more importance than to know how to build the lofty rhyme.

Then there were frequent nutting expeditions, fishings, flower-gatherings, quilting parties, and husking bees, when—

> " We laughed round the corn-heap, with hearts all in tune,
>   Our chair a broad pumpkin,—our lantern the moon,"

as Whittier sings. And good Aunt Mercy, the mother's sister, in her spotless Quaker cap,—what absolutely de-licious pumpkin pies she used to make ! " None sweeter or better e'er smoked from an oven or circled a platter ! "

> " O fruit loved of boyhood ! the old days recalling,
> When wood-grapes were purpling and brown nuts were falling !

*   *   *   *   *   *

What moistens the lip and what brightens the eye,
What calls back the past, like the rich pumpkin pie?"

—Whittier.

On First-days the old one-horse shay was got out, and father and mother drove off to meeting, sometimes taking one of the children with them. There, while their Puritan neighbors were wrestling with the "long nineteenthlies poured downward from the sounding-board," they sat in silence, worshiping God often with the heart alone. As for John Greenleaf, he says he thinks he generally preferred to worship in the fields in those days, being in this respect like his Quaker friend Mary Howitt, who says in her recently published autobiography that the only thing she enjoyed in the horribly plain old meeting-house of her childhood was looking at the reflection of certain windows in a certain other window, and imagining that the reflected ones were the windows of heaven. Sabbath afternoons the mother gathered her children about her, like the good man in the "Cotter's Saturday Night," and read and expounded a portion of Scripture. It was in order to be nearer the little Friends' "Meeting" that she removed to Amesbury after the death of her husband and the sale of the farm in 1840. A beautiful character—the mother; serene, dignified, benign, practical, and fond of reading the best books. A neighbor, speaking of her natural refinement, says that whenever she saw him she always politely inquired for the health of himself and mother: "How do thee do, Charles?—and how is thy mother?"[1] Mrs. Whittier died in 1857 at Amesbury, the tender and intimate relation between

---

[1] Underwood's "Whittier," p. 48.

herself and her poet-son having never been in the least degree weakened. To such a mother a son owes more than can be expressed. An excellent picture of her is given in Mr. Francis H. Underwood's careful work on Whittier, and an oil-portrait hangs in the little parlor at Amesbury.

John Whittier, the father of the poet (or " Quaker Whycher," as he was called by some of his neighbors), was a rough, decisive, but kind-hearted and devout man. He was several times in the public service of the town of Haverhill (selectman, *e. g.*), and was intimate with its prominent men, such as the Minots, the Wingates, and the Bartletts. He was often called upon to act as arbitrator in matters of dispute between neighbors. He is included in the portrait gallery in "Snow-Bound." He married Abigail Hussey when he was forty-four, and John Greenleaf, their second child, was born three years later. The father died in 1832, tenderly cared for to the last by his children.

Mr. Whittier's only brother, Matthew Franklin Whittier, was for many years a resident of Boston. His humorous verses and satirical dialect articles, signed " Ethan Spike, from Hornby," were mostly contributed to the Portland " Transcript," but some of them to Boston papers. I should not advise anyone to take the trouble to hunt them up. They prove incontestably that but one genius is born in a family. Matthew died at the age of seventy, at the Maverick House in East Boston, January 7, 1883, after a long and painful illness, leaving a wife and three children, and grandchildren. Until a few months before his death he had been a clerk in the Naval Department of the Boston Custom House,—his service covering a period of thirteen years,—and his retirement was made the occasion of a formal testimonial of esteem from his fellow-clerks, among whom he was very popular for his cheery humor. He is described as having been "very different from his brother," in many characteristics. He did not use the Quaker mode of speech,—its "thee's" and "thou's." He was an omnivorous reader, and, like his brother, an out-and-out anti-slavery man. He was associated with B. P. Shillaber in the attempt to float that unfortunate journalistic craft, the "Carpet Bag." He resided for many years in Portland, where he was book-keeper for certain mercantile houses, and where he married Miss Jane Vaughn. "Frank," as his associates called him, was, like his brother, inclined to seclusion, yet had the same geniality and quaint, quiet humor. Mr. Charles O. Stickney[1] once asked him of his relation to his brother the poet. "'The only relationship existing between John Greenleaf Whittier and myself,' said he, in solemn deliberative tones, 'is, we each had the same father and the same mother.'"

Aunt Mercy was a person of great sweetness and refinement of nature and of a playful disposition. She removed with the family to Amesbury, and died there in 1846. She was betrothed in her youth, says Mr. S. T. Pickard,[2] to a young man every way

---

[1] In the Boston "Evening Transcript," January 2, 1892, where a specimen of Ethan Spike's comic writing is given, with references.

[2] In the Portland "Transcript." Mr. Pickard's wife is Whittier's niece, and Mr. Pickard himself is the nephew of Joshua Coffin, Whittier's old schoolmaster.

worthy of her, but not a member of the Friends' society. Late one evening, as she sat musing by the fire, after all the rest had gone to bed, she felt mysteriously impelled to go to the window and look out, and in a moonlit space under the trees she saw a horse and rider coming down the hill toward the house. She recognized her lover. He drew rein at the yard entrance, and she went out at once to meet him. While she was unbolting the door in the little porch, she happened to turn her head to look out of the window opposite her, and plainly saw her lover on his horse ; but, when the door was opened, no trace of man or horse was to be seen. Bursting into tears, she called up Mrs. Whittier, and told her story. Her sister said, " Thee had better go to bed, Mercy ; thee has been asleep and dreaming by the fire." But Mercy was sure she had not been asleep ; and, in afterwards recalling the circumstances of the vision, she remembered that *she had heard no sound of hoofs.* Some time after she received a letter from a distant city, stating that her lover had died on the very day and hour of her ghostly visitation ! This is the story of Aunt Mercy, as told in the family.

Whittier's elder sister, Mary, married Mr. Jacob Caldwell, at one time publisher of the Haverhill " Gazette." She died in 1861.

A member of the household who was beloved by all the children was Uncle Moses Whittier, " innocent of books, but rich in lore of fields and brooks,"—a sort of Rollo-book Jonas, " a tall, plain, sober man," far less stout than the father of the household. His portrait, like that of all the others, is drawn in

"Snow-Bound." His tragic death in 1824 has often been mentioned by writers on Whittier. He had gone out in the morning with his axe to cut wood, turning into a path on the right of the Haverhill road. He was missed at dinner time, and presently his dog came up to the house barking frantically, and then off again to the woods. The unfortunate man was found under a fallen tree. In attempting to get to the ground a lodged tree he had cut, he felled the one on which it rested, and the two dropping at the same time, and taking unexpected directions, he was caught and pinned to the ground by one of them. He lived but a short time after being taken home, and was buried on a bitter winter's day in the little family burial-lot a few rods from the house.

Of the poet's sister, Elizabeth, it seems almost profanation to speak at all, so sacred was the bond between the two. Yet a few words may help readers of her poems, "Hazel Blossoms," to enjoy them better. She was her brother's intellectual companion, his critic and his guardian angel both, and a co-worker with him in the cause of the slave. When in good health, she is said to have been gay-hearted. Her Batchelder eyes were large and wondrous deep, looking from under a broad, noble brow. The crayon sketch of her face in the Amesbury parlor wears a smile of sweetness and patience. She had a vivid imagination, and was a delightful story-teller. Says an acquaintance of hers, "She sometimes visited at my father's house, and all of us children used to climb upon the bed of an invalid sister and listen, rapt, to Elizabeth, who, sitting at the foot, told us stories by the hour." Says Mrs. Harriet Prescott

Spofford:[1] "Mr. Whittier's sister Elizabeth, sympathizing with him completely, of a rare poetic nature and fastidious taste, and of delicate dark-eyed beauty, was long a companion that must have made the want of any other less keenly felt than by lonely men in general. The bond between the sister and brother was more perfect than any of which we have known, except that between Charles and Mary Lamb; and in this instance the conditions were of perfect moral and mental health. To the preciousness of the relationship the pages of the poet bear constant witness, and Amesbury Village is full of traditions of their affection, and of the gentle loveliness and brilliant wit of Elizabeth, whom the people admired and reverenced almost as much as they do the poet himself." At the time of her death in 1864 a Newburyport paper said: "The tidings of the death of Elizabeth Whittier went to the hearts of many in this community with a pang like that of personal loss. Regard for the delicacy of a nature that held itself shrinkingly aloof from publicity forbids more than a passing tribute to its rare loveliness." Miss Whittier had been a semi-invalid for some years, and for a few months before her death her sufferings were extreme.

Perhaps one should not take leave of the household of " Snow-Bound " without a few words on the " not unfeared, half-welcome guest," whose portrait is so well drawn by Whittier,—namely, the self-styled pilgrim-stranger with a violent temper, the half-

----

[1] In a valuable article in " Harper's Magazine " for January, 1884, to which I am indebted for facts used in this volume.

crazy religious enthusiast and evangelist, Harriet
Livermore :—

> "She blended in a like degree
> The vixen and the devotee,
> Revealing with each freak or feint
>   The temper of Petruchio's Kate,
> The raptures of Siena's saint.
> Her tapering hand and rounded wrist
> Had facile power to form a fist ;
> The warm dark languish of her eyes
> Was never safe from wrath's surprise."

In 1884 a distant kinsman of Harriet Livermore
(the Rev. S. T. Livermore of Bridgewater, Massachusetts) published a little book about her, as a vindica-
tion of her character from what he morbidly conceives
to be the distorted account given by Mr. Whittier
in " Snow-Bound." He calls the " epithets heaped
upon her " in that poem " an assault upon a pious
female's character," and the portrait of her " a cruel
caricature," and hints that he would like to use the
" flexors and extensors of his right arm in her protection." The item about her visiting Lady Hester
Stanhope in Palestine, and

> " Startling on her desert throne
> The crazy Queen of Lebanon
> With claims fantastic as her own,"

he pronounces to be " a slanderous myth," and quotes
Missionary Thompson, author of " The Land and the
Book," as saying that the statement of the person
who informed Mr. Whittier that Harriet Livermore
was at one time head of a Bedouin tribe " is a lie."

We shall, further on, find the Rev. Mr. Livermore
attempting to whitewash the Ethiopian skins of the

old Block Island wreckers. A good strong infusion
of positive wickedness, sparkling at the eyes, is his
abhorrence, and rightly so in real life. The poet,
too, abhors it. But the antithesis of right and
wrong, light and darkness, is needed in art. That it
furnishes the dramatic contrast and shading indispensable to a poet is no concern of Mr. Livermore's,
he thinks, and he indignantly asks why we are not
presented with a list of Harriet Livermore's virtues.
It is curious that nearly every authority brought into
court by him to prove his fanatical female relative a
saint only serves to fix more ineffaceably the colors
of Whittier's portrait of her. He entirely ignores,
also, the benignant spirit of the poet, who adds to
his sketch twenty-seven lines of charitable excuses
for her failings:—

> " Where'er her troubled path may be,
>   The Lord's sweet pity with her go !
>   The outward wayward life we see ;
>   The hidden springs we may not know.
>   Nor is it given us to discern
>   What threads the fatal sisters spun,
>   Through what ancestral years has run
>   The sorrow with the woman born," etc.

The following interesting letter by Mr. Whittier
was written in answer to inquiries on the subject: '—

DANVERS, MASS., 9th mo., 18, 1879.
DEAR FRIEND,—Harriet Livermore, when I was a young
boy, was for some considerable time a resident of Rocks Vil-

---

¹ Livermore's " Harriet Livermore," p. 15. Another good
authority on Harriet Livermore is the booklet of Miss Rebecca I.
Davis, of East Haverhill.

lage, Haverhill; I think a visitor of Dr. Weld's in that place, and was often at our house—a brilliant, dark-eyed woman—striking in her personal appearance and gifted in conversation. The tradition of her disappointment [in love] was current in our neighborhood, and the name of the gentleman was Dr. Elliot, of the U. S. Army, who, I think, died in Florida, or in some part of the extreme South. He was Haverhill born.

After boyhood I never saw her until she came to see me at Philadelphia, on her return from the East, in 1829 [1839]. I interested myself with J. R. Chandler, and others, to get an audience for two lectures by her. She gave one, and declined to give the other because the audience was smaller than the first. She spent some days at my boarding-house, alternating from an agreeable and interesting guest to a violent-tempered woman of indomitable will. She told us of her stay with Lady Hester Stanhope, and that Lady H. S. kept two white horses with a red mark on the back of each in the shape of a saddle, ready waiting for the coming of the Lord—one of them to be ridden by herself to Jerusalem. It seems that H. L. insisted that *she* was to accompany the Lord on the spare horse; and therefore a quarrel arose which ended in their separation.

The lecture procured her, I believe, about $150. She said she must go back to Jerusalem and meet *the coming* there. Even then she was a noble-looking woman.

A friend of mine, years afterwards, met her in Syria, with a fragment of a Bedouin tribe, of which she was the head—its spiritual and temporal chief. I do not think I have exaggerated her character in " Snow-Bound." I certainly did not intend to.

Thy friend,
JOHN G. WHITTIER.

It is not desirable to go minutely into the story of Harriet Livermore's life here,—of her early education by her father, the Hon. Edward St. Loe Livermore, judge and United States Senator; of her disappointment in love; her temper; her teaching in

the Whittier neighborhood ; her authorship of religious books ; or how she charmed the social circles
of Washington by her beauty and brilliancy, and,
later, when an evangelist, preached in the House of
Representatives with such eloquence that many were
moved to tears and sobs. Her portrait shows an exquisitely moulded face, and wide, wild eyes, though
it does not show the wealth of moist raven-black hair
which once adorned her head. At one time she had
a crazy notion of preaching to the Indians, and
actually made her way as far as Fort Leavenworth,—
as she says, "urging her way to the West, undis-
mayed by cholera, sand-bars, or floating timbers,
commissioners, or the Devil." Here is a stanza of a
hymn she wrote for her imaginary Indians :—

> " I'll tell them whiskey to forsake,
>   Crying 'tis Satan's bait to kill.
>   Oh, Choctaw, Cherokee, come take
>   Pure water from the forest rill ! "

She made four or five trips to Jerusalem, the first
in 1836. In 1841 she was living in part of a house
owned by a Gibraltar Jew, near Hezekiah's Pool.
She was given food by the Protestant missionaries.
Dr. Selah Merrill, American Consul in Jerusalem in
1883 (who got his information from those who had
known her there), wrote that " she was very irritable
and exacting, and would often insult people in their
houses or in the streets." She was well known to be
crack-brained, and was not allowed to preach in
Jerusalem. Dr. Van Dyke, who was living in Jerusalem, says she told him one day that she had spent
the previous Sunday in an olive-tree on the Mount of
Olives. She also thought that she and Joseph Wolff

were the two witnesses of Revelation xi., and identified Bonaparte with Mehemet Ali.

Mr. Livermore's attempt to discredit the statement of Mr. Whittier as to the Lady Hester Stanhope story is not at all successful. It all reduces to this: she could not have visited that lady, he thinks, because she was in Palestine only a month on the occasion of her first trip. But this is no argument. Lady Hester lived only eight miles from Sidon, in her mountain villa of Djoun, and Mr. Livermore admits that the American pilgrim passed through Sidon, either on her journey to Jerusalem or on her return to take ship at Beirut. A day or two at Djoun would have afforded more than sufficient opportunity for these two half-crazy and high-stomached dames to see that they could not dwell under the same roof. Dr. Van Dyke says he would have given his little finger to have witnessed the meeting between the two, although he does not think they did actually meet. "It would have been diamond cut diamond,—the haughty aristocratic Englishwoman and the fearless republican." The truth of the incident is attested by Mr. Whittier, by a Mr. Thomas, who knew Miss Livermore for years in Philadelphia,[1] and by another old acquaintance, who wrote an article on her for a Philadelphia paper at the time of her death in 1867.

Lady Stanhope was a niece of Pitt, the English Minister, and at his death she received a government pension of £1,200 annually. She died in Syria in 1839. She inherited her wayward and imperious disposition from her father. Her life, as revealed in her Memoirs and Travels, was certainly one of the most

---

[1] See S. T. Livermore's book, p. 82.

3

romantic and eccentric ever lived by mortal. She was withal benevolent in disposition, and often saved the lives of fugitives in Syria. She had a stronger character and a more versatile mind than had Harriet Livermore. Her special hobby was her belief in the coming of a Messiah and the ride to Jerusalem on her pet mares ; and we may be sure that any audacious handling of that theme by the pilgrim-saint would have caused instant rupture of all relations between them. A physician who was Lady Stanhope's most trusted friend, who lived with her at Djoun, and compiled the volumes of her Memoirs, gives a description of the famous mares ; but neither he nor Dr. Wm. M. Thompson, who, after her death, went up to bury her, and saw the favored animals, says anything about the red spots like saddles which are mentioned by Mr. Whittier in his note. Neither was their color white, as Mr. Whittier states.

It appears from the Memoirs that a village doctor named Meta, on Mt. Lebanon, predicted that on the coming of the " Mahedi " he would ride a horse born saddled, and that " a woman would come from a far country to partake in the mission." (This explains how Harriet Livermore, as well as Lady Hester, could plausibly lay claim to horse number two.) Dr. Thompson, in " The Land and the Book " (i. 113), thus speaks of these wondrous steeds, compared with which the mares of Diomed, or that Persian horse of brass on which the Tartar king did ride, were naught in the eyes of Lady Hester :—

" She had a mare whose backbone sank suddenly down at the shoulders and rose abruptly near the hips. This deformity her vivid imagination converted into a miraculous saddle, on which she was to ride to Jerusalem as queen by the side of some sort of Messiah, who was to introduce a fancied millennium. Another mare had a part to play in this august pageant, and both were tended with extraordinary care. A lamp was kept burning in their very comfortable apartments, and they were served with sherbet and other delicacies." She lavished her choicest affections on them for fourteen years.

She never suffered any one to mount them. The hollow-backed one was a chestnut, named Läila, and the other, Lulu, was a gray. They had each a groom, and were daily exercised on a green plot of ground near the house-wall. No servant was even allowed to look at them while they were at exercise, on pain of being dismissed from her service. She once said that in her pecuniary trouble she would have quitted the country, had it not been for these mares and her desire to remain and see the outcome of the prophecy. After her death, the poor creatures were soon worked to death by the rapacious villagers.

There can scarcely be a doubt that the statement made to Mr. Whittier and repeated in the latest edition of "Snow-Bound" (1888)—that Harriet Livermore was at one time the spiritual and temporal head of a fragment of a Bedouin tribe—is a mistake. A poor and obscure fanatic, living almost wholly upon charity in Jerusalem, would not have been accepted by Arabs as their chief. This might have happened if she had had abundance of money and power, like Lady Stanhope, but not otherwise. Dr. Thompson, with whom she lived for a time, denies the story *in toto*, as we have seen.   Still, there might have been a slight basis of fact for it,—some momentary freak of hers, like that attempt to take up her life among the American Indians.

We may now give a glance at the outward surroundings of Whittier when a boy on the farm.   In a brief autobiographic paper, he relates that from the top of " Job's Hill," which rose abruptly from the brook that passed the house, he could see the blue outline of the Deerfield mountains in New Hampshire, and the solitary peak of Agamenticus on the coast of Maine.   The valley of the Merrimack could be traced by a long line of morning mist, and on the breeze was borne from the village of Haverhill the sound of its two church bells.   The view of the house from the road was once obscured by oak woods. Not far away, on the cross-road stood one of those old garrison houses which were formerly established in New England towns for protection against the Indians. Sometimes private houses were fortified and made to serve as garrisons.   Such was the one near the Whittier farm.   I condense two separate accounts given of it by Mr. Whittier,—one in " Harper's Magazine " and the other in his prose works.   It was, says he, a massive, venerable structure, built of solid oak logs, with the walls double, and filled in with bricks between.   There was a double-thick plank door, made bullet-proof and studded with iron nails.   Over the door and projecting from the second story was a species of balcony, also of thick planks, with a bullet-proof breastwork around it, through which were cut loopholes, so that the defenders could creep from the interior of the house and fire down upon those who might be about the door. The windows were narrow, and had small diamond-shaped panes, set in lead. The door opened upon a stone-paved hall, or entry, leading into the huge single room of the basement, which was lighted by two small windows, the ceiling black with the smoke of a century and a half, a huge fireplace, calculated for eight-foot wood, occupying one entire side; while overhead, suspended from the timbers, or on shelves fastened to them, were household stores, farming utensils, fishing-rods, guns, bunches of herbs gathered perhaps a century ago, strings of dried apples and pumpkins, links of mottled sausages, spareribs and flitches of bacon, the firelight of an evening dimly revealing the checked woolen coverlet of the bed in one far-off corner, while in another shone the pewter plates on the dresser.

This old relic was destroyed some years ago,— more 's the pity, for it showed not the least sign of decay, and would have been a thing of joy unspeakable to antiquaries.

The birthplace of a man of genius is always worth looking at, but is not so interesting as are the *lares et penates* of his later years. It is not worth while to gaze with rapture into the empty husk of the nut: the kernel is the essential thing. Nevertheless, a word once again on the old Quaker grange where the best friend of the slave passed his boyhood. I suppose among those whose forbears were the original settlers of New England one could count upon the fingers of both hands the persons who, like Whittier, lived until manhood in the house built by the founder of their family in the New World. The old home at Haverhill is over two hundred years old. It is a severely plain, not to say ugly, old two-story box, the rooms, like those of so many other similar houses in New England (Thoreau's birthplace, for example), having heavy beams running across the ceilings, which are so low as to be easily touched. The front door opens into a small, square entry, with steep staircase. On the right is the room where Whittier used to study,—the *salon* of the old grange. Here he used to sit by a bright wood fire,—the fireplace being the one luxury he has always allowed himself,—absorbed in the books and newspapers that covered a little table in the centre of the room. A neighbor says that he was a great reader: " He used to load me down with papers for my father to read; he was as good as a library." In the room on the opposite side of the entry Whittier was born. In the rear is the kitchen, with its enormous Old World fireplace, broad enough to admit benches on each side, and with accessories of brick oven and mantel-piece; here is the inset cupboard where shone the pewter dishes; and here yet are the broad-headed wrought-iron nail on which hung the bull's-eye watch, and the circle worn on the wall by the warming-pan. The original barn was behind the house, in a sheltered spot near the old orchard. At the roadside is the stone horse-block, built into the stone fence, and containing circular depressions, made by generations of children cracking hickory-nuts and butternuts there. From the boards of the original garret floor of the house boxes and paper-weights are now made, and varnished penholders from the twigs of the great elm. In reply to a suggestion recently made by Miss Frances E. Willard, that the old homestead be bought from its present owners and perpetually preserved in its present state, Mr. Whittier wrote: [1]—

MY DEAR FRIEND,—I have just received thy note respecting the old Whittier homestead in Haverhill. I do not know how to thank thee for thy interest in the matter. It is very generous and noble on thy part. I am at present confined here by illness, and have no certain knowledge of the willingness of the owner to sell the property. I will be glad to have the old place—the home built by my American ancestor more than 200 years ago—secured in the way proposed. I think the Whittier Club of Haverhill might feel interested in the plan. I will send them the extracts from the Chicago paper. If the thing can be done without too much trouble, I shall be glad. I will give $100 toward it.

I am most gratefully thy old friend,

JOHN G. WHITTIER.

Whittier first attended the district school when he was a little chap in his seventh winter. The schoolhouses of that time were warmed by a fireplace, the wood for which was split and piled up and brought in by the boys as needed. There were no writing-books, but a strong coarse paper of foolscap size was used, either in single sheets or the sheets stitched together. Lead-pencils were unknown; a chunky plummet of lead was used instead, and it was usually made at home and cut into various shapes to suit the owner's taste. Whittier's first schoolmaster was Joshua Coffin, who was teaching that winter in a private house, as the schoolhouse was undergoing repairs. This explains a mysterious passage in the

---

[1] Letter published in the "Literary World," Feb. 4, 1888.

poem " To my Old Schoolmaster," in which we read of the sound of the cradle-rock, and squall coming through the cracked and crazy wall, and " the goodman's voice at strife with his shrill and tipsy wife." What young reader of Whittier has not racked his brain, hitherto, for explanation of occurrences so queer in a school? In succeeding winters little John and his brother learned their lessons in the brown schoolhouse that stood a half-mile from home, but is now no more. For pictures of these school-days read the poems " In School Days," " My Playmate," " Snow-Bound," " The Barefoot Boy," and the lines mentioned above, " To my Old Schoolmaster." Joshua Coffin was the poet's life-long friend. He was born in Newbury in 1792, was graduated at Dartmouth College in 1817. He became the historian of Newbury, held various offices in that town, and was one of the twelve resolute men who formed the first anti-slavery society in New England (one stormy night, in Boston). Some one speaks of Coffin as " that huge and voluble personification of good humor." His fine massive face is pictured in " Harper's Magazine," July 25, 1875, together with a view of his residence in Newburyport. He died in that city in 1864.

In the first four of the autobiographic poems above mentioned—which seem to me of unsurpassable beauty in their kind—are found shy references to school loves. Of course he had them. All poets have. You remember Burns's first love ?—the bonnie, sweet, sonsie lass, who initiated him into " that delicious passion which, in spite of acid disappointment, gin-horse prudence, and book-worm philosophy," he held to be "the first of human joys, our dearest blessing here below." Whittier's pines of Ramoth Hill (an imaginary place), the song the veeries sang, the violet-fringed mossy seat, the tangled golden curls, the trembling voice, the falling blossoms,— what yearning emotions, what strangely thrilling memories, these beautiful verses excite !

The dawn of the poetic instinct came rather early, through the accident of his becoming acquainted with the poetry of Robert Burns. Here is the story as he told it to Robert Collyer : [1]—

"Whittier said to me " (writes Mr. Collyer), "'I hear thee is lecturing this winter on Burns. I should like to hear thee. Burns is to me the noblest poet of our race. He was the first poet I read, and he will be the last. Our people did not care for poetry when I was a boy. We had in our house an American reader, quite popular at that time, in which I found some pieces of the old school of singers; and, besides that, we had a poem called the "Davideis," written by a "Friend," and held in great esteem by our body. But somehow these did not seem to touch me; they were not what I wanted. One day one of our preachers came to stay all night; and noticing, as we sat by the fire, that I was intent on a book, he said, "I will read to thee, if thee likes, some poems by Robert Burns. I have a copy with me." [2] So he got the book

---

[1] See " Every Saturday," June 3, 1871.

[2] In his autobiographic notes, Mr. Whittier states that it was *Joshua Coffin* who first introduced him to Burns. He says:—

" When I was fourteen years old, my first schoolmaster, Joshua Coffin, the able, eccentric historian of Newbury, brought with him to our house a volume of Burns's poems, from which he read,

and **began to read.** It was the first I had heard of
Burns, and my wonder and delight over what I heard
is as fresh still as if it were yesterday. I had heard
nothing up to that moment, it seemed to me, that had
any right to be called poetry; and I listened as long
as the old man would read. I noticed he left the
book on the table, so I rose at gray dawn next morning, and read for myself. I was hanging over the
book when the Friend came down, and then he told
me he was going farther, to visit such and such
meetings, would be back at such a time, and, if I
liked, would leave the book with me. Thee may be
sure I gratefully accepted his offer. I read Burns
every moment I had to spare. And this was one great
result to me of my communion with him: I found
that the things out of which poems came were not, as
I had always imagined, somewhere away off in a
world and life lying outside the edge of our own New
Hampshire sky,—they were right here about my feet

---

greatly to my delight. I begged him to leave the book with me
and set myself at once to the task of mastering the glossary of the
Scottish dialect at its close. This was about the first poetry I had
ever read,—with the exception of that of the Bible, of which I had
been a close student,—and it had a lasting influence upon me. I
began to make rhymes myself, and to imagine stories and adventures. In fact, I lived a sort of dual life, and in a world of fancy,
as well as in the world of plain matter of fact about me."

As Mr. Collyer's account was from memory, we must give the
preference to Mr. Whittier's deliberately written statement.

It should be noted that in one of his prose sketches Mr. Whittier
relates that he first heard words of Burns as uttered by an old
Scotch tramp, who, after eating his bread and cheese and drinking
his mug of cider, sang, with a full, rich voice and with spirit,
" Auld Lang Syne," " Bonnie Doon," and " Highland Mary."

and among the people I knew. The common things of our common life I found were full of poetry.'".

Mr. Collyer continues: "He told me also what such a man only can say in good faith, that he could not understand what the critics mean when they say there are things in Burns not fit to be read,—things impure and vile, the spume of a fallen spirit. 'I never found such things,' he said. 'I read all Burns, every line of him; and, while there is a difference, of course, to me every line is good.' I know Whittier could not have thought, as he told me this, that Paul said once, 'To the pure all things *are* pure'; and how purely true his commentary on Burns was to the great old text!"

Mr. Whittier did not state his whole opinion of Burns to Robert Collyer (conversation is so fragmentary). We are not, of course, to understand that he did not know and disapprove of Burns's peculiar failing, did not know that "eating love inhabits in the finest wits of all." This is clear from the following stanzas in his poem "Burns," written nearly twenty years previous to the Collyer talk:—

> "And if at times an evil strain,
>   To lawless love appealing,
>   Broke in upon the sweet refrain
>   Of pure and healthful feeling,
>
> "It died upon the eye and ear,
>   No inward answer gaining;
>   No heart had I to see or hear
>   The discord and the staining!
>
> "Let those who never erred forget
>   His worth, in vain bewailings;
>   Sweet Soul of Song!—I own my debt
>   Uncancelled by his failings!"

"I began to make rhymes myself," he says. Let us see to what purpose. In 1882 Mr. Whittier sent a letter and poem to Friends in Chester, Pennsylvania, who were commemorating the bicentennial of the landing of Penn in America. The poem is not included in his collected works, latest edition,[1] and has not before appeared in a book. "Looking over some old papers recently," writes the poet, "I found some verses written by me when a boy of sixteen, nearly sixty years ago. Of course the circumstances under which they were penned alone entitle them to notice, but I venture to send them as the only response to thy request which I can make."

WILLIAM PENN.

The tyrant on his gilded throne,
   The warrior in his battle-dress,
The holier triumph ne'er have known
   Of justice and of righteousness.

Founder of Pennsylvania ! Thou
   Didst feel it, when thy words of peace
Smoothed the stern chieftain's swarthy brow,
   And bade the dreadful war-dance cease.

On Schuylkill's banks no fortress frowned,
   The peaceful cot alone was there ;
No beacon fires the hilltops crowned,
   No death-shot swept the Delaware. .

In manners meek, in precepts mild,
   Thou and thy friends serenely taught
The savage huntsman, fierce and wild,
   To raise to Heaven his erring thought.

---

[1] Reference is had to the elegant "library" edition, published by Houghton, Mifflin & Co. In this edition the poems are newly grouped, and many of them are accompanied by new introductory notes by Whittier.

How all unlike the bloody band
    That unrelenting Cortez led
To princely Montezuma's land,
    And ruin 'round his pathway shed.

With hearts that knew not how to spare,
    Disdaining milder means to try,—
The crimson sword alone was there:
    The Indian's choice to yield or die.

But thou, meek Pennsylvanian sire,
    Unarmed, alone, from terror free,
Taught by the heathen council fire
    The lessons of Christianity,

Founder of Pennsylvania's State,—
    Not on the blood-wet rolls of fame,
But with the wise, the good, the great,
    The world shall place thy sainted name.

1824.

This is not stuff to be ashamed of. Pretty strong verse for a novice! And (with the exception of verses, often of a humorous character, written on his slate at school, and sometimes passed around by his fellow-pupils somewhat against his will) they are the first known poetry of his. There is a relish in them of better things. His two years' study of Burns is beginning to bear fruit. But now comes the second important event in his literary life,—his discovery by young William Lloyd Garrison, then editing a paper in Newburyport. Garrison is described as being at that time a neatly dressed youth, popular with young ladies; having rich dark-brown hair, forehead high and very white, cheeks ruddy, lips full and sensitive, wide hazel eyes, active movements, and a bright and happy disposition.

Father Whittier had subscribed for Garrison's "Free Press," and was much pleased with its humanitarian tone. Greenleaf's elder sister, Mary, had, unknown to him, sent to the "Free Press" by the postman, in 1826, a poem of her brother's, probably that called "The Deity."

One day, as he was mending stone fence by the road, the postman threw him the family copy of the "Free Press"; and he was dumfounded to find a piece of his own in the poet's corner. He wrote and sent others; but let William Lloyd Garrison himself tell the story :—

"Going upstairs to my office, one day, I observed a letter lying near the door, to my address; which, on opening, I found to contain an original piece of poetry for my paper, the 'Free Press.' The ink was very pale, the handwriting very small; and having at that time a horror of newspaper 'original poetry,'—which has rather increased than diminished with the lapse of time,—my first impulse was to tear it in pieces without reading it, the chances of rejection after its perusal being as ninety-nine to one; . . . but, summoning resolution to read it, I was equally surprised and gratified to find it above mediocrity, and so gave it a place in my journal. . . . As I was anxious to find out the writer, my post-rider one day divulged the secret, stating that he had dropped the letter in the manner described, and that it was written by a Quaker lad named Whittier, who was daily at work on the shoemaker's bench with hammer and lapstone at East Haverhill. Jumping into a vehicle, I lost no time in driving [with a friend] to see the youthful rustic bard, who came into the room with shrinking diffidence, almost unable to speak, and blushing like a maiden. Giving him some words of encouragement, I addressed myself more particularly to his parents, and urged them with great earnestness to grant him every possible facility for the development of his remarkable genius." [1]

Elsewhere Mr. Garrison writes : "I found him a bashful boy covered with blushes, from whom scarcely a word could be extracted."

It seems that young Whittier had been at work in the field, and, on being called, he had come up to the back door, and got on his coat and shoes, and exchanged a few words with his callers, when the father appeared on the scene.

"'Is this friend Whittier?'

"'Yes.'

"'We want to see you about your son.'

"'Why, what has the boy been doing?'"(anxiously).

On learning that the crime was nothing more than verse-making, his alarm was quieted. He informed Mr. Garrison that the boy had been writing verse almost as soon as he could write at all, and, when pen and ink failed him, he would resort to chalk and charcoal,—but all with so much secrecy that it was only by removing some rubbish in the garret that his concealed manuscripts had been brought to light. When Garrison urged the father to give him an education, and allow him to follow his guiding star, the father answered with deep emotion, " Sir, poetry will not give him *bread*," and begged him not to put such notions into his son's head.

---

[1] Life of William Lloyd Garrison, by his children, i. 67.

Garrison's mouth was closed by what he himself felt to be the truth of the old man's words, and he took his leave.

But the seeds of ambition had been sown, a quench-less ardor set aflame in the young man's breast. It seemed utterly out of the question for the father to afford a single term's schooling away from home. But Greenleaf set his wits to work. It happened that the young man who helped on the farm in summer was accustomed to make ladies' shoes and slippers during the winter, and he agreed to instruct Whittier in the mysteries of the "gentle craft of leather," and thus enable him to get money for a term of schooling at Haverhill Academy.

Behold, then, our deep-eyed, sunny-tempered lad of genius seated on his bench amid shoemakers' wax, bristles, pincers, paste-horns, rosin, and waxed ends!

> "Rap, rap! upon the well-worn stone
>   How falls the polished hammer!
> Rap, rap! the measured sound has grown
>   A quick and merry clamor.
>
> "Now shape the sole! now deftly curl
>   The glossy vamp around it,
> And bless the while the bright-eyed girl
>   Whose gentle fingers bound it!"
>
> *—Whittier.*

He had probably known something of the art pre-viously, judging from Mr. Garrison's account above quoted. For it was a common thing for some member of every farm to mend the horses' harness and make the home shoes. Garrison himself had, when a boy, been apprenticed for a short time to the shoe business in Lynn, and actually learned how to make a shoe. To these two illustrious shoemakers add the names of Noah Worcester, Henry Wilson, Roger Sherman (one of the signers of the Declaration of Independence), Jacob Boehmen, and many others, whose lives are sketched in William E. Winks's work on Illustrious Shoemakers.[1] Coleridge, too, had a great idea in his youth of turning shoemaker! The introduction of machinery for making shoes has now almost annihilated the old-style shoemaker with leather apron and hands redolent of wax ; his place is taken by the cutter and clicker and riveter and machine-girl of the great factory,—more's the pity!

Mr. Moses E. Emerson, who was one of Whittier's teachers in the district school and lived for a year in the Whittier family, gave, at the age of eighty-two, some interesting reminiscences of his school-teaching days. The occasion was the reunion in 1885 of the class of 1827–30 of the Haverhill Academy. "Whittier loved his fun and joke as well as the rest of us," said he. "If my memory serves me rightly, Mr. Whittier, with others on the farm, made shoes in one of those little shops you see now at country farm-houses. I remember that he used to sit on a low bench that had a little draw[2] at the side. When I have entered

---

[1] This book can claim the proud preëminence of containing the most atrocious caricature portrait of Whittier extant in the world, the work, evidently, of a 24-carat donkey. It looks as if its subject were afflicted with an aggravated case of mumps, and had been stung about the eyes by yellow-jackets. No shoemaker reading the book but would turn sadly away from any incipient intention he might have formed of purchasing Whittier's poems.

[2] A New England local expression for "drawer."

4

the shop for a chat with those I was sure to find there, I remember that often Mr. Whittier would pull out the little draw and hand me some loose sheets of paper, with the poems he had [written] on them during the day. He usually offered no comment, but continued steadily at his work." [1]

Whittier entered Haverhill Academy in April, 1827, and remained six months, returning home every Friday evening. It was the first year of the school's existence, and the building had never been occupied. He wrote the dedicatory ode, and acquired respect thereby. He roomed and boarded with the family of Mr. A. W. Thayer, editor and publisher of the Haverhill "Gazette." Numerous poems—some of them in the Scotch dialect—were contributed by him to this paper. Here is one composed a year or two later, in imitation of Burns : [2]—

THE DRUNKARD TO HIS BOTTLE.

" Hoot !—daur ye shaw ye're face again,
 Ye auld black thief o' purse and brain ?
 For foul disgrace, for dool an' pain
  An' shame I ban ye :
 Wae 's me, that e'er my lips have ta'en
  Your kiss uncanny !

" Nae mair, auld knave, without a shillin'
 To keep a starvin' wight frae stealin'
 Ye'll sen' me hameward, blin' and reelin',
  Frae nightly swagger,
 By wall and post my pathway **feelin'**,
  Wi' mony a stagger.

---

[1] Boston Advertiser, 1885 (about September 11).

[2] From the library edition of the poems, 1888.

" Nae mair o' fights that bruise an' mangle,
Nae mair o' nets my feet to tangle,
Nae mair o' senseless brawl an' wrangle,
Wi' frien' an' wife, too,
Nae mair o' deavin' din an' jangle
My feckless life through.

" Ye thievin', cheatin', auld Cheap Jack,
Peddlin' your poison brose, I crack
Your banes against my ingle-back
Wi' meikle pleasure.
De'il mend ye i' his workshop black,
E'en at his leisure !

*   *   *   *   *

' Cock a' ye're heids, my bairns fu' gleg,
My winsome Robin, Jean, an' Meg,
For food an' claes ye shall na beg
A doited daddie.
Dance, auld wife, on your girl-day leg,
Ye 've foun' your laddie ! "

The master of the school, Oliver Carlton, could
with difficulty be made to believe that the first composition handed in by Whittier had been written by
him without assistance. But the matter was soon
put beyond question by the production of many more
of equal or greater merit. The lad indulged in not a
single luxury this first winter; for at the end of the
half-year he still had the Mexican quarter of a dollar
which remained as surplus after he had calculated
and apportioned his expenses.'

The most important thing that happened to him
during this and the following year (for the next year
he taught school in West Amesbury and got enough

' Underwood, p. 69.

money for another six months at the Academy) was
his being offered the use of two good private libraries. Genius without knowledge will go but a little
way. Whittier, like Abraham Lincoln and Henry
Wilson, wrested his intellectual education from
between the covers of books read often by stealth,
outside of college walls. And it is well. University
men are good, and field men and mountain men are
good. Great men, like great trees, grow far apart,
and draw their nutriment from a wide area of soil
and circumambient air. If they are to have a distinctive savor, or *race*, they must be of different
species and grown on different soils. That the scho-
lastic culture of Longfellow and Bryant and Lowell
was not Whittier's, or Whitman's, or Lincoln's, is the
world's gain. The daughter of Mr. Thayer of Haverhill speaks of the great delight Whittier took in
reading books from her father's library, being often
so absorbed in thought that the noise of three children playing around him did not serve to drive him
from his pursuit. He was always an eager reader,
and would walk miles, he says, to borrow a book he
had heard of. The other library placed at his disposal in Haverhill was that of Dr. Elias Weld, the
"wise old doctor" of "Snow-Bound," and the one to
whom "The Countess" is dedicated. "He was the
one cultivated man of the neighborhood," Mr. Whittier has said.

A fellow-student at the Academy, the Hon. Jackson
B. Street, has interesting remembrances of Whittier:—

"As I remember, he came in for recitations only,
and did his studying elsewhere. I can picture him

now standing beside the master's desk, reciting in a subdued tone. To my boyish fancy, the knowledge that he was gifted enough to write the ode read at the dedication of the Academy, and also poems for the village paper, raised him to a high place in my estimation. His presence in the room had a great attraction for all of us. As for myself, I remember that I used to sit and gaze at him,—a habit that often brought down Master Carlton's displeasure upon my innocent head. I could n't help it, however. I only know it was impossible for me to do any studying when Mr. Whittier was in the room."

Rev. Charles Wingate, as a lad of thirteen, was with Whittier at the Academy. Says he:—

"I remember him as a big boy whom we were all proud to know, and by whom we all esteemed it the greatest of honors to be noticed. Many and many a time I remember seeing his slate going about from hand to hand with some little poem that he had struck off in school. I used always to deem it an exquisite pleasure, as well as a deep honor, if the slate were passed to me. I do not remember if Mr. Whittier ever approved of this proceeding on the part of his schoolmates. He was always modest in showing his productions, and when his slate was passed on from hand to hand, as I have told you, it was generally the result of some breach of confidence on the part of some one of his particular friends who sat near him. These verses were often of a humorous nature, and often had as subjects things to be found in the schoolroom. Many, however, were of a more serious and thoughtful character." [1]

---

[1] Boston Advertiser, Dec. 17, 1887.

The pupils at the Academy were of both sexes, and from ten to twenty-five years old. The first preceptress in charge of the young ladies was Miss Arethusa Hall, who is, I believe, still living in Northampton, Massachusetts. She has all her life been a teacher in private schools and academies of Massachusetts and Brooklyn, Long Island. As an educator she holds high rank. She has published one or two educational works, as well as the "Thoughts of Blaise Pascal," and a life of the Rev. Sylvester Judd, in whose family she lived when a girl. For a class reunion of the Haverhill Academy, in 1885, she wrote the following interesting letter, being then over eighty years of age:—

NORTHAMPTON, MASS., Sept. 3, 1885.

THE REV. MR. WINGATE:

DEAR SIR,—I have your circular inviting me to meet Mr. Whittier at a reunion of his schoolmates of Haverhill Academy. It would give me great pleasure not only to meet one of the most distinguished of our American poets, whom I for the moment assume the honor of calling one of my pupils,—but also to see again his young lady schoolmates, who were directly under my care and instruction. I remember Mr. Whittier well, as he was then, having enjoyed few opportunities for academic culture, and whom Mr. Duncan introduced to my attention as "a young man who, at the shoemaker's bench, often hammered out fine verses." I recollect the assiduity with which he was reported to study, and I have vividly pictured in my memory his appearance at a public examination, in an embarrassed attitude, undergoing the well-sustained ordeal. From that time I followed his literary career with interest, imbued as it was with the noblest principles of humanity no less than with the deepest poetic feeling. Only a few days ago I reread with intense delight, summer though it was, his "Snow-Bound," picturing in many points my own early experiences. I regret very much that I do not see the probability of my being present at the proposed reunion. Failing in this, you will please present my highest appreciation and regard to Mr. Whittier, and my kind wishes to any of my old pupils who may be at the gathering.

Respectfully yours,

ARETHUSA HALL.

Friends who knew Whittier at the period of which we are now treating describe him as being earnest, conscientious, witty, quick to help in righting a wrong; never flattering or to be flattered; a love of fun and teasing lurking under his grave exterior; cold and embarrassed in general society, but in a small, congenial circle a fine converser. In person he was tall and slender, with a shy beautiful face, as innocent and modest in appearance (judging from his portrait) as the boy Milton or Longfellow. The portrait painted by Bass Otis ten years later (engraved for the library edition of the poems) shows well his amiability and geniality of disposition. Friends of the Academy days describe Whittier as a silent, thinking boy, neatly dressed, rather lionized at school, especially by the girls; one whom you would turn to look at a second time on the street. At the Wednesday afternoon meetings of the scholars for social and literary entertainment he was usually present, and entered into the spirit of the hour with zest, freed for the time being from the bashful reserve which usually characterized him in public.

In the village he was a member of the group of progressive intellectual people who met at Judge Pitman's and Judge Minot's. It is said that he was the

central figure at these gatherings, the one whose
coming was always waited for; and here he threw off
his natural reserve and took part in the conversation,
always intensely interested, a good listener, and
biding his time to utter his own thought. When his
distant kinsman, Daniel Webster, was a young man
at Portsmouth, New Hampshire, he exercised a curiously similar influence upon social circles. All who
knew Webster at that time speak of his tenderness,
gayety, exceedingly rich humor, and fine social powers. A lady who knew him says : "He soon formed
a circle around him of which he was the life and
soul." Yet, in basic traits, how dissimilar the two !—
Webster conservative, prosaic, unimaginative ; Whittier the exact opposite. In each, however, fervid
intensity of emotion is balanced by a shrewd practical humor,—a sense of the ludicrous which saves
them from extravaganza.

There are discernible in Whittier (as in Webster)
many of the distinctive New England traits,—something of the shrewd caution and conservatism that
plow so deep a line of separation between the East-
erner and the sanguine-audacious and nonchalant
Westerner. But, when all is said, Whittier stands
unique,—a curious cross between Quaker, Yankee, and
Saracen, and yet fibred with the purest Americanism.

The foregoing reminiscences of Whittier's school-
days help us to understand a little matter that otherwise would seem very mysterious; namely, how Wil-
lis Gaylord Clarke could have written of Whittier, in
1830, to the London "Literary Gazette," as "a young
poet-editor of great promise."[1] To us, the couple of

---

[1] James Grant Wilson, in "Bryant and his Friends," p. 46.

dozen of immature poems the boy had published up to that date seem to furnish too slight a basis for such praise. But poets were scarce in those days, and were more highly valued than at present, as the picture of Haverhill society just given makes evident. Furthermore, William Lloyd Garrison tells us that Whittier's early verses, printed in Garrison's Newburyport "Free Press," were "readily copied by other papers," and thus helped to spread his fame.

CHAPTER II.

"Now, when I know how far this world's happiness can reach; now, when all the stars of good fortune shine over me, fair and propitious; *now*, is it, by my God, a noble spirit which stirs in me; now do I give a mighty proof that no offering is too great for man's highest blessing—the freedom of his country! The great movement calls for great hearts; and within me do I feel the power to be a rock amidst this raging of the waves of nations. I must away—and throw my breast with fearless force against this storm of seas."—KÖRNER, *Letter to his Father*.

FOR five years—1828 to 1833—Whittier watched the career of his friend William Lloyd Garrison before he decided to cast in his lot with the despised Abolitionists, in the meantime employing his pen in purely literary work. Undoubtedly there was a struggle in his mind as to just where his duty lay. He had, as he once said to the writer, political ambitions and literary aspirations in those days, and he would seem to have doubted whether he was adapted to the rough work of reform. Let it be remembered, too, that his mind matured slowly, that his educational advantages had been slender, and that to enter upon public work with success it was necessary to have a disciplined and well-furnished mind.

Not that hatred of oppression was not always strong in his breast : he had from boyhood up fed his mind with accounts of the oppressions endured by his fellow-Quakers, and had inherited from persecuted ancestors instincts of freedom. Even a hundred years after active persecution of the Quakers had ceased in New England the old Puritan bitterness and bigotry still existed, and Thomas Chalkley, whose works were cherished and frequently read to her children by Mrs. Whittier, says in his Travels, "I, being a stranger and traveler, could not but observe the barbarous and unchristianlike welcome I had into Boston. 'Oh, what a pity it was,' said one, 'that all of your society were not hanged with the other four!'" It is to be supposed, also, that that classic of the Friends, Besse's "Sufferings of the Quakers," was read by Whittier when a boy. The influence of those old tomes must have tinctured his very blood, and been built into every fibre of his being. They alone were enough to determine the whole course of his life as a friend of the oppressed.

As editor of three different journals, during the years 1828–1833, Whittier must have studied with considerable thoroughness the political situation, and got well informed on the subject of slavery. Then in 1833 he publishes, at his own expense, his anti-slavery pamphlet "Justice and Expediency," and takes his stand, for life or for death, with the friends of the slave. As soon as he had fairly faced the matter, his poetic insight let him see the shallow sophistry of the defenders of slavery. He believed in the dignity of

human nature and in the Golden **Rule** of Christ.
Therefore it was that

> "He went
> And humbly joined him to the weaker part,
> Fanatic named, and fool, yet well content
> So he could be the nearer to God's heart,
> And feel its solemn pulses sending blood
> Through all the widespread veins of endless good."

His first journalistic work was done as editor of
the "American Manufacturer" of Boston,—a position for which he was indebted to his friend William
Lloyd Garrison, who was at that time editing in
Boston the "National Philanthropist," the first paper
in the world established expressly to advocate total
abstinence from intoxicating liquors. The founder
of this paper was the Rev. William Collier, a Baptist
city missionary, who kept a kind of boarding-house
at 30 Federal Street, near Milk. Whittier and Garrison both boarded with "Parson Collier," who was
also the proprietor of Whittier's "Manufacturer,"—
a protectionist paper, and friendly to Henry Clay. It
was to Parson Collier's also that Benjamin Lundy
came in 1828, and first interested Garrison in the
cause of the slave. Whittier had gone to Boston to
study and read, 1828-29, and he accepted this editorial work, at $9 a week, because it enabled him to
carry on his studies. He confesses that he always
had to study up his subjects before writing his editorials for this journal.

The next year, 1830, he is at home, editing the
Haverhill "Gazette." From July, 1830, to January,
1832, he is editor of George D. **Prentice's** "New Eng-

land Weekly Review," published in Hartford, Connecticut. When at the Haverhill Academy, he had sent some of his "compositions" to Prentice, who liked them and published them with commendatory notice. Young Whittier was at work in the field when the letter of the Hartford publishers was brought to him, asking him to edit their "Review." He was overwhelmed with astonishment at the request, yet accepted. He says the publishers, on their part, were much surprised at his youth, when they first met him. He let them do most of the talking in the first interview! The Hartford episode was a period of quiet gestation and study, during which he wrote poems and sketches, and edited the literary remains of his friend J. G. C. Brainard. In March, 1831, he made a trip home, to be with the good father during his last illness. The publishers of the "Review" were so pleased with his sketches and poems that they had shortly before issued a collection of them in a small volume,—Whittier's first published work, now suppressed,—entitled "Legends of New England, in Prose and Verse." The trip to Haverhill was of course by stage-coach. There were no rosewood, upholstered boudoir cars to ride in then,—not a single railroad in New England, and but two in the United States, and they just built.[1] Mr. Whittier

----

[1] One in South Carolina and one in New York, the latter being the Mohawk & Hudson Railway, on which the queer, little De Witt Clinton locomotive had been drawing rude passengers-cars for about two months. On some of these early railways they had open cars for people of small means. As many of the Abolitionists were numbered among this class, they occasionally availed themselves of the open cars. See the fascinating Life of Garrison by his sons.

wrote at the time an amusing account of the hardships and miseries of his journey.

From 1832 to 1837 Whittier toiled on the farm and
finally succeeded in paying off the debt with which it
was encumbered. It is stated that he used to drive
over to the head of tide-water on the Merrimack with
apples and vegetables, which he exchanged for salt-
fish with the owners of coasting vessels. Hard work
and little yield is the rule on most Massachusetts
farms. In the intervals of farm work he managed to
print "Moll Pitcher" (of which more hereafter) and
"Mogg Megone." His hero "Mogg" he has styled
"a big Injun strutting around in Walter Scott's
plaid." He says that for his early poems and literary
articles he received absolutely nothing, with the
exception of a few dollars from the "Democratic Review" and "Buckingham's New England Magazine,"
his pronounced views on slavery making his name
too unpopular for a publisher's uses. In a prefatory
note to "Moll Pitcher," he humorously owns up to
the unremunerative nature of his literary work: "I
have not enough of the poetical in my disposition to
dream of converting, by an alchemy more potent
than that of the old philosophers, a limping couplet
into a brace of doubloons, or a rickety stanza into a
note of hand." All this time, it is to be understood
that he was by no means indifferent to the subject of
slavery, but was earnestly examining it in all its
aspects. Some time early in 1833, while he was thus
engaged, Garrison, as if divining his thoughts, wrote
as follows to three young ladies of Haverhill:—

"You excite my curiosity and interest by informing me that
my dearly beloved Whittier is a *friend* and townsman of yours.

Can we not induce him to devote his brilliant genius more to
the advancement of our cause, and kindred enterprises, and
less to the creations of romance and fancy, and the disturbing
incidents of political strife? . . . You think my influence
will prevail with Whittier more than yours. I think otherwise.
If he has not already blotted my name from the tablet of his
memory, it is because his magnanimity is superior to neglect.
We have had no correspondence whatever for more than a
year with each other! Does this look like friendship between
us? And yet I take the blame all to myself. He is not a
debtor to me—I owe him many letters. . . . Pray secure
his forgiveness, and tell him that my love to him is as strong
as was that of David to Jonathan. Soon I hope to send him a
contrite epistle, and I know he will return a generous pardon."[1]

Presently, as if in response to the appeal in this
letter, Whittier publishes at his own expense, in June,
1833, his "Justice and Expediency; or, Slavery Considered with a View to its Rightful and Effectual
Remedy, Abolition." An edition of 5,000 copies was
afterwards issued by Lewis Tappan, for gratuitous
distribution. Tappan wrote Whittier a very kind
letter about the essay, and it was appreciatively
reviewed by the anti-slavery editor, Nathaniel P.
Rogers. A notice of it in a Virginia paper called
forth two long and noble responses from its author.
They were published in the "Liberator," and are
included in the latest edition of his prose works. In
a foot-note to the pamphlet Whittier calls the attention of his friends to "'Thoughts on Colonization,' a
very able and eloquent pamphlet by a much-traduced
and noble-hearted philanthropist, William L. Garrison, of Boston." Garrison returns the compliment

____

[1] Life of Garrison, i. 331.

in a little paragraph in his paper, to the effect that "John G. Whittier, of Haverhill, a member of the Society of Friends, and a gentleman distinguished as a writer, has published an excellent pamphlet on the subject of slavery. . . . Friend Whittier deserves to be called the Stuart of America."

"Justice and Expediency" is a thorough piece of argument, terribly in earnest, abounding in italicised and capitalized sentences (as first printed), and solemn appeals to the religious nature. In Great Britain the long struggle for emancipation in the West Indies was just drawing to a close, and the writings of the British anti-slavery chiefs were drawn upon by Whittier for material and illustrations, although perhaps not quite so tellingly as in Mrs. Child's "Appeal," published four months later in the same year. A few sentences from "Justice and Expediency" will give an idea of the treatment:—

"But it may be said that the miserable victims of the system have our sympathies.

"Sympathy!—the sympathy of the Priest and the Levite, looking on, and acknowledging, but holding itself aloof from mortal suffering. Can such hollow sympathy reach the broken of heart, and does the blessing of those who are ready to perish answer it? Does it hold back the lash from the slave, or sweeten his bitter bread?

"Oh, my heart is sick—my very soul is weary of this sympathy—this heartless mockery of feeling. . . .

"No—let the TRUTH on this subject—undisguised, naked, terrible as it is, stand out before us. Let us no longer seek to cover it—let us no longer strive to forget it—let us no more dare to palliate it. . . .

"Sisters, daughters, wives, and mothers, your influence is felt everywhere, at the fireside, and in the halls of legislation, surrounding, like the all-encircling atmosphere, brother and father, husband and son! And by your love of them, by every holy sympathy of your bosoms, by every mournful appeal which comes up to you from hearts whose sanctuary of affections has been made waste and desolate, you are called upon to exert it in the cause of redemption from wrong and outrage. . . .

" In vain you enact and abrogate your tariffs; in vain is individual sacrifice, or sectional concession. The accursed thing is with us, the stone of stumbling and the rock of offense remains. Drag, then, the Achan into light; and let national repentance atone for national sin. . . .

" But a few months ago we were on the verge of civil war. . . . The danger has been delayed for a time; this bolt has fallen without mortal injury to the Union, but the cloud from which it came still hangs above us, reddening with the elements of destruction."

Soon after the publication of " Justice and Expediency " there appeared in the Haverhill "Gazette" Whittier's first anti-slavery poem,—the lines to Garrison, "Champion of those who groan beneath oppression's iron hand,"—a poem which had, however, been in his portfolio since 1832, and which was quickly followed by " Toussaint L'Ouverture " and " The Slave-Ships," the handsel of a long and remarkable series of poems of freedom, extending over a period of thirty years, during which the stirring music of these northern pibrochs never ceased to be heard. Whittier has now unfurled his flag and taken his place in the ranks of freedom, and it behooves us to ascend to some elevated point and sweep the horizon with our glass,—in other words, get some idea of the situation, appreciate the sacrifice made, understand the obloquy and danger undergone by the reformers, the sufferings of the slave and the attitude of society and the Church toward the doctrine of immediate emancipation. In short, I purpose to forecast the years, and briefly touch on the more salient features of the Abolition struggle, so that those who were not of it may better understand the part played by Whittier in the movement. I shall then give an account of the poet's adventures and sufferings as a member of the anti-slavery band, and of his anti-slavery poems and the enthusiasm of humanity they awakened in the minds of all true men.

In brief, the situation was this: The nation at large was lulling a guilty conscience with the music of the cotton-gin, stopping its ears against the languid protests and half-forgotten example of the Quakers, and paying no attention at all to the timid voice of Benjamin Lundy,—but had been suddenly startled and angered by the loud voice of William Lloyd Garrison of Massachusetts calling for Immediate Emancipation. Garrison had been imprisoned in Baltimore for opposition to the slave-trade, and a price of $5,000 set on his head by the Legislature of Georgia. The "Liberator" had been conducted by him in Boston for two years and a half, and he had put forth a crushing pamphlet against the iniquitous Colonization Society, which, with full apology for existing slavery, and cheerfully recognizing the status of the slave as a chattel, was filled with bitter prejudice against the free "niggers," and sought their unjust expulsion from the country. Finally, the school of Prudence Crandall, established in Canterbury, Connecticut, for the education of young colored girls, after a long struggle against insane prejudice, had at last been closed by the State authorities.

Of the stainless moral integrity of Garrison, by whose side Whittier now stood bravely forth, there can be no question. That to Garrison more than to any other single individual was due the creation of the public sentiment that made possible the Emancipation Proclamation, and sustained Congress in the passing of the Constitutional Amendment forever abolishing slavery in this country, it seems to me fatuous to deny. His words were " sparkles hot and seed ethereal " dropped into the moral nature of the American people, to kindle there an undying flame. In half a dozen years, the society founded by him in Boston had multiplied to eight hundred, three hundred of which were in Ohio alone, and one of these societies numbered four thousand members. All bear witness to the purity of Garrison's character, his beautiful domestic life, his gay-heartedness, and his gentleness and moderation in private conversation. Harriet Martineau deemed him to be " one of God's nobility," "covered all over with the stars and orders of the spiritual realm." It is related of Charles Sumner that shortly after the assault upon him by Brooks, and while the wounds on his head were yet new and of a dangerous character, and his physician had strictly charged him not to take off his hat out of doors, yet, when he caught sight of William Lloyd Garrison on a street of Boston, he took off his hat to him, and to him alone of all he met. Intensely positive souls Garrison attached to his own by the strongest ties. But people who did not know him personally were incensed by the violent language of his editorials and speeches. He wrote with very strong ink, his words were not musk-scented by any means, and the lip of the medicine-glass he offered the South was not smeared with honey. Like most journalists of that day, he could speak daggers and make every word stab. He was almost as headstrong in his attempts to defend and enforce his doctrines of Perfectionism, Non-Resistance, Non-Political Action, and Disunion, as in his battle against the slave-power. He caused a split in the ranks of the Abolitionists, alienated many stanch friends, and poured his scorn upon such advocates of gradual and conciliatory anti-slavery measures as Dr. William Ellery Channing and Henry Ward Beecher.

Now, there are thousands of Southern gentlemen who were as humane in their treatment of their slaves as ever was Thomas Jefferson or George Washington. They did not therefore quite fancy being described in the columns of the "Liberator," in staring capitals, as THIEVES, ROBBERS, and MAN–STEALERS, "man-hyenas," "fiends in human shape," "assassins of bleeding humanity." Vituperative epithets such as these bespatter all the early pages of the "Liberator." For example, alluding editorially to an article in the "Colonization Herald" of Philadelphia, written just after the burning by a mob of the Abolitionists' splendid new Pennsylvania Hall, the "Liberator" speaks of its "brutally contemptuous and fiendishly malignant" language, its "vulgar billingsgate," and thinks that "the man who can write such an article is a ruffian capable of any crime." But now the article, as reprinted on the same page, contains no billingsgate whatever, and no fiendish language: it is only quietly satirical. The clergy the "Liberator" styles "a brotherhood of thieves." A certain Dr. Baird is delicately alluded to as " this lickspittle of European despotism and aristocracy." In reference to Rev. William S. Plummer, D.D., a slaveholder of Virginia, the "Liberator's" Philadelphia correspondent remarks, "Can there be a more detestable, a more infamous, and more diabolical character on earth than a professedly man-stealing minister?" Caleb Cushing is styled by Garrison "an impudent, canting demagogue," "a fool," "a political adventurer," "a shallow sophist," "a dissimulator," and "a recreant son of Massachusetts" ("Liberator," Feb. 5 and 19, '58). Nathan Hale, father of Edward Everett Hale, and editor of the Boston "Advertiser," wrote some temperate and not unkindly articles on the evils of the intermarriage of distinct types, *i. e.*, on race degeneration (with reference to the amalgamation laws of Massachusetts); whereupon Garrison bestows upon him some tender and charitable appellations,—as, "the twaddling, cowardly, doughfaced editor of the 'Advertiser'" ("Liberator," xv. 1); "impertinent intermeddler," "impudent," "shameless," "depraved"; "this man aspires to the level of respectable society, though in spirit he seems to be as degraded as the lowest frequenters of Billingsgate"; "in the struggle for liberty, he will distinctively espouse the side of villainy" ("Liberator," Feb. 24, '43).

However, the "Liberator's" intemperate language, although regretted by the more judicious of the Abolitionists, was by no means disliked by all. And, in truth, it may be doubted whether mild language would have excited any attention. Language both fierce and loud was needed to pierce to the conscience of a people whose ears were stopped with

Southern cotton. And then observe, please, that the Abolitionists got rough language as well as gave it. Throw a scoop-net back into almost any part of the anti-slavery brine, and you will fetch up grewsome proofs of this, live and quivering. Here, for example: In one of the martyrical lecturing tours of apostles Stephen Foster and Abby Kelley they had been stoned by the boys of a certain town; the local paper blames the boys for putting themselves on a level with " most consummate blackguards." If Saint Stephen called them robbers and nigger-baby thieves and their ministers servants and ambassadors of the devil, they retorted in kind. Abby and Stephen charge two cents for the privilege of signing a petition of theirs for the dissolution of the Union; the local paper exclaims, " *Dissolve the Union!*—may the heart that could conceive the thought be torn from its resting-place, and thrown to the dogs!" The Abolitionists' tongues are likened to " serpents' fangs bedabbled in corruption's foulest dregs." [1]

Abolition was a religion to those who believed in it, a sublime consecration, a solemn sacrament. They called each other brother and sister, and sang their Abolition hymns with all the fervor of Methodist revivalists. Said Miss Martineau, after her first acquaintance with the Abolitionists: " Ordinary social life is spoiled for them; but another which is far better has grown up among them. . . A just survey of the whole world can leave little doubt that the Abolitionists of the United States are the greatest people now living and moving in it." [2] So Lydia Maria Child

---

[1] Liberator, Oct. 17, 1845.

[2] Westminster Review, xxxii. 59 (1839).

says, somewhere in one of her published letters, that socially she lost nothing by her advocacy of Abolitionism, for she made thereby the acquaintance of the noblest people, morally and intellectually, that she had ever known. Miss Martineau especially notes the "bright faces" and continual cheerfulness and courage of the Abolitionists. Wendell Phillips said that Garrison's life was the happiest he ever knew, and all of Mr. Garrison's friends say the same. So Oliver Johnson is called by his friend, John Chadwick, "the happiest of men."

Of course the movement brought out the long-haired fraternity and the cranks ("long-heels," the Boston boys dubbed them), but in no greater number than in the case of every unpopular moral reform.[1] The justness of a cause is not impeached

---

[1] Oliver Johnson tells an amusing story of good Abigail Folsom, an innocent monomaniac on the subject of free speech, who used to annoy anti-slavery meetings by her grotesque interruptions, but was respected for her generous gifts to deserving folk. She was very witty, and was always roundly cheered by the hostile characters that usually fringed the anti-slavery meetings. On one occasion when, seated in a chair, she was being gently carried out of a meeting by Wendell Phillips, Oliver Johnson, and another, she said to the crowd in the aisle, " I 'm better off than my Master was: he had but one ass to ride, I have three to carry me."

Mr. Whittier has recently told another story which matches this. They were having a stormy anti-slavery meeting in New York. Difference of opinion threatened to break up the meeting. But it so happened that near each other on the platform were Garrison, whose head was very bald; William A. Burleigh, whose hair fell in heavy masses to his shoulders ; and a coal-black negro. " All at once," says Mr. Whittier, " during a brief lull, some man

by the imperfections of its defenders. There were
all kinds of apples in the Abolition barrel. There
was plenty of raving fanaticism in the brains of the
anti-slavery lecturers, and a plenteous lack of judgment and high breeding. On the one hand, you have
the fiery indignation, tempered by courtesy and charity, of such men as Whittier, and such women as
Lucy Stone, the Grimké sisters, and Lucretia Mott;
and, on the other, such fanatical apostles as poor,
meek, non-resistant Stephen S. Foster, and brawny
Parker Pillsbury,—"reviled and pelted Stephen"
(who became thoroughly familiar with the odor of
rotten eggs and the nature of brickbats and sole-
leather), and "brown, broad-shouldered Pillsbury,"
whose book, full of shrieks and superlatives and denunciations, on the anti-slavery crusade, as waged
in the schoolhouses and churches of country towns
by himself and brethren, must be read by all who
want to know what Abolitionism was in all its phases.
A little incident in the career of one of these minor
prophets of the cause, Stephen Foster, will help us to
understand why he was "chucked" into lamp closets
and kicked out of churches so often. He was one
evening sitting on the platform waiting for his audience, when a woman came up to the front seat with a
child in her arms. Foster pointed his finger at her,

---

in the back part of the hall shouted at the top of his voice, 'Mr.
Speaker! Mr. Speaker! I 've only a word to say. I want that
negro to shave Burleigh and make a wig for Garrison!' The
whole house immediately broke forth into roars of laughter, which
had the effect to avert all trouble, which had seemed imminent,
and good humor was restored." As Mr. Whittier finished relating
the incident he laughed heartily until the tears ran down his cheeks.

and said to the audience, " There are babies in the South stolen from the cradle *much whiter* than the one that lady holds in her arms." The poor creature sank down abashed and terror-stricken, as all eyes were bent upon her to see what kind of a black child she had given birth to.[1] Is it any wonder that when sound eggs were worth two cents, rotten ones were worth four cents apiece for certain Abolitionists' heads ?

I have unwillingly dwelt upon the darker side of the Abolition movement in order to make it clear that, when Whittier espoused the cause of the slave, he had counted the cost, and knew that he was burying all hope of political preferment and literary gains. Those who gave themselves to the work knew not but that it might be for a lifetime. To be shunned and spat upon by society, mobbed in public, and injured in one's business,—this was what it meant to become an Abolitionist. When Miss Martineau avowed her sympathy with them, society shut its doors in her face. When Longfellow put forth his little pamphlet of poems on slavery, weak and harmless as they were, the editor of " Graham's Magazine " wrote to him to offer excuses for the brevity of a guarded notice of the poems, saying that the word " slavery " was never allowed to appear in a Philadelphia periodical, and that the publisher of the magazine had objected to have even the name of the book appear in his pages. This recalls the notorious mutilations made in foreign books republished in America by the American Tract Society. Several of

---

[1] *Liberator*, Oct. 10, 1845.

their books were "doctored" by cutting out the word "slave" and other matter, and the insertion of harmless equivalents that would give no offense to slaveholders. See Pillsbury's "Acts of the Anti-slavery Apostles," where the details are given. Allusion only can be made to a few of the innumerable persecutions endured by the friends of the black race. How Lydia Maria Child was deprived of the use of the Athenæum library in Boston, because the first use she had made of it was to prepare her "Appeal"; how Dr. Follen was deprived of his professorship in Harvard College for his brave espousal of Abolitionism; how Prudence Crandall's schoolhouse was defiled with filth, and its windows broken; how Arthur Tappan's house was sacked and his life threatened; how Dr. Reuben Crandall (teacher of botany in Washington, D. C., and brother of Prudence Crandall), for having, at his own request, lent to a white citizen a copy of Whittier's "Justice and Expediency," was kept in the damp city prison for eight months, until the seeds of consumption were sown, and his life made a sacrifice; how Amos Dresser was flogged in the public square of Nashville, and his fellow-student of Lane Seminary, the eloquent Marius R. Robinson, was dragged from his bed at night, and tarred and feathered by ruffians,—all these things are matters of history.

But those of the faithful Abolition band who still survive have had ample revenge. Looked upon then as the scum of the earth, they are now regarded as heroes and martyrs. Stone in those days was violently applied to their persons: to-day it is used to carve their statues and busts. Brickbats were then employed against them as *a posteriori* arguments: they are now used for such objects as erecting a $200,000 hall to the memory of Wendell Phillips. Frederick Douglass was at that time a fugitive slave hunted by bloodhounds: recently he was United States Minister to Hayti. A "nigger" then was deemed a soulless ape, a malodorous beast of burden: to-day a monument to the black man Crispus Attucks stands on Boston Common. The very community that regarded Garrison as an intolerable nuisance made him a present of $30,000; and he and Whittier lived to see themselves regarded, with John Brown and Abraham Lincoln, as the saviours of the colored race, and to receive, by ovations and public letters, the grateful reverence of that rapidly rising and affectionate class of American citizens. When the first number of the "Liberator" was issued, it was a deadly crime to teach a negro to read or to write; but since the year 1865 more than fifty million dollars have been expended in the education of Southern negroes, and in 1888 there were fifteen thousand primary schools and some seventy academies, colleges, and professional schools in the South, established for the education of the colored race. The colored people now edit over one hundred and fifty newspapers. As for the opponents of the Abolitionists, *they* are now the obscure and despised. Whittier says, in a pleasant rhymed epistle to his fellow-bard John Pierpont,—

> " Where now are all the 'unco good,'
> The Canaan-cursing 'Brotherhood,'
> The mobs they raised, the storms they brewed,
> And pulpit thunder ?

> Sheer sunk like Pharaoh's multitude ;
>   They 've all ' gone under !' " [1]

Some of Whittier's strongest poems (for stern sar-
casm and ironical rebuke) were inspired by the opposition of the canting pro-slavery clergy, North and
South. That for many years after the anti-slavery
agitation had begun the American Church was the
bulwark of slavery, has been proved again and again
by such writers as Charles K. Whipple, Oliver Johnson, Parker Pillsbury, and the Garrison brothers.
Nothing surprised William Lloyd Garrison more
than the discovery of this fact. A hired priesthood
has often been the conservator of the popular will.
If the pulpits had been occupied by unsalaried speakers,—as with the Quakers,—the Abolitionists would
not have encountered a hundredth part of the opposition they did. Some of the preachers, however,
were on the right side from the start,—Beriah Green,
Moses Thacher, Amos A. Phelps ; Dr. Samuel H.
Cox and J. R. W. Sloane of New York City ; John
Rankin, William H. Furness, and others.[2] The
clergy as a body wheeled into line after a time. As
early as 1845, one hundred and seventy ministers of
Massachusetts signed a protest against slavery, which

---

[1] Liberator, April 28, '65; not reprinted.

[2] I am glad to remember that the house of my father, Rev.
William Sloane Kennedy, of Sandusky, in the Western Reserve,
was a station on the Underground Railroad. One of my earliest
recollections is that of seeing a group of fugitive slaves, black as
coal, standing in our wood-shed waiting for their breakfast,—and
we children enjoined for our lives not to mention the matter to
anyone.

had been drawn up by James Freeman Clarke.[1] Whittier tells of a minister in the old town of Newbury, Massachusetts, who startled and shamed his brother-ministers, who were zealously preaching the enforcement of the Fugitive Slave Law, by drawing up for them *a form of prayer* for use while engaged in catching runaway slaves.

The record of the Quakers on the slavery question in Abolition times is not one for their body as a whole to be proud of. They had fallen away from the high position they occupied nearly a century previous, when they had voluntarily freed all their slaves, and were become as worldly and selfish as the other churches. Having removed slavery from among themselves, they felt no call to interfere with the conscience of Southerners in the matter, especially as their wealth was acquired largely by Southern trade; and Daniel Webster could boast, without fear of contradiction, that he had the support of the sober and "respectable" part of the Society of Friends in his action in support of the Fugitive Slave Law. Yet the work accomplished by such ardent anti-slavery people as the Grimké sisters, Lucretia Mott, John Kenrick, Thomas Shipley, Lindley Coates, and John Greenleaf Whittier atones for much that is hard to forgive in the attitude of the Quakers toward slavery at that time.[2] And one is glad to remember the deed

---

[1] See his "Anti-slavery Days," p. 131. The protest, with all the names, is in the "Liberator," Oct. 10, '45.

[2] A pleasant picture of the domestic life of an anti-slavery Quaker family during Abolition days is given by Lillie B. Chace Wyman in the "Atlantic Monthly," August, 1889.

of the brilliant philosophical writer and wealthy manufacturer, Rowland G. Hazard of Rhode Island, a
Quaker by birth, who in 1841, being in New Orleans,
obtained, by great effort and in the face of threats,
the liberation of one hundred free colored men who
belonged to ships from the North, and had been placed
in the chain-gang as slaves.

The system of slavery was atrocious, Thomas Carlyle to the contrary notwithstanding. "Enslave but
a single human being,"said Garrison, " and the liberty
of the world is put in peril." And another said,
" Slavery has a guilt the blackness of which can never
be painted except by a pencil dipped in the midnight
of the bottomless pit." To deprive a human being of
self-respect, to cut the houghs of his manhood, to
regard him as a beast of burden to be fed on a peck
of corn a week and occasionally given a shirt of coarse
bagging and a pair of trousers to hide his nakedness;
to make of a woman a breeding-animal, and forbid
her the rite of marriage; to tear children from their
mother's knees to be carried off where they would
never see them again; to whip a human being to
death, to tear out his nails by the roots, brand him,
cut the tendons of his heels, and burn him to death,[1]
—not very pleasant things these, and not exactly cal-

---

[1] This seems to be a favorite amusement with lynchers of the
negro in the South. The case of the negro McIntosh who was
burned to death in slow agony by the whole street populace of St.
Louis, in 1836, is well known. In the month of September,
1889, the New York " Nation" copied from a Southern paper an
account of the recent burning to death of a negro lad, for the crime
of rape. There are on record other cases of negro-burnings.

culated to make Northern lovers of freedom moderate in their opposition.

And yet there was a sunny side to slavery. Human nature is at heart good, and much the same everywhere. The writer, in looking over a manuscript lecture of his father's (written in 1858, shortly after his return from a trip to New Orleans, whither he had gone as a delegate to the General Assembly of the Presbyterian Church), finds several statements that furnish interesting testimony to the general humanity of the slaveholders. Speaking as one known to be anti-slavery in his sentiments, he yet says: " A traveler in the South will learn that there is vastly more creature comfort and contentment amongst the mass of the slaves than he supposed. Their general appearance gives no indication of oppression." (Opinion based upon observations in several cities.) He attended several slave sales, and found no exhibition of brutality, no inhumanity. The physical condition of the blacks was fine: " Their strict regimen and discipline and their restraint from vice tend to develop and perfect their physiques." " Had we been at the South and the planters at the North, unquestionably we should have been the slaveholders, and they the Abolitionists. In habits, appearance, intellectual culture, morals, and religion they are our equals; in hospitality and liberality, our superiors."

There can be no doubt that kind treatment of the slave was the rule in nearly all parts of the South. The Abolitionists never forgave Dr. Nehemiah Adams, of Boston, for revealing, in his " South-Side View of Slavery," the brighter side of the institution;

and yet he did not refuse to give the darker side also.
I am not defending the clerical sophistry by which
Dr. Adams shored up the institution, trying to put
out a volcano with a shovelful of Northern snow; but
any one who has seen a good deal of negro life in
the South cannot help having his risibilities excited
by the opening pages of Dr. Adams's book, in which
he tells how, on going South for the first time, with
fearful apprehensions, expecting to meet on all sides
the painful evidences of suffering,—chains, manacles,
the whip, and looks of woe and despair,—he landed
at Savannah, and, instead of finding negroes on
bended knees, with manacled hands raised implor-
ingly, and saying, "Am not I a man and a brother?"
—a common picture on anti-slavery broadsides and
tracts,—he found on the wharf a lot of blacks so
polite, jolly, and full of catching "hi-his!"—lifting
one leg as they laughed—that he began to laugh with
them in spite of himself. He then goes on to tell of
the pleasant relations existing between master and
slave, as he noticed them in traveling about.

The most deeply rooted prejudice encountered by
the Abolitionists was "colorphobia." It was something that could not be argued with. The cutting
irony of Garrison's Shorter Catechism fell upon deaf
ears :—

"Why are slaves not fit for freedom? Because they are
black. Why does the Bible justify American slavery? Because its victims are black. Why are the slaves contented and
happy? Because they are black. Why are they not created
in the image of God? Because they are black."

Negrophobia is, even now, almost as strong among

the vulgar class of whites as it was twenty-five years ago. We have educated colored people now by the thousand—singers, authors, judges, journalists, statesmen even—both North and South. It matters not: the least strain of darker blood stamps them as of the pariah caste. Europeans laugh at this color-nervousness, and it is about time we had got rid of it. A few years ago, Prof. Richard J. Greener and Mr. Robert A. Terrell, of Washington (both colored), sons of Harvard College, wished to join the Washington Club of Harvard graduates : they were black-balled on account of their color, so it is said. And yet, in 1889, the Senior Class of Harvard College elected a gifted black man, Clement H. Morgan, to the class oratorship,—the highest honor at its disposal. This is encouraging, even if it was the result of ballot-and-nomination cabals, as I learned at Harvard. In the same year, also, Yale students chose a colored man for one of the college base-ball nine. Not long ago, I stood in a car of the Old Colony Railroad in Boston, waiting to see a friend off for New York. The seats were all taken but one, and that was partly occupied by a mulatto *lady*, with fine massive, intellectual face, and an expression of matronly dignity. Nobody would share the seat with her. One white boor stood a moment eying the seat wistfully; she moved her package ; he walked away without a word of thanks. The face of the lady only took on a look of deeper patience and suffering. She was used to such insults.

A few years ago a beautiful and intelligent lady was attending a private school in Pittsburg. She stood for a year at the head of the school, and

6

was the favorite pupil of the master. One day it transpired that she had a few drops of unsuspected African blood in her veins: she was at once expelled by the poltroon pedagogue.[1]

Again, for the heinous crime of allowing white and colored students to be educated together within its walls, the Atlanta University was refused its annual appropriation of $8,000 by the Georgia Legislature, a short time ago, and this despicable act was heartily approved by the Southern press.

As the negroes move upward in the social scale, they feel social ostracism more keenly. In the South, the Jim Crow car is still in existence. No negro is allowed to ride first-class. A colored preacher in South Carolina not long ago brought complaint against a Southern railroad before the Interstate Railway Commission for being ejected from a first-class car; negro murders and riots are common at the South; the negroes are refusing to work for the whites, and the relations between the two races are strained to breaking in some sections. Some of the leaders of the negroes advise emigration, and in their journals utter foolish threats against the " white trash," who are their bitterest enemies. At the celebration of the twenty-fifth anniversary of the Emancipation Proclamation in Boston, Bishop H. M. Turner, the first colored chaplain commissioned in the United States Army, said, " Twenty-five years have made us more enlightened than any freed people on the face of the earth; another twenty-five years, and the white man will tremble at the injustice he has done us." And

---

[1] The Forum, October, 1889.

the Hon. George P. Downing, of Newport, Rhode Island, said: "For sixty years I have felt myself to be the victim of injustice. Although I have never committed any crime, I have never seemed to breathe the free air of my native country. . . . A fire of dissatisfaction and grief burns in my breast. The conservative speech I am now making would endanger my life in some States. While my son is spurned from your counting-room, your art-museum, and your church, and while my wife is forbidden to ride with you in the railway car, while my countrymen are murdered in the South, can you expect me to be mild?" Evidently, the work of Abolitionism is not over yet. There are wrongs demanding its attention nearer home than Africa, and quite as cruel as the Arab slave-trade (if more subtle and more hidden from view). A leading colored man of this country, having recently returned from Europe, where no invidious and galling discriminations were made against him on account of his color, feels the change to our bigoted atmosphere so bitterly that he has made calls on a large number of the leading men of his race in the vicinity of New York, and secured their coöperation in the formation of a national defensive league of all the colored people of America. It is clearly the duty and privilege of the surviving Abolitionists and their children to support them in such steps as this. It is a curious fact that the old colonization scheme is coming to the front again, and is by no means dead and buried, as Garrison thought. The plan is advocated not only by some of the blacks themselves, but by Senator Wade Hampton and others. In Texas a plan was recently broached (approved of and subsidized by the Mexican Government) to colonize the blacks of Texas in Vera Cruz, Mexico, for the raising of cotton and sugar-cane.

To return now to Whittier. He first saw service in the field as one of the secretaries of the Philadelphia Anti-slavery Convention of '33. Portions of his own graphic sketch of the meeting cannot be condensed or restated without loss. I shall therefore without apology make somewhat copious quotations, filling in the picture with an incident or two from Samuel J. May's " Recollections " and other sources:—

" In the gray twilight of a chill day of late November," says Whittier, " forty years ago, a dear friend of mine, residing in Boston, made his appearance at the old farm-house in East Haverhill. He had been deputed by the Abolitionists of the city—William Lloyd Garrison, Samuel E. Sewall, and others— to inform me of my appointment as a delegate to the Convention about to be held in Philadelphia for the formation of an American Anti-slavery Society, and to urge upon me the necessity of my attendance.

" Few words of persuasion, however, were needed. I was unused to traveling; my life had been spent on a secluded farm ; and the journey, mostly by stage-coach, at that time was really a formidable one. Moreover the few Abolitionists were everywhere spoken against, their persons threatened, and, in some instances, a price set on their heads by Southern legislators. Pennsylvania was on the borders of slavery, and it needed small effort of imagination to picture to one's self the breaking up of the Convention and maltreatment of its members. This latter consideration I do not think weighed much with me, although I was better prepared for serious danger than for anything like personal indignity. I had read Governor Trumbull's description of the tarring and feathering of his hero, MacFingal, when, after the application of the melted tar, the feather-bed was ripped open and shaken over him, until

> ' Not Maia's son with wings for ears,
> Such plumes about his visage wears,
> Nor Milton's six-winged angel gathers
> Such superfluity of feathers,'

and I confess I was quite unwilling to undergo a martyrdom which my best friends could scarcely refrain from laughing at. But a summons like that of Garrison's bugle-blast could scarcely be unheeded by one who, from birth and education, held fast the traditions of that earlier Abolitionism which, under the lead of Benezet and Woolman, had effaced from the Society of Friends every vestige of slave-holding. I had thrown myself, with a young man's fervid enthusiasm, into a movement which commended itself to my reason and conscience, to my love of country, and my sense of duty to God and my fellow-men. My first venture in authorship was the publication, at my own expense, in the spring of 1833, of a pamphlet entitled 'Justice and Expediency,' on the moral and political evils of slavery, and the duty of emancipation. Under such circumstances, I could not hesitate, but prepared at once for my journey. It was necessary that I should start on the morrow, and the intervening time, with a small allowance for sleep, was spent in providing for the care of the farm and homestead during my absence."

The expenses of so long a journey were no slight matter, and he had written to Mr. Garrison, when the first proposal was made to him, that he would like to go. "But," said he, "the expenses of the journey will, I fear, be too much for me : as thee knows, our farming business does not put much money in our pockets." In the end his expenses were borne by the generous Samuel E. Sewall.[1]

---

[1] Life of Garrison by his sons.

Taking the stage for Boston, he put up at the old Eastern Stage Tavern, and next morning started for New York by the stage-coach in company with William Lloyd Garrison. On arriving in Philadelpia, the delegates first held an informal meeting at the house of the Abolition Quaker, Evan Lewis. The chairman of the meeting was Lewis Tappan, one of the pillars of Abolitionism, a handsome, intellectual-looking man, with clear incisive tones, cool self-possession, fine business qualities, and a pleasant laugh. There were sixty-two members eventually present, representing eleven different States, although only forty were at this preliminary meeting. Their object was one which would subject them to annoyance and insult, if not danger (threats had already been made, and the police had notified them that their meetings must be held in the day-time, as they could not protect them at night). Accordingly, it was thought best to try to secure a presiding officer from among the prominent philanthropists in the city. So six or seven of the members were delegated to wait upon Thomas Wistar and Robert Vaux, wealthy Quakers. Of their call upon the latter gentleman, Samuel J. May says : " I wish I had some wit that I might be able to do justice to the scene. But I need not help you to see it in all its ludicrousness. There were at least six of us—Beriah Green, Evan Lewis, editor of the anti-slavery journal in Philadelphia, called the 'Advocate of Truth,' Eppingham L. Capron, Lewis Tappan, John G. Whittier, and myself— sitting around a richly furnished parlor, gravely arguing by turns with the wealthy occupant, to persuade him that it was his duty to come and be the most prominent one in a meeting of men already denounced as 'fanatics, amalgamationists, disorganizers, disturbers of the peace, and dangerous enemies of the country.' Of course our suit was unsuccessful. We came away mortified much more because we had made such a request than because it had been denied. As we left the door, Beriah Green said in his most sarcastic tone, ' If there is not timber amongst ourselves big enough to make a president of, let us get along without one, or go home and stay there until we have grown up to be men.'"

At the meeting next morning, in the Adelphi Theatre, Beriah Green was chosen president, and Whittier and Tappan secretaries. Mr. Whittier has sketched some of the more prominent persons present, many of whom were young men, enthusiastic and solemnly consecrated to the cause. Beriah Green is described as an eloquent speaker, "a fresh-faced, sandy-haired, rather common-looking man"; then there was the genial, large-hearted, and brave Samuel May ; " that tall, gaunt, swarthy man, erect, eagle-faced, upon whose somewhat martial figure the Quaker coat seemed a little out of place, was Lindley Coates, known in all eastern Pennsylvania as a stern enemy of slavery ; that slight, eager man, intensely alive in every feature and gesture, was Thomas Shipley, who for thirty years had been the protector of the free colored people of Philadelphia; . . . beside him sat Thomas Whitson, of the Hicksite school of Friends, fresh from his farm in Lancaster County, dressed in plainest homespun, his tall form surmounted by a shock of unkempt [brown] hair, the odd obliquity of his vision contrasting strongly with the clearness and directness of his spiritual insight. [When **he** spoke, says **Mr.** McKim, "his matter **was** solid and **clear as a** bell, **and** was moreover **pat to the** point **in** question."] Elizur Wright, **the** young professor **of a Western** college, who **had** lost his place **by** his bold **advocacy of** freedom, with **a look of** sharp concentration **in** keeping with **an** intellect keen as a Damascus blade, closely **watched** the proceedings through **his** spectacles, opening **his** mouth only **to** speak directly to the purpose."

Directly in front of **Mr.** Whittier, who **sat on the** platform, **was** Joshua Coffin, **his old teacher.** The best **speech in the Convention, all** allowed, was made **by** Lucretia **Mott, whose marvelously** beautiful, **sharp-cut, and intellectual face was** radiant with thought. **She was** dressed in plain **but** rich **Quaker** costume, **and had a** dignified **and** earnest manner. Only on the subject of slavery was her habitual placidity of manner disturbed. When she first **rose** to speak, she hesitated **in** deference to the supposable prejudices **of** the non-Quaker part **of** the **audience,** among **whom it was then an** unheard of **thing for a** woman to speak **in public. But** Beriah Green called out encouragingly, **"Go on,** ma'am, **we shall** all be **glad to hear you."** And **"Go on, go on !"** was echoed **by many more.**

A Constitution was written **out and** adopted, and officers chosen. **Mr.** Garrison sat up all night in the attic of his colored host, Lewis Evans, to draft the Declaration **of** Sentiments, which urged immediate emancipation as **a moral** duty, **to** be attained **by** peaceful measures, and conceded the right **of the** separate States **to manage** their **own** domestic interests, asserting, however, that it was the duty of the general government to suppress the slave-trade between the several States, and to abolish slavery altogether in that territory over which it has exclusive jurisdiction. After the Declaration had been discussed, amended, and engrossed on parchment, the sixty-two members (twenty-one of whom were Quakers) signed it one by one. The oldest of the signers, David Thurston, of Maine, lived to see the emancipation of the slaves. Mr. Whittier's words in relation to the Declaration have often been quoted: "I set a higher value on my name as appended to the Anti-slavery Declaration of 1833 than on the title-page of any book." In the little study at Amesbury hangs a copy of the Declaration, in a frame made of wood from Pennsylvania Hall. Of this Hall more anon.

In December, 1863, the thirtieth anniversary of the founding of the American Anti-slavery Society was held in Philadelphia, and interesting addresses were given by Mr. Garrison, J. Miller McKim, and Lucretia Mott.[1] In 1883, the fiftieth anniversary was celebrated (after a fashion) in the same city. Only three of the original signers of the Declaration were alive; namely, Robert Purvis, Elizur Wright, and John G. Whittier. The latter could not come, and sent a letter of regret, so that the meeting consisted of two persons,—Robert Purvis the chairman, and Elizur Wright the audience.

The years 1834 and 1835 are often spoken of in anti-slavery writings as the mob years. Mr. Whittier

---

[1] Stenographic report of the proceedings in "Liberator," Dec. 25, 1863, including an interesting letter by Whittier.

suffered in two of the mobs and riots of these years, and was present at a third. In 1834 the mobs in New York City were so numerous and violent that the time in which they occurred is spoken of as the Reign of Terror. In 1835 the post-office of Charleston, South Carolina, was broken open by citizens, and all papers judged by them to be of an inflammatory nature were seized and burned. This act was condoned by the United States authorities. At the famous mobbing of Garrison in Boston, October 21, 1835, Mr. Whittier was present, being then in Boston with his sister Elizabeth, his duty as a member of the legislature requiring his presence there. He was at the State House on Beacon Hill when the mobbing took place ; and he at once hastened down to the old State House where the broadcloth mobocrats were surging wildly to and fro in the attempt to secure possession of the person of Mr. Garrison. After he was lodged in jail, he was visited by Mr. Whittier and other friends, who found him to be in good heart. Mr. Whittier was staying with his sister at the house of Samuel J. May, and, hearing that the crowd had threatened to attack the house, he saw his sister safely bestowed for the night at another friend's, and he and Mr. May passed a sleepless night in the latter's dwelling. Harriet Martineau, in her "Views of Slavery," is amazed at the indifference shown by the "respectable" classes toward this outrage ; and sore amazed, too, was young Wendell Phillips, who witnessed it : the mob decided his life-work. Miss Martineau writes that an eminent lawyer of Boston said to her:—

"'Oh, there was no mob. I was there myself, and

saw that they were all gentlemen. They were all in fine broadcloth.'

" ' Not the less a mob for that,' said I.

" ' Why, they protected Garrison. He received no harm. They protected Garrison.'

" ' From whom, or what ? '

" ' Oh, they would not really hurt him. They only wanted to show that they would not have such a person live among them.' "

We are next called upon to notice two mobs that occurred farther north, and both on the same evening. In the Haverhill mob Mr. Whittier's sister Elizabeth was in danger of her life ; and in that of Concord, New Hampshire, directed against Mr. Whittier himself and his friend George Thompson (the English orator, afterwards member of Parliament), these two men were in serious danger. At Haverhill, it was a Sunday evening lecture by Samuel J. May that brought out the lewd fellows of the baser sort. Amid terrible yells and other noises a stone came crashing through the window, after the lecture had begun, and struck a lady on the head. She uttered a shriek, and fell bleeding into the arms of her sister. Mr. May closed the meeting, and escaped by walking out between Elizabeth Whittier and the daughter of a wealthy and determined citizen of the place.

The mob-ordeal through which Whittier and George Thompson passed in Concord, New Hampshire, in 1835, was perhaps not excelled in thrilling and picturesque incident by any other during the anti-slavery struggle.' It happened in this wise :

____

' I have constructed the narrative of the Concord mob not only

George Thompson, the English lecturer, was visiting Mr. Whittier at Haverhill; and, thinking they would not be recognized, they determined to take a drive up into New Hampshire to visit N. P. Rogers. They stopped over night in Concord at the house of George Kent, a brother-in-law of Mr. Rogers. After they had gone, Mr. Kent, being an Abolitionist, determined to try to hire a hall for a meeting, to be held when the friends should return. Accordingly, it was arranged that they should be back on the Friday following. The use of the Court House was obtained for the meeting, and handbills were posted announcing that George Thompson and John G. Whittier would address the citizens, setting forth the aims and views of the Abolitionists. Now, nobody had anything against the little-known young man Whittier; but the mention of Thompson created tremendous excitement and wrath; for it was then the implicit belief of the people that Thompson, " the carpet-bagger," was an emissary of the British Government, sent over here to foster dissension between North and South, and

---

from a description of it given to me by Mr. Whittier himself some years ago, but from the accounts of others to whom he has told the story. My thanks are due to the D. Lothrop Co., of Boston, for the use of material embodied in their " Whittier " ; I am also indebted to Underwood's " Whittier " ; to reminiscences of Mrs. Julia Ward Howe (" Cosmopolitan," July, 1889); to Rossiter Johnson's " Short History of Secession " ; the reminiscences of John M. Barbour (Boston " Transcript," August, 1889) ; letter of Mr. Whittier to J. W. Powell (New York "Tribune," 1885); a letter by the same to the Haverhill "Gazette," reprinted in the " Liberator," Oct. 3, '35 ; and Bouton's " History of Concord," pp. 434, 435, which is good for names and dates, but glosses over or is silent about the worst features of the outrage.

so cripple our industries. The indignation of the townsmen was so strong that Gen. Robert Dana, chairman of the Board of Selectmen, called on George Kent, and advised that the meeting should not be held, and directed that the door of the Court House be locked.

Nevertheless, at the appointed time, the Abolitionists and their opponents began to assemble around the building. Whittier and Thompson had arrived and put up at George Kent's beautiful residence ; and, not knowing that their arrival had been bruited abroad, Whittier, in company with Mr. C. Hoag (a Quaker) and editor Joseph H. Kimball, started just at dusk down the street. As they passed along the principal thoroughfare, they met a large concourse of men all crazy with liquor, and shouting and yelling furiously. They had just subjected to rough treatment a poor traveling Quaker preacher who was passing through the town. They took him to be Whittier, the Abolitionist.

"The good people," writes Mr. Whittier, "were lashing each other into a fine frenzy, cursing the Abolitionists as Federalists, etc. The cry was raised, ' *To George Kent's and the wine in his cellar !*' Fearing an attack on our friend's house, we turned to go back and give warning of the danger. But our friends, the mobites ["our friends, the enemy !"] followed us, and insisted that I, notwithstanding my Quaker coat, must be the identical incendiary and fanatic, George Thompson. A regular shower of harmless curses followed, and soon after another equally harmless shower of stones [dirt, and gravel]. These missiles were hurled with some force, and might have done us some injury, had not those who projected them been somewhat overdone by their patriotic exertions in drinking destruction to the Abolitionists."

We know from other sources that Mr. Whittier's hat was knocked off and lost, and that he was bruised in the face by a large stone hurled at him. He was afterwards told by one of the mobbers that it was their intention to catch him and paint his face black. As the trio were retreating, Whittier heard an Irishman say, " They 've killed the Englishman, and now they 're going for the Quaker."

The pelted three were followed up Washington Street and down State, where they found it necessary to take shelter in the house of the Hon. William A. Kent. Although he was not an Abolitionist, the rioters knew him to be a brave man. He barred his door, and addressed the crowd, assuring them they had mistaken their man, that George Thompson was not in the house, and that they should have Whittier only over his dead body.

In the meantime it had grown dark ; and Whittier, remembering the remark of the Irishman in the crowd concerning Thompson, became so anxious as to his fate that he borrowed a hat, succeeded in passing the enemy's lines, and arrived safe at George Kent's, where he found Mr. Thompson unhurt and cheerful.

After some delay on the part of the mob, the cry "Onward!" was raised, and they moved off to George Kent's. After some stone-throwing and much blasphemy, they were decoyed away by a stratagem. But after parading the town for an hour or two, "refreshed with Deacon Giles's best," they once more returned (having discovered the trick), provided with drums, fifes, muskets, and a cannon, and threatened to blow up the house if the d—d Abolitionists were not delivered up to them, in the meantime keeping up a continuous uproar of braying, cat-calling, and swearing.

Now, it so happened that a little group of anti-slavery people were met that evening at George Kent's,—among them being two nieces of Daniel Webster. They all felt that the lives of Whittier and Thompson were in danger, and that they ought to try to get away. To this proposal Whittier, at least, was able to agree unhesitatingly ; for he had always had a nervous dread, not of death, but of suffering gross personal indignities. The mob filled the street just below Mr. Kent's carriage-gate, leaving a way of possible escape through it. Accordingly, the horse and carriage were drawn up quietly in the shadow of the house. It was a bright moonlight night, and the glint of the musket-barrels could be seen just below. Suddenly the two friends jumped into the carriage, the gate was opened, and the horse driven off at a gallop amid the yells and shots of the rioters.

After the escape, these fellows paraded an effigy through the streets, and afterwards burned it in the State House yard, concluding the orgie with a display of fire-works and discharges of cannon.

The two friends left the city by way of Hookset Bridge, the only way open to them, and took the road to Haverhill. They had received minute and careful directions from their friends, and got further directions at the house of an anti-slavery man three miles out from Concord. In the morning they stopped at a tavern to give themselves and the horse a breakfast. While they were eating, the landlord entertained them with a report of the Haverhill mob. Said one of the friends to the host,—

" What kind of a fellow is this Whittier ? "

" Oh, he 's an ignorant sort of chap, a Quaker farmer."

" And who is this Thompson they 're talking about ? "

" Him ? He 's a man sent over here by the British government to make trouble between the North and the South."

As the two gentlemen were stepping into the carriage, Whittier, with one foot on the step, turned and said to the landlord :—

" You 've been talkin' about Thompson and Whittier. This is Mr. Thompson, and I 'm Whittier. Good morning."

" And, jumping into the carriage " (said Mr. Whittier to the writer, with a twinkle in his eye), " we stood not on the order of our going." The good Boniface looked stupefied with wonder. " And for all I know," said the poet, " he 's standing there still with his mouth open."

After this adventure, Mr. Thompson was kept quietly at the Whittier farm-house for a couple of weeks. For the indignities he suffered at Concord, Whittier had ample revenge, in that stinging way in which men of the pen have always defended their sensibilities; namely, by the publication of a brace of satirical ballads,—the " Letter Supposed to be Written by the Chairman of the Central Clique at

Concord" (1846), and the following verses, which, indeed, appeared a year previous to the mobbing of Whittier and Thompson, but were published in the first edition of the poems in 1837, and have not since been reprinted :—

APOLOGY

TO THE " CHIVALROUS SONS OF THE SOUTH," FOR THE FORMATION OF THE LADIES' ANTI-SLAVERY SOCIETY, IN C———D, N. H.

Most chivalrous gentlemen, pardon us, pray,
  And pity our present condition,—
The *lady fanatics* have carried the day,
  And openly preach Abolition !
The petticoat-plotters, with might and with main,
Are tearing the bonds of the Union in twain !

We knew, to our sorrow, that over their tea
  These ladies, for months, had been brewing
A plot to dismember the Union, and free
  Your slaves, to their positive ruin:
But who would have dreamed that they ever would dare,
In the face of New Hampshire, their purpose declare !

Oh, where had the fear of the P———t gone
  From the eyes of these turbulent ladies ?
And where Parson F———k's indignation and scorn
  Which overwhelmed all, when he made his
Great speech at our Democrat gathering, when
Abolition was working its way with the men ?

Alack and alas ! that we live to relate
  How these Amazons gathered together,
Consulting each other, in solemn debate,
  About loosing the slave from his tether;
And gravely resolving your negroes to be
Created like all of us—*equal* and *free.*

7

But think not, dear sirs, that with conduct so base
   " The Democracy " rested in quiet :
No, it rose in its strength to redeem from disgrace
   The town by a regular riot !
And, surrounding the house where the mischief went on,
Plied well the "fanatics " with brickbat and stone.

Through door and through window our missiles went in,
   Disturbing the laces and trimming,—
Oh, would that " our dear Southern brethren " had seen
   How " Democracy " pelted the women !
And had heard, midst the crashing of brickbats, its shout—
" Hurrah for the Union !—you women, clear out ! "

Yet it grieves us to say that in spite of our great
   And most patriotic exertion,
These petticoat-traitors regarded our feat
   As merely a cause of diversion ;
And still they went on, without let or disaster,
To spoil " the relations of servant and master."

But, though foiled in its efforts to drive away
   This bevy of gossip and beauty,
" The Democracy " feels, and rejoices to say,
   That it fully performed its duty ;
And it trusts that its friends will with cheerfulness own
That all that it *could* do, *in safety*, was done !

We are sadly disheartened, and all in a fret—
   Parson F——k is about to absquatalize,
And B—t—n beneath the State's Prison debt
   Is hiding himself from mortal eyes ;
Even H——ll cannot help us—his hands are too full,
Making C—h—n a " Democrat died in the wool."

WHITE SLAVE, DOUGHFACE, & Co.[1]

---

[1] The verses first appeared in the " Liberator " Jan. 3, 1835.

In February, 1836, some five months after the event of the mob, we find Whittier addressing an open letter to Edward Everett (printed in " Liberator," February 20, of that year).

" TO EDWARD EVERETT, GOVERNOR OF MASSACHUSETTS :—

" Exercising, while yet I may, the unsurrendered right of a free citizen of Massachusetts, with due respect for thy official station, but with the frankness which becomes a republican, I feel myself called upon to address thee, in relation to that portion of thy late Message which is devoted to the subject of Slavery."

Whittier disagrees with Governor Everett as to his statement that at the time the United States Constitution was formed the question of slavery was an open one. He affirms that the signers simply left the slavery question as it was, without at all desiring to perpetuate it. In proof, he cites the fact that Benjamin Franklin, although a signer of both the Declaration and the Constitution, also signed another Constitution not long after ; namely, that of the Pennsylvania Society for the Abolition of Slavery. He continues :—

" George Washington was another signer of the Constitution. I know that he was a slaveholder ; and I have not forgotten the emotions which swelled my bosom, when in the metropolis

---

and refer to a mob which occurred in Concord, New Hampshire, Nov. 14, 1834 (not noticed in the " History of Concord," but date recoverable from " Liberator" Dec. 13, '34, which contains an article on the affair). " Parson F——k " is undoubtedly Rev. Wilbur Fisk, one of the most "abusive and malignant" of the opponents of George Thompson. "C—h—n" is evidently for Calhoun.

of New England, the Cradle of Liberty, a degenerate son of the Pilgrims pointed to his portrait, which adorns the wall, with the thrice repeated exclamation,—' That Slaveholder!' I saw the only blot on the otherwise bright and spotless character of the Father of his Country held to open view—exposed by remorseless hands to sanction a system of oppression and blood. It seemed to me like sacrilege. I looked upon those venerable and awful features, while the echoes, once wakened in that old Hall by the voice of ancient Liberty, warm from the lips of Adams and Hancock and the fiery heart of James Otis, gave back from wall and gallery the exulting cry of ' Slave-holder,' half expecting to see the still canvas darken with a frown, and the pictured lips part asunder with words of rebuke and sorrow.[1] I felt it, as did hundreds more, on that occasion, to be a reproach and a cruel insult to the memory of the illus-trious dead. Did not the speaker know that the dying testi-mony of Washington was *against* slavery ? "[2]

---

[1] **The** famous sentence of Wendell Phillips —" I thought those pictured lips would have broken **into voice,** to rebuke the recreant American "—was clearly plagiarized, by an unconscious act of memory, from **the** above eloquent passage by Whittier written nearly two years previous to the Faneuil Hall speech by Phillips. Young Phillips had been mightily aroused by **the** Garrison mob, some **months before** the date of Whittier's open letter to Everett, and **had resolved to** devote his life **to the cause of Freedom. He had** undoubtedly, therefore, **read Whittier's strong and manly letter to the Governor, and remembered, dimly, the passage** in question.

[2] **By** the will of Washington all his **slaves were to be freed on the death of his wife. It** was his ardent desire **to free** his own slaves during his life, but their intermarriage with the dower slaves of his **wife caused** " insuperable difficulties,"—so he said. It is evident **that** both **he** and his wife were guilty of weakness **and** cowardice in **this matter.** There were *no* insuperable difficulties in **the way of** doing **right.** However, **we** must have charity. **No** doubt they acted in accordance with all the light given them. To an aristocratic Virginia gentleman and lady **of** the eighteenth

Whittier then quotes from several letters of Washington, in which that statesman expresses an ardent desire for the abolition of slavery :—

"I come now to that portion of thy remarks which of all others seems most reprehensible. After admitting the repugnance of our people to laws impairing the liberty of speech and of the press, 'the patriotism of all classes of citizens is invoked' 'to abstain from a discussion 'of the subject of Slavery. Abstain from discussion !—What more does the Holy Alliance require ?—What more does Gov. McDuffie demand ? Is this the age—are ours the laws—are the sons of the Pilgrims the men—for advice like this ?—What !—when the whole world is

---

century, living in something like patriarchal or feudal style, on an isolated estate, emancipation presented itself in a different light from what it does to us now. There is extant a curious open letter addressed to Washington on this subject by a certain Edward Rushton, of Liverpool, in 1797, two years before Washington's death. The reason why Washington returned his pamphlet to Rushton "under cover, without a syllable in reply," will appear from the following sentence in it : "The hypocritical bawd who preaches chastity, yet lives by the violation of it, is not more truly disgusting than one of your slave-holding gentry bellowing in favor of democracy." Rushton's letter is not mentioned in any of the numerous Lives of Washington, which, like nearly all biographies, are careful whitewashes. In 1835 a visitor to Mount Vernon found several of Washington's freed slaves—Sambo Anderson, Dick Jasper, and others—engaged in gratuitous work for the improvement of the turf about his tomb. They stated that they had offered their services as the only way in which they could show their love for the man who had been more than a father to them ("New Eng. Anti-sl. Almanac," 1841, p. 2). See in "Liberator," March 22, '34, a long letter from Washington's degenerate nephew, who tries to excuse himself for selling fifty of *his* slaves south, and separating wives and husbands. He talks of them as if they were so many hogs, "my property," etc.

moved—when the very foundations of principalities and powers
are upheaving with the one great impulse of the age—the ir-
resistible workings of Free Inquiry—is it in Massachusetts,
over the graves of Adams and Warren and Hancock and Otis,
that the spirit of free investigation is to be arrested and stricken
dumb? . . . Is this the advice of a republican magistrate
to a community of freemen? Far fitter is it for the banks of
the Bosphorus and the Neva than for those of the Connecticut
and the Merrimack."

Whittier then alludes to Edward Everett's atrocious assertion of his willingness to buckle on a
knapsack and shoulder a musket to help fight the
battles of the slaveholders, and closes with the re-
fusal to yield the home-bred right of free discussion
to the demands of interested politicians. "We can
neither permit the gag to be thrust in our mouths by
others, nor deem it the part of 'patriotism' to place
it there ourselves."

The next mob by which Mr. Whittier, in common
with others, was made a sufferer was that which was
guilty of the burning of the Pennsylvania Hall, in
Philadelphia, in the spring of 1838. He had been
appointed in 1836 one of the Secretaries of the American Anti-slavery Society, and had gone to New York
City in the autumn of 1837, remaining there three
months. His colleagues were Henry B. Stanton and
Theodore D. Weld. Late in the autumn he went on
to Philadelphia to write for the "Pennsylvania Freeman," a paper that had formerly been edited by
Benjamin Lundy, under the title of the "National
Enquirer." Mr. Whittier became editor of the "Freeman" in March, 1838. He tells us that at this time
he used often to be attracted from the heat and

bustle of the city by the quiet and beautiful scenery
of the village of Frankford, where was the residence
of Thomas Chalkley, the West India merchant and
Friends' minister, "gentlest of skippers, rare sea-
saint," who is spoken of in "Snow-Bound," and in
Whittier's "Chalkley Hall." In Philadelphia, too, he
met his old friends, the Thayers, of Haverhill.

The little group of anti-slavery people in Philadelphia had united with other progressive philanthropists in the building of a large hall for free discussion. It stood on the corner of Sixth and Cherry
Streets, near the Adelphi Theatre. It had cost $40,-
000; and the painter, plumber, and clockmaker were
just giving it the last touches when a three days' convention—May 15, 16, and 17—was begun in it by way
of dedication ceremony. Garrison, Burleigh, Whittier,
and other leading Abolitionists were present. The
building was large and commodious, the main hall
(with the galleries) having a seating capacity of two
thousand. On the front were to be seen, in large
gilded letters, occupying nearly the whole width of
the structure, the words PENNSYLVANIA HALL.
On the ground floor were various offices, including
the anti-slavery bookstore, and the office of Whittier's
"Freeman," which he had just had removed thither.

During the first day's session there was little dis-
turbance. On the second day was held an Anti-
slavery Convention of American Women in the new
hall, five hundred women being present. William
Lloyd Garrison opened the meeting with a short
speech. Attempts were made by a mob outside to
break up the convention by hurling showers of stones
against the windows. The glass was broken, but the

inside blinds prevented the stones from entering the room. Amid the uproar and confusion, Mrs. Maria W. Chapman, of Boston, rose and addressed the audience. Sarah Grimké wrote at the time: "She is the most beautiful woman I ever saw; the perfection of sweetness and intelligence being blended in her speaking countenance. She arose amid the yells and shouts of the infuriated mob, the crash of windows, and the hurling of stones. She looked to me like an angelic being descended amid that tempest of passion in all the benignity of conscious superiority."[1]

The next speaker was Angelina Grimké Weld, who, three days previous, had been married to Theodore D. Weld.[2] She spoke for over an hour on the sin of slavery. The influence of her pure, beautiful presence and quiet manner was such that in a few moments the noise *within* the hall had ceased. But stones continued to crash against the windows. "What is a mob?" she said. "What would the breaking of every window be? Any evidence that we are wrong, or that slavery is a good or wholesome institution? What if the mob should now burst in upon us, break up our meeting, and commit violence upon our persons,—would this be anything compared with what the slaves endure?"

At the close of the meeting each colored woman present was taken for protection between two white ones ; and thus, amid showers of missiles and jeering words, they passed out.

The immediate cause of the disturbances of this

---

[1] Life of the Grimké Sisters, p. 239.

[2] Mr. Whittier is so strict a Quaker that he obeyed the rules of the church, which forbade his attendance at this marriage of two dear friends of his, one of whom, the lady, was a Quaker.

day and of the crowning catastrophe of the day following lay in the spread of a ridiculous rumor that
the meeting was held in the interests of amalgamation.
Amalgamation was the great bugbear (or cantingly
feigned to be such) in those days among the unedu-
cated populace. Not to believe that Abolitionists
were all rank amalgamationists was as great a heresy
as disbelief in the Plot was during the Lord George
Gordon riots. Several incidents unfortunately tended
to inflame the popular ideas on this occasion. A
wealthy and educated young colored farmer happened to come to the Women's Convention in a carriage with his wife, who was darker than himself;
whereupon the report went out that a white man had
brought a colored girl with him in his carriage to the
hall. Again, the wife and sister-in-law of a respectable colored citizen (who was the son of a governor
of one of the Southern States) were seen walking
with their own cousin, who was darker than they,—
and the mob had it that a black man was seen walking with two pretty white girls. Said the "Colonization Herald": "In our quiet city of Philadelphia, in
which masquerades are forbidden by legislative
enactment, there has been, notwithstanding, a season
of carnival. Some hundreds of persons of both sexes
and all colors, the more prominent of whom were
white, black, and yellow, had agreed to keep high
festival in honor of a hybrid and piebald equality,
which they invoked in a new and spacious edifice
recently erected by some of their associates in the
idolatrous worship. . . . But when there was
seen here *a black beau escorting two interesting and
pretty white females*—there a white man, more advanced

in years, *parading up and down a street with a sable dame on each arm*, and a procession in the most public street *of black and white duly intermixed* [the trios of women before mentioned] the people began to express their dissatisfaction."

All through the next day the meetings in Pennsylvania Hall were disturbed by the mob. The presiding officer was Dr. Daniel Neall. An incident of the day is thus related by Mr. Whittier:—

"I was standing near Dr. Neall while the glass of the windows, broken by missiles, showered over him, and a deputation of the rioters forced its way to the platform and demanded that the meeting should be closed at once. Dr. Neall drew up his tall form to its utmost height.

"'I am here,' he said, 'the president of this meeting, and I will be torn in pieces before I leave my place at your dictation. Go back to those who sent you. I shall do my duty.'"

About sunset, a mob of twenty-five thousand men surrounding the hall, the mayor, John Swift, appeared, and told the president that, if the keys of the building were given to him, he could induce the rioters to disperse. This was done, and he spoke as follows to the crowd: "There will be no meeting here this evening. The house has been given up to me. The managers had the right to hold the meeting, but as good citizens they have, at my request, suspended their meeting for this evening. We never call out the military here! We do not need such measures. Indeed, I would, fellow-citizens, look upon you as my police! I trust you will abide by the laws and keep order. I now bid you farewell for the night."

The crowd of course understood the double meaning conveyed in these crafty and ambiguous words, and immediately shouted, "The mayor won't hurt us—the mayor is our friend—the mayor hates Amalgamation and Abolition as bad as we do!"

About seven and a half o'clock the rioters (conspicuous among whom were a number of Southern medical students) burst open the door, broke out all the windows to let the air have free circulation, tore down the blinds and piled them around the speaker's desk, adding books and papers from the basement, then set fire to the heap, turned on the gas, and left the room. The crowd gave a great shout of joy as the smoke and flame appeared. The now thoroughly alarmed mayor reappears with the High Sheriff; they are hustled unceremoniously about by the crowd. A number of hand fire-engines are tardily brought along; but the "gallant" firemen take their cue from the crowd, and the exact truth is represented in the quaint engraving by Sartain, in the pamphlet history of the hall, where the firemen are shown throwing streams of water upon every other building in the vicinity except the hapless hall of liberty. "The fire-companies," says a Southerner, writing to the Augusta "Chronicle," "repaired tardily to the scene of action, and not a drop of water did they pour upon that accursed Moloch until it was a heap of ruins. Sir, it would have gladdened your heart to have beheld that lofty tower of mischief enveloped in flames."

Whittier's office in the basement was looted, and all his papers, books, and other property destroyed, as were also Benjamin Lundy's effects,—his papers, books, and all his clothing except what he was wearing at the time. The publication of the "Pennsylvania Freeman" was not, however, suspended, but continued to be edited by Whittier for over a year. The day after the fire, the members of the Anti-slavery Society met by the smoking ruins, amid the howling mob, and calmly transacted the business of the day. The tumult continued for a week, during which the Shelter for Colored Orphans was partially burned. It was also the intention of the ruffians to loot the house of James and Lucretia Mott. They accordingly made preparations to receive the mob by sending away the children and a part of their furniture. They then sat down in the parlor, with a few neighbors, to await the result. About eight o'clock in the evening the shouts of the mob could be heard not far off, now here, now there ; but they finally concluded to make the Home for the Orphans the object of their attack, and so the Motts escaped.[1]

The next number of the "Pennsylvania Freeman" contained a full account of the burning of the hall.[2] I transcribe from Whittier's editorial a few glowing sentences :—

"Not in vain, we trust, has the persecution fallen upon us. Fresher and purer for the fiery baptism, the cause lives in our hearts. . . . Woe unto us if we falter through the fear of man ! . . . Citizens of Pennsylvania ! your rights as well as ours have been violated in this dreadful outrage. . . . In the heart of your free city, within view of the Hall of Independence, whose spire and roof reddened in the flame of the

---

[1] Life of the Motts by Mrs. Hallowell, p. 129.

[2] Quoted in the "Liberator," June 1, 1838.

sacrifice [with shame, perhaps?] the deed has been done,—and the shout which greeted the falling ruin was the shout of Slavery over the grave of Liberty. . . . Are we pointed to the smoking ruins of that beautiful temple of Freedom, which we fondly hoped would have long echoed the noble and free sentiments of a Franklin, a Rush, a Benezet, a Jay; and as we look sadly on its early downfall, are we bidden to learn hence the fate of our own dwellings if we persevere? Think not the intimation will drive us from our post. . . . We feel that God has called us to this work, and if it be his purpose that we should finish what we have begun, He can preserve us, though it be as in the lions' den, or the sevenfold-heated furnace."

Whittier's lyrics of freedom were written in the strength of his mature and seasoned manhood, and were either read at anti-slavery gatherings or published in the Abolition papers of the time. They often appeared anonymously, but were always recognized, copied in paper after paper, and quoted again and again in speeches and essays. Occasionally, when recited in public meetings, their cutting satire would cause the tumult of the men of Alsatia to break out with redoubled fury. They were imitated freely and copiously by the poetlings of the day, and the old files of newspapers contain many and many a poem written in Whittier's honor by these worthy people. As appeals to manhood and womanhood and spurs to ideal action,—the slogans, or war-cries, of the march,—the influence of Whittier's voices of freedom was deep and permanent. Like grains of ambergris or pungent spices, they diffused their fiery quality through the mind and stole softly and unperceived into the heart. A whole generation drew heroic nourishment from them, as the thirsty roots of the willow draw water from the brook. In many families Whittier's poems were learned by the children for declamation, and recited in concert around their mother's knee.[1] Said Prof. J. B. Thayer, of Harvard College, to an instructor at the Friends' School in Providence, in 1884, " Tell your boys and girls that, however much they admire and love Whittier, they cannot know what a fire and passion of enthusiasm he kindled in the hearts of the little company of anti-slavery boys and girls of my time, when they read his early poems." And Thomas Wentworth Higginson, in a poem to Whittier, writes:—

> " At dawn of manhood came a voice to me
>   That said to startled conscience, ' Sleep no more ! '
>
> *   *   *   *   *   *
>
> If any good to me or from me came
> Through life, and if no influence less divine
> Has quite usurped the place of duty's flame ;
> If aught rose worthy in this heart of mine,
> Aught that, viewed backward, wears no shade of shame ;
> Bless thee, old friend ! for that high call was thine."

Shortly after the appearance of Whittier's superb poem, " Massachusetts to Virginia,"—

> " We hear thy threats, Virginia ! thy stormy words and high
>   Swell harshly on the Southern winds which melt along our
>   sky,"—

an imitative response, in the same metre, was printed. Its allusions are very interesting as showing how Whittier's lyrics influenced people:—

-----

[1] Lillie B. Chace Wyman, in " Atlantic Monthly," August, '89

"We greet thee, eldest sister, that from thy lip has broke
The voice of warning and rebuke, as if a prophet spoke—
Unshackled as the mountain winds that o'er thy valleys sweep,
And, mingling with the swelling waves, their ocean-anthem
    keep.

"Our yeomanry have paused to catch the spirit-thrilling tone,
The poet's soul around thy words has beautifully thrown,
And the maiden stops her busy wheel to cast her flashing eye
Along the page that seems to ring the Bay State's banner cry.

"The schoolboy up among our hills has caught its words of
    truth,
And shouts them with the fiery heart and eloquence of youth,
And moves the souls and stirs the blood of gray and aged men,
As if they heard the voice of Stark, or Langdon's words again." [1]

The following note to the '37 edition of the poems
was probably penned by Garrison, who is thought to
have edited the volume. The book was put forth in
Boston during Whittier's absence. The editor says :
"On the appearance of these stanzas ["Our fellow-
countrymen in chains!"] in the 'Liberator,' it was
predicted by Garrison that 'they would ring from
Maine to the Rocky Mountains,' and the prophecy
has been fulfilled. They have been circulated in
periodicals, quoted in addresses and orations, and
scattered broadcast over the land, beneath the kneel-
ing slave and motto ' Am I not a man and a brother?'
—the device of Cowper and the English Abolition-

---

[1] Other metrical imitations were written from Vermont, Ohio,
and Pennsylvania. Indeed, their name was legion. Whittier
must have got pretty sick of these parrot-echoes before the fever
subsided.

ists.[1] In this last form, they have roused the consciences of slaveholders in New Orleans, have been held up to a Boston audience by the sophist Gurley, after a fruitless endeavor to create a tumult by one of his strong appeals to prejudice and selfishness, and have been displayed by the noble-souled May before a Massachusetts legislature, as a refutation of the charge of incendiarism cast on the Abolitionists by the legislature of the South."

A reviewer in 1848 said of the poems of freedom: "We know nothing of the physical mould of this J. G. Whittier; but if he can *speak* his poems, breathing into the delivery the same living fire which is embodied in them, and if he will do it, even in the strongholds of conventionalism, in the hearing of 'brave men and fair women,' the former may restrain their indignation at the wrong upon which he pours his scathing reproof, and the latter may forbid their tears to flow for the suffering which he commiserates, if they can."[2]

There is a striking resemblance between the portrait of Whittier and that of Ebenezer Elliott, the English Corn-Law rhymer. Elliott's poems were published in 1834 in book form, and were often quoted in anti-slavery journals. There can be little doubt that Whittier's style was influenced pretty strongly by Elliott's. He and the Corn-Law rhymer were both ardent admirers of Burns, and wrote many of their reform poems in Burns's eight-line stanza.

---

[1] The reference is to a huge broadside containing the poem, and headed by the picture of a prodigious manacled black.

[2] D. March, in "New Englander," 1848, p. 63.

Out of the half hundred or more of the voices of freedom I would indicate the following round dozen as by far the best, and would advise those first making Whittier's acquaintance to read and re-read these: "The Virginia Slave-Mother's Lament," "Massachusetts to Virginia," "The Branded Hand," "Pæan," "Stanzas for the Times," "The Hunters of Men," "Clerical Oppressors," "The Slave-Ships," "Stanzas" ("Our fellow-countrymen in chains!"), "Ichabod," "The Rendition," and "Laus Deo!" The American who can read these splendid lyrics without quickened pulse may consider that his patriotism and his moral sense are dead beyond recall. "The Virginia Slave-Mother's Lament," wrote John Bright to a friend in this country, "has often brought tears to my eyes. It is short, but it is worth a volume on the great question. . . . These few lines were enough to rouse a whole nation to expel from among you the odious crime of slavery."

The poem "Ichabod" ("So fallen! so lost!" etc.), concerning Daniel Webster's notorious *volte-face* on the slavery question, was much admired by Emerson. It was written at a white heat of indignation, just after Webster's famous 7th of March speech, 1850, in which he argued that no further restrictions on the extension of slavery into the Territories of California and New Mexico were needed, that the Fugitive Slave Law must be obeyed, that colonization of the free negroes was desirable, and that the labors of the Abolitionists had served only to fasten the system of slavery more firmly than ever on the South. After reading this speech, Whittier wrote to Garrison, "The scandalous treachery of Webster and the *backing* he

8

has received from Andover and Harvard [1] show that
we have nothing to hope for from the great political
parties and religious sects." All Abolitionists received the blow with wrath and terror, but not with
surprise. Webster had been for ten years leaning
toward apostasy. I find in an old file of anti-slavery
papers (as early as 1840) such sentences as these:
" Daniel Webster has at length bowed the knee to
Baal" (*Advocate*); " Daniel Webster, the 'champion
of the Constitution,' has at length consented to receive the mark of the beast in his forehead" (*Philanthropist*); " he has at length yielded a freeman's birthright for a chance at the Presidency" (*Liberator*).
Then when the final blow came, in 1850, " the Free-
Soil party quivered and sank for the moment beneath the shock. The whole anti-slavery movement
recoiled."

But Mr. Whittier, at least, cherished no lasting re-
sentment. He has stated that the poem was composed after an entirely sleepless night, and that, if he
had waited a couple of months, he probably should
not have written it. He thinks that, if Webster had
lived till the outbreak of the war, he would have in-
evitably been found on the right side, and would
have recovered his ancient renown; and he has said
as much in his poem, " The Lost Occasion." Elsewhere he writes:—

" My admiration of the splendid personality and
intellectual power of the great Senator was never

---

[1] An address of congratulation was presented to Webster, signed
by eight hundred prominent citizens of Massachusetts, including
Rufus Choate, Wm. H. Prescott, and Jared Sparks, and Prof.
C. C. Felton of Harvard College.

stronger than when I laid down his speech, and, in one of the saddest moments of my life, penned my protest. I saw, as I wrote, with painful clearness, its sure results,—the slave-power arrogant and defiant, strengthened and encouraged to carry out its scheme for the extension of its baleful system, or the dissolution of the Union, the guaranties of personal liberty in the free States broken down, and the whole country made the hunting-ground of slave-catchers. In the horror of such a vision, so soon fearfully fulfilled, if one spoke at all, he could only speak in tones of stern and sorrowful rebuke." "Ichabod" should be read in connection with the strong and indignant "Stanzas for the Times: 1850," written on the same subject. The poem "Ichabod" has been compared to Browning's "Lost Leader":—

"Just for a handful of silver he left us,
    Just for a riband to stick in his coat—

 * * * * * *

He alone breaks from the van and the freemen,
    He alone sinks to the rear and the slaves.

 * * * * * *

Deeds will be done—while he boasts his quiescence,
    Still bidding crouch whom the rest bade aspire;
Blot out his name, then, record one lost soul more."

Mr. Stedman has also compared, or rather contrasted, "Ichabod" with William W. Lord's remarkable lines "On the Defeat of a Great Man," suggested by Polk's victory over Henry Clay in the presidential campaign of 1843 :—

Fallen !   How fallen ?   States and empires fall ;
     O'er towers and rock-built walls,
And perished nations, floods to tempests call
With hollow sound along the sea of time :
     The great man never falls,—
He lives, he towers aloft, he stands sublime ;
     They fall who give him not
The honor here that suits his future name,—
     They die and are forgot.

O Giant loud and blind ! the great man's fame
   Is his own shadow, and not cast by thee :
     A shadow that shall grow
As down the heaven of time the sun descends,
     And on the world shall throw
His godlike image, till it sinks where blends
   Time's dim horizon with Eternity.

There are a few other of the anti-slavery and reform pieces that need words of comment or illustration other than those given by Whittier in his latest edition.

For example, " The Burial of Barber " (spelled " Barbour " in early editions).   Thos. W. Barber, the second martyr of freedom in Kansas, was shot dead, Dec. 6, 1855, near Lawrence, by Geo. W. Clarke, Indian agent.   The impressive funeral services were held in the dining-room of a newly erected building. The walls of the room were of rough unplastered limestone, and seats of plank were placed in rows its entire length.   The funeral cortège was a long and solemn one, stretching nearly a mile over the prairie, many riding in ox-carts and mule-carts, and the soldiers marching with arms reversed.[1]

---

[1] " Annals of Kansas," 1856.

"The Branded Hand" refers to Captain Jonathan Walker of Harwich, Massachusetts. While working as a railroad contractor in Florida (having emigrated thither with his family), he became interested in the slaves, employed them, treated them like men, and won their affection. In 1844 he took seven of these slaves in his open boat south along the coast from Pensacola, hoping to get them to one of the West India Islands. But he fell very ill, it being hot July, and the whole party was captured. Walker was put in irons, carried back to Pensacola, subjected to the ignominy of the pillory, branded on his right hand by a United States marshal with the letters S. S. (slave-stealer), kept for eleven months chained to the floor of a cell bare of all furniture, ill and emaciated as he was, and only released after the payment of his fine of $150 by Northern Abolitionists. The branding was done by binding his hand to a post and applying a red-hot iron to the palm, which left the letters about an inch long and an eighth of an inch deep, as shown in the cut.[1] The brander was a Maine man named Dorr,—another proof of the frequent assertion that New Englanders made the cruelest slaveholders. "Lift up that manly right hand," cries the poet,—

"Hold it up before our sunshine, up against our northern air,—
  Ho! men of Massacnusetts, for the love of God, look there!

---

[1] The cut is from a daguerreotype of Captain Walker's hand, owned by Dr. Henry I. Bowditch. Reproduced in the " Liberator," xv. 132, to accompany Whittier's poem on the subject ; also given in one of the anti-slavery almanacs.

Take it, henceforth, for your standard, like the Bruce's heart
    of yore,
In the dark strife closing round ye, let that hand be seen be-
    fore!"

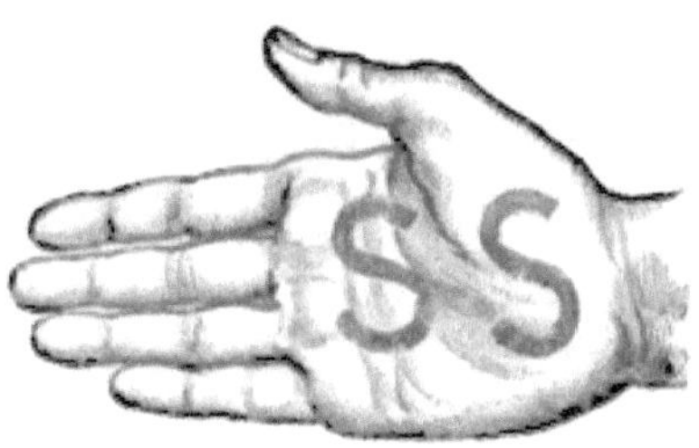

Captain Walker removed to Muskegon, Michigan.
His branded hand got him much respect among his
townsmen, and at his death he received marked civic
honors. A granite monument costing $700 was
erected over his grave by Photius Fiske of Boston,—
that eccentric, good, rich little Greek fellow, whose
benefactions to unfortunates have been innumerable,
and who has also erected a monument to Charles T.
Torrey in Auburn's Field of God, and others to other
anti-slavery martyrs. When his tomb and theirs are
mossy with age, may some Old Immortality be as
kind to them as he has been to the memory of the
heroic dead!

Whittier's poem "Texas," as first printed, may be
seen in the "Liberator," April 19, 1844. One of its
stanzas was afterwards so altered as not to put the
North in the position of a people demanding disunion. Then the following new lines were added:—

"Vainly shall your sand-wrought rope
    Bind the starry cluster up,
    Shattered over heaven's blue cope."

The phrases changed in other stanzas seem to me

weakened. In the third triplet from the end, as the poem now stands, the line " as the lost in Paradise " was " as the damned in Paradise "; and a line in the following cluster stood, " Freedom's brown and honest hand " (" brown " changed to " strong "). Other lines in other poems have been clearly injured by revision,—as the first in the " Lines " on the Pinckney Resolutions, " Men of the North-land ! where 's the manly spirit," which originally read, " Now, by our fathers' ashes ! where 's the spirit." [1]

" Rantoul " was penned in grief over the death of Robert Rantoul, the orator and statesman of Beverly, Essex County, Massachusetts. He was a fellow-member of Whittier in the Massachusetts legislature in 1835. He became Webster's successor in Congress, was a leader in the Free-Soil party, and a man of rare political genius and promise.

> " One day, along the electric wire
> His manly word for Freedom sped ;
> We came next morn : that tongue of fire
> Said only, ' He who spake is dead ! ' "

" William Francis Bartlett " commemorates General Bartlett, another brave and lamented soldier of Essex County. He was the son of a Boston merchant, though born in Haverhill. He was appointed captain in the 20th Massachusetts Regiment while yet a student at Harvard. He was in the battles of the

---

[1] Good " Saint James " Freeman Clarke, in his Louisville " Western Messenger " of December, 1836, says the Pinckney lines are " almost equal to anything in Campbell "! " Although no friend of Abolitionism," he says, " we like good poetry on any and every subject."

Wilderness, and lost a leg and was otherwise wounded in the service. He died in 1876:—

> "Mourn, Essex, on thy sea-blown shore
>   Thy beautiful and brave,
>   Whose failing hand the olive bore,
>   Whose dying lips forgave!"

The poem "To Ronge" opens with the tremendous apostrophe:—

> "Strike home, strong-hearted man! Down to the root
>   Of old oppression sink the Saxon steel!
>   *Thy* work is to hew down. In God's name then
>   Put nerve into thy task!"

Jean Ronge (Le Curé Ronge) of Silesia may be styled the founder of the Old Catholic movement of religious reform, of which Dr. Doellinger is a more recent leader. In 1844 Ronge published a remarkable letter (said to have been written by another) in the "Feuilles Nationales," in which he ridiculed the superstitious credulity of the hundreds of thousands of pilgrims who were visiting Trèves, by invitation of its Bishop, Arnoldi, to see the seamless robe of Christ. Ronge advocated complete separation of all true Christians from the Church of Rome, and a new organization was actually formed. But in 1848 came the democratic uprisings all over Europe, turning men's thoughts into new channels. Ronge adopted radical views, was made a member of the National Assembly at Frankfort, but in '49 (in consequence of certain incoherent articles published by him) was compelled to fly, with many other political exiles, to the shores of England.[1] He had married a divorced lady, the sister-in-law of Carl Schurz. Martineau and other Unitarians in England had thought highly of Ronge, but his personal presence and ways disenchanted them, and they soon dropped him. He seems not to have had the Lutherian qualities necessary for leadership, although Whittier in America hailed his movement as one calculated to advance the interests of freedom in Europe.

One of the most graphic of the slavery lyrics is the poem "To Governor McDuffie," which has not been reprinted since 1838 or 1840. Probably it is regarded by the poet as too personal, too severe in tone, to say nothing of its two blunders in grammar and quantity. But poets are not always the best judges of the merits of their own work. There is a fierce sharp rhythm and clash as of steel in this poem,—a kind of

"Suono l' un brando e l' altro, or basso, or alto,"—

which, joined with the fact that Whittier's friends have besought him to include it in his works, leads me to venture to present it here. The full statement by Governor George McDuffie, as given in his message of 1835, was this: "Domestic slavery, instead of being a political evil, is the corner-stone of our republican edifice,"—a sufficiently exasperating statement, surely, to an Abolitionist. McDuffie's dictum was "indorsed without reserve" by Governor Ham-

---

[1] Larousse, "Dictionnaire Universel." The best article about Ronge appeared in the "Unitarian Review," of Boston, January, 1888, by John Fretwell.

mond of South Carolina. It was McDuffie who said
that "the institution of slavery supersedes the
necessity of an order of nobility."

TO GOVERNOR McDUFFIE.

" The patriarchal institution of slavery,"—" the corner-stone of our republican edifice."—*Gov. McDuffie.*

King of Carolina—hail !
　Last champion of Oppression's battle,
Lord of rice-tierce and cotton-bale,
　Of sugar-box and human cattle !
Around thy temples, green and dark,
　Thy own tobacco-wreath reposes ;
Thyself, a brother Patriarch
　Of Isaac, Abraham, and Moses !

Why not ? Their household rule is thine ;
　Like theirs, thy bondmen feel its rigor ;
And thine, perchance, as concubine,
　Some swarthy counterpart of Hagar.
Why not ? Like patriarchs of old,
　The priesthood is thy chosen station ;
Like them thou payest thy rites to gold,—
　And Aaron's calf of Nullification.

All fair and softly ! Must we, then,
　From Ruin's open jaws to save us,
Upon our own free workingmen
　Confer a master's special favors ?
Whips for the back—chains for the heels—
　Hooks for the nostrils of Democracy,
Before it spurns as well as feels
　The riding of the Aristocracy !

Ho ! fishermen of Marblehead !
　Ho ! Lynn cordwainers, leave your leather,

And wear the yoke in kindness made,
   And clank your needful chains together!
Let Lowell mills their thousands yield,
   Down let the rough Vermonter hasten,
Down from the workshop and the field,
   And thank us for each chain we fasten.

SLAVES in the rugged Yankee land!
   I tell thee, Carolinian, never!
Our rocky hills and iron strand
   Are free, and shall be free forever.
The surf shall wear that strand away,
   Our granite hills in dust shall moulder,
Ere Slavery's hateful yoke shall lay,
   Unbroken, on a Yankee's shoulder!

No, George McDuffie! keep thy words
   For the mail-plunderers of thy city,
Whose robber-right is in their swords;
   For recreant Priest and Lynch-Committee!
Go, point thee to thy cannon's mouth,
   And swear its brazen lips are better,
To guard " the interests of the South,"
   Than parchment scroll or Charter's letter.[1]

We fear not. Streams which brawl most loud
   Along their course are oftenest shallow;
And loudest to a doubting crowd
   The coward publishes his valor.
Thy courage has at least been shown
   In many a bloodless Southern quarrel,
Facing, with hartshorn and cologne,
   The Georgian's harmless pistol-barrel.[2]

---

[1] See speech of Governor McDuffie to an artillery company in Charleston.

[2] [The allusion is to a ridiculous affair of honor between McDuffie and Colonel Cummings, of Georgia, for which the two men fortified themselves with eau de cologne and spirits of hartshorn.]

No, Southron! not in Yankee land
    Will threats like thine a fear awaken;
The men who on their charter stand
    For truth and right, may not be shaken.
Still shall that truth assail thine ear;
    Each breeze, from Northern mountains blowing,
The tones of Liberty shall bear,—
    God's " free incendiaries" going!

We give thee joy! Thy name is heard
    With reverence on the Neva's borders;
And " turban'd Turk," and Poland's lord,
    And Metternich, are thy applauders.
Go, if thou lov'st *such* fame, and share
    The mad Ephesian's base example,—
The holy bonds of UNION tear,
    And clap the torch to FREEDOM's temple!

Do this—Heaven's frown, thy country's curse,
    Guilt's fiery torture ever burning,
The quenchless thirst of Tantalus,
    And Ixion's wheel forever turning—
A name for which " the pain'dest fiend
    Below" his own would barter never,—
These shall be thine unto the end,
    Thy damning heritage forever!

Another poem that was dropped from the collected works some forty-five years ago is " Stanzas for the Times." It appeared in '39, and was called out by the apostasy of David R. Porter, Governor of Pennsylvania, to the cause of freedom. He had once cast his vote in the Pennsylvania legislature in favor of suppressing slavery in the District of Columbia, but afterwards swung over to the pro-slavery side. Whittier's indignation bursts forth in the following fiery verses :—

"Go, eat thy words.   Shall Henry Clay
    Turn round,—a moral Harlequin?
And arch Van Buren wipe away
    The stains of his Missouri sin?
And shall that one unlucky vote
Stick burr-like in *thy* honest throat?

"No: do thy part in putting down
    The friends of Freedom,—summon out
The parson in his saintly gown,
    To curse the outlawed roundabout,
In concert with the Belial brood—
The Balaam of 'the brotherhood!'

"Quench every free discussion light,
    Clap on the legislative snuffers,
And caulk, with 'resolutions' tight,
    The ghastly rents the Union suffers!
Let Church and State brand Abolition
As Heresy and rank Sedition.

"Choke down at once each breathing thing
    That whispers of the Rights of Man:
Gag the free girl who dares to sing
    Of Freedom o'er her dairy pan;
Dog the old farmer's steps about,
And hunt his cherished treason out.

"Go hunt sedition.   Search for that
    In every pedler's cart of rags;
Pry into every Quaker's hat
    And Dr. Fussell's saddle-bags,
Lest treason wrap, with all its ills,
Around his powders and his pills.

"Where Chester's oak and walnut shades
    With slavery-laden breezes stir,
And on the hills and in the glades
    Of Bucks and honest Lancaster,

Are heads which think and hearts which feel,—
Flints to the Abolition steel!

"Ho! send ye down a corporal's guard
    With flow of flag and beat of drum,—
Storm Lindley Coates's poultry-yard,
    Beleaguer Thomas Whitson's home!
Beat up the Quaker quarters,—show
Your valor to an unarmed foe!

"Do more.   Fill up your loathsome jails
    With faithful men and women,—set
The scaffold up in these green vales,
    And let their verdant turf be wet
With blood of unresisting men,—
Ay, do all this, and more,—WHAT THEN?

"Think ye one heart of man or child
    Will falter from its lofty faith,
At the mob's tumult, fierce and wild,—
    The prison cell,—the shameful death?
No, nursed in storm and trial long,
The weakest of our band is strong.

"We cannot falter!   Did we so,
    The stones beneath would murmur out,
And all the winds that round us blow
    Would whisper of our shame about.
No, let the tempest rock the land,
Our faith shall live, our truth shall stand.

"True as the Vaudois, hemmed around
    With Papal fire and Roman steel,—
Firm as the Christian heroine, bound
    Upon Domitian's torturing wheel,
We 'bate no breath, we curb no thought:
Come what may come, WE FALTER NOT!"

Of the anti-slavery verses written for special occasions or drawn out by startling events, Mr. Whittier says :—

"Of their defects from an artistic point of view it is not necessary to speak. They were the earnest and often vehement expression of the writer's thought and feeling at critical periods in the great conflict between Freedom and Slavery. They were written with no expectation that they would survive the occasions which called them forth ; they were protests, alarm-signals, trumpet-calls to action, words wrung from the writer's heart, forged at white heat, and of course lacking the finish and careful word-selection which reflection and patient brooding over them might have given. Such as they are, they belong to the history of the anti-slavery movement, and may serve as way-marks of its progress." [1]

Some of the most glowing of the poems of freedom were printed as broadsides or on cards. Such were "Stanzas" ("Our fellow-countrymen in chains !"), and the "Kansas Emigrants" song. The circumstances that gave birth to this famous marching song were as follows : Kansas and Nebraska had been opened up for settlement, and a stream of emigration had set in. The hope of the Free-Soilers was that it would be settled by an anti-slavery population. Eli Thayer of Massachusetts caught up the idea, and, apparently from interested motives, organized a company, raised money, and sent out band after band of New England Free-Soil settlers to hold Kansas for the North. With him were asso-

---

[1] Preface to the edition of 1888.

ciated **Edward Everett Hale** and others. Thayer has written an intemperate **and** boastful book, in which, like another **Colossus,** he bestrides the Union, and dares it to **say** he did n't save it, **by saving Kansas.**[1] But we are not concerned **as to** the exact amount of his service **to the** government. Suffice **it to say that,** directly **or** indirectly, he sent out some four or five thousand **men to** Kansas and settled **them there.** The departure of the **first band** from Boston, by railroad, **was** witnessed **by an** immense and enthusiastic crowd, extending **along the** track for several blocks. **All through New England** and the Middle and Western Middle States the progress **of the** party was **a** continued ovation from **cheering crowds.** This first **company founded the city of Lawrence.** Before they started, **Mr.** Whittier **sent them his " Kansas Emigrants "** song,—

> " We cross the prairies as of old
>> The Pilgrims crossed the sea,
>> To make the West as they the East
>> The homestead of the free."

The song was actually sung, says **Mr.** Hale,—sung when they started, **sung as** they journeyed, and sung in their new home. **To better adapt it to a** company of persons, **a chorus was originally appended to each** stanza, thus :—

> *Chorus.*—" The homestead of the free, my boys,
>> The homestead **of the free.**
>> To make the West as they the East
>> **The** homestead of the free."

---

[1] See a caustic review of his book in " Nation," Nov. 7, 1889, probably by **Wendell** Phillips **Garrison.**

In virtue of this song, as well as his "Marais du Cygne" and "Burial of Barber," Whittier to-day holds a warm place in the affections of the people of Kansas.

During the Civil War many of the poems of Whittier were committed to memory and a few of them sung by the Union soldiers.[1] A signal testimony to the power of his verse is attested by the case of the Hutchinson family and Whittier's "Ein' Feste Burg." This war lyric was published in the New York "Independent" in July, '61, in the very first days of the war. It was at once adopted by the people as a campaign song. In the early period of the contest the members of the Hutchinson family (already long known and admired by the public), divided into several bands, were accustomed to visit recruiting stations and sing for the purpose of inspiring patriotic valor and encouraging volunteer enlistments. After the discouraging defeat of Bull Run, they went to Virginia, very properly thinking, I suppose, that that was the place where they were most needed. They entered the national lines, but were expelled by General McClellan for singing Whittier's "Ein' Feste Burg," the spirited third stanza (given below) being especially dangerous, thought McClellan, who still hoped, with Lincoln, that a peace might be patched up with the South :—

> " What gives the wheat-field blades of steel ?
> What points the rebel cannon ?

---

[1] Collections of patriotic songs of that time generally contain only two or three poems by Whittier, such as " The Crisis," and " Ein' Feste Burg." His verses were read more than they were sung.

9

> What sets the roaring rabble's heel
>   On the old star-spangled pennon?
>   What breaks the oath
>   Of the men o' the South?
>   What whets the knife
>   For the Union's life?
> Hark to the answer: Slavery!"

The Hutchinson family appealed to President Lincoln. The poem was formally read in Cabinet meeting by Secretary Chase, and the President said, "It is just the kind of a song I want the soldiers to hear." By the unanimous vote of the Cabinet, then, and by order of the President, the singers were readmitted to the national camps.[1]

But, however marked may have been the influence of Whittier's poems in the war days, let us beware of claiming for him or for any one person an undue share in the honor of having saved the country. Nothing could shock his modesty or hurt his feelings more than such a claim. It was, indeed, not the labor of Benjamin Lundy, or of John Brown, or Mrs. Stowe, or Eli Thayer, or William Lloyd Garrison, or John G. Whittier, or Abraham Lincoln, that saved the Union and abolished slavery,—not the work of any one of these alone, nor of the armies of the North alone, nor of the farmers and merchants who furnished food, clothes, and weapons; but it was the toil of all these together that brought about the result.

Mr. Whittier's feeling about the war was regret mingled with resignation to "God's will," and a

---

[1] Appleton's Cyclopædia of Biography, iii. 334.

patriotic acquiescence in what seemed an unavoidable calamity. He recognized that God is sometimes in the whirlwind as well as in the still small voice. He believed that the mission of the Friends in the war was to care for the slave and the freedman and for the wounded. He, as well as Garrison, was sadly tried by President Lincoln's cautious and conciliatory measures as to slavery. Those shackles and chains, those fellow-men in bondage,—these were the matters that fretted and chafed him. Garrison and Phillips were even ready for disunion, if our skirts could not be cleared of the sin of slavery in any other way. Not so Lincoln,—a man of much profounder statesmanship than any one of the three Abolition chiefs. The blood circulated slowly through his gigantic frame, and he was slow in reaching his conclusions. But he early saw the vital necessity of preserving the union of the States. The recently issued lives of him by his law partner and by his private secretaries show how deeply he abhorred slavery. But he felt his way slowly and cautiously to emancipation. He sagaciously refused to move in national matters until he felt that the inertia of the people was overcome and that they were ready for change. He was a profound calculator of forces and events. There was that in him that matched the long sufferance and taciturnity of nature. Undoubtedly, his feelings about slavery were not so fiery-indignant as those of the Abolitionists. He viewed everything intellectually. Like Carlyle, he did not consider slavery absolutely the worst thing under the sun. In his public letter to Horace Greeley he affirmed that, while he wished all men to be free, he could only

work for immediate emancipation if he were convinced that it would help to save the Union. And,
although he cherished a secret ambition to go down
to posterity as the emancipator of the North American slaves, he would by no means allow emancipation to get between his feet and trip him up while he
was trying to save the country. He never abolished
slavery at all in the loyal border States, always shun-
ning to exasperate the feelings of these States, and
promptly annulling the premature proclamations of
freedom by Generals Frémont and J. J. Piatt in Missouri and Maryland respectively. Lincoln, in his
large-hearted charity, pitied the masters of the slaves,
and the Abolitionists did not,—that was the great
difference between them. He even favored colonization, and kept bringing forward his scheme of gradual
emancipation, with the issue to the planters of indemnity bonds, or immediate emancipation, with a
remuneration in cash from the national treasury for
each slave freed (the very measures once proposed by
Washington). And when the war was practically
over, just a few weeks before the insane act of his
assassination, this best friend of the South proposed
to his Cabinet a measure for creating a fund of $400,-
000,000 for the indemnity of Southern planters. All
along, his idea was to hold the raft well together by
patience and tact. Broken eggs can never be mended,
was his homely illustration. His Emancipation
Proclamation, when it came, was only an incident of
war, and slavery was only completely abolished years
afterwards by the Amendment to the Constitution.
It was natural for such men as Whittier, with whom
the slave question was of most concern, to be queru-

lous and impatient with the President. In a moment of disgust, Garrison once said that Lincoln had not a drop of anti-slavery blood in his veins. And at another time he wrote, "Lincoln is very weak in the joints, and wholly unqualified to lead or inspire." But this was in 1861. He learned to put greater trust in him later. In September, 1861, Whittier wrote to Lydia Maria Child, apropos of Frémont's proclamation of freedom :—

"I am afraid the Government will tie up the hands of Frémont. I was just thinking of trying to thank him for his noble word 'free,' when, lo! the papers this morning bring us Lincoln's letter to him, repudiating the grand utterance. Well, if the confiscated slaves are *not* free, then the Government has turned slaveholder, that is all.

"I am sick of politicians. I know and appreciate the great difficulties in the way of the administration, but I see neither honesty nor worldly wisdom in attempting *to ignore the cause of the trouble.*

"They tell us we must trust, and have patience; and I do not like to find fault with the administration, as in so doing I *seem* to take sides with the secession sympathizers of the North."

But when at last came the Amendment forever abolishing slavery, and that Black Idol was "blown hellward from the cannon's mouth, while Freedom cheered behind the smoke," Whittier felt that all had been for the best,—

> "We prayed for love to loose the chain,
> 'T is shorn by battle's axe in twain."

And in his supreme exultation and exaltation of mind

he poured forth, as if by a sublime improvisation, that Miriam's song of triumph, "Laus Deo!" in which there is not a weak line from beginning to end. The poem took shape in Whittier's mind as he sat in the Friends' meeting-house in Amesbury and heard the clang of the bells rung in celebration of the event. It is a poem that ought to endure as long as the human race itself. The dungeon of Giant Despair was at last forced open, and the grim iron key presented to the man who best deserved it.[1]

Before passing on from the topic of the Civil War of 1861–65, it is desirable to inquire a little more closely into Whittier's theory and practice as to war, —its right or wrong, and its disciplinary value, especially as the imagery of war is so frequently employed in his anti-slavery poetry and elsewhere.

General J. J. Piatt, in a lecture delivered in Cork, Ireland, some years since, on the personality and poetry of Whittier, read to the audience a note he had received from the Quaker bard, as follows:—

"MY DEAR FRIEND,—I see thee are selecting Geo. D. Prentice's poems, and find in the New York 'Evening Post' the following extract from the advance sheets. [The newspaper slip was appended.] The term war-poet—especially that of Quaker war-poet—is a misnomer, and, in my case, I have never written a poem in favor or in praise of war. If possible, strike out the phrase, as I do not wish to be represented as false to my life-long principles."

Mr. Whittier's statement is true in the main, but

---

[1] The iron key of the Richmond slave-pen was sent to Whittier when the city was occupied by Union troops.

will bear some discussion. It is a fact that he has never intentionally written in praise of war, and his prose and his poetry are full of passages reprobating or deploring it. In a note to his poem on Kossuth the soldier, he is careful to state that he believes no political revolution was ever worth the price of human blood; and, in a remark appended to his poem on the storming of the city of Derne, he affirms his belief in a higher and holier heroism than that of war. In "Massachusetts to Virginia," he says, "We wage no war, we lift no arm," against the South; in "Barclay of Uri," he lauds the non-resistant Quaker; in "Stanzas," his bugle-call is not to clash of arms, but to the contest of Truth and Love with Error; he praises peaceful arbitrament in "The Peace Convention at Brussels"; in "Disarmament," the sentiment is that "hate hath no harm for love, and peace unweaponed conquers every wrong"; and in "Brown of Ossawatomie" essentially the same idea is developed. In a letter to Lydia Maria Child, under date of Oct. 21, 1859, he writes:—

"We feel deeply (who does not?) for the noble-hearted, self-sacrificing old man [John Brown]. But as friends of peace as well as freedom, as believers in the Sermon on the Mount, we dare not lend *any* countenance to such attempts as that at Harper's Ferry. . . . I have just been looking at one of the *pikes* sent here by a friend in Baltimore. It is not a Christian weapon; it looks too much like murder."

Garrison took Whittier to task for the lukewarm tone of his "Brown of Ossawatomie." He thought he did not so much honor the liberty-loving heroism of Brown as he had the heroes of the Revolution.

There was undeniable truth in this criticism, and the poet makes but a lame defense in his reply.[1] But we will let all that rest. The war, right or wrong, has come and gone, and—

"Old John Brown's body is a-mouldering in the dust,
  Old John Brown's rifle 's red with blood-spots turned to rust,
  Old John Brown's pike has made its last, unflinching thrust,
        His soul is marching on ! "

Writing on another occasion to Mrs. Child, Whittier says :—

" I know nothing nobler or grander than the heroic self-sacrifice of young Colonel Shaw. The only regiment I ever looked upon during the war was the 54th [colored] on its departure for the South. I shall never forget the scene. As he rode at the head of his troops, the very flower of grace and chivalry, he seemed to me beautiful and awful as an angel of God come down to lead the host of freedom to victory. I have longed to speak the emotions of that hour, but I dared not, lest I should indirectly give a new impulse to war." (A contemporary account of the embarkation of this regiment says that not a sneer or an unkind word marred the occasion. Streets and balconies were thronged with cheering crowds, flags were hung out, and a lady in Essex Street presented Colonel Shaw with a handsome bouquet.)

But there is another side to the shield. If Whittier has written no poem in praise of war, he has assuredly written poems full of the warlike spirit. There is a touch of the fighting parson or Friar Tuck in him.

---

[1] See " Liberator," Jan. 13 and 27, 1860.

The elder Hawthorne wittily spoke of him as "a fiery Quaker youth to whom the Muse has perversely assigned a battle-trumpet." His favorite metaphors are those of battles and the sword. To an essay on William Leggett he prefixes as motto some strong lines in which the poet Bryant apostrophizes Freedom, not as a fair girl with curls flowing from under her Phrygian cap, but as a strong, bearded man, "armed to the teeth," one hand grasping the shield and the other the sword. Mr. Whittier is himself perplexed over the outbursting of the war-spirit in him :—

"Without intending any disparagement of my peaceable ancestry for many generations, I have still strong suspicions that somewhat of the old Norman blood, something of the grim Berserker spirit, has been bequeathed to me. How else can I account for the intense childish eagerness with which I listened to the stories of old campaigners who sometimes fought their battles over again in my hearing? Why did I, in my young fancy, go up with Jonathan, the son of Saul, to smite the garrisoned Philistines of Michmash, or with the fierce son of Nun against the cities of Canaan? Why was Mr. Greatheart, in Pilgrim's Progress, my favorite character? What gave such fascination to the grand Homeric encounter between Christian and Apollyon in the valley? Why did I follow Ossian over Morven's battlefields, exulting in the vulture-screams of the blind scald over his fallen enemies? Still later, why did the newspapers furnish me with subjects for hero-worship in the half-demented Sir Gregor McGregor, and Ypsilanti at the head of his knavish Greeks? I can only account for it on the supposition that the mischief was inherited,

—an heirloom from the old sea-kings of the ninth century.

"Education and reflection have indeed wrought a change in my feelings. The trumpet of the Cid, or Ziska's drum even, could not now waken that old martial spirit. . . . It is only when a great thought incarnates itself in action, desperately striving to find utterance even in the sabre-clash and gun-fire, or when Truth and Freedom, in their mistaken zeal and mistrustful of their own powers, put on battle-harness, that I can feel any sympathy with merely physical daring."

Some curious facts connected with the American Civil War of 1861–65 show that the old war-instinct troubles other Quakers besides Whittier. It was Mr. John S. Gibbons, a Hicksite Quaker, it will be remembered, who wrote the popular war lyric,—

> " We are coming, Father Abraham,
> Three hundred thousand more."

During the early days of the war the good Friends of Philadelphia were greatly scandalized at finding their sons rushing to arms with the rest; so that, we are given to understand, there was scarcely a Quaker household from which one or more sons had not gone forth to the conflict.[1] In northern New Jersey the famous Quaker Regiment, of a full thousand men, was formed in 1862. After two hundred of these men, all wearing straight coats and broad-brimmed hats, had offered themselves and been accepted, their conduct was sharply criticised at the next quarterly

---

[1] Life of Garrison, iv. 37.

meeting, whereupon one of them, who was present, arose and told a little story. He said that his grandfather once had dealings with an obstreperous "man of the world," who provoked him until his patience was worn out. All at once he threw off his coat and laid it on the ground, saying, " Lie there, Quaker, till I give this rascal his dues ! " and then proceeded to give him a good drubbing. During the later days of the war the Quakers were not exempt from the draft, and some of them strove hard to avoid it; but others were willing to send substitutes. It is recorded that a Quaker merchant of New York said to one of his clerks, "If thee will enlist, not only shall thee have thy situation, but thy salary shall go on while thee is absent. But, if thee will not serve thy country, thee cannot stay in this store."

It is, one gladly admits, moral heroism alone that Whittier has sometimes seemed to praise, in spite of himself, when he finds it in men with the weapons of death in their hands. Read in illustration a half-dozen or more poems produced in the flower of his manhood and in the heat of the anti-slavery struggle,—1846 to 1858,—" What the Voice Said," " Pæan," " Yorktown," " Stanzas for the Times," " The Branded Hand," " Lucknow," and " Derne"; also some rollicking verses " written to beguile a rainy day on the farm," about sixty-three years ago. They were published anonymously in some paper, but have not since been admitted into any collection of his works.[1] The poem is called—

---

[1] The time of the poem is in the early days when Vermont was struggling for independent existence, under the lead of Ethan Allen

THE SONG OF THE VERMONTERS.

Ho! all to the borders! Vermonters, come down,
With your breeches of deerskin and jackets of brown;
With your red woolen caps, and your moccasins, come
To the gathering summons of trumpet and drum!

Come down with your rifles! let gray wolf and fox
Howl on in the shade of their primitive rocks;
Let the bear feed securely from pig-pen and stall;
Here 's a two-legged game for your powder and ball!

On our south come the Dutchmen, enveloped in grease,
And arming for battle, while canting of peace;
On our east, crafty Meshech has gathered his band,
To hang up our leaders and eat out our land.

Ho! all to the rescue! For Satan shall work
No gain for his legions of Hampshire and York!
They claim our possessions,—the pitiful knaves!—
The tribute *we* pay shall be prisons and graves!

---

and other Green Mountain Boys. The poem is given in Henry W.
De Puy's " Ethan Allen," Buffalo, 1853, and in " Littell's Living
Age," March 22, 1856.   Under date of March 19, 1887, Whittier
wrote to the Boston " Transcript " a letter, in which he said: " ' The
Song of the Vermonters, by Ethan Allen,' was a piece of boyish
mystification, written sixty years ago and printed anonymously.
The only person who knew its authorship was my old friend
Joseph T. Buckingham, and I supposed the secret died with him.
We were both amused to find it regarded by antiquarian authorities
as a genuine relic of the old time.   How the secret was discovered a few years ago I have never known. I have never intentionally written anything in favor of war, but a great deal
against it."

Let Clinton and Ten Broek, with bribes in their hands,
Still seek to divide us and parcel our lands:
We 've coats for our traitors, whoever they are;
The warp is of *feathers*, the filling of *tar!*

Does the " Old Bay State " threaten? Does Congress com-
  plain?
Swarms Hampshire in arms on our borders again?
Bark the war-dogs of Britain aloud on the lake?
Let 'em come! what they *can*, they are welcome to take.

What seek they among us? The pride of our wealth
Is comfort, contentment, and labor and health;
And lands which as Freemen we only have trod,
Independent of all save the mercies of God.

Yet we owe no allegiance; we bow to no throne;
Our ruler is law, and the law is our own;
Our leaders themselves are our own fellow-men,
Who can handle the sword or the scythe or the pen.

Our wives are all true, and our daughters are fair,
With their blue eyes of smiles and their light flowing hair;
All brisk at their wheels till the dark even-fall,
Then blithe at the sleigh-ride, the husking, and ball!

We 've sheep on the hillsides; we 've cows on the plain;
And gay-tasselled corn-fields, and rank-growing grain;
There are deer on the mountains; and wood-pigeons fly
From the crack of our muskets, like clouds in the sky.

And there 's fish in our streamlets and rivers, which take
Their course from the hills to our broad-bosomed lake;
Through rock-arched Winooski the salmon leaps free,
And the portly shad follows, all fresh from the sea.

Like a sunbeam the pickerel glides through his pool,
And the spotted trout sleeps where the water is cool,
Or darts from his shelter of rock and of root
At the beaver's quick plunge or the angler's pursuit.

And ours are the mountains which awfully rise
Till they rest their green heads on the blue of the skies:
And ours are the forests, unwasted, unshorn,
Save where the wild path of the tempest is torn.

And though savage and wild be this climate of ours,
And brief be our season of fruits and of flowers,
Far dearer the blast round our mountains which raves
Than the sweet summer zephyr which breathes over slaves.

Hurrah for VERMONT ! for the land which we till
Must have sons to defend her from valley and hill ;
Leave the harvest to rot on the field where it grows,
And the reaping of wheat for the reaping of foes.

Far from Michiscom's valley to where
Poosoomsuck steals down from his wood-circled lair,
From Shocticook river to Lutterlock town,—
Ho ! all to the rescue ! Vermonters, come down !

Come York or come Hampshire,—come traitors and knaves ;
If ye rule o'er our *land*, ye shall rule o'er our *graves ;*
Our vow is recorded,—our banner unfurled ;
In the name of Vermont, we defy *all the world !*

There is an interesting parallelism between Ruskin
and Whittier in their latent sympathy with war and
yet their open reprobation of it.   The truth is, we
are in a transition state from the era of battle to the
era of peace.   And while to the old soldier-nations
the fatal ordeal of the sword—man to man and shield
to shield—seemed the sole condition of high mental

attainments, to us a more excellent way presents itself ; namely, battle with the hostile forces of nature, and moral struggle and emulation. But at present we must charitably allow our poets of peace the mere imagery of the old ages of strife ; for poetic material is not easy to obtain unless the whole range of life is open to the poet's use.

The moral quality of the Quaker poet which leads him to abhor war reveals itself in a milder form in his dislike of the strife and noise of the professional politician's life. Although taking a deep interest in elections and in all questions concerning the nation's welfare, he says that, as a rule, he has declined overtures for acceptance of public station; and adds, "I have not been willing to add my own example to the greed of office." In 1842 he was nominated as a Liberty party candidate for Congress from Massachusetts, as we shall see. The only offices he has actually held, however, have been unsought by him. He was twice elected to the Massachusetts legislature, and served twice as member of the government Electoral College. He has also been on the Board of Overseers of Harvard and Brown Universities. In 1845 he was a Vice-President of the Massachusetts Society for the Abolition of Capital Punishment. He made a few anti-slavery speeches,[1] but was more successful as a lobbyist ("a superb hand at it," said

---

[1] A reviewer of Whittier in 1849 ("Littell's Living Age," January 13) says, "We have small sympathy with him as a lecturer," and gives as his reasons that he does n't like the "fierce anathemas and savage denunciations" of the Puritans ! Rather amusing that !— "the savage Whittier" is much like "the ferocious turtle dove." The reviewer continues, "As is generally the case with ultra-liberals, Mr. Whittier exhibits a most vindictive intolerance."

Wendell Phillips) and as an organizer of voters. His keen insight into men's characters, taken in connection with his winning address, was what made his election services so highly prized by party managers. He must have startled and almost terrified the quiet-loving Longfellow by proposing to him that he should accept a nomination to Congress on the Liberty party ticket in 1844. Longfellow had just published his Poems on Slavery, which had pleased Whittier, and he wrote to thank him for them, saying they had been of important service to the party. " Our friends," said he, " think they could throw for thee one thousand more votes than for any other man." Longfellow answered, "At all times I shall rejoice in the progress of true liberty, and in freedom from slavery of all kinds; but I cannot for a moment think of entering the political arena. Partisan warfare becomes too violent, too vindictive, for my taste; and I should be found but a weak and unworthy champion in public debate." [1]

In 1834 Whittier was Corresponding Secretary of the Haverhill Anti-slavery Society; and his Reports as Corresponding Secretary of the Essex County Anti-slavery Society in 1837 are extant.[2] In April, '37, he spoke at a meeting of the Massachusetts Society in Lynn, and at the anniversary meeting of the American Anti-slavery Society, in that year, he introduced a resolution advocating no political support to any party candidate who was unwilling to work for the abolition of slavery. In February of this busy year,

---

[1] Life of Longfellow, by Samuel Longfellow, ii. 20.

[2] In " Liberator," Jan. 14, '37, and May 5, '37.

'37, he is at Harrisburg, Pennsylvania, attending a convention of the Pennsylvania Society, and writes glowing letters to the papers, saying that Thomas Whitson was there, "firm as rock and true as steel"; Charles C. Burleigh, with his eloquence and his plain homespun appearance, was "moving all before him"; and "sturdy farmer Ritner," the Governor, had flung out on the mountain breezes of Pennsylvania the banner of free discussion. We are told that one of the delegates (honor be to his name!) had the good sense to hold that the negroes had a right to fight for their freedom, and he indignantly withdrew from the convention when the doctrinaires refused to agree with him, saying it was nothing but a Quaker meeting. In 1839, at the anniversary of the American Society, we find Whittier introducing a resolution (successfully passed) favoring the ballot as a weapon in the hands of Abolitionists. At a business meeting of the society in January, 1840, he was present and took part in the proceedings; and in July of the same year he serves on a business committee at the Albany Convention.

He was an ardent supporter of Caleb Cushing in his thirteen attempts to secure election to Congress. (Cushing was finally successful.) In 1828, when a mere boy, Whittier, as editor of the "American Manufacturer," supported Henry Clay, in a sort of perfunctory way; but, when afterwards his eyes were opened more fully to the wrongs of slavery, he declined to give him his support, because he was a slaveholder,—and told him so frankly in a cordial interview he had with him once in Washington.[1]

[1] Life of Garrison, i. 190.

10

Mr. Whittier helped to organize the Liberty party, which was the precursor of the Free-Soil party (in the essential matter); and that in turn was merged in the present Republican party. The real founder of the Liberty party was Myron Holley of New York State. The party came into existence in entire independence of the New Organization faction of the Abolitionists, but that faction at once fraternized with it on political grounds. In the ethical field the founding of the American and Foreign Anti-slavery Society, and its organ, the "American and Foreign Anti-slavery Reporter," by the New Organizationists, was one of the minor results of division in the Abolition ranks, primarily on the question of woman's rights, and secondarily on the subjects of political action, non-resistance, and moral perfectionism. Garrison and his party thought the Constitution of the United States to be a covenant with death and an agreement with hell, and could not conscientiously vote under it or recognize its authority. But such Abolitionists as Whittier, Samuel E. Sewall, James G. Birney, Gerrit Smith, the Tappans, Joshua Leavitt, Elizur Wright, Henry B. Stanton, Amos A. Phelps, and Rev. John Pierpont were willing to work under the Constitution, and vote under it; and they therefore joined themselves to the Liberty party, and founded their own journals, — among them the "Reporter," above mentioned. This short-lived monthly, founded by Lewis Tappan, published in New York, and edited by Whittier, had no great strength or following. Whittier was also placed on the executive committee of the new society, but excused himself on account of his health. The

Garrisonians, and notably the keen-witted Edmund Quincy, fought the come-outers with tooth and nail; and the list of names above given shows that well was their need, if they would keep alive after so alarming a defection. As for the American and Foreign Society, if it had done nothing else, we should owe it a debt of gratitude for the founding and nursing into self-support of the " National Era," which furnished a medium for the publication of a large part of Whittier's best poems (ninety-five of them) and— most important of all—Mrs. Stowe's " Uncle Tom's Cabin."

The split in the Abolition ranks, which is of very little interest to most of us now, occupies a conspicuous place in the history of Abolitionism, and created a good deal of hard feeling and not a little bitter speaking between members of the different factions. Whittier was often spoken of as a good editor for projected organs of the new party, and did actually do editorial work both on the " Emancipator " of Joshua Leavitt and the " American and Foreign Anti-slavery Reporter," as has been stated. Garrison was extremely jealous of the new journals, and pretty severe in his language about them. He said he was certain that " the grand design was to supplant the ' Liberator,' and establish a paper upon its ruins that would be less offensive to the clergy, and less free in its spirit, and that would not dare to utter a word upon any other question of reform—unless it were popular!" This was a most unfair statement, but Garrison firmly believed it. The relation of friendship between him and Whittier was strained, but never entirely broken by these differences of opinion. It was hard to quarrel with so gentle and amiable a man as the Quaker poet.

Still, between the years 1839 and 1861, the columns of the "Liberator" contain from time to time little flings at Whittier as one of the leaders of the political Abolition party.

At the beginning of the difficulty, Whittier, as editor of the "Freeman," wrote in February, 1839, a piece in which, as always, he poured oil upon the troubled waters. He said, in substance: Let us tolerate and forgive one another everything but wilful and deliberate treachery to the cause. Our merely personal differences must be buried "deeper than plummet ever sounded." "Are we not all brethren, Abolitionists all? . . . Like the fabled stone of Scio, which Pliny speaks of, that floated on the waves when whole, but sunk like lead beneath them when broken asunder, our strength and safety lie in our union and brotherhood of spirit."[1]

In his comment on this Mr. Garrison characteristically said: "All this is certainly in a very amicable spirit. Its object is pacification, but somewhat in the Henry Clay style, when Missouri was admitted into the Union as a slave State, for the sake of peace."

Whittier wrote in reply in the next number of the "Liberator" but one:—

AMESBURY, 24th, 2d mo., 1839.

MY DEAR GARRISON,—As sickness, in thy opinion, does not always "subdue the temper and chasten the spirit," was it not somewhat hazardous, on thy part, to make an experiment upon my complacency and good nature while suffering from pro-

---

[1] Liberator, Feb. 22, 1839.

tracted indisposition ? There are times when "the grasshopper is a burden"; and therefore it ought not to surprise thee, that, without fully indorsing the erudite Dogberry's theory in relation to comparisons, I should take exceptions to one in thy last paper, likening my efforts for the "pacification" of conflicting "Boston notions" to those of Henry Clay on the Missouri question; and that the idea of being held up alongside of the "Great Pacificator," right on the heel of his late "surrender" to John C. Calhoun, is peculiarly unsavory. It may have been nothing more than a figure of speech, or a flourish of rhetoric; but if it was intended to impeach me with having, for the sake of peace, or for any other reason, yielded up one of those great and glorious truths for which for the last six years we have contended side by side, it was unworthy of William Lloyd Garrison—far more injurious to himself than to his friend; and in the free spirit of an Abolitionist, I tread it as the dust under my feet and leave it.

It may be, however, that, in this matter, my heart will be excused at the expense of my judgment. My views of the existing difficulty may be attributed to a defect of moral vision. Well, be it so. I confess that the habit of my mind is somewhat confiding and unsuspicious. No visions of future treachery haunt and disturb me in my communion with my anti-slavery brethren: no shadows and omens of thick-coming disasters throng before me: no ghosts of treason, wearing the similitude of loved and familiar friends, scowl on me from the Shadow World of the Future. My sphere of vision is mainly limited to the Actual and the Present. For me, "sufficient unto the day is the evil thereof." Yet, when real difficulties come,—when the ploughshares of a fiery ordeal lie hot and glowing in the very path of duty,—I trust I shall not evince more hesitancy and faltering than those of my brethren who, more clear-sighted than myself, have seen the danger afar off. . . .

But enough—I have written far more than I intended when I commenced this note. Make such comments upon it as thou mayst deem proper, or none at all. One thing I would state in advance. However I may differ from him, I shall not quarrel with the friend of twelve years' standing, whom I have known and loved in prosperity and adversity—who first stimulated me to active exertion in the cause of the slave. . . .

Truly thy friend,
JOHN G. WHITTIER.

To this genial avowal the fiery Garrison, who was in a state of great irritation, appended a half-column of ungracious accusations against the seceded party, headed by the following remark to Whittier, in which he rubs the sore when he should apply the plaster: "We sympathize with our dear friend in his illness. In our allusion to Henry Clay's manner of 'pacification,' we only meant that J. G. W. is for obtaining peace at the expense of consistency, if not of principle."

Matters were evidently grown to be a little serious between the two friends, and it is easy to see on which side intolerance existed. One could imagine Whittier as saying with Landor, "I do not like your great men who beckon me to them, call me their begotten, their dear child, and their entrails; and if I happen to say on any occasion, 'I beg leave, sir, to dissent a little from you,' stamp and cry, 'The devil you do!' and whistle for the executioner." Whittier had sailed quite into the north of Garrison's good opinion, and that reformer took no pains to conceal the fact or to breathe the faults of his friend quaintly, but keeps twitting him and pricking him. He calls members of the new party "the sightless and priestless dupes of a bigoted clergy."[1] When Whittier was annoyed at

---

[1] Liberator, xiii. 51.

the circulation in the presidential campaign of 1842 (as if they were then first written) of some highly encomiastic lines on Henry Clay penned by him in 1829 or 1830, Garrison slyly asks why Whittier or any of his friends should marvel at this, since " all's fair in politics." In 1859, when the hanging of John Brown occurs, Garrison keenly remarks that Whittier can't complain of Brown, since he himself votes under a constitution which upholds war. In 1841 there appears on the first page of the "Liberator" a paragraph from the "Pennsylvania Freeman" which Whittier had recently edited. The writer of the paragraph expresses regret that " the soul of John G. Whittier should choose to be cramped within such narrow limits" as the editorship of the "American and Foreign Anti-slavery Reporter" imposes. Then comes a veiled sneer about the feeble health of Whittier being just suited to a task of such slight magnitude. Again, the "Liberator" itself says editorially: " Where is John G. Whittier? At home, we believe, but incapable of doing anything important for the cause — except to write political electioneering addresses for the 'Liberty party'! New Organization has affected his spirit to a withering extent, and politics will complete his ruin, if he 'tarry long in all the field.'"[1] In the "Liberator" for Nov. 11, 1842, Garrison holds Whittier up to ridicule. " The most ludicrous feelings are excited within us," he says, "on looking over the Liberty party's list of Congressional nominations." After speaking of three of the nominees as " Methodist priests," wholly untrustworthy

---

[1] Liberator, Aug. 12, 1842.

for the work of Abolitionism, he continues: " In District No. 3, John G. Whittier is the Liberty party candidate. Like the other two, if elected, he would be speechless on the floor of Congress,—not, like them, for the want of intellectual ability, but because public speaking is not his gift. Whittier, it is well known, is a member of the Society of Friends. He is professedly opposed to war, defensive as well as offensive, and to capital punishment. As a member of Congress, he would be compelled to promise, under the pains and penalties of perjury, to support the U. S. Constitution AS IT IS. By that Constitution, the life of man may be taken, and war declared and prosecuted—the army and navy must be maintained —piracy is made lawful, in the granting of letters of marque and reprisal—and the judiciary, which sentences human beings to be hanged by the neck till they are dead, is regarded as the sheet-anchor of ' law and order,'—to say nothing about the clauses allowing slaveholders to represent their slaves, and to recover fugitives in any part of the Union. How can Whittier promise to support such a bloody instrument, either as a philanthropist or a Christian ?"

Now, Whittier was of course sensitive to censure, and quick as lightning to perceive coldness or hostility in a friend. He showed the old party the back seams of his stockings in an unmistakable way, when he found out their animus. From about 1840 to 1854 no direct communications whatever from Whittier appear in the " Liberator," though his poems continue to be regularly quoted from other journals. Still, the trouble between Garrison and his friend was not unsolderable, but was only of the nature of

a marked coolness (for a number of years). A little
incident is in point here. In the latter part of 1841
Whittier happened one day to be in Garrison's office
in Boston, after the headquarters of the old American
Anti-slavery Society had been removed to that city.
"Why can't we all go on together?" said Whittier.
"Why not indeed?" said Garrison: "*we* stand just
where we did. I see no reason why you cannot
coöperate with the American Society." "Oh," replied
Whittier, "but the American Society is not what it
once was: it has the hat and the coat and the waistcoat
of the old Society, but the life has passed out of it."
"Are you not ashamed," laughingly replied Mr. Garrison, "to come here wondering why we cannot go
on together! No wonder you can't coöperate with a
suit of old clothes."[1]

At heart, however, Whittier often suffered poign-
antly over the disagreements of the two parties. In
1840 he wrote to Joshua Leavitt:

"My dear Brother Leavitt,—I have just returned to
the quiet of my home, and have barely had leisure to glance
over the anti-slavery newspapers which have accumulated during my absence.

"Last year I attended the Annual Meeting of the American
Anti-slavery Society in New York. It was to me a painful
season. The distrust and jealousy which were manifested, and
the impeachment of motives which was indulged in, were to
me a source of regret, mortification, and sorrow unfeigned.
And when, previous to the late Anniversary, I saw the parties
mustering for strife,—signals and watchwords passing and
repassing over the land,—and every indication of a desperate
struggle for the mastery of numbers, I could not find in my

---

[1] Life of Garrison, iii.

own mind any freedom to attend the meeting. Even had I
resolved otherwise, the state of my health must have prevented
me from any active participation in the business proceedings,
and I felt no disposition to be a spectator of dissension and
strife among friends.

"Of the result of that meeting I need not speak. The anti-
slavery host has been severed in twain. The thing which I
have greatly feared has come upon us. The original cause of
the difficulty—a disposition to engraft foreign questions upon
the simple stock of immediate emancipation—I early discovered,
and labored to the extent of my ability to counteract. That in
so doing I have been compelled to dissent from the views of
some of my dearest personal friends has been no ordinary trial
to me."

Whittier then begs leave, on account of his health,
to be excused from serving on the Executive Committee of the American and Foreign Anti-slavery
Society, and closes with a pious exhortation and expression of faith in the cause. [1]

A few months later than the time of the above
letter, Whittier had a brilliant word-duel with N. P.
Rogers, whose second was Garrison. As the give
and take game went on, it was merged into a discussion of the right or wrong of the New Organization for political action, and the motives of the different parties, and will therefore give us an opportunity to investigate the case a little ourselves, and
see if we can, at this distance of time, reach the truth
about it.

The immediate occasion of the clash was a letter of
Whittier's written to the " Pennsylvania Freeman,"

----

[1] Emancipator, July 2, 1840.

under date of Sept. 24, 1840,[1] criticising N. P. Rogers for certain published statements about the London Convention of Abolitionists, to which he was a delegate. But it is necessary to go back a little further, in order to see the matter in all its bearings.

About half a year previously, Whittier had written a poem on the proposed Convention, couched in beautiful terms and breathing a spirit of charity and peace,—

> " Yes, let them gather ! Summon forth
> The pledged philanthropy of earth.
>
> *   *   *   *   *
>
> Let them come and greet each other,
> And know in each a friend and brother."

Alluding to this poem, Garrison, with characteristic hard obstinacy and intolerance, said, " Amen, yes, let them all come,— . . . all but those who refuse to associate for the slave's redemption with others who do not agree with them as to the divinity of human politics, and the Scriptural obligation to prevent woman from opening her mouth in an anti-slavery gathering for ' the suffering and the dumb,'— and *they* cannot come, *conscientiously*—they are *par excellence* New Organizationists ! "

This was slamming the door in Whittier's face with a vengeance ! Yet the difficulty suggested so delicately by Garrison did not seem to be insuperable to the New Organizationists, for they sent two of their number—James G. Birney (at that time a can-

----

[1] Quoted in " Liberator " Nov. 27, 1840. None of the letters of Whittier written at this time have been reprinted.

didate for the Presidency) and Henry B. Stanton—to the Convention, and no doubt invited Whittier, but he was very ill at home and could not go, and was besides, as we have seen, in a state of disgust over the everlasting wrangle and *jaw* of the Garrisonians and their opponents.

Well, off to London, in high feather, had gone Garrison and Rogers, Lucretia Mott and Wendell Phillips, Birney and Stanton. They were having a grand time there, and sending home letters about it all.

When the British delegates refused to admit women to the Convention, Garrison declined to take his seat with them, and remained a spectator of the proceedings. Now, as the ostensible ground for the split in the Abolition host had been difference of opinion on the desirability of women taking part in conventions and meetings, of course Whittier, in his letter to the "Freeman," above mentioned, takes the position that the action of the British in rejecting the women delegates affords no ground for sweeping condemnation of the great meeting. He himself, as a Quaker, was used to women speaking in meetings, and has always been what is called a woman's rights man. But, seeing the state of public opinion on the subject, he thought it wise to defer the question, and not swamp the Abolition boat by loading her too heavily with other reforms. And he was right. He repels with warmth, also, the assertion of William Howitt that the Orthodox Friends voted " No " because they were unwilling to associate with Lucretia Mott, a heterodox Quaker. He takes issue with Mr. Rogers as to the latter's assertion that the great mass

of British Abolitionism was more despotic, as well as
more servile, than our republican pro-slavery folk.
"They have no freedom in England, and how can
they have anti-slavery?" said Rogers.

To this Whittier replies:—

"Logical and convincing might this be, did not
800,000 FACTS to the contrary, in the redeemed and
disenchained islands of the West Indies, start up
before us—did not the voices of emancipated men
and women, and children, in those islands, rising
above the roar of many waters, bemurmuring the
'still vexed Bermoothes,' invoke blessings upon the
heads of the men whom our brother has termed 'despotic' and 'servile'—less worthy than 'our pro-
slavery mob.' . . . The truth is, our friend Rogers
has little sympathy with anything staid, sober-paced,
prosaic, and formula-fettered; and we suppose he
found most of our English brethren mere non-con-
ductors of his fervid, imaginative, electric-sparkling
Abolitionism. He went dreaming of setting a whole
world free from all kinds of oppression—mental,
physical, social, religious, and political; millennial
fire-shadowings fell about him in his pathway across
the waters; he went to receive and in turn communicate an enthusiasm which was to go round the
world, the *pharmakon nepenthes* for all its evils—and
they gave him dull reports, plans for abolishing the
slave-trade—and for cotton-growing in the East—
passionless, and *figurative* only in tables of statis-
tics. . . .

"They came to welcome American Abolitionists to
their hearts and homes, and join them in promoting
the extinction of chattel slavery. They did not, how-

ever, come prepared to adopt our new doctrines of
human equality; and probably knew little of them
—our declarations, immortal in lithograph and satin;
our ' platform ' on which men and women lose their
distinctive character, and become ' souls without sex '
—our long ' reports,' and indignant ' protests '—old
and new organization tactics—hair-splitting meta-
physics of the Joseph Tracy school—poetical and
rhetorical flourishes—transcendentalism engrafted
upon puritanism; Cousin's ' Progress and Reform '
and Cromwell's ' sword of the Lord and of Gideon '
—our discussions of ethics, theology, politics, ' fore-
knowledge, will and fate,' ' long drawn out,' although
not always with the ' linked sweetness ' Milton speaks
of ! The faintest possible rumor of all this had alone
reached our British fellow-laborers. They came to
meet American Abolitionists, as men altogether like
themselves,—intent upon the one common object.
That object they supposed might be attained without
subscribing to our Yankee doctrines of equality, or
sexless democracy. For was not Wilberforce himself
a Tory? Did he not with one breath denounce the
slave-trade, and with the next defend that church
establishment which Milton, eloquently indignant in
the name of his abused and plundered countrymen,
declared had been ' for twelve hundred years a sad
and doleful succession of blind guides to the souls of
Englishmen: a wasteful band of robbers to their
purses '? Was it to carry into practice any abstract
doctrine of equality that the measure of West India
emancipation received the votes of the Lords Spiritual
and Temporal in Parliament ? Did William IV., in
giving his royal assent to that Bill, become a radical

democrat—a second Monsieur Égalité? And now when members of the Royal Family, Lords and Knights and Right Honorables,—England's chivalry and her highest born,—grace the platforms of anti-slavery meetings, will Ireland find redress for her wrongs—will China, swallowing opium-poison, under the guns of the British navy, obtain a respite—will the starving murmur of the miserable Chartists be answered less sternly with pistol-shot and sabre-cut? Not at all. It were as unreasonable to suppose it as that we ourselves, by reason of our Abolitionism, should be found perfect patterns of consistency, meekness, self-denial, and kind-dealing—with no segment wanting to complete the circle of our perfectibility. Our British friends, I suspect, after all, upon a rigid scrutiny, will be found quite as consistent as ourselves."

The communication closes with the expression of a hope that his old friend Rogers will take what is said in a spirit of kindness. Garrison spoke of this letter as "very reprehensible" and "somewhat contemptuous." Charles C. Burleigh also replied to it in a long and admirably cool review, in which he regretted the over-statements of his Orthodox Quaker friend, Whittier, and offered indubitable proof (taken from private letters) that William Howitt was right in saying that Lucretia Mott had been given the cold shoulder by many of the Orthodox Quakers in England.[1] Mr. Rogers's reply also soon appeared in the "Anti-slavery Standard":—

---

[1] This is now confirmed by the recently published Autobiography of Mary Howitt, who says, "The English Quakers will not receive Lucretia Mott because she is a Hicksite."

" Who could have thought, while contemplating the lofty
effusions of our anti-slavery bard, that 'new organization'
would ever be able to 'tame' or to 'catch' his ethereal spirit,
or fetter his free limbs in its narrow harness? Alas! has it
not caught him, and reduced him, and tamed him, as to all
further coöperation in the enterprise of which he has ever been
the ornament and pride? It may be to humble us in the dust,
that star after star in our enterprise is thus starting from its
sphere in the anti-slavery firmament, and disappearing like an
exploded meteor. Whittier at length goes out, we fear, among
the other wandering luminaries. We speak it with grief, for
we have gloried in his light and beauty. But, henceforth, we
look for him no longer blazing in the anti-slavery van, bearing
his shield gallantly abreast of the ' Liberator '—celebrating the
triumphs of freedom in deathless verse, and bursting forth on
tyranny in volcanic explosion, as it developed itself from time
to time, under the Ithuriel-touches of our movement. We look
no longer for his banner in the anti-slavery field. He is transferred to another service."

And in a succeeding letter Mr. Rogers adds:—

" He tolerated New Organization [political Abolitionism]
and threw the whole weight of his powerful influence against
the editor of the ' Liberator,' and the movement he had from the
beginning singly (as an Abolitionist) pursued, and cast it into
the scale with this new type of clerical appealism, called New
Organization ; the most wolfish, as by experience we have elsewhere found, of any sheep-clad hostility that has waylaid the
anti-slavery movement."   .   .   .

" We ask dear friend Whittier to down with his classic pride
and up among us again—again to unfurl his beauteous white
streamer to the wind—once more to be the ornament, the admiration, of our thinned but deathless ranks. May God send
him health, and with it his ancient vision and spirit, is our sincere, our earnest prayer."

In Mr. Whittier's rejoinder to this he says that he
has received a copy of Mr. Rogers's paper, in which
he is officially informed that he is no longer an Abolitionist.

"I am likened to a star shooting madly from its
sphere,—launching, like Carazan of the Eastern
story, into the abyss of infinitude—

> ' A comet shorn,
> Out into utter darkness borne.'

And a mock lamentation is set up over me, which
would be pathetic, did it not partake so largely, under
all the circumstances of the case, of the ludicrous.

"Now, if the editor of the 'Standard' means by all
this simply that he and myself disagree on some
points in reference to anti-slavery movements, and if
believing, as a matter of course, that his views are
correct and mine wrong, he chooses to express in this
way his dissent from my conclusions, and to expose
their folly and fallacy, I have nothing to say. Let him
argue down or laugh down my heresies, if he can.
He may rest assured that I can do justice to a sound
argument, even if it overthrows a favorite doctrine ;
and relish good-natured wit and humor, even when
exercised at my expense, consoling myself, like Falstaff, with the reflection, that if I have not wit myself,
I am 'the cause of wit in others.' Even if brother
Rogers should so far shut up the bowels of his com-
passion as to quote *my* own poetry against me, and,
as in the case of poor Cinna, the poet in Shakspeare's
'Julius Cæsar,' 'condemn me for my bad verses,'
however I might writhe under the infliction, I do n't
know as I should complain.

11

"But if Nathaniel P. Rogers means (what his language somewhat strongly implies) to impeach my
character as an honest man—to assail my moral integrity—to brand me with the foul suspicion of treachery and hypocrisy ; as one wilfully recreant to the
cause of emancipation—I have only to say that his
recent voyage 'in search of a World's Convention'
has wrought in his head and heart a 'sea-change'
which would have astonished the tenants of Pros-
pero's island—transforming the generous and high-
minded Christian gentleman into a false ' accuser of
his brethren '—a Titus Oates swearing away more
than the life of his friend.

"I am told, in unqualified terms, that I shall never
be able to do anything more for that cause to which
I have devoted the morning of my life—on whose
altar I have laid all that I possessed. Indeed, it may
be so. He who, in His ' dealings with the children
of men,' has seen fit to visit me with lingering pain
and illness, knows whether more labor will be required at my hands in that cause, and, if so, will give
me strength to perform it."

It must be granted that Whittier, like another Ivan-
hoe, wielded a respectable weapon in this single-
handed fence with his group of opponents. And
the enemies of the Liberty party were by no means
puny men of their hands. To those named should
be added the witty Edmund Quincy, who described
the New Organization as the Devil's own. As his
Majesty was sitting once on a time (says he) in moody
meditation, "gnawing his bitter nail," and pondering
how he could destroy the usefulness of the Abolitionists, "on a sudden, a happy thought flashed into his

mind: 'Go to,' he exclaimed, rubbing his claws, and wagging his tail in an ecstasy of infernal glee,—'go to,—I have it ! I will make *fun* of them !' And, even as he spoke, out from his teeming brain, as did Sin of old, leaped forth the Liberty party." [1]

In sober truth, the Liberty party was far from being despicable, as the Garrisonians affirmed, and still affirm. Oliver Johnson, as well as the sons of Garrison, claim too much for their party, it seems to me. It is with them, just as it ever was with William Lloyd Garrison, all or nothing. *Orna me !* was his continual cry, and he often tripped over the perpendicular pronoun. His undying glory lies in his having created, as none other did, unless it was Whittier, the moral sentiment that finally destroyed slavery. Everything that he said was interesting ; his editorials are trenchant pieces of reasoning (thought clear-cut and lucid, no hair on the nib of his pen); he towers up above everybody in his faction in moral earnestness and strength. But he was unelastic, was lacking in the mobility and tact of genius ; and when, after ten years of agitation, the anti-slavery party was clearly ripe for political action (as the issue demonstrated), he and his adherents made the strategic mistake of remaining stationary. Looking back, we can now see that the despised and ridiculed Liberty party, like the Independents of to-day, was on the right track. Like the little Spartan band of John Brown, their plans were not so wild as they have been represented to be. John Brown knew well enough that his force was small, but he expected to draw to it

---

[1] Liberator, Jan. 5, '43.

thousands of blacks along the great Alleghany range.
So the new party of Liberty, seeing the South marching on from victory to victory, and the great question
of Texas looming up, saw that the time was come to
send the electric current through the nation and
crystallize the discordant elements into the serried
ranks of a great party : they expected to be joined
by hundreds of thousands of Whigs and Democrats
who should find their organization the nucleus of
union. "They judged, *and the event has proved that
they judged wisely*" (says Henry Wilson, in his " Rise
and Fall of the Slave Power ") "that by narrowing
the platform, even if it did not contain all that the
most advanced Abolitionists desired, if such men as
John P. Hale, Wilmot, Giddings, Palfrey, Seward, and
Mann could be drawn from the Whig and Democratic
parties and be thus arrayed in a compact and vigorous organization against the Slave Power, there
would be great gain."

The declaration of objects and principles of the
Liberty party, as set forth in their journals,—and
notably in their Almanac for 1846,[1]—shows that their
plans were well seasoned and not unfeasible, and
reveals their essential identity with the platform of
the Free-Soil party that came later. The Almanac
announces that their aim was to secure an anti-
slavery Congress and Executive, and thereby abolish
slavery in the District of Columbia, do away the
slave-trade, annul the Fugitive Slave Law, and, by
excluding slaveholders from all offices in the gift of

---

[1] This seems to be the best and fullest statement of the objects
of the party that has been made.

the appointing power, virtually disfranchise the South, and render it imperative to close out the business of slavery altogether.

Now, the party did not succeed exactly in the way it had hoped to do, yet indirectly did succeed. For it was the elder brother of the Free-Soil party, and got so mixed up with it in the bath-tub of the Buffalo Convention of 1848 that its identity disappeared. It is well known that at this Convention the members of the Liberty party, after due consultation, dissolved their organization (they were met in the same city, at the same time) and took their seats among the delegates of the just-born Free-Soil party; and it was remarked by one of the speakers—and the *mot* was applauded—that "without tasting death the Liberty party had been translated."[1] But, now, remember that the Free-Soil party was merged in the Republican party, which held Kansas for the North, abolished slavery, and saved the Union.

Internal dissension was what killed the Liberty party. In 1844, however, in voting for James G. Birney, it held the balance of power in New York, and decided the presidential election against Clay, who had expressed himself as willing to see Texas annexed as a slave State. Says Schouler, "Had half of the Birney votes of the election of 1844 been given to Clay, he would have won the State."[2] This is a matter of figures, and has not been disputed. It seems to me that, if this Third party could have been held together by some great leader, it would have drawn

---

[1] Wilson's "Rise and Fall of the Slave Power," ii. 157.

[2] History of United States, iv. 479.

to it all the elements that afterwards went to make
up the Republican party. It is idle to say that it did
not represent genuine anti-slavery principles because
it affiliated with Free-Soilers, who were many of them
only half-way anti-slavery. The fact remains that
the fiery thread of freedom ran through all the parties, — Liberty, Free-Soil, and Republican, — either
darkling or in the light, until it burst into flame in the
Emancipation Proclamation of 1863. Then, it is in
fact a great mistake to say that the Free-Soil party
was not anti-slavery. In their platform of 1852, article five demands that there shall be no new slave
territory; article seven, "immediate and total repeal
of the Fugitive Slave Act of 1850"; and article six
declares that "slavery is a sin against God, and a
crime against man, which no human enactment or
usage can make right; and that Christianity, humanity, and patriotism alike demand its abolition." Can
language be stronger or more unequivocal than this?
Honor, then, to the gallant little Liberty party! And
let it never be forgotten that, while the Garrison and
Phillips faction of the Abolitionists was resting in
masterly inactivity (politically speaking) and coun-
selling disunion, the Whittier and Birney party (as a
part of the Republican host) was rushing on amid the
whirl of events, and gathering in the Great West the
votes that saved the Union.

We have faithfully recorded, as a matter of history,
the differences of opinion and the partial alienation
of Garrison and Whittier; and we now note with
pleasure the gradual growth of reconciliation.

When in 1854 the souls of lovers of freedom in
Massachusetts were deeply stirred by the remanding

of Anthony Burns to slavery, Whittier wrote to Garrison that Abolitionists must forget all past differences and unite their strength for the conversion of the North. "If I had any love for the Union remaining," he writes, "the events of the last few weeks have 'crushed it out.' But I do not forget that the same power which is needed to break from the Union may make the Union the means of abolishing slavery. At any rate, what we want now is an abolitionized North. To this end Unionists and Disunionists can both contribute. At least let us have union among ourselves. In our hatred of slavery, our sympathy for our afflicted colored brethren, and in our indignation against the oppressor, we are already united; and let us now unite, as far as may be, in action. For one, my heart goes out to all who in any way manifest love of liberty, and pity for the oppressed."[1]

In 1856 Whittier sends Garrison a copy of a new edition of his poems, inscribed to his "old and affectionate friend," and Garrison graciously acknowledges the gift in a review in his paper.

With the outbreak of the Civil War, which took the work of emancipation out of the hands of the Abolitionists altogether, the last vestige of variance disappears from the mind of Garrison (Whittier, as we have seen, never had any hard feeling at all), and henceforth all is concord. At the anniversary meeting of the American Anti-slavery Society in 1863, Whittier was warmly eulogized by Garrison, who said, "There are few living who have done so much to operate upon the public mind and conscience and

---

[1] Liberator, June 9, '54.

heart of our country, for the abolition of slavery, as John Greenleaf Whittier." And, when the poet's seventieth birthday was celebrated in 1877, Garrison wrote some cordial lines (which by a stretch of imagination might be called verses) in his honor.

It is almost needless to say that John G. Whittier cast his vote and used his influence in favor of the election of Abraham Lincoln to the presidential chair. There are some humorous, ringing campaign verses written by him for the first of the two Lincoln election struggles. They have not heretofore appeared in book form, but only as a campaign leaflet, or broadside, and in newspapers thirty odd years ago.[1] They were read at a Republican meeting in Georgetown, Massachusetts, in the autumn of 1860 :—

THE QUAKERS ARE OUT.

Not vainly we waited and counted the hours,
The buds of our hope have burst out into flowers.
No room for misgiving—no loop-hole of doubt,—
We 've heard from the Keystone! The Quakers are out.

The plot has exploded—we 've found out the trick;
The bribe goes a-begging; the fusion won't stick.
When the Wide-Awake lanterns are shining about,
The rogues stay at home, and the true men are out!

The good State has broken the cords for her spun;
Her oil-springs and water won't fuse into one;
The Dutchman has seasoned his Freedom with Krout,
And slow, late, but certain, the Quakers are out!

---

[1] The leaflet is headed "A Voice from John G. Whittier." The poem may also be found in the "Liberator," 1860.

Give the flags to the winds ! set the hills all aflame !
Make way for the man with the patriarch's name !
Away with misgiving—away with all doubt,
For Lincoln goes in when the Quakers are out !

By way of response, somebody, assumed to be a
Quaker, wrote some verses in reply :—

" The Quakers are out ! They had better stay in
  Than mix with the world in political din ;
  What though the earth's potsherds together may smite ?
  Keep the eye firmly fix'd and unmoved on the right," etc.

Since the war, brief letters from Mr. Whittier, in
support of candidates for the Republican party, have
appeared from time to time in the journals, and some
of them are included in the latest edition of his prose
writings. Every autumn, regularly, he goes down to
Amesbury, where he is a legal voter, and casts his
vote. He also takes a live interest in the struggles
of other peoples for freedom and for republican forms
of government,

CHAPTER III.

WHITTIER AT HOME.

WHITTIER is tall and erect in form, with quick movements and alertness of glance. The strict old Quaker régime forbade bows of salutation. The Quaker poet's jerky nod is therefore a concession to the world, but its deficiencies are amply supplied by the pleasant smile that generally accompanies it. He inherited one of those enviably sweet and lovable natures that so often serve to insure success in life. He is somewhat hard of hearing now, and his face is grave and sad when not animated by conversation. But ever and anon, as you talk with him, the features are illumined by a sweet and sudden smile and a kindly flash of the dark eyes. His "thee's" and "thou's" and quaint rural solecisms of speech come with the shock of a surprise when you first meet him. But you like him all the better for them. The more liberal Quakers have discarded the broad brims and antique drab garments of Charles the Second's time. Mr. Whittier generally wears a black or drab tile hat and black undercoat. I have seen him on the street in Amesbury, wearing a cinnamon-colored overcoat and a small gray tippet around his neck. The long backward and upward slope of the head gives it just the shape of Walter Scott's and Emerson's. Mr. Wasson keenly observes that this feature, together with the dark deep eyes full of shadowed fire, the Arabian complexion, the sharp-cut, intense lines of the face, the light tall stature, and quick axial poise of movement, shows that Whittier is of the Saracenic type. Mr. J. Miller McKim, who was with Whittier at the Philadelphia Convention of 1833, says that at that time, with his dark frock-coat with standing collar, black flashing eyes, and black whiskers, he had something of a military look, and was a noticeable figure in the convention.

The next pen-portrait, in order of time, is given by Thomas Wentworth Higginson.[1] He describes an interview he had with Whittier in 1843, "when the excitement of the 'Latimer Case' still echoed through Massachusetts, and the younger Abolitionists were full of the 'joy of eventful living.'[2] I was then nineteen," writes Mr. Higginson, "and saw the poet for the first time at an eating-house, known as Campbell's, then quite a resort for reformers of all sorts. I saw before me a man of striking personal appearance ; tall, slender, with olive complexion, black hair, straight black eyebrows, brilliant eyes, and an Oriental, Semitic cast of countenance. This was Whittier at thirty-five. I lingered till he rose from the table, and then, advancing, I said with boyish enthusiasm,— and I doubt not with boyish awkwardness also,—' I

---

[1] In the "Literary World," December, 1877.

[2] The reference is to the attempt made in 1842 by James B. Gray, of Norfolk, Virginia, to carry back from Boston his fugitive slave George Latimer. A tremendous excitement was the result, and meetings were held in Faneuil Hall, at which Wendell Phillips, Frederick Douglass, and others made speeches. The excitement was repeated on the floor of Congress.

should like to shake hands with the author of " Massachusetts to Virginia." '   The poet, who was, and is,
one of the shyest of men, broke into a kindly smile,
and said briefly, ' Thy name, friend ? '   I gave it, and
we shook hands, and that was all.   But to me it was
like touching a hero's shield ; and though I have
since learned to count the friendship of Whittier as
one of the great privileges of my life, yet nothing has
ever displaced the recollection of that first boyish
interview."

A writer in the " Democratic Review " for 1845
notices in Whittier the " union of manly firmness and
courage with womanly sweetness and tenderness,
alike in countenance and character."   Fredrika Bremer writes in 1847 of his over-strained nervous system, his " nervous bashfulness."   And here is a rather
flattering picture of him at forty-five, by George W.
Bungay : " His temperament is nervous-bilious ; [he]
is tall, slender and straight as an Indian ; has a superb
head ; his brow looks like a white cloud under his
raven hair ; eyes large, black as sloes, and glowing
with expression,—   .   .   .   those starlike eyes flashing under such a magnificent forehead."

The truest picture of all, it seems to me, is given
by genial Robert Collyer : [1]—

" When you see Whittier, you see instantly it is the
Whittier of the pictures, only more thin and gray.
The pictures give you a larger head, yet not so fine
in the lines that mean most in a man of genius ; and
no picture can give you the eyes, smaller than those
we see in the portraits of Burns, but dark, intense,

---

[1] *Every Saturday*, June 3, 1871.

and tender, and, when he speaks of what touches him intensely, all aglow with the light of his soul,—such eyes, indeed, as you only see now in a picture by one of the great masters. There is a hint of the Quaker, you notice, in the cut of his dress, but not in the color, which is black,—not new at all, but so spotless as to make you wish he would take all your new garments and put them through a course of training for a few months, that they might get the habit of looking as pure and sweet as that when you came to wear them. A Quaker in his speech, but using 'thee' and 'thou' with such a shy sweet grace as to make you wonder whether the finest manners may not lurk, after all, within the homely old Saxon terms; quick with his words, contrary to all his traditions and training, and with no hint of the sacred sing-song his sect has always held in such profound esteem, especially in meet'n'."

And here is a little photograph showing the poet among the voters of his own town of Amesbury. It may go down to posterity to interest admirers of his "After Election,"—a marvelous improvisation, a triumph over what to all but a poet would have seemed hopelessly prosaic material.[1] When George M. White was in Amesbury on election day in November, 1883, he went to the town-hall where farmers, tradesmen, and mechanics were discussing in groups,

---

[1] The strong phrases of this poem are familiar. The poet represents himself as awaiting telegraphic election returns: "Hark!—there the Alleghanies spoke "—" That signal from Nebraska sprung "—" Is that thy answer strong and free, O loyal heart of Tennessee?"—" In that wild burst the Ozarks spoke ! Cheer answers cheer from rise to set of sun. We have a country yet !"

larger or smaller, the local issues: "Among these figures there was pointed out to me the tall thin figure of an old man wrapped in a long brown coat, with a high fur collar and woolen mantle around his neck, almost coming up to the brim of his tall black hat. He was talking with the various groups around him. He is much above the average height of men, and few of his pictures that I have seen resemble him. His hair and beard are quite white, he wears no moustache, and his lips are set with an expression of much decision and energy, which is emphasized by a short quick utterance."[1]

Of late years Mr. Whittier has passed the greater part of each winter in Boston, taking rooms in some quiet hotel, such as the Winthrop, in Bowdoin Street, on the northern slope of Beacon Hill. When he reads a book, he usually takes up old and tried favorites; and, although very near the Athenæum library, neither he nor Dr. Holmes (so far as I know) is often seen there, eagerly browsing among the latest books and journals, as is their friend, Dr. Bartol. Occasionally Mr. Whittier can be entrapped into taking an early tea with a Boston friend; but he never feels able to stand the excitement of a large company and late hours.

It was formerly his custom, and I believe still is such, to spend a few weeks of each summer amid the sublime and yet quiet and pastoral scenery of the outskirts of the White Mountains. He used to put up at the old Bearcamp House before this was burned down. This old inn commanded a view of rough and

---

[1] Harper's Monthly, February, 1883.

savage Chocorua Mountain, and Mounts Israel and Whittier. "There is an atmospheric bloom over all the jagged ridges," writes Mr. S. J. Pickard, "which is to the eye like the softness of velvet, but which hides no outline and does not obliterate the distinction between rock and forest. The colors change from hour to hour: rich blues and dark purples alternate during the day, varied with cloud-shadows and drifting gray mists." In the valley through which the tree-fringed Bearcamp flows are orchards loaded with fruit; the tinkle of cow-bells is heard on the mountain slopes. In the autumn the wayside fences are festooned with clematis in bloom. By the roadside are masses of golden-rod and purple asters, and the trees are crimson with woodbine.

Whittier's "Sunset on the Bearcamp" gives the higher inspiration of this mountain scenery. There was an inspiration equally strong, too, in the open fireplaces of the inn. Your hot and ruddy wood fire is a great thawer-out of conventional frigidities; and the fireplace of the Bearcamp Inn parlor was not inferior to its fellows in this good work. Around it used to gather not only Whittier and his friends, but such celebrities as Lucy Larcom and Gail Hamilton, with their relatives and acquaintances; and in the basking heat the merriment often waxed deep and subtle. Comic verses were improvised on rainy days, and Whittier's gift of impromptu composition was drawn upon for nonsense verses to season the feast.

Amesbury was Whittier's home for many years before the death of his mother and sisters, and he still owns the old home there. It is occupied by friends. Portraits of mother and sister hang in the little parlor; and he keeps in his study a few books and pictures. The region round about has been celebrated in his verse. From the study window the green dome of Powow Hill is to be seen,—an elevation which he frequently climbed with friends; across the Merrimack rise "The Laurels"; and near by is the Powow River, and farther off the Artichoke, Lake Attitash, and the green hills of Newbury. The introductory lines of "Miriam" describe the view from Powow Hill. The town contains manufactories of cloth and of carriages. It is said to be named after Ambresbury in England. It is a quiet peaceful old village, especially in its outskirts of orchards and meadows. Mr. Whittier's wooden house on Friend Street is as plain as plain can be. It was originally a one-story structure, but a second story with attic has been added. A few hundred yards from it, in the delta formed by the meeting of two streets, stands the wooden meeting-house of the Friends, where the poet has worshiped God after the ways of his fathers ever since he was a boy. When the family first came to Amesbury, he had with him his mother, sister, and Aunt Mercy: the brother, Matthew, seems early to have married and set up his own household apart. After mother, aunt, and sister had successively passed away, Greenleaf's niece kept house for him until her marriage with Mr. S. T. Pickard. Whittier then removed to Oak Knoll, a fine estate in Danvers, nearer Boston, which is the property of cousins of his.

On the table in the tiny parlor at Amesbury stands, or stood, Rogers's group, "The Fugitive's Story," representing Whittier, Garrison, and Henry Ward

Beecher listening to a black woman as she relates the story of her flight from bondage. On the wall used to hang a large picture of Longfellow facing one of Whittier himself. The gracious and benignant face of his mother, who is clothed in spotless drab, looks down upon you, as does a crayon of the loved sister. Here is a sketch of the little parlor as seen through the eyes of an Englishman in 1885:[1]—

"The small parlor into which the visitor is shown is furnished with the dreary and prim commonplaceness of horsehair upholstery and the old-fashioned conventional ornaments under glass shades. It might be a Dissenting Minister's front room in some provincial English town, like Leicester or Northampton, not yet reached by the iconoclasm of modern æstheticism. But Mr. Whittier's kindly greeting of 'How do thee do? I'm glad to see thee,' dispels all surprise by recalling the fact that he is not only a New Englander, which means simple living from necessity, but also a Quaker, which means simple living from choice."

The study, or garden room, in the Amesbury house is in the rear, one of its windows giving upon a long strip of garden full of pear-trees and grape-vines, and the other (a glass door) opening upon a little side porch. Above was formerly his sleeping-room. The Franklin stove with brass andirons furnishes the open fire which is loved by all poets, but especially by this one. Near the sashed door is the writing-desk. Six book-shelves are fitted into the space between the chimney and the side of the house, and

---

[1] Quoted from the "Pall Mall Gazette."

12

contain such works as Charles Reade's novels, Irish ballads, and the poems of Browning. A side shelf on the wall is completely filled with a blue-and-gold edition of the poets. On the walls hang a pen-and-ink sketch of his brother Matthew, a portrait of Emerson, paintings of Essex County scenes,—including water-colors by Harry Fenn and Celia Thaxter, fringed gentians painted by Lucy Larcom, and Hill's picture of the old farm-house. To this shrine of poetry have come in days past such men as Garrison, Longfellow, Sumner, Bayard Taylor, Wendell Phillips, James T. Fields, Higginson, Wasson, Emerson, Whipple, and many more as famous men. "To this nook," says Mrs. Spofford, "came Alice and Phœbe Cary on their romantic pilgrimage, and here have come many others of the illustrious women of the day, most of whom he reckons as his friends in this generation, as he did Lydia Maria Child and Lucretia Mott and their contemporaries of the last. Here the poet has taken his ease in the slippers that Gail Hamilton made for him, the cunning fingers reconciling his belligerency with his principles by clothing in Quaker drab the enraged American eagle wrought upon them; here he has amused himself teaching tricks to the house animals, which, if he does not love, he loves to play with; here has this verse been struck off like a spark, and that one painfully labored after ; and here, in spite of his laurels, have the thunder-bolts of the gods twice sought the wearer, the last time felling him to the floor as he stood in the doorway, prostrating his niece at the same time, shattering a mirror, and piercing a rolled-up window-shade till it left the burned mark of a dozen jagged bullet-holes. After that the treacherous lightning-rods were removed, his nephew tells us, but the pertinacious vender of a new variety, who could not make the poet his victim, had his revenge by heading his prospectus with a cut of the lightning descending upon Mr. Whittier's house, and doing the havoc it could not have done, had the house owned this peculiar and particular protector." [1]

Whittier is as deeply loved by the people of Amesbury as was Emerson by his neighbors in Concord, or as was the Good Gray Poet by the citizens of Camden. And the same is true of Whittier's neighbors in Danvers,—his other home, which is an hour's ride by cars from Amesbury, by the leisurely local train.

The old Boston path to Newburyport once led, by an alternate and scarcely secondary line, directly by the estate of Oak Knoll. Here once lived the Rev. George Burroughs, who was pressed to death with heavy weights for questionable dealings with Satan in the days of the witchcraft delusion. The sounding-board of the pulpit in the church where the witches of the neighborhood were tried now covers the mouth of a well on the estate. Oak Knoll is a farm of some sixty acres, and lies about a mile and a half northwest of the village of Danvers. The stately house, with its great Doric pillars, fronts the south, and stands on elevated ground commanding a view of distant hills and farms and towns. At some distance, on the opposite side of the road, are the farm buildings. The charms of landscape-gardening vie with the wildness of nature to render this a place of

---

[1] Harper's Monthly, January, 1884.

delightful quiet and seclusion. The carriage-way winds upward through bosky lawns kept trim by the horse lawn-mower.

"Directly in front of the house," says Mr. Pickard, "and completely encircled by the curving approaches, is a picturesque knoll in the form of a dome, covered with a luxuriant carpet of grass, making one of the most charming lawns it is possible to imagine. This knoll, the summit of which is a little higher than the site occupied by the house, is crowned by two magnificent trees, an oak and a hickory. The estate might well have been named for either of these noble trees. The grounds slope toward the east, the south, and the west, with just enough of irregularity to heighten the beauty of the landscape in each direction. Trees, in clumps and singly, deciduous and evergreen, are placed with careful reference to artistic effect. The variety of trees is very great, many of them being rarely seen in New England. There is a fine magnolia near the house, and farther off a tulip-tree. The rich dark hue of a purple beech calls attention to a fine grove in the western distance. There are English elms and English oaks, an immense Norway spruce, also hemlocks, pines, chestnuts, and almost every other tree that can be made to grow in this climate. There are great orchards of apples and pears ; a garden flanked with luxuriant grape-vines, and yielding all the smaller fruits, as a matter of course, also roses in abundance. Near the eastern piazza of the house is a large circular flower garden surrounded by a neat hedge, with great green arches for gateways to it. In the centre of this garden is

a fountain throwing a fine spray to a considerable
height. In this garden Mr. Whittier is to be seen at
work each pleasant morning before breakfast, with
rake, hoe, and broom. All the beds and walks are
kept exquisitely neat, for the poet is thorough in
everything he undertakes."

No shooting is allowed on the estate, and squirrels
and birds sometimes come to the window to be fed.
The squirrels, says Mrs. Spofford, take liberties that
" puzzle such fellows as the little Dandie Dinmont
who has the care of the house upon his shoulders,
and who darts after them in a terrible fury, and
when he has treed them, in his wrath stands on his
hind feet, waves his paws, and whines, begging them
to come down." Mrs. Bolton writes, in one of her
books for young people, of one of the dogs coming
out to welcome her and holding up a bruised paw
for sympathy, while the mocking-bird on the porch
talked so much louder than she and Mr. Whittier
that he was obliged to cover up its cage

Among the ornaments of the roomy parlor are
a portrait of Whittier painted when he was about forty,
a statuette of Charles Sumner, and a verd-antique
statue of Hercules once owned by Mr. Sumner. A
little library, opening on the western veranda, was
built especially for Mr. Whittier. On its walls are
hung paintings of the Bearcamp and Ossipee region.
"Above the parlor," says Mrs. Spofford, "is his
spacious sleeping-room, furnished after Mr. East-
lake's ideas. Here hang a fine marine view, a sketch
of the Shoals, and a portrait of Hawthorne, another cherished friend. The windows, which are on
three sides of the room, command all the beauty

of the place—flower-garden and fountain, the velvet
turf of the knoll, the stately groups of trees against
a western sky, and the lofty lawns about the turreted
asylum on the distant hill."

In the autumn of 1889 Sir Edwin Arnold published in his paper, the London "Telegraph," brief
notes of a visit paid by him to Oak Knoll :—

"Mr. Whittier's conversation, which was of the
Quaker fashion, full of 'thees' and 'thous,' was
pointed, animated, and marked by the felicity of
his printed works ; nor can any cultured person
need to be told how classic and lucid and happy
are many of Whittier's best lines. He smiled, half
sadly, when I expressed the wish that he could
come across the Atlantic to see, under the memorial
window to Milton, in St. Margaret's Church at Westminster, his own admirable verse :—

'The New World honors thee, whose lofty plea
    For England's freedom made her own more sure.
    Thy page, immortal as its theme, shall be
    Their common freehold, while the worlds endure.'

He dropped a bright epigram in the course of our
chat. I had been praising Emerson, and lamenting
that a great authority—known to us both—dis-
sented, and compared the Concord philosopher's
style in prose to 'the shooting forth of stones from
a sack.' 'Ah ! but,' replied instantly the old poet,
'thee knows well, friend, they are all precious
stones.' And I was happy enough to obtain an
interesting avowal from his lips. He had been
speaking of the enduring and gloomy influence of
the old accustomed Puritan doctrines upon the

minds of New Englanders, of their pernicious dark-
ening of life and literature, and how he himself had
come under the cloud of Calvinism and its terrors.
'But you,' I said, 'sir, born in the purple of the
Muses, never were, and never could have been, a
Calvinistic Puritan.' 'Nay, thee are right,' he answered, 'the world was much too beautiful and God
far too good. I never was of that mind.'"

In the midsummer of '89 the veteran Abolitionist
John M. Barbour published in the "Watchman"
some reminiscences of Whittier and Oak Knoll which
have the charm of old-fashioned graciousness and
entire unconsciousness of any infringement of the
laws of propriety. Indeed, the privileges of age and
life-long friendship bar that. Mr. Barbour says what
I should not dare to say, and I shall therefore let
him speak:—

"On Tuesday, June 4, I was at the depot at the
hour named. The coach was there: the lovely young
daughter of the genial and accomplished Mrs. Woodman (who has just published the charming book,
'Picturesque Alaska,'' which everybody should read)
jumped from the carriage with the buoyancy of health-
ful youth, and gave me a hearty welcome. We soon
arrived at 'Oak Knoll,' one of the most delightful
spots on earth. The copious rains seemed to have
drawn the living verdure from the ground, while the
century-old oaks and elms shading the old mansion
made everything beautiful in the extreme. The five
ladies and the venerable poet gave me a genuine wel-

---

1 "Picturesque Alaska," by Abby Johnson Woodman, Houghton, Mifflin & Co., 1889. Introductory note by Mr. Whittier.

come ; though they feared 'Uncle Greenleaf' was too tired to enjoy my company, as nineteen unexpected callers had been there yesterday. I told them I would behave as well as I knew how ; that they must not allow me to trespass upon his time or strength. We then retired to his sanctum. He seated me in a large, plush arm-chair, convenient to his best ear. We began the eventful history of mutual friends by whose agency, through God's mighty purpose, the dark stain of slavery was swept from our country. Alvan Stewart, Gerrit Smith, Pierpont, Adams, Garrison, Phillips, Sumner, Rantoul, Leavitt, Colver, Webster, Cushing, and others now with the great silent majority, were discussed. We threw aside all restraint, were young again, reviewed the past, when, as disciples of Wilberforce, Clarkson, Buxton, and Sturge, we knew it was wrong to buy and sell human souls, before Garrison and Phillips came on the active stage of life. He said, 'Friend Barbour, I can remember but *four* of the old Abolitionists—Bowditch, Sewall [Samuel E. Sewall has since passed away], thyself, and myself—now living. Did thee ever get hurt in any of the mobs that have so disgraced our country?' I told him I had been driven from many places by violence. I inquired whether he had ever suffered personal injury. 'Yes,' said the good man, 'I was pelted by the mob and badly hurt in my face by a large stone. I was subsequently told, by one of the party, that their purpose was to catch me and paint my face black, so that I would be a "real nigger." But it was not accomplished.'

"The little silver bell rang for dinner. Mrs. Woodman called me from the library, and placed us in proper order at the table. I was near the poet, whom they almost idolize. The six ladies and two men bowed their heads in silent prayer, for about the space of three or four minutes of marked solemnity. Then the most social, genial, cheerful conversation marked the more than an hour of the admirably prepared and highly appreciated dinner. Mrs. Mary A. Livermore was announced at the door. Mr. Whittier retired with her to the library. The others of this sweet domestic circle, with myself, gathered in a large room nearly filled with cherished memorials and valuables, presented to him by hosts of friends and admirers from all parts of the world. At this moment in rushed 'Robin Adair,' the huge Scotch collie which I had known in my former visits. He seemed to know me, was quite familiar, but the grand-niece of Whittier mildly rebuked him for his ardor. I invited him to rest his head in my lap, fondled him, and he seemed as happy as the rest of the family, of whom he is a decided pet.

"Mr. Whittier has just passed his eighty-first year, is feeble, and suffers much from neuralgic pains. When I told him that at eighty-four I was unacquainted with pain of any kind, never spent a whole day in bed in my long life, he said, with an expressive smile, that I 'ought to be a better man, however good I might be.'

"I was after this led by the young lady to the home of the valued Jersey cows, with their young calves. They never slaughter any of their animals. 'Robin Adair' accompanied us, and was directed to call them from their hiding-places under the barns, which he did with vociferous alacrity. She asked me if they were not beauties. I candidly acknowledged that they were. I told her that one of my grandsons had 'a string of twenty-five such Jerseys' in Oregon, which he milked every morning and evening, and had a personal acquaintance with each cow.

"The time for my departure seemed near. She said, 'No, not yet, I am posted as to trains; at the proper moment I will have the coach at the door.' I was then led to the garden surrounded by the old-fashioned box-plant, trimmed to about eighteen inches high. It was filled with magnolia and tulip trees, and flowers of various kinds in all their lavish beauty. They pressed upon me an armful to be taken to my home for my grandchildren, which, after examination, the venerable poet said was not complete; he added a new variety which he thought they had not seen. This delightful family is based upon the religion of Jesus Christ; its members believe in the constant influence of the Holy Spirit. They are Friends in word and deed, of high culture and intelligence."

The young lady spoken of by Mr. Barbour above, Phœbe Woodman, assists "Uncle Greenleaf" with his correspondence, and he in turn has presented her with a beautiful horse.

Mr. Barbour's paper may be supplemented by a few notes on the poet's personal traits.

I have already alluded to his rural peculiarities of speech. This is something that elicits the sympathy of the farmers and laborers who meet him. A friend[1]

---

[1] Mr. William M. Fullerton, ex-editor of the Boston "Advertiser."

once got on his track up somewhere by Mt. Monadnock. "Why," said an old farmer, "he 's just as natural and like folks as can be. He wrote some poems [!] right out here in the yard, on a board he picked up, and he was sittin' in a kitchen chair he brought out, lookin' toward 'Chusett yonder. His poems we can understand, though we 're not book people; he 's like folks, Whittier is."

Mr. George M. White gives in " Harper's Monthly " some amusing chat by Whittier on onions and boiled dinners, etc. He never uses tobacco in any shape, nor drinks alcoholic liquors, it seems, but stated that he had once, when he was unwell, and nothing tasted good, derived much benefit from cider. Cabbage and cucumbers he eschews as abominations. Cabbage cooked in the house makes the most diabolical smell that was ever invented; you have got to burn your house down to get rid of the odor ("and Whittier, who was sitting near the open-stove grate, upon the top of which he had deposited his tall hat, folded his hands and laughed a hearty, silent laugh"). Onions he thought not quite so bad, for you can get the odor of those out of the house after three or four days.

"Then," said his friend, "you would not approve of the old-fashioned boiled dinner?"

"*No.* I think that is a detestable dish. I remember that my father used to have it, in which cabbage, onions, beets, potatoes, turnips, and carrots were all boiled up together, and turned out into a great dish all in a heap, with a great greasy piece of meat in the middle. I think that is the reason why the present generation is not so strong as the former. It is owing to the way the parents lived, eating so much pork and potatoes. Our last war showed that. The farmers were not nearly so strong as the men recruited in the cities,—Portland, Portsmouth, and Boston."

Recent investigations are showing that color-blindness affects vastly more people than was imagined. And the same is true of the newly talked of astigmatization, or inability to rightly estimate the dimensions of objects. A lady friend of the poet (Mrs. Harriet Prescott Spofford) tells us that he must be classed with the color-blind. Once when the library fire had damaged the wall-paper near it, he matched the pattern at the store " and triumphantly replaced it before detection." But great was the amusement of the women to find that he had substituted a crimson vine for a green one.

Mr. Whittier's health has always been delicate. He says he thinks he was born with a headache. Since the Philadelphia mob he has only at intervals been free from pain ; and this accounts for his almost invariably having to decline invitations to public gatherings.

Writing to Garrison in 1855 to enclose a contribution to the Vigilance Committee fund for helping on the cause of resistance to the Fugitive Slave Law, Whittier says: "Does thee remember Felicia Hemans's lyric of the Captive Crusader? From his cell the prisoner hears the march of his troop, the ringing of bridle chains, and the sound of trumpets, and sees the flash of their spears, and the flutter of their pennons in the sun and wind. I think I can appreciate the captive's state of mind, since illness, for the most part, has made me a spectator where I would fain have been an actor, for the past three or four years."[1]

In another place he writes: "I inherited from both my parents a sensitive, nervous temperament; and one of my earliest recollections is of pain in the head, from which I have suffered all my life. For many years I have not been able to read or write for more than half an hour at a time, often not so long. Of late, my hearing has been defective. But in many ways I have been blessed far beyond my deserving, and, grateful to the Divine Providence, I tranquilly await the close of a life which has been longer, and on the whole happier, than I had reason to expect, although far different from that which I dreamed of in youth."

Such sentiments as these last give the key to his temperament, which is never morbid or melancholy, but light and cheerful, in spite of ill health. The sense of the ludicrous is very keen in him. This is remembered of him by his old associates of the Haverhill Academy days; and everybody who has talked with him perceives it. In his writings it appears in such verses as "The Demon of the Study," "The Pumpkin," and "The Double-headed Snake." When on his vacations, he likes to sit on the piazza of the hotel, noting with keen eye the foibles and idiosyncrasies of people who go and come. Speaking once of his early anti-slavery toils and sufferings, he said, "I try to remember only the bright and good." Then, with merriment in his eye, "I have forgotten all the mischief I did." If the letters of Whittier shall any

---

[1] Liberator, April 6, '55.

of them be published hereafter, the genial humor of
his nature will be seen to be a very conspicuous trait.
Two letters, already printed, are here given. To the
National Carriage Builders' Association of which he
and Holmes were oddly made members in 1880, he
wrote as follows:—

"I am not a builder, in the sense of Milton's phrase
of one who could 'build lofty rhyme.' My vehicles
have been of humbler sort, merely the farm-wagons
and backwoods of verse, and not likely to run so
long as Dr. Holmes's 'One-Horse Shay,' the construc-
tion of which entitles him to the first place in your
Association. I should not dare to warrant any of my
work for a long drive."

To an officer of the Egypt Exploration Fund
society he wrote in 1884:—

"I am glad to have my attention called to the ex-
cavation of Zoan. The enterprise commends itself
to every reader of the Bible, and every student of the
history and monumental wonders of Egypt. I would
like to have a hand in it. I hesitate a little about
disturbing the repose of some ancient mummy, who,
perchance, 'hobnobbed with Pharaoh, glass to glass,
or dropped a halfpenny in Homer's hat, or doffed his
own to let Queen Dido pass.' But curiosity gets the
better of sentiment, and I follow the example of Dr.
Holmes by enclosing an order on Lieut.-Gov. Ames
for one of his best shovels."

In reference to his bachelorhood and early loves,
some have thought they were on the right trail in his
poems "Benedicite," "My Playmate," and "Memories."
But he guards his secret well. He was evidently interested, like all young men, in a good many girls in

his neighborhood. In 1832 he wrote the following stanzas, which are perhaps autobiographic: [1]—

" I do not love thee, Isabel, and yet thou art most fair !
I know the tempting of thy lips, the witchcraft of thy hair,
The winsome smile that might beguile the shy bird from his
    tree ;
But from their spell I know so well, I shake my manhood free.

" I might have loved thee, Isabel ; I know I should, if aught
Of all thy words and ways had told of one unselfish thought ;
If through the cloud of fashion, the pictured veil of art,
One casual flash had broken warm, earnest from the heart.

    *   *   *   *   *   *   *

" I do not love thee, Isabel ; I would as soon put on
A crown of slender frost-work beneath the heated sun,
Or chase the winds of summer, or trust the sleeping sea,
Or lean upon a shadow, as think of trusting thee."

Some years ago an article appeared in a Western paper stating that a lady who had recently died was the fair one once beloved of Whittier. He wrote to the editor that the article was very interesting, but decidedly imaginative, since he had not seen the person mentioned since she was nine years old.[2]

His love of children is very marked. He has written several children's poems (" Red Riding Hood," " King Solomon and the Ants," etc.) and stories in prose, and published two books of Selections for children's reading. He will take a hand in children's sports, and has been known to lose an important train that he might give a ride to a group of village

---

[1] From the library edition of the poems, 1888.

[2] Mrs. Sarah K. Bolton's " How Success is Won," p. 54.

children who besieged the door of his hack.   He was
known among the children of Amesbury as the man
with the parrot.   He describes this bird in one of his
poems:—

> " Behind us at our evening meal
>   The gray bird ate his fill,
>   Swung downward by a single claw,
>   And wiped his hookèd bill.

> " He shook his wings and crimson tail,
>   And set his head aslant,
>   And, in his sharp impatient way,
>   Asked, ' What does Charlie want ? ' "

This plaintive bird also had the habit, we are told,
of crying " Whoa ! " when teams passed the house,
and " Run in, boys ! run in ! " to the schoolboys when
their bell rang.   Another little incident will show
Whittier's popularity among the boys.   In the summer
of 1876, while he was staying at the Sturtevant farm-
house, back of Centre Harbor on Lake Winnepesaukee, word was sent to him that a lot of boys from
Camp Chocorua in Holderness would make their
picnic rendezvous next day under the great Whittier
pine on Sunset Hill.   He gladly complied with the implied invitation to be present ; and, shortly after the
boys got there, he was seen approaching in a carriage
through the woodland road, and was greeted with a
round of tremendous cheers.   He of course re-
sponded by shaking hands all around and enjoyed it
as much as did the boys.[1]

---

[1] Boston Advertiser, Dec. 17, 1887.

His kindness to children is matched by his tender sympathy for unfortunate men and women, and his generous toleration of opinions and customs different from his own (smoking, for instance). He says he always reads a book with sympathy for the author; that it is easy to tear it to pieces by criticism, but he tries to find its merits. His purse has always been open for the relief of the destitute,—$50, for example, to the sufferers by a recent fire in Lynn. His hospitable nature he inherits from his mother, and will put himself to serious inconvenience rather than turn away a worthy guest. And yet he is keen to detect mere curiosity-hunters and spongers. Though even these he is too tender-hearted harshly to rebuff. Mrs. Child writes amusingly of his attempts to get rid of bores. "I was amused," she says, "to hear his sister describe some of these irruptions [of genteel tramps] in her slow Quakerly fashion. 'Thee has no idea,' said she, 'how much time Greenleaf spends in trying to *lose* these people in the streets. Sometimes he comes home and says, " Well, sister, I had hard work to lose him, but I have lost him."' 'But I can never lose a *her*,' said Whittier. 'The women are more pertinacious than the men; don't thee find them so, Maria?' I told him I did. 'How does thee manage to get time to do anything?' said he. I told him I took care to live away from the railroad, and kept a bulldog and a pitchfork, and advised him to do the same." Like all prominent literati, Whittier is deluged with manuscripts for his perusal and opinion, and with applications for autographs. His patience is unfailing; and, notwithstanding his almost constant headaches, he reads and returns, often at his own expense, many long manuscripts sent to him. He used to answer, it is stated, as many as two thousand applications for autographs in a year. To an English friend he said, " My letters average twenty-five and thirty a day, and when I 'm sick they accumulate ; and then, when I get well, I make myself sick again trying to catch up with my answers to them."

As the years roll on the bores increase with alarming rapidity. Whittier's life at present is said to be made a burden to him by inroads of gaping tourists, who push into his house to look at the curiosity, but have no adequate idea of himself or his works.

Speaking of bores, a little story about his poem " The Barefoot Boy " is in point : Mr. Whittier once wrote to Prang, the publisher of chromos, some words of praise for his chromo of " The Barefoot Boy." His words were stolen by rival publishers and affixed to a mean imitation of the Prang picture, —a piece of baseness which elicited the following indignant letter to Mr. Prang: " I have heard of writers who could pass judgment upon works of art without seeing them ; but the part assigned me by this use of my letter to thee, making me the critic of a thing not in existence, adds to their ingenuity the gift of prophecy. It seems to be hazardous to praise anything. There is no knowing to what strange uses one's words may be put. When a good deal younger than I am now, I addressed some laudatory lines to Henry Clay ; but the newspapers soon transferred them to Thomas H. Benton, and it was even said that the saints of Nauvoo made them do duty in the apotheosis of the Prophet Joseph Smith. My opinions

as an art-critic are not worth much to the public ;
and, as they seem to be as uncertain and erratic in
their directions as an Australian boomerang, I shall,
I think, be chary in future of giving them. I do n't
think I should dare speak favorably of the *Venus de
Medici*, as I might expect to find my words affixed to
some bar-room lithograph of the bearded woman." [1]

It is a happy custom nowadays in America publicly
to celebrate the birthdays of our elder poets. Mr.
Whittier has been at least five times the recipient
of this honor. His seventieth birthday was celebrated
by a grand symposium of writers in the " Literary
World " newspaper, and by a banquet given in his
honor at the Hotel Brunswick in Boston by his publishers. Mr. Garrison returned the compliment that
had been paid him by Whittier forty-five years before,
and wrote some lines in honor of his life-long Quaker
friend. So did Longfellow and Holmes. Emerson
read Whittier's "Ichabod" to the company. Whittier's " Response " (" Beside that milestone where the
level sun ") is a fragment of verse of great power.
Over the centre of the dining-table was hung a new
portrait of Whittier wreathed with ivy, and opposite
it was a view of his birthplace. It is interesting to
note that the negro waiters took a deep interest in
the proceedings, delighted with the reverence paid to
the man who had done so much for them.

About the same time a Whittier Club was formed
in Haverhill, and the ladies of Amesbury presented
their distinguished townsman with a portfolio of
water-color views of many scenes in the Merrimack
Valley that he has described in his poems.

---

[1] Evenings in the Library, by George W. Stewart, Jr., p. 138.

Mr. Whittier's seventy-fifth birthday, in 1882, was passed quietly in his rooms at the Hotel Winthrop in Boston. The citizens of Amesbury wished him to spend the day in Amesbury and hold a reception, but he was obliged to decline on account of indisposition. He said that it seemed a rather queer thing to congratulate a man that he was seventy-five years old. He thought the weather of Boston very trying. "I am a New Englander, and I love New England," said he ; " but my seventy-five years of life here have failed fairly to acclimate me."

On the day when he attained his seventy-seventh year many friends called to congratulate him at Oak Knoll, more than forty letters were received from friends abroad, and baskets of roses and a huge birthday cake from nearer friends. A few weeks before he had written to a friend apropos of public congratulations: "I have reached an age when flattery ceases to deceive and notoriety is a burden, and the faint shadow of literary reputation fails to hide the solemn realities of life."

On Sept. 10, 1885, a reunion of the Haverhill Academy class of 1827-30 was held in the rectory of St. John's Church, in Haverhill. The central figure and theme was the poet Whittier. A representative of the Boston "Advertiser" who was present says: In the company was one man who seemed neither to accept nor comprehend the situation. That man was John G. Whittier. His face and demeanor would have afforded study for a psychologist. The face was one on which was "a look of shyness, of surprise, of perplexity, withal; a countenance irradiated by reciprocal affection and pleasure in seeing others pleased.

That it was fifty-seven years since he had entered Haverhill Academy he remembered with a certain sweet melancholy. That everybody was vying with everybody else in making love to him he could not help observing. But what it was all about, and why people would persist in talking of him when he wanted other more congenial topics to be uppermost,—these things evidently puzzled him." The reporter speaks of the winning way in which Whittier seemed to take him into his confidence as he placed in his hands the manuscript of the verses he had written for the occasion, explaining to him the motives for various lines as called forth by old memories. A few days after this meeting Mr. Whittier was presented with an album containing photographs of many of his old classmates.

By 1887 Whittier could say with the old man in " Macbeth ":—

> " Threescore and ten I can remember well:
> Within the volume of which time, I have seen
> Hours dreadful, and things strange."

But not more dreadful hours than hours delightful, surely, if one may judge by those of his eightieth birthday. James Parton wrote of him [1] that he was carrying his burthen of eighty years with considerable ease and with constant cheerfulness, walking with alert step, and seeming better than he was five years before. His birthday was celebrated by the school

---

[1] In the pleasant memorial tribute which occupied several pages of the Boston " Advertiser " of Dec. 17, 1887, and which has been several times quoted in this volume.

children of the whole country. The Essex Club of Boston presented him with a large album containing a eulogy by Senator Hoar and other papers. At Oak Knoll there was a busy day. The morning was clear and brilliant, air bracing, skies high and blue. Every room in the house was adorned with gift-baskets and bouquets of roses and other flowers. An overflowing basket of fruit arrived, and was placed on the dining-room table opposite the great birthday cake. In the library stood a basket of eighty roses edged with ferns,—the gift of ladies of Boston. On an open book of Cornelia Cook roses, margined with yellow ones and intersprinkled with violets, lay a pen of violets; on the broad white satin book-mark was inscribed the closing stanza of " My Triumph":—

> " I feel the earth move sunward,
>   I join the great march onward,
>   And take, by faith, while living,
>   My freehold of thanksgiving."

The colored students of Hampton sent a sofa cushion; and from the new town of " Whittier " in California came an advance copy of the town's newspaper, with an editorial greeting. The Governor of the Common-wealth cut the birthday cake and offered pieces to each visitor. All day the poet passed to and fro among the guests, now greeting a bevy of children in the parlor, now conversing with old friends in the library, and again in the dining-room offering refresh-ments to some new caller.

Contributors to the " Boston Advertiser's " sym-posial Whittier number were such friends as Edward Everett Hale, Oliver Wendell Holmes, Walt Whit-

man, Dr. Bartol, Senator Hoar, and T. W. Higginson.
Here is Walt Whitman's striking bit of verse:—

> " As the Greek's signal flame, by antique records told,
> Rose from the hill-top, like applause and glory,
> Welcoming in fame some special veteran, hero,
> With rosy tinge reddening the land he 'd served,
> So I aloft from Mannahatta's ship-fringed shore
> Lift high a kindled brand for thee, Old Poet."

And here are some of the lines of Dr. Holmes:—

> " Friend, whom thy fourscore winters leave more dear
> Than when life's roseate summer on thy cheek
> Burned in the flush of manhood's manliest year,
> Lonely, how lonely! is the snowy peak
> Thy feet have reached, and mine have climbed so near !
> Close on thy footsteps 'mid the landscape drear
> I stretch my hand thine answering grasp to seek,
> Warm with the love no rippling rhymes can speak !

On Dec. 17, 1889, Whittier's health was so poor
that he was obliged to ask his editorial friends to
state his inability to endure the excitement of birthday demonstrations or to answer many letters. The
day was celebrated by a flag-raising at a Whittier
School, and by a general observance of Whittier Day
in the public schools of the country.

On Dec. 17, 1891, the fullest and most enthusiastic birthday celebration of all — and the last — was
held at the home of Joseph Cartland in Newburyport
(also once the home of the Harriet Livermore of
" Snow-Bound "). Mr. Whittier exercised all his old-
time hospitality, and stood the fatigue very well. The
" Boston Advertiser " and the " Boston Journal " published notable Whittier numbers in honor of the
New England poet.

LAST HOURS.

And here, alas. our narrative of the poet's life must draw to a close. For the fell sergeant Death has laid his mace upon the shoulder of the revered minstrel, the beloved citizen-poet of New England, and summoned him away. It but remains briefly to tell of his last hours, and then to let the curtain fall.

Mr. Whittier had been passing the summer of 1892 in quiet enjoyment at "Elmfield," in Hampton Falls, N. H., the town where his Batchelder and Hussey ancestors once lived, the home of his young Quaker friend, Miss Abby Gove. Miss Gove is a member of the once flourishing society of Friends in Hampton Falls, but has of late years worshiped in· the little Friends' church in Amesbury. Mrs. Edward Gove was an eloquent preacher, and Whittier wrote a memorial poem on her death.[1] What drew him to Miss Gove's was his desire to escape summer visitors. One day, after meeting, he said to her, " Abby, has thee a spare room up at thy house?" Her answer was Yes. His room opened on a balcony commanding a view of the sea near Rivermouth Rocks and Hampton Beach, scenes of his earlier poems. He and his friends took their meals at the tavern adjoining, reached by a moment's walk through a pine grove.

The Gove residence on "the hill" is rich in treas-

---

[1] So Mr. F. B. Sanborn says, who, as well as Whittier, is a descendant of Stephen Batchelder, and lived as a boy in this neighborhood.

ures of old Colonial days. It stands a little off of the winding road with its venerable elms. Across the way is an old orchard containing paths and rustic seats. Here Whittier often strolled, or from the piazza watched through a glass the sails upon the blue sea, or conversed with friends, or read the papers and magazines. It had been his intention to return with the Cartlands to their home in New-buryport on September 6. He was first taken ill on August 31. By Saturday, September 3, a remarkable irregularity of the heart's action was experienced, and he grew suddenly worse. Dr. John A. Douglas of Amesbury, and Dr. Frances E. Howe of Newburyport, and Dr. Sarah Ellen Palmer of Boston were the physicians called to his bedside. Mr. Whittier was conscious and able to recognize those about him, but was at first unable to articulate, and seemed to be suffering from partial paralysis of the left side. He made several unavailing attempts to communicate something to his nephew, Mr. Pickard, apparently on some matter of business. On September 5 he seemed slightly better and took a little nourishment. He was fully aware of his critical condition, and whispered to the loving friends who were constantly bathing his head, "It is of no use." To his niece, Mrs. Pickard, who asked him if he knew her, he replied, "Yes, I have known you all the time."

A cable message of sympathy was received on Wednesday from friends in England. Neighbors calling were, however, not allowed to enter the room of the dying man.

At 4.30 of the 7th of September Whittier calmly breathed his last, surrounded by some of his closest relatives. In Amesbury and Haverhill, as soon as the news was known, bells were tolled and flags displayed at half-mast. The funeral occurred at the Whittier home in Amesbury on Saturday at 2.30. Memorial exercises were held and addresses made (in place of the usual funeral exercises) in the pretty garden in the rear of the house, while the dead poet lay within, flower-surrounded, in the little front parlor. E. C. Stedman, Elizabeth Stuart Phelps, Parker Pillsbury, Mrs. Spofford, and many other personal friends were present. Whittier was buried in the Friends' Cemetery in the family lot. Thousands of people visited the grave on the days immediately following the funeral. The old farmhouse at Haverhill was draped in mourning and the public offices closed during the hour of the funeral, while the city schools at the same time gave up the hour to exercises appropriate to the occasion. Memorial services were also held in Danvers and Salem and by citizens of Amesbury.

By his will Whittier bequeathed to relatives some $50,000 or more in sums ranging from $500 to $15,000, the largest bequest being to his niece, Mrs. Lizzie T. Pickard, who kept house for him so long in Amesbury. He left her $15,000, his two houses in Amesbury, and two or three minor gifts. The list of relatives remembered by cash gifts is a long one— no one forgotten (good, kind Uncle Greenleaf!). To Lucy Larcom he left $500 and the copyright of two of his works, and to Sarah Orne Jewett and Annie Fields a painting each. His Amesbury furniture and pictures and books go to Mrs. Pickard, and the same at Oak Knoll to the members of that household.

Various charitable organizations of Essex County and the Hampton (Virginia) school each received legacies. His manuscripts and other papers go to his literary executor, Mr. S. T. Pickard. The amount of property he left—from $75,000 to $100,000 about—will be a surprise to those who suppose poetry never pays. But to be a popular poet *and* a Quaker means thrift and wealth.

On the day of Whittier's death a Boston paper gave some interesting gossip about his old winter haunt, the Hotel Winthrop in Boston. It seems that he got acquainted with this quiet hostelry through the accident of going there to call on Celia Thaxter in 1881, and in November of that year he joined the ladies of his Oak Knoll home at this hotel in Boston and passed his first winter there. The fire-escape of his room made a little balcony looking out upon the ivied old church of St. John the Evangelist. His reception-room was the parlor. His method of getting about for long distances was to take a herdic. Writing from Amesbury in 1884, he said, alluding to the severe winters of New England, "I wish the Pilgrim Fathers had drifted around Cape Horn and landed at Santa Barbara instead of Plymouth Rock, and I had in consequence been born in a land of flowers instead of ice." However, to the same correspondent he wrote that "life at four-score was worth living." Mr. Whittier said he liked the Winthrop because of its quiet and because in the great hotels he was overwhelmed with service, but here it seemed more like home. He had always been used to waiting upon himself, and he liked a place where they would let him do so.

Little facts of interest that transpired after his
death were such as that he never spent more than
$50 a year on his dress; that his income was "about
that of the average college professor"; that he was
fond of splitting wood for exercise; that his tea was
imported especially for him, and kept in a painted
porcelain jar; that he had no musical sense and didn't
know one tune from another; that he never attended a theatrical performance in his life nor
(so the tradition in Amesbury runs) ever rose to
speak on religion in the Friends' meetings; that he
once or twice expressed regret that he had never
married; and that his reason for never having traveled
was that the reading of books of travel left such a
vivid picture in his mind of the scenes described as
made it seem superfluous for him to visit them himself.

Those who know something of Elizabeth Whittier
will thank me for closing these final and supplement-
ary notes with a rarely drawn portrait from the pen
of the most accomplished and scholarly of living
American essayists.[1]

"Elizabeth Whittier," he says, "was one of the
rarest of women, her brother's complement; possess-
ing all the readiness of speech and facility of inter-
course which he wanted; taking easily, in his presence, the lead in conversation which the poet so
gladly abandoned to her, while he sat rubbing his

---

[1] Thomas Wentworth Higginson, in New York "Evening Post,"
September 7, 1892.   Higginson was the friend of Whittier because
he knew him, but the bitter and malignant enemy of Walt Whitman
(a greater than Whittier) because he did not know him.   Such is
the limitation of the human mind!

hands and laughing at her daring sallies. She was as unlike him in person as in mind: for his dignified erectness, even amounting to stiffness, she had endless motion and vivacity; for his regular and handsome features she had a long Jewish nose, so full of expression that it seemed to enhance instead of injure the effect of the large and liquid eyes that glowed with merriment and sympathy behind it. There was something bird-like in Elizabeth Whittier's look and in the movements of her head; her quick thoughts came like javelins; a saucy triumph gleamed in the great eyes; the head moved a little from side to side as with the quiver of a weapon; and, lo! you were transfixed. Her poems, tragic, sombre, imaginative, give no impression of this side of her nature; but it was as if long generations of parents who had 'held the Quaker rôle' had broken into reactionary sunshine and rollicking gayety in her. Her wit had play upon the grave Friends themselves, as they gathered at the time of 'Quarterly Meetings' under the roof which latterly held all of Quakerism that was left in Amesbury; she wound them round her finger in spite of themselves, and did not hesitate to discipline the most venerable Friend on the high seats until she had compelled him to rise and close the meeting by shaking hands in good season, lest the dinner should be overdone. She was a woman never to be forgotten; and no one can truly estimate the long celibate life of the poet without bearing in mind that he had for many years at his own fireside the concentrated wit and sympathy of all womanhood in this one sister."

CHAPTER IV.

To speak of all of Mr. Whittier's friends would require an enumeration of several thousand names ; for every one who has ever known him loves him. Among the eminent persons with whom he has been on terms of intimate association are Dr. Samuel G. Howe, Edwin P. Whipple, George L. Stearns, Samuel Sewall, Theodore D. Weld, James T. Fields and Mrs. Annie Fields, Bayard Taylor, N. P. Rogers, Nathaniel Hawthorne, Longfellow, Emerson, Holmes, and Lowell ; Mary Howitt, Harriet Prescott Spofford, Gail Hamilton, Celia Thaxter, Elizabeth Stuart Phelps, Charles Sumner, John Bright, and Dom Pedro, the late Emperor of Brazil.

The occurrence of poets' names in this list would seem to falsify Landor's affirmation, that poets hate poets the world over.

Whittier admired Sumner for his noble advocacy of peace doctrines, in "The True Grandeur of Nations" and other orations, and for his magnanimous attitude toward the South after the close of the Civil War.

Longfellow's Journals record frequent visits paid by him to Whittier and by Whittier to him. Not a great while before Longfellow died he wrote to his friend to come and see him. Mr. Whittier was not able to go at once ; and, when he did at last come, it was too late : Longfellow was then too ill to see any one, and died shortly afterward.

Emerson, too, was a frequent visitor at Amesbury. Elizabeth Whittier used to say that she liked him better than any man who visited them, because he never talked over her head. And her brother has said, " Emerson was a delightful companion, and was often here. No matter who remained, when he left there was a void." [1]

Of the genial relation existing between Holmes and Whittier the following from a letter of the Amesbury poet to Dr. Holmes on occasion of one of Dr. Holmes's birthday celebrations is ample witness : " My father," says he, " used to tell of a poor innocent in his neighborhood who, whenever he met him, would fall to laughing, crying, and dancing: ' I can't help it, I can't help it; I 'm so glad you and I are alive.' And I, like the poor fellow, can't help telling thee that I am glad thee and I are alive ; glad that thy hand has lost nothing of its cunning and thy pen is still busy ; and I say to thee, in the words of Solomon of old, ' Rejoice, O young man, in thy youth, and let thy heart cheer thee in the days of thy youth.' But do n't exult over thy seniors who have not found the elixir of life and are growing old and past their usefulness. I have just got back from the hills and am tired, and a pile of unanswered letters are before me this morning ; so I can only say, God bless thee."

The charmed circle must be drawn to include James Russell Lowell, also, who on occasion of the

---

[1] Conversation with Frank A. Burr, Boston " Herald," Nov. 18, 1883.

unveiling of a life-size portrait of Whittier by Edgar
Parker in the Friends' School in Providence, in 1884,
wrote a prose greeting, accompanied by these poetical
lines: [1]—

> " New England's poet, rich in love as years,
>   Her hills and valleys praise thee, and her brooks
>   Dance to thy song : to her grave sylvan nooks
>   Thy feet allure us, which the wood-thrush hears
>   As maids their lovers, and no treason fears.
>   Through thee her Merrimacks and Agiochooks,
>   And many a name uncouth, win loving looks,
>   Sweetly familiar to both Englands' ears.
>   Peaceful by birthright as a virgin lake,
>   The lily's anchorage, which no eyes behold
>   Save those of stars, yet, for thy brother's sake,
>   That lay in bonds, thou blew'st a blast as bold
>   As that wherewith the heart of Roland brake,
>   Far heard through Pyrenean valleys cold."

To a young lady who visited him in 1887 Whittier
said : "I remember the first time that I saw Hawthorne. I went to make him a visit, and Mrs.
Hawthorne called him in to see me. He came into
the room with a look on his face that made me feel
as though he had been sitting writing for a long time
in a dark place." Whittier's face lighted up as he
added, in homely, telling phrase, "He looked as
though he had just come up from down cellar."
Elsewhere alluding to this same call, apparently,
Whittier says that Hawthorne remarked of the plot of
a book he was writing, "It darkens damnably."

To Harriet Prescott Spofford, who is a not very
distant neighbor of Whittier's, in her home,—

---

[1] As published in Boston " Advertiser," Oct. 25, '84.

> "Set like an eagle's nest
> Among Deer Island's immemorial pines,
> Crowning the crag on which the sunset breaks
> Its last red arrow,"—

to this dear friend Whittier dedicates his "Bay of Seven Islands."

For the Quaker writer Mary Howitt Mr. Whittier had a hearty regard. Her Autobiography records the reception from him, in 1874, through Mrs. A. D. T. Whitney, of verbal greetings and a letter of friendship. To William Howitt, author of the fine Whittieresque lyric of freedom,—

> "The land for me, the land for me,
> Where every living soul is free,"—

our poet does not seem to have been so much attracted. Both the Howitts were ardent in the anti-slavery cause, and we are told of Mary's good old mother knitting "a quantity of nice things for the anti-slavery bazaar in Boston." Whittier, no doubt, would say "Amen" to this effusion of Kit North's shepherd, in the "Noctes": "The twa married Hooitts I love just excessively, sir. What they write canna fail o' bein' poetry, even the most middlin' o' 't. For it 's aye wi' them the ebullition o' their ain feeling and their ain fancy; and, whenever that 's the case, a bonny word or twa will drap itsel' intil ilka stanzy, and a sweet stanzy or twa intil ilka pome, and sae they touch, and sae they sune win a body's heart."

John Bright, a Quaker, was naturally an admirer of the Quaker poet of America. Writing in 1884, he said : " In the poem of ' Snow-Bound ' there are lines on the death of the poet's sister which have nothing superior to them in beauty and pathos in our language. I have read them often, with always increasing admiration. I have suffered from the loss of those near and dear to me, and I can apply the lines to my own case and feel as if they were written for me. The ' Eternal Goodness ' is another poem which is worth a crowd of sermons which are spoken from the pulpits of our sects and churches, and which I do not wish to undervalue."

Mr. Bright told James Grant Wilson that he valued Whittier's poems more than those of any other poet of the present century. When Garrison and John Bright were one sunny afternoon standing in the Library of the House of Parliament conversing, and watching the busy scene on the Thames, Mr. Bright repeated " with exquisite feeling " Whittier's apostrophe to his sister Elizabeth above mentioned.[1]

I have mentioned Dom Pedro's love of Whittier. He had translated some of his poems into Portuguese, and, when he was in America in 1876, he paid Mr. Whittier a visit of affection. Later, on hearing that slavery was at last abolished in Brazil, Mr. Whittier cabled these words to the Emperor, who was then lying ill at Milan : " With thanks to God, who has blessed your generous efforts, I congratulate you on the peaceful abolition of slavery in Brazil."

Bayard Taylor, who was a Quaker by descent, on his father's side, was a welcome guest in Amesbury. There was in Bayard Taylor's hearty, robust phy-

---

[1] Life of Garrison, iv. 279.

sique just that complement of Whittier's invalid, feminine nature needed by the latter in a friend. Taylor's letters seem to me the most vivacious and interesting in our published literature, and only to be matched for verve and snap (so far as my epistolary experience enables me to judge) by those of his friend E. C. Stedman or by William Douglas O'Connor of Washington. Taylor is the traveler described in the "Tent on the Beach" ("one whose Arab face was tanned by tropic sun," etc.).

Writing in July, 1850, Mr. Taylor says : " Friday morning, early, Lowell and I started for Amesbury, which we reached in a terrible northeaster. What a capital time we had with Whittier, in his nook of a study, with the rain pouring on the roof and the wind howling at the door ! " [1] On the day of the publication of Taylor's " Faust," Mr. and Mrs. James T. Fields gave a dinner in the translator's honor. Whittier wrote to Mr. Fields : " I take up the lamentation of Falstaff : ' There are but few of us good fellows left, and one of them is not fat, but lean, and grows old.' It would be pleasant to sit down with thy special guest, my dear friend Taylor, and with others whose poetical shoestrings I hold myself quite unworthy to untie,—the wisest of philosophers and most genial of men from Concord ; the architect of the only noteworthy ' Cathedral ' in the new world ; and his neighbor, the far-traveled explorer of Purgatory and Hell, and the scarcely less dreary Paradise of the great Italian dreamer." The last parting of these two friends, Whittier and Taylor. took place

---

[1] Life and Letters of Bayard Taylor, i. 176.

under the elms of Boston Common, after a visit they
had just been making at the house of Richard H.
Dana.

Whittier has a general poem on Taylor :—

> " 'And where now, Bayard, will thy footsteps tend ? '
> My sister asked our guest one winter's day.
> Smiling, he answered in the Friends' sweet way
> Common to both : ' Wherever thou shalt send !
> What wouldst thou have me see for thee ? '   She laughed,
> Her dark eyes dancing in the wood-fire's glow :
> ' Loffoden isles, the Kilpis, and the low,
> Unsetting sun on Finmark's fishing-craft.'
> ' All these and more I soon shall see for thee ! '
> He answered, cheerily ; and he kept his pledge."

One of Mr. Whittier's earliest friendships was that
between himself and Edwin P. Whipple. He wrote
in 1886 of Whipple : "I cannot now dwell upon his
authorship while thinking of him as the beloved member of a literary circle now, alas ! sadly broken. I recall
the wise, genial companion and faithful friend of
nearly half a century, the memory of whose words
and acts of kindness moistens my eyes as I write."
And again, in another place : " To him more than to
any other person I was indebted for public recogni-
tion as one worthy of a place in American literature,
at a time when it required a great deal of courage
to urge such a claim for a proscribed Abolitionist.
Although younger than I, he had gained the reputation of a brilliant essayist, and was regarded as the
highest American authority in criticism." Mr. Whittier refers to the critical review written by Whipple in
1848 or earlier. Whipple, in this paper, quotes the
old saying of John Dennis, of Queen Anne's time,

that genius is "a furious joy and pride of soul on the conception of an extraordinary hint," and keenly notes that Whittier has this "furious joy and pride of soul" even when the hints are not extraordinary. He observes that his vehement sensibility does not allow his inventive faculties fully to complete what they have begun. "Whittier has the soul of a great poet, and we should not be surprised if he attained the hight of excellence in his art."[1]

We have seen how close was the friendship between William Lloyd Garrison and Greenleaf Whittier. Mr. Garrison had an extremely amiable, cheerful nature, and was domestic in his tastes. The same is true of Whittier. In their younger years, especially, was the bond that knit them together strong. In the work of reform they were at that time like two heads under one hat. For seven years at least, they toiled shoulder to shoulder in the anti-slavery harness. Garrison was often at Whittier's home, and Whittier more than once shared the bowl of bread and milk of the editor of the "Liberator," in the dingy little printing-room in Boston. They ate at the same table when both were young men editing Boston papers; together they drafted the Magna Charta of the nation's anti-slavery society, worked often in the same conventions, wrote poems in each other's praise, and together shared the plaudits of the world on the overthrow of slavery.

Whittier's many letters to Lydia Maria Child, some of which have been published, sufficiently indicate the sympathy that bound these two together. Dear

---

[1] Whipple's Essays, i.

Mrs. Child, with her beautiful sweet face under that funny, old-fashioned bonnet that made the children snicker,—what a pleasant life she led with her brave, though semi-invalid husband!—they two alone in Wayland in their little home on the quiet by-road overlooking broad green meadows.

James T. Fields was the constitutional complement of Whittier, had the strong, healthy, rich nature in which such temperaments as Whittier's love to bask. Fields, with his full, jet-black beard, and with chest thrown out, reciting " Douglas, Douglas, tender and true ! " is a memory in my mind only matched by the equally powerful recital of Byron's " Sennacherib " by Bayard Taylor.   One can imagine how Fields and Taylor must have rivaled Demosthenes in spouting poetry along the Salisbury sands in that episode of the Tent on the Beach.   In the poem, Fields is—

> " A lettered magnate, lording o'er
>   An ever-widening realm of books.
> In him brain-currents, near and far,
>   Converged as in a Leyden jar ;
> The old, dead authors thronged him round about,
> And Elzevir's gray ghosts from leathern graves looked out.

> " Pleasant it was to roam about
>   The lettered world as he had done,
>   And see the lords of song without
>   Their singing-robes and garlands on."

It seems a regrettable thing that Mr. Whittier should have felt impelled to destroy a large mass of his correspondence with friends.   He might have appointed a literary executor in whose judgment he had perfect confidence. No literature is so valuable as contemporary memoirs and letters. There is such a thing as being morbidly sensitive as to the privacy of a letter. Ruskin has said that he never wrote a letter in his life that all the world are not welcome to read if they will. Mr. Whittier's act and the motives that led to it are spoken of by him in the following note published in the "Brooklyn Magazine" in the spring of 1886:—

"The report concerning the burning of my letters is only true so far as this: Some years ago I destroyed a large collection of letters I had received, not from any regard to my own reputation, but from the fear that to leave them liable to publicity might be injurious or unpleasant to the writers or their friends. They covered much of the anti-slavery period and the War of the Rebellion, and many of them I knew were strictly private and confidential. I was not able at the time to look over the mass, and thought it safest to make a bonfire of all. I have always regarded a private and confidential letter as sacred, and its publicity in any shape a shameful breach of trust, unless authorized by its writer. I only wish my own letters to thousands of correspondents may be as carefully disposed of."

Undoubtedly the distinguished friends, from the "world's people," who have maintained constant intimacy with Whittier have been of great benefit to him in getting him partially out of the rut of narrow sectarianism. Whittier is not only an Orthodox Quaker by birth, but from heart-felt conviction. He is a constant attendant at Quaker meetings, submits to the authority of the Quaker discipline, and for Sunday wear has an Orthodox Quaker coat made in Philadelphia. His Westminster Abbey is a little white wooden box of a church, in the fields, capable of holding forty persons. In winter the congregation sometimes dwindles to seven or three members. His soul here communes with God more closely, he finds, than when distracted by the fuss and talk and music of the great churches, or even by the shows of nature. This is all well, and even beautiful. For the Quaker doctrine of the Inner Light there is a sound psychological basis. Philosophical and religious thinkers of all times have found silence indispensable to the mind's best working. But it is the thousand and one narrowing, unmanly, old-woman rules and discipline of the Quakers that Whittier needed friends to free him from. And, as it is, he has never succeeded in permanently throwing off the dead weight he came into life handicapped with. Indeed, when you consider Quakerism on its weak side,—its phlegmatic utilitarianism, its icy formalism, selfishness, reprobation of music, poetry, painting, the theatre, the dance, hunting, fine manners, rich dress, nearly all that makes life noble and distinguished,—you wonder that Whittier ever produced any great poetry at all. Fiery lyrics by a Quaker are like passion flowers in Nova Zembla; 't is a miracle that such bitter cold should yield such tropic blooms. It is largely due to Quakerism that Philadelphia has never produced a genius. Of Mr. Whittier we must affirm that the very depth and intensity of his religious nature have been an injury to his work as an artist. Always in proportion to the strength and tenderness of the religious feeling of the artist is the weakness of the art. Great art is a depicting of man's noble deeds and emotions; but the artist must himself have passed through the stage of distracting emotion when he gives his ideas final shape. Religious emotion is especially apt to becloud and agitate the mind, unhinges it, blurs the impressions (as of a sensitized chemical plate) that fall upon it. While many of Mr. Whittier's religious hymns are of exquisite beauty, and are found in large numbers in the hymn-books, it is still true that the vast mass of his verse is injured by weak religious didacticism. "Prythee, Señor Curedo, let God's finger alone. Very worthy men are apt to snatch at it upon too light occasions: they would stop their tobacco-pipes with it."

It is only the Quakeristic atmosphere in which he has grown up, the unconscious influences of his secluded life, that have crippled his genius. His creed is a broad one; his religious sympathy, or tolerance, is as wide as Christianity; his gonfalon has always fluttered in the van of all progressive and liberal movements. To the Principal of the Friends' School in Providence he wrote in 1884: "Though I am a Quaker by birthright and sincere convictions, I am no sectarian in the strict sense of the term. My sympathies are with the Broad Church of Humanity." Elsewhere he has said, "I have never felt like quarreling with Orthodox or Unitarians who were willing to pull with me, side by side, at the rope of Reform." In the "Liberator" of Sept. 22, 1837, he wrote: "In the anti-slavery cause I have cheerfully held counsel with Catholic and Protestant, Unitarian and Trinitarian, Jew and Christian; and have done so, without, on the one hand, sacrificing my own principles, and, on the other, without doing violence to the feelings and consciences of others. I have, it is true, heard and read many things at lectures and conventions, and in anti-slavery publications, which, as a member of the Society of Friends, I could not approve of, and which have been as unwelcome to me as anything in the 'Liberator' can possibly have been to the signers of the Protest.' But I have not felt free to denounce my friends of other denominations, and withdraw from them, on that account.

In 1889 he said in the "Jewish Messenger," "I do n't know what it is to be a Jew, but I know what it is to be a Christian, who has no quarrel with others about their creed, and can love, respect, and honor a Jew who honestly believes in the faith of his fathers, and who obeys the two great commandments 'Love to God and Love to Man.'"

Mr. Whittier's confession of faith is perhaps most fully set down in two public letters of his published in 1870.[2] Here are a few key sentences which breathe a pretty liberal spirit:—

"A very large proportion of my dearest personal friends are outside of our communion; and I have learned with John Woolman to find 'no narrowness respecting sects and opinions.' But, after a kindly and candid survey of them all, I turn to my own Society, thankful to the Divine Providence which

---

[1] Reference is had to a disagreement in the ranks of the Abolitionists at the time of a certain " Clerical Appeal."

[2] Included in his prose works, edition 1889.

placed me where I am; and with an unshaken faith in the one distinctive doctrine of Quakerism,—the Light within, the immanence of the Divine Spirit in Christianity. . . . I am not blind to the short-comings of Friends. I know how much we have lost by narrowness and coldness and inactivity, the over-estimate of external observances, the neglect of our own proper work while acting as a conscience-keeper for others." The remedy is "not in setting the letter above the spirit; not in substituting type and sym-bol, and Oriental figure and hyperbole, for the simple truths they were intended to represent; not in schools of theology; not in much speaking and noise and vehemence; nor in vain attempts to make the 'plain language' of Quakerism utter the Shibboleth of man-made creeds: but in heeding more closely the Inward Guide and Teacher ; in faith in Christ, not merely in His historical manifestation of the Divine Love to humanity, but in His living presence in the hearts open to receive Him; in love for Him mani-fested in denial of self, in charity and love to our neighbor. . . .

"Quakerism, in the light of its great original truth, is 'exceedingly broad.' As interpreted by Penn and Barclay, it is the most liberal and catholic of faiths. . . .

"They fail to read clearly the signs of the times who do not see that the hour is coming when, under the searching eye of philosophy and the terrible analysis of science, the letter and the outward evi-dence will not altogether avail us; when the surest de-pendence must be upon the Light of Christ within."

One cannot but admire in Whittier his stanch loyalty to the faith of his fathers, in respect of confessing it before men. He has never been ashamed of his religion. His attitude recalls an anecdote told of Thomas Ellwood. As he was one day coming out of meeting, among a hostile crowd, some one called out, "Do n't stone that man, he is not a Quaker, see his fur cap!" Ellwood instantly snatched his cap from his head and dashed it to the ground, saying, "I *am* a Quaker!"

A writer in the Chicago "Inter-Ocean" in the autumn of 1880 reports Whittier as having said in conversation that he believed in an absolute religion above all written revelations : all revelations presuppose and appeal to it. "There is an absolute basis of truth in all minds, which is the same ; and in all difficulties growing out of the relations of old religious ideas to new facts we shall have enough of absolute truth to carry us through. . . . Authority as a ground and element of religion must wholly disappear. . . . The claims for Christ must be based on the perfect character of His life and teachings, and not on His authority." For a right nurture of the religious nature the sensibilities must be brought more into cultivation and active influence. "After early childhood, the cultivation of the sensibilities begins to give place to intellectual training, and soon ceases entirely, and the young mind is left to train its own sensibilities. It is also taught to smother and conceal the impressions and sensibilities, and eventually it hardens into a spiritual indifference."

On the doctrine of Predestination and Endless Punishment he has written as follows to the Universalists : "I recognize the importance of the revolt of your religious society from the awful dogma of pre-destined happiness for the few and damnation for the many, though in the outset that revolt brought with it something of the old fatalistic belief in the arbitrary will and power of the Almighty. Assuming that a favored few can be saved by a divine decree irrespective of any merit on their part, it was logical at least to suppose that all might be saved in the same way. If I mistake not, this view has been greatly modified by the consideration that the natural circumstances of death cannot make any real change of character ; that no one can be compelled to be good or evil; that freedom of choice belongs to both worlds, and that sin is, by its very nature, inseparable from suffering. I am not accustomed to attach very great importance to speculative opinions, and am not disposed to quarrel with any creed which avoids the danger, on the one hand, of attributing implacable vengeance and cruelty to the heavenly Father, and on the other of underrating the 'exceeding sinfulness of sin' and its baleful consequences. Slowly but surely the dreadful burden of the old belief in the predetermined eternity of evil is being lifted from the heart of humanity, and the goodness of God, which leadeth to repentance, is taking the place of the infinite scorn which made love well-nigh impossible."[1]

In his poem "The Minister's Daughter" will be found a strain of thought similar to this.

A contributor to the Syracuse "Journal"—in the summer of '82—writes that in a conversation with

---

[1] The Critic, June 5, '86.

Whittier the talk drifted into the topic of death and the nearness or distance of the departed to different individuals.

"'I have never felt the influence you describe,' said the poet; 'no one who has passed away seems near to me now. Life is such a mystery that I do not ask to penetrate the secrets of eternity; but I can imagine that you and others are conscious of the unseen presence of those whom you have loved and lost.'

"'And who are eternally happy,' I added.

"'Well, I am not certain about that,' he continued, with an expression of abstraction. 'I believe that we may have troubles there, as well as here ; if not, the contrast would not be so sweet. The difference will be that we shall be better enabled to bear them. Heaven is a place of harmony. Everything will be harmonized there.'

"'Then you do not admire a state of complete bliss?'

"'No, why should I, any more than I like clams at high tide,'[1] and, after joining me in a moment of merriment, he turned suddenly and said,—

"'When are you the happiest?'

"'You will laugh, Mr. Whittier, but it is when I hear the first note of a robin in the early spring-time.'

"'No, I shall not laugh; for I understand that pleasure, too.'

---

[1] Those who have never lived by the sea may need to be told that clams are only obtainable when the water has receded, at low tide.

" Then I described the meadows of Central Park, which he said was all new to him, and he had not supposed any one would go there to hear a robin's song. A merry twinkle came in his eyes as he added,—' I like Boston Common because they hung some Quakers there once upon a time.' "

Here are some cheerful thoughts of Whittier's from a talk on Communism and the Shakers : [1]—

" You young men will have your trials, too," he said, " and your conflicts will be with subtler difficulties than ours."

" Is Professor Goldwin Smith's ' Moral Interregnum ' probable ? " asked his questioner.

" I think there is some prospect of it," said Whittier. " The breaking of old forms has begun. I have no fears for the result." The communism of the French Revolution is impossible with us.

" The most successful form of communism," said he, humorously, " is the Shaker Community. They have broken down the family, and have common property; but they also have industry, frugality, purity, and temperance. They have the spirit of thrift and cleanliness. But even in this form communism is not a good thing. It would extinguish the race in time.

" The Shakers have always been very careful about running after strange notions; but they publish a paper now called ' The Shaker Manifesto,'—a rather smart title,—in which they give their views of things in

---

[1] From the New York " Tribune," Oct. 4, 1880 (the Inter-Ocean " conversation above referred to).

general. They send it to me, and I take some interest in looking at it, and seeing what they are thinking about. They have a column of poetry in it that is interesting reading. They have a machine for making poetry as well as everything else; and they compose tunes of their own for these songs. I do not think the world will steal their music. It is the most singular music I have ever heard."

Quakerism, in virtue of its doctrine of Inward Illumination, is the sworn foe of caste and class privilege. Every man and woman may receive the honor of inspiration from above. Hence perfect equality among classes of men, and—the unavoidable corollary—the co-equality of the sexes. Whittier favored "woman's rights" from the start, though during the anti-slavery struggle he deemed it unwise to keep introducing the subject into the meetings of the Abolitionists. It was irrelevant, and hurt the cause. "Let other reforms stand on their own intrinsic merit," he said. "The Abolition car moves heavily enough already, without dragging after it everything which our thousand and one reformers may choose to hitch to it." [1]   In 1880 his words are reported as follows: [2]—

"Woman suffrage I regard as an inevitable thing, and a good thing. Women in public life will bring it up more than it will bring them down. There will be considerable floundering about before society will be completely adapted to the change; but, after it shall be fairly accomplished and in working order,

---

[1] Liberator, Oct. 27, '37.

[2] New York Tribune, Oct. 4, 1880.

the work of society will go on without any deteriora-
tion, and with a gain of purity in motives and unself-
ishness of law-makers and administrators. I fear its
effects in large cities, where bad women will come
forward. Women are so intense that bad women will
be worse in public life than bad men. But the difficulty is in the nature of the city. Yet I do not believe that woman's work will be done mainly by
voting. Disinterested lives are the things needed in
society, and women will do most in showing the
practicability and value of such lives in all forms of
work."

Similarly he speaks in a published letter: '—

"I frankly confess that I am not able to foresee all
the consequences of the great social and political
change proposed. But of this I am at least sure: it is
always safe to do right, and the truest expediency is
simple justice. . . . I have no fear that man will be
less manly or woman less womanly when they meet on
terms of equality before the law. On the other hand,
I do not see that the exercise of the ballot by woman
will prove a remedy for all the evils of which she
justly complains. It is her right as truly as mine;
and, when she asks for it, it is something less than
manhood to withhold it. But unsupported by a
more practical education, higher aims, and a deeper
sense of the responsibilities of life and duty, it is not
likely to prove a blessing in her hands any more than
in man's."

---

[1] Prose Works (edition 1889), iii. 228.

CHAPTER V.

"TELLING THE BEES," AND OTHER BALLADS.

" I knew a very wise man that believed that if a man were permitted to make all the ballads, he need not care who should make the laws, of a nation."—FLETCHER OF SALTOUN.

INASMUCH as I have elsewhere published a critical estimate of Mr. Whittier's poems, pointing out the gradual growth of his art away from homiletical, or didactic, work until it culminated in the beautiful ballads of his riper years, I do not purpose to go over that ground again in this volume, but will content myself with quoting (by the tacit permission of its writer) the following weighty and condensed bit of criticism from an eminent fellow-poet and contemporary of Mr. Whittier, and will then pass on to annotate and illustrate some of his most fascinating stories in verse: " Whittier's poetry stands for *morality* (not its *ensemble*, or in any true philosophic or Hegelian sense, but) as filter'd through the positive Puritanical and Quaker filters; is very valuable as a genuine utterance; with many capital local and Yankee and *genre* bits—all unmistakably hued with zealous partisan anti-slavery coloring. Then the *genre* bits are all precious; all help. Whittier is rather a grand figure—pretty lean and ascetic—no Greek— also not composite and universal enough (does n't wish to be, does n't try to be) for ideal Americanism." [1]

If the Essex poet is not composite and universal, he is at least very near the heart of the people, and never more so than in his best ballads,—such as "Telling the Bees," "Maud Muller," "Barbara Frietchie," "Skipper Ireson," "The Witch's Daughter," and "The Witch of Wenham." These musical arrows, shot as with the miraculous bow of Rama, are undoubtedly feathered for a far flight into the future. And a chief reason for their perpetuity lies in the fact that they are free from the disfigurement (from an artistic point of view) of so many of Whittier's descriptive pieces; namely, the moral at the end. A direct homiletical application of a story, instead of pointing it, weakens its point: it is the button on the sword. A poem with a moral reminds one of Edward Lear's "scroobious snake, who always wore a hat on his head for fear he should bite anybody."

The determination of Whittier upon the moral is complete and radical. The roots, trunk, branches, and blossoms of his life are steeped in the sense of duty. The obligation to high daring and heroic doing rests upon his soul like a solemn sanction. He has received a commission from on high. Will the Commander-in-chief approve of his sitting down to write pretty ballads in the heat and burden of the day? he keeps anxiously asking himself. To an

------

[1] The poet of Camden, letter to the author, Oct. 10, '89. It is a significant and historically fitting circumstance that the three chief democrats of the New World—Whitman, Lincoln, and Whittier —should all be, remotely or immediately, of Quaker stock.

edition of his poems published in 1849 he prefixes
these lines of Coleridge:—

> " Was it right,
> While my unnumbered brethren toiled and bled,
> That I should dream away th' intrusted hours
> On rose-leaf beds, pampering the coward heart
> With feelings all too delicate for use ? "

In the dedication of one of his prose works to his
sister Elizabeth he is still seen to be debating the
question in his mind, but leans to the opinion that
it is all right :—

> " And knowing how my life hath been
>   A weary work of tongue and pen,
>   A long, harsh strife with strong-willed men,
>   Thou wilt not chide my turning
>   To con, at times, an idle rhyme,
>   To pluck a flower from childhood's clime,
>   Or listen, at Life's noon-day chime,
>   For the sweet bells of Morning ! "

Had he consulted his *choice*, he would not have entered
into the political field at all, but would have loved all
his life to drift idly up and down among the drowsy
Venetian canals of legendary lore.   As he says at the
close of " The Panorama ":—

> " Oh, not of choice, for themes of public wrong
>   I leave the green and pleasant paths of song.
>
> *   *   *   *   *   *
>
>   More dear to me some song of private worth,—
>   Some homely idyl of my native North."

The quaint and touching European custom, described in " Telling the Bees," of informing the occupants of the hives of a death in the family, and draping the hives with crape in order that the swarms may not take their departure, has been transplanted to our country, and is still observed by isolated individuals here and there among the country folk, especially in New York State. It is a pretty idea, and a very natural one, that those marvelous little waxen-thighed flower-riflers, those winged geometers and potters whose whirling wheel turns out such cunning vases of scented sweets, should have the power of comprehending all that men do and say. It is among the peasantry of Europe, of course, that the idea is most prevalent. Some of them think that the bees' sense of smell, which is known to be very acute, is offended by the presence of a dead body. At any rate, it is imperative to inform them of the death and invite them to the funeral. Some drape the hives with shreds of black, and some do not ; some also place on the alighting-boards of the hives fragments of the funeral cake or bread, soaked in beer, wine, or honey. Bees also expect to be invited to a wedding, and to have their hives decorated with wedding favors. In Buckinghamshire, England, on the occasion of a death, the nurse of the family, or a servant, goes to all the beehives in the garden and taps gently three times, saying each time in a low voice, " Little brownie, little brownie, your master's dead," whereupon the bees begin to hum, showing that they understand and are willing to remain. In Derbyshire and Wilts the custom is a common one. Three taps are made on the hive with the house-key, and the informant says, " Bees, bees, your master [or mistress] is dead, and you must work for ——," naming the heir or successor. A piece of black crape is then fastened to the hive. An old farmer's wife in Cheshire, England, had from fifteen to twenty hives of bees.

"Well," said a friend one day to her, "how have the bees done this year?"

"Ah!" she replied, "they are all gone. When our Harriet lost her second child, a many of them died. You see they were under the window where it lay; and then when Will died, last spring, the rest all died, too. I always say that bees are very curious things."

In some parts of France, on the day of Purification women read the gospel to the bees, and it is believed that, if children or grown people swear within earshot of them, they will swarm out and attack them. The belief is alluded to by Béranger in one of his *chansons*. In Westphalia, when the death of the master of the household occurs, the servant puts on a *Bienenhelm*, or bee-bonnet, and, going out into the garden to the hives, stoops down and says in a low voice, "The mistress sends her best compliments, and the master is dead." In some parts of Germany they say,—

> "Bienchen, unser Herr ist todt,
> Verlass mich nicht in meiner Noth."

"Little bee, our master is dead. Forsake me not in my distress."[1]

---

[1] See Farrer's "Primitive Manners and Customs," p. 281; English "Notes and Queries" (consult the indexes); "American Notes and Queries," i. 312, and ii. 328, 374; "Scribner's Monthly," May, 1879 (article by Burroughs); "Open Court," Sept. 12, 1889 (article by L. J. Vance); and Brand's "Popular Antiquities."

In regard to the ballad "Maud Muller," Mr. Whittier tells us that the name Muller he took from the descendants of a Hessian deserter in the Revolutionary War. "The poem," he says, "has no real foundation in fact, though a hint of it may have been found in recalling an incident, trivial in itself, of a journey on the picturesque Maine seaboard with my sister some years before it was written. We had stopped to rest our tired horse under the shade of an apple-tree, and refresh him with water from a little brook which rippled through the stone wall across the road. A very beautiful young girl in scantiest summer attire was at work in the hay-field, and, as we talked with her, we noticed that she strove to hide her bare feet by raking hay over them, blushing as she did so through the tan of her cheek and neck." [1] "Maud Muller" was first published in the "National Era," December, 1854. It is a poem sweeter and purer in sentiment than Browning's "Statue and the Bust"; the root-idea of this poem also is embodied in the phrase, "It might have been." The name, being German, should have been written Müller. The English author Walter Hamilton says in volume five of his "Parodies" that Mr. Whittier pronounces it as if written Müller. Mr. Hamilton adds a remark of the poet: "If I had had any idea that the plaguey thing would have been so liked, I would have taken more pains with it."

The story of Skipper Ireson [2] was first told to

____

[1] Note to the library edition of 1888 of Whittier's poems.

[2] The sources of information for this ballad are as follows: History of Marblehead, by Roads, Jr., p. 233; article by John Chad-

Whittier by a schoolmate, a young girl from Marblehead, when he was attending the Academy in Haverhill. He says he remembers thinking it over while walking to and fro under Hugh Tallant's sycamores, which formed a leafy archway beside the river. Thirty years later he wrote and published the ballad. For doing so, he has excited the unappeasable wrath of the good Marbleheaders, especially the women, who in reality had nothing to do with the "torring" of the skipper, and do not like their portrait as sketched by the balladist. As for the "men-folks," they have been laboring for years to convince the world that it was n't Skipper Ireson who was to blame for leaving the shipwrecked sailors to perish: it was his men. But, as these were also Marbleheaders, one cannot see how the reputation of the town would be in any way bettered by shifting the odium onto the shoulders of Ireson's crew.

The refrain of "Skipper Ireson" was originally written without the use of the queer local pronunciation, but was afterwards changed to its present form at the suggestion of Mr. Francis H. Underwood, then editor of the "Atlantic Monthly," in which the poem first appeared. The event chronicled in the ballad took place in 1807 ; and, when Mr. Whittier took up the story for literary purposes, it had been talked about and sung about in Marblehead for a generation, and

---

wick in "Harper's Monthly," July, 1874, and one by George M. White in the same for February, 1883; Underwood's "Whittier," p. 219; Boston "Evening Transcript," Sept. 23 and Oct. 3, 1889; and a note by Mr. Whittier in the library edition (1888) of his poems. The poem first appeared anonymously in the "Atlantic Monthly" in 1857.

was regarded by him as a legend. The original doggerel, as sung by the boys of Marblehead, is said to have run in this wise :—

> " Old Flud Oirson, for his horrd hort,
> Was torred and feathered and corried in a cort ;
> He left foive men upon a wrack,
> And was torred and feathered all over his back."

By 1837 this had got changed and amplified (according to the Gloucester " Telegraph " of that year) into—

> " Old Flood Ireson, for his hord hort,
> Was torr'd and feathered and corried in a cort !
> Old Flood Ireson, for leaving the wreck,
> Was torr'd and feathered all up to his neck !
> Old Flood Ireson, for his great sin,
> Was torr'd and feathered all up to his chin !
> Old Flood Ireson, for his bad behavior,
> Was torr'd and feathered and corried to Salem !'

In the early part of this century the Marblehead vessels usually made three fishing trips in a season to the Grand Banks, from March to December. A crew generally consisted of the skipper, five men, and a cook. In the autumn of 1807 a capable and intelligent young Marbleheader of twenty-three years of age, named Captain Benjamin Ireson (Flood, or Flud, or Floyd, was a nickname), was placed by her owner in charge of the schooner " Betty " and despatched to the Grand Banks. As he was homeward bound on his third trip, he found himself one midnight with Cape Cod under his lee, and a high sea running and a strong wind blowing. The situation was not a pleasant one to the sailors, who were anxious to get home. Presently the lumber-schooner " Active," of

Portland, was descried in a sinking condition, lying on her beam ends, and the crew were clinging to the rigging. As to what took place next there is considerable uncertainty. The defenders of Captain Ireson say that he ordered the crew to lie by the wreck till "dorning" (dawn), and then turned in for a little sleep. Another account says that he and one other were for immediately rendering assistance ; but the rest of the crew (being part-owners in the cargo) refused to do so. The crew themselves, when they returned, said the captain deserved all the blame. It is pretty clear that they were all alike guilty. As for the skipper, the damning fact is not denied that he never by a word repelled the charge of having abandoned the ship. The "Betty" arrived in Marblehead October 30, and the very next day who should come sailing into the port, aboard the sloop "Swallow," but the captain of the "Active." He had been rescued, with three of the passengers, by Mr. Hardy of Truro, in a whale-boat ; but four of his crew had gone down to Davy Jones's locker.

The story of the abandonment gradually spread through the town. But no steps were taken at first, although the wrath and excitement grew more intense (it being now the idle season with the fishermen). The fare of fish was unloaded and dried on the flakes (or platforms of sticks), the "wessel" laid up for the winter, and "the v'yage sittl'd."

For some days previous to the tarring and feathering, a restless, unsettled spirit was manifested by the more indignant ones, and finally a deputation waited upon young Captain Ireson, as he was walking to and fro on Pitman's Wharf, to inquire into the truth or falsity of the accusation against him. He is said to have been a very taciturn man, and to their interrogatories returned no answer, maintaining a dogged silence to the last. This seemed to them proof positive of his guilt.

Accordingly, the Freemasons held secret meetings to discuss the matter. Their plan of action was soon matured, and on the following day the conspirators suddenly sprang upon him, threw him into a condemned dory lying on the wharf, where he was held by one Morse until his hands were tied behind his back. He made no resistance. A bucket of tar had been prepared, and the crowd, to the number of a hundred, laid hold of the long rope tied to the boat's painter and started on a run through the town, halting at the corner of Darling Street. They had received a gift of two feather pillows as they came along, from the wife of Captain David Bruce,[1] and, proceeding to the outskirts of the village, they applied the tar and feathers, rubbing it in well, and dabbing two huge lumps of tar on each temple, wherein were stuck goose feathers. The march was then resumed toward Salem, and, when the bottom of the dory came out, the skipper was placed in a cart. The Salem authorities refused to allow the crowd to enter that town, whereupon they returned to Marblehead, and unbound their prisoner, who said, "I thank you for my ride, gentlemen; but you will live to regret it." This was the only word he spoke during the proceedings. He did not return to

----

[1] From this circumstance, the mythical story of the women being engaged in the matter possibly took its rise.

his home until night set in, reaching it by a round-about way.

One of his contemporaries, on being asked what effect the tarring had on Ireson, answered, "Cowed him to death, cowed him to death." He never went skipper but once more, and that was the next year. Thereafter he earned his living by dory-fishing in the bay, selling his daily catch in a wheelbarrow trundled from door to door. He appeared to become reckless of his life. On one occasion—the story goes —he landed near the house of one of his old persecutors, and deliberately made fast a noose to a large log, which he then towed away into deep water, hurling bad names at the owner, who called out,—

"Stop, Ireson, or I'll shoot you!"

To which he replied,—

"Fire away, old man! You can't hit me!"

Another old salt tells of having once picked Ireson up far out at sea, where he had been driven in his dory by a storm. His savior took him into Gloucester. He had not a cent with which to buy a meal or to get back home. A benevolent individual gave him his supper, kept him over night, and next day took up a subscription to pay his fare to Marblehead. When Ireson had gone, he informed the subscribers who he was, whereupon they swore, in great wrath, that, if they had known it, they would not have given him a penny.

When old age and blindness at last overtook him, and his last fishing-trip had been made, his old dory was hauled up into the lane by his house, and there rotted away. Whittier's ballad appeared in 1856, a year or two after his death.

As has been stated, the "women of Marblehead" have a very poor opinion of the Quaker poet. In the autumn of 1889 some young ladies from Salem went over to Marblehead, on a boating trip, and, while there, went in search of Floyd Ireson's house. As they were inquiring their way, a woman thrust her head out of the window, exclaiming:—

"Want to find Flood Ireson's house, do ye? Well, you won't find out here, I can't tell ye! Flood Ireson was every bit as good as you be; and you treatin' his house 's if 't was a curiosity! You better go right away from here!"

The young ladies declined to take the advice, and were not molested. But shortly after another party on the same errand were pelted with mud by street gamins.

Mr. Whittier, who has been pained by the way the ballad has been received, has written a note to Samuel Roads, Jr., the historian of Marblehead (and has taken the pains to prefix it to the ballad as published in the latest edition of his poems), in which he says,—"My verse was founded solely on a fragment of a rhyme which I heard from one of my early schoolmates, a native of Marblehead. I supposed the story to which it referred dated back at least a century. I knew nothing of the participators, and the narrative of the ballad was pure fancy. I am glad for the sake of truth and justice that the real facts are given in thy book [Mr. Roads follows the popular feeling of the town, and attempts to exonerate the skipper]. I certainly would not knowingly do injustice to any one, dead or living."

Mr. Charles T. Brooks, the genial Unitarian divine

of Newport, and translator of Richter, wrote some
compassionate verses about "Old Flud," the best of
which are given below. One cannot but feel, however, that his pity is just a little misplaced (like a
good deal of Unitarian philanthropy), and that those
four poor sailors, drowned through the crime of the
skipper, would be fitter subjects for the poet's sympathies :—

> "Old Flood Ireson ! all too long
>   Have jeer and jibe and ribald song
>   Done thy memory cruel wrong.
>
> "Old Flood Ireson sleeps in his grave ;
>   Howls of a mad mob, worse than the wave,
>   Now no more in his ear shall rave.
>
> "Gone is the pack and gone the prey,
>   Yet old Flood Ireson's ghost to-day
>   Is hunted still down Time's highway.
>
> "Old wife Fame, with a fish-horn's blare
>   Hooting and tooting the same old air,
>   Drags him along the old thoroughfare.
>
> "Shall Heaven look on and not take part
>   With the poor old man and his fluttering heart,
>   Tarred and feathered and carried in a cart ?"

"Barbara Frietchie"[1] is a ballad that cannot be
read by an American without deep emotion. It has

---

[1] The name is properly spelled Fritchie, judging from the in-
scriptions on the tombstones of Barbara and her husband in
Frederick.

been twice translated into German,[1] and was highly valued by the ex-Emperor of Brazil, Dom Pedro, who, shortly after its appearance, read it repeatedly in English in the presence of members of his Court, and then brought it to the notice of the Princesses and their husbands,—the Count d'Eu and the Prince of Saxe-Coburg-Gotha,—as one of the rarest specimens of poetry in any literature in its portrayal of the heroic patriotism of woman.

Not long after the publication of the ballad, in 1863, while sympathy for the South was still strong and determined in Maryland, the Secession relatives of Dame Barbara, not relishing such extreme Northern patriotism as hers, united with the disloyal citizens of Frederick in spreading reports of the unauthenticity of the incident pictured by the poet ; and it is surprising to see with what ingenuity they have wrenched the facts, so as to make them fit their version of the affair. A dozen and one accounts have been put forth, and each is inconsistent in one or more points with the others.

Now, Mr. Whittier wrote to a friend in 1872 that a nephew of Barbara had visited him and had confirmed the authenticity of the incident.[2] To the editors of the "Century" he also wrote, in the autumn of 1886:—

"My attention has been called to an article in the

---

[1] The free rendering of the late Hon. Theodore S. Fay, in his work, "Die Sklavenmacht," is not unspirited,—

"Frisch vom Septembermorgen umhaucht,
Aus goldenen Aehrenwogen taucht,
Umgrünt von den Hügeln Maryland's,
Der Kirchthurm Frederick's im Sonnenglanz," etc.

[2] Potter's American Monthly, 1875, p. 416.

June number of the 'Century,' in which the writer, referring to the poem on Barbara Frietchie, says: 'The story will perhaps live, as Mr. Whittier has boasted, until it gets beyond the reach of correction.' Those who know me will bear witness that I am not in the habit of boasting of anything whatever, least of all of congratulating myself upon a doubtful statement outliving the possibility of correction. I certainly made no 'boast' of the kind imputed to me. The poem of Barbara Frietchie was written in good faith. The story was no invention of mine. It came to me from sources which I regarded as entirely reliable; it had been published in newspapers, and had gained public credence in Washington and Maryland before my poem was written. I had no reason to doubt its accuracy then, and I am still constrained to believe that it had foundation in fact. If I thought otherwise, I should not hesitate to express it. I have no pride of authorship to interfere with my allegiance to truth."

The writer referred to by the poet is Colonel Henry Kyd Douglas of the Confederate army, who, in his article on General Jackson in the "Century," June, 1886, p. 287, goes out of his way to affront Mr. Whittier. He says no such incident ever happened, since he was with General Jackson at the time. He shows how much he knows about the matter by adding contemptuously that there was such an old woman as Barbara Frietchie, but that she was bed-ridden. The falsity of the latter part of this affirmation will appear as we unfold the true account. It is very clear from the tone of this Confederate colonel's remarks that such stanzas in the ballad as—

"'Shoot, if you must, this old gray head,
But spare your country's flag,' she said,"

must have pricked hard the consciences of the Southerners. 'T was a home thrust,—especially to soldiers, who are sensitive to the approval or the disapproval of woman, and who are placed by the poet in the light of naughty boys being spanked by their mamma, Dame Columbia (typified, one may say, in old Barbara Frietchie).

Now, the poet Whittier has been considerably disturbed by the rumpus kicked up by the Southerners over this ballad, and, wishing to be obliging, has prefixed a note to it in the recent library edition of his poems, in which he makes unnecessary concessions, as I think I shall show. He says: "The story was probably incorrect in some of its details. It is admitted by all that Barbara Frietchie was no myth, but a worthy and highly esteemed gentlewoman, intensely loyal, and a hater of the Slavery Rebellion, holding her Union flag sacred and keeping it with her Bible; that when the Confederates halted before her house, and entered her dooryard, she denounced them in vigorous language, shook her cane in their faces, and drove them out; and, when General Burnside's troops followed close upon Jackson's, she waved her flag and cheered them. It is stated that May Quantrell, a brave and loyal lady in another part of the city, did wave her flag in sight of the Confederates. It is possible that there has been a blending of the two incidents."

Mrs. Mary A. Quantrell was a pretty, black-haired woman of thirty-two at that time. She stood at her gate with her daughter "Virgie," and both courage-ously waved Union flags in the face of the Confederates. As the little girl was flourishing a small flag, an officer cut the stick in two with his sword. She picked up another, and that, too, was cut out of her hand, the men exclaiming, " Throw down that flag!" Mrs. Quantrell waved a larger flag, and was not molested. Some of the officers, with characteristic Southern politeness, raised their hats, saying, " To you, madam, not your flag." [1]

Reports of Barbara Frietchie's patriotism and valor were carried to Washington by citizens of Frederick. It was Mrs. E. D. E. N. Southworth, of Washington, who first sent an account of her to Whittier, enclosing a newspaper slip about her spirited treatment of the Confederates under Jackson, as described by Mr. Whittier above. Mr. Whittier was afterwards assured by Miss Dorothea L. Dix, who had been caring for the wounded in a hospital in Frederick, that the story was true, virtually as he has sung it. Later he was presented with a cane made from the wood of Barbara's house.

About the year 1881, Mrs. Caroline H. Dall went to Frederick and made an exhaustive study of the whole matter. [2] The result of her investigation was a conviction that the poem has an historic basis. The deniers of its authenticity affirm that Jackson was not riding at the head of his troops at all. But Mrs. Dall learned that he had only ridden hastily back for

---

[1] Article by Joseph Walker in Baltimore " Herald," Sept. 29, 1884; quoted in " American Notes and Queries," Oct. 6, 1888.

[2] See the Boston " Evening Transcript," June, 1888, Query 12,827.

a few moments to leave a note at the door of a friend with whom he intended to pass the Sunday following, and overtook the column just as the guns were pointed at Barbara's flag. In continuation of their subterfuges and quibbling with the literal text of the ballad, the Southerners affirm that Jackson's army did not enter Frederick at all. This is literally true, but practically false. The army did not pass through the town, but did pass within fifteen or twenty feet of one of its boundary lines. Frederick town is separated from Frederick County by Carroll Creek, a very narrow stream (about the width of an ordinary street), and the road traversed by Jackson's soldiers lay along the farther side of that creek. But Barbara Frietchie's house overhung the stream. Her husband was a glover, and the house had been so constructed that the trimmings of the shop might be swept into the stream through a trap door. There was but one window on the side of the house next to the creek, and that was in the attic. It was here that she waved the flag, and in the photographs sold in the town it is always represented as fluttering from this window. The little flag is about 12 x 18 inches, has but thirty-four stars, is of silk, and is attached to a staff some three feet long. It is still preserved by her niece, Mrs. Handschue. This good lady affirms that the incident is apocryphal, for she was in the house and saw nothing of it. But Mrs. Dall said she learned on inquiry that the niece was at the time hidden under the bed, saying her prayers in German! Mrs. Handschue's daughter, Mrs. Abbott, writes that, when later the Union troops under Burnside marched by the front door, the old lady stood on her porch, leaning on her cane, and waving her silken flag of the Union. She was then over ninety-six. The men cheered her again and again. Some even ran into the yard to shake hands, exclaiming: " God bless you, old lady! May you live long!" On the opposite side of the narrow street stood a white-haired German pastor, over a hundred years old, and it was said that the tears of joy streamed down the cheeks of both as they waved their flags.

We are told also that on other occasions, if, on going out, she found rebel soldiers encumbering her door steps, she would strike them right and left, crying, " Off, off, you lousy Rebels !" [1]

Let it be noted that General Jackson passed through Frederick, *en route* to capture Harper's Ferry, on Sept. 6, 1862, and that *on December* 18, *three months later, Barbara Frietchie died*, and was buried in the cemetery of the German Reformed Church in Frederick.[2] Whittier's ballad did not appear until October, 1863, when it was published in the " Atlantic Monthly," *nearly a year after Barbara had passed away*. Mr. Joseph Walker, her son-in-law, claims to know all about the matter, and speaking, probably from hearsay or remembrance, twenty-two years after the event, says Barbara never claimed the credit of the General Jackson incident nor even alluded to it. Perhaps not. But why should she? It would not have seemed to her anything very extraordinary to do. She may have said nothing to the Confederate

---

[1] Sunday Afternoon Magazine, April 8.

[2] The Century Company's " War Book," ii. 618 ; article by George O. Seilheimer.

soldiers, and there may possibly have been no firing at the flag,—or, if there was, she would have deemed it prudent not to mention it to her terrified niece. Her well-known patriotism makes it nearly certain that she would not have allowed a Confederate army to pass under her window without rebuking it (as she did in the case mentioned by Mr. Whittier). Very well. The incident of the flag happened, and was forgotten. Gradually, as we know, her reputation for patriotism spread; and then some citizen or one of Jackson's soldiers recalled that little scene at the attic window; the account reached Washington, and later was sent on to Mr. Whittier. In the hurly-burly of war it may well have happened that her own niece remained in ignorance that the flag-story was circulating elsewhere. Then in three months the old lady was beyond the reach of questions.

In further confirmation of the incident Mrs. Dall states ("Unitarian Review," September, 1878) that she had received a letter from an Englishman of education, a member of the Shakespeare Society, who was a soldier in the Union Army and member of Burnside's Ninth Army Corps. He states that on September 18, 1862, twelve days after the entrance of Jackson into Frederick, he passed through the town with an ambulance of wounded men. Stopping for refreshments at a restaurant, they were told by a pretty Irish girl the story of the firing on the flag. The girl was a Confederate sympathizer, and exclaimed, "Bully for Jackson!" This shows that the story was common talk twelve days after the event. This Englishman went South after the war, and once read the ballad aloud at a public meeting. Persons present testified to their personal knowledge of the countermanding by Jackson of the order to fire. In 1868 a Union officer, one of the convalescent patients in the Frederick hospital at the time, told Mrs. Dall that he himself saw the shot fired at the flag.

One day, shortly before her death, says Mrs. Dall, two friends called on Barbara Frietchie to pay her some money owed her. They found her sitting by the window knitting. She wore a black satin dress and a snow-white cap; a white kerchief was pinned over her shoulders. When the money had been paid, a pen was put into her hand, and she was shown where to make her mark. She pushed back her gold spectacles, and with a smile drew her pen through the name that had been written for her, writing it herself with a steady hand, saying to her friend, " Honey, I wrote my name before you were born."

There is another ballad of Whittier's founded on an incident the authenticity of which is denied by certain authorities. I refer to the poem " Brown of Ossawatomie," and especially to the second stanza, in which are embodied the subject and *raison d'être* of the whole piece:—

" John Brown of Ossawatomie, they led him out to die ;
   And lo ! a poor slave-mother with her little child pressed
      nigh.
   Then the bold blue eye grew tender, and the old harsh face
      grew mild,
   As he stooped between the jeering ranks and kissed the
      negro's child ! "

Mr. Thomas Hovenden, of Philadelphia, has put this scene into a powerful realistic painting, containing twenty-two figures, eight or nine of them carefully finished studies. It is a great historical work, the value of which will enormously increase with time. My description of this painting in successive numbers of the Boston "Index" in 1885 brought out important evidence as to the authenticity of the story upon which the painting is based,—especially a long editorial in the New York "Sun" of September 27th of that year, written by Edward F. Underhill. Mr. Underhill thinks that my belief in the truth of the story of the child-kissing by Brown is built upon sand. It may be so, but let us see. No one knew before the appearance of Mr. Underhill's editorial where the famous passage came from which was taken by Redpath from the New York "Tribune" for his Life of John Brown, and thence extracted by Greeley for his History of the Civil War, and which formed the basis of Whittier's poem and Hovenden's painting. The truth is now revealed: it came from the journalistic brain of Mr. Underhill. In his "Tribune" article, he tells a number of journalistic falsehoods, assumes to have been an eye-witness of everything he relates, speaks of the very expression of Brown's face, his smile, the elasticity of his step, and says he (the writer) was present at the scaffold. But Mr. Underhill now tells us that this was only a journalistic trick. He was detailed by the editor-in-chief to write the article, and to put it in the form of correspondence, in order to deceive the vigilant Southerners at Charleston, who were ready to string up the authors of all letters to Northern papers. The information for his article Mr. Underhill got from the Abolitionist, Mr. J. Miller McKim, who came to the

16

"Tribune" office two days after the hanging, in company with Mrs. John Brown. Mr. McKim had not been allowed to go to Charleston where Brown was, but waited at Harper's Ferry while Mrs. Brown went on to see her husband. After her return to the Ferry, and while they were both waiting there for Brown's remains to be delivered to them, McKim heard, in conversation with others, the statement about the kissing of the slave-child. It did not come at first or even second hand to him. But somehow it had got abroad. Was it true? Only two persons whose word is entitled to any weight have denied it. These are Mr. Redpath and John Brown's jailer, Captain Avis. Brown's best biographer, Mr. F. B. Sanborn, wrote to me, in 1885: "Redpath, who gave currency to the story, told me five years ago that it was not true. He depended on Ned House (the 'Tribune' correspondent) for it (as he said), and he had discovered that House invented it." Now, Edward H. House was present during the entire trial and execution, and sent on letters, by secret channels, to the New York papers. But we have just seen that it was not he who furnished the narrative to the "Tribune." So that Mr. Redpath was mistaken. House did *not* invent the "Tribune" narrative. As for Captain Avis, he testified in 1882 as follows: "Brown was between Sheriff Campbell and me; and a guard of soldiers surrounded him, and allowed no person to come between them and the prisoner, from the jail to the scaffold, except his escorts." But may we not believe that in the confusion of the party as they emerged from the jail through the narrow little porch, and just before the formal positions of the march to the wagon had been assumed, the rough old hero, who had helped so many slaves out of bondage, stooped, with his usual alertness, although his arms were tied behind him, to kiss the slave-child (as a last example to the world), and passed on, Captain Avis being at that instant separated from him by an intervening body, or having his attention drawn to the military before the door?

"The most charming and best authenticated of all our traditions," says Edward Everett Hale, "is that commemorated in Whittier's beautiful ballad 'The Palatine.'" It is a story of the pillage and burning of a ship by wreckers, and of its annual reappearance as a phantom ship of fire. The scene of the legend is Block Island, called by the Indians Manisees, "the Isle of the Little God." Here once, it is remembered, came bold Captain Underhill, and in an Indian fight received an arrow against his helmeted forehead. Picturesque in its bluffs and in its fifteen miles of surf-beaten sea-coast, encircled by seas always blue, there it lies, menacing alike in its smile and its frown, with its death-scented traditions of innumerable wrecks and wreckers, and pirate deeds, planted right athwart the track of ships sailing out of and into Long Island Sound, not the fabled Symplegades shunned more by mariners (even now with its fine lighthouses and brilliantly lighted summer hotels),—such is Block Island. Leagues north from the mainland,

> "Point Judith watches with eye of hawk;
> Leagues south, thy beacon flames, Montauk."
>
> —*Whittier.*

We have a picture of the sea view in Walt Whitman's " From Montauk Point " :—

" I stand as on some mighty eagle's beak
    Eastward the sea absorbing, viewing, (nothing but sea and
       sky,)
    The tossing waves, the foam, the ships in the distance,
    The wild unrest, the snowy, curling caps—that inbound
       urge and urge of waves,
    Seeking the shores forever."

That Nestor of American poets, the elder Dana, describes Block Island in his " Buccaneer " :—

" The island lies nine leagues away,
    Along its solitary shore,
    Of craggy rock and sandy bay,
    No sound but ocean's roar,
Save where the bold wild sea-bird makes her home,
Her shrill cry coming through the sparkling foam.

" But when the light winds lie at rest,
    And on the glassy heaving sea
    The black duck, with her glossy breast,
    Sits swinging silently,—
How beautiful ! no ripples break the reach,
And silvery waves go noiseless up the beach."

So far as can be discovered, the essential facts of the wreck of the " Palatine," as handed down by tradition, are these :[1] The " Palatine " was a German

---

[1] I have consulted the following authorities: William P. Sheffield's " Historical Sketch of Block Island," 1876; S. T. Livermore's " History of Block Island," 1877 ; Charles Lanman's " Recollections of Curious Characters and Pleasant Places," pp. 297–304; Drake's " New England Legends," p. 406; Edward E. Hale's " Christmas in Narragansett," p. 285; and the Poems of Richard H. Dana, Sen.

emigrant ship, though many of her passengers were quite wealthy. The captain had either died or been murdered on the voyage hither, and the diabolical crew had caused the ship to lie off and on, skirting the coasts of Delaware for weeks, while they robbed the passengers of all they could extort by the process of starving them nearly to death and then charging exorbitant rates for morsels of food and drink. When they had got all they could, the crew forsook the ship, which drifted ashore on Block Island one bright Sabbath morning, between the festivals of Christmas and New Year's. The wreckers boarded her, and found that some of the miserable passengers were delirious. They landed them all except one woman, Mary Vanderline, who had much gold and silver plate aboard, and who refused to leave the ship. Many of the suffering emigrants died shortly afterwards, and were buried on the island. The wreckers towed the ship into a little cove, where, having pillaged her, they set her on fire and let her drift out to sea with the unfortunate woman on board (probably having stolen her treasure-chest, as we shall see). The ship drifted away into the darkness of a stormy winter night, her spars and cordage painted in flame on the sky, and the waves blood-red below, while the surf boomed on the shore, the wind flung the swirling sand about, and (as tradition says) the shrieks of the abandoned woman could be heard far off, growing each moment fainter and fainter.

> "In their cruel hearts, as they homeward sped,
>   'The sea and the rocks are dumb,' they said;
>   'There 'll be no reckoning with the dead.'

> " But the year went round, and when once more
>   Along the foam-white curves of shore
>   They heard the line-storm rave and roar,
>
> " Behold! again, with shimmer and shine,
>   Over the rocks and the seething brine,
>   The flaming wreck of the Palatine! "
>
> *—Whittier.*

There can be little doubt that the poet Dana had heard this legend of the phantom ship, which he thus describes in his hysterical, blood-and-thunder poem, " The Buccaneer ":—

> " 'T is near mid-hour of night :
> What means upon the waters that red light?
>
> " Not bigger than a star it seems,
>   And now 't is like the bloody moon !
>   And now it shoots in hairy streams !
>   It moves !—'T will reach us soon !
> A ship ! and all on fire !—hull, yard, and mast !
> Her sails are sheets of flame !—she 's nearing fast !
>
> " And now she rides upright and still,
>   Shedding a wild and lurid light
>   Around the cove, on inland hill,
>   Waking the gloom of night.
> All breathes of terror ! men, in dumb amaze,
> Gaze on each other in the horrid blaze."

No phenomenon is better authenticated than this of the moving flame of Block Island. It is probably to be classed with such electrical appearances at sea as the St. Elmo's light so often seen on the tips of spars and masts. I notice that Winthrop, in the first volume of his History of New England, speaks of a great light seen in the night on a river near Boston :

" When it stood still, it flamed up, and was about three yards square ; when it ran, it was contracted into the figure of a swine. It ran as swift as an arrow toward Charl[es]ton, and so up and down about two or three hours."

In 1811, Dr. Aaron C. Willey, who then lived on Block Island, wrote a letter to Dr. Samuel Mitchell, of New York City, in which he described the "Palatine" light. His letter was printed in a publication called "The Parthenon." Following are extracts from this letter :—

"The people who have always lived here are so familiarized to the sight that they never think of giving notice to those who do not happen to be present, or even of mentioning it afterwards, unless they hear some particular enquiries are made.

" This curious irradiative rises from the ocean near the northern part of the island. Its appearance is nothing different from a blaze of fire. Whether it actually touches the water, or merely hovers over it, is uncertain, for I have been informed that no person has been near enough to decide accurately. It beams with various magnitudes, and appears to bear no more analogy to the *ignis fatuus* than it does to the Aurora borealis. Sometimes it is small, resembling the light through a distant window ; at others expanding to the highness of a ship with all her canvas spread. . . .

" When most expanded, this blaze is generally wavering like the flame of a torch. At one time it appears stationary, at another progressive. . . .

" It is often seen blazing at six or seven miles' distance, and strangers suppose it to be a vessel on fire. . .

"The first time I beheld it was at evening twilight, in February, 1810. It was large and gently lambent, very bright, broad at the bottom and terminating acutely upward. . . .

"I saw it again on the evening of December the 20th. It was then small, and I supposed it to be a light on board of some vessel, but I was soon undeceived. It moved along, apparently parallel to the shore, for about two miles, in the time that I was riding one at a moderate pace."

In his treatment of the tradition of the "Palatine," Mr. Whittier has been charged with having accused the now dead and gone wreckers of Block Island of acts of which they were never guilty. Rev. S. T. Livermore thinks that "the representing of an entire community of law-abiding Christian people as barbarians and pirates is intolerable." But his attempts to invalidate the tradition seem quite weak. He says that after the appearance of Mr. Whittier's ballad researches were made in the customs archives of Rotterdam and Amsterdam, but that no record of any ship named the "Palatine" could be found, except of one that was wrecked in the Bay of Bengal in 1784. This proves conclusively, thinks Mr. Livermore, that the "Palatine" was not wrecked on Block Island! But is it not ridiculous to assume that there was in the world but one ship of that name? There were probably many. Two ships of the same name were once wrecked on Block Island itself, and on the same day. Then the attempts that have been made to bolster up the character of the old islanders have not been very successful, it seems to me. Mr. Samuel Adams Drake (one of the first authorities on New

England traditions) says of Block Island: "Somehow, the reputation of the island was never good." "Sailors always shook their heads when they spoke of Block Island. A bad lee shore, a place of no good hap for the unlucky mariner who might be driven upon it, were prevailing notions,—and firmly rooted ones,—to which dark hints, and still darker traditions, concerning shipwrecked crews and valuable cargoes, give a certain color and consistency. 'I would rather be wrecked anywhere than on Block Island,' became a common and significant saying in the forecastle or the midnight watch, when the dark mass of the island heaved in sight."[1]

"As a general rule, most wreckers would be called hard characters," says Mr. W. F. G. Shanks.[2]   Charles Lanman, in his valuable chapter on Block Island, states that there have been as many as one thousand wrecks on the island during the past century, and that the wreckers have grown rich from them.

The hint for his poem "The Palatine" came to Mr. Whittier from James Hazard, of Newport. When complaints of the islanders came to the poet in 1876, he wrote to Charles E. Perry, a Block Islander, as follows :—

"In regard to the poem 'Palatine,' I can only say that I did not intend to misrepresent the facts of history.   I wrote it after receiving a letter from Mr. Hazard, of Rhode Island, from which I certainly inferred that the ship was pillaged by the islanders. He mentioned that one of the crew, to save himself,

---

[1] New England Legends, p. 406.

[2] Harper's Monthly, xxxviii. 433.   See also xviii. 577.

clung to the boat of the wreckers, who cut his hand off with a sword. It is very possible that my correspondent followed the current tradition on the mainland. . . .

"Mr. Hazard is a gentleman of character and veracity, and I have no doubt he gave the version of the story as he had heard it."

The reader will notice that a part of the letter is withheld from the public by Mr. Perry.

Now, what is the value of the traditions as handed down? The occurrence of the wreck is known to have been about the year 1750. The gulf of time from that day to this is spanned by two or three lives, and the chain of tradition is admitted to be unbroken. Two of the women who were saved had the same name,—Kate,—and were styled by the islanders Short Kattern and Long Kattern. It was Long Kattern who told of the starving of the emigrants by the crew of the ship. Her descendants are living to-day. The tradition is traced back along two or three other threads. It must be remembered that the Block Islanders were for a hundred and seventy years without mails or printing-press,— entirely cut off from regular communication with the mainland. In such cases traditions are always tenacious and of great historical value. Memory is cultivated by fishermen to an astonishing extent. I once talked with one of this class living at the mouth of the Connecticut River who could quote by the hour from all the great English poets.

Again, if the "Palatine" were not wrecked, how is it, I would ask, that logs of *Lignum vitæ* from her cargo were obtained by the islanders, worked up into mortars for grinding corn, and transmitted to the descendants of the original wreckers? These mortars are to be seen still, and no one has denied that they were from the "Palatine." Then it is not denied that a number of the silver cups which belonged to the passengers are still shown on the island, and Mr. Whittier was presented with a plate which is said to have come from the ship. It seems pretty evident that these silver cups were from the treasure-box of poor Mary Vanderline, the woman who perished on the burning vessel. The poet Dana, who lived comparatively near the island, and was born only about thirty-five years after the wreck, has in his poem "The Buccaneer" a Spanish lady who is murdered for her gold by the Block Island cut-throat, Lee. That Dana had in mind the "Palatine" tradition when he wrote is proved not only by this incident, but by other correspondences too close to be the result of chance. For example, in the poem, as by the tradition, the vessel is set on fire and then abandoned; and in both the spectre ship appears.

It is a curious thing,—this bitter determination of our times to deny the possibility of heroic deeds, and, conversely, to soften down or wholly excuse great crimes. There is no such thing as genius, they are happy to inform us; and self-sacrificing heroism is laughed at, unless interest is somehow spied as a motive. Homer never wrote the Iliad, nor Shakspere his plays; Christ never really existed; Joan of Arc was no heroine at all; Cromwell was a humbug, and so was John Brown; grand old Walt Whitman is a disgrace to the earth; William Lloyd Garrison was only actuated by love of fame; the pipers did n't pipe at Lucknow, Barbara did n't wave her flag, and Sheridan rode only eight miles, not twenty. The diluted ethical wash is applied with a broad brush to nearly every great personality and noble deed in history. There is the story of John Brown magnanimously kissing the little slave-child in its mother's arms. Assuming the incident to be true, we may suppose he did it on purpose to rebuke the shameful color-caste which makes America as provincial and as inferior to England in social ethics as she is in the matter of free trade and copyright.' But the very idea of such an act excites our repugnance. Oh, no! John Brown never did such a thing. Christ had a darker skin than thousands of negroes in America, but he would never have taken a little negro child in his arms and blessed it, poor thing! And little Eva caressing and kissing Uncle Tom,—what a shocking matter! You may hug and kiss your poodle dogs, my dear children, but do n't touch even with the tongs such persons as Frederick Douglass, or Crispus Attucks, or Toussaint L'Ouverture, or Alexandre Dumas.

Precisely the same spirit that would drag down the great to the common level seeks to lift up to that level those who have fallen below it,—the great criminals of history, from Napoleon and Henry VIII. down to Boss Tweed and Jim Fiske and the whole

---

' Strong, robust natures never have this hysterical-morbid horror of the negro. Louisa M. Alcott, in her " Hospital Sketches " (p. 76), tells how her Abolition blood took fire one day in Washington and, just to give a lesson to a *nase-weis* Southern woman, she caught up a funny little black cherub and kissed it. She was henceforth regarded as a dangerous fanatic.

rogues-gallery brigade of American plutocratic scoundrels. There, for example, is Skipper Ireson, the poor fellow! Do you know it is all a mistake about the young skipper's leaving those men to drown? It was n't he, after all: it was somebody else. And there were those men of Block Island a hundred and fifty years ago,—not savage, stony-hearted wreckers at all, but God-fearing, benevolent gentlemen of the sea, who tenderly cared for shipwrecked crews, and were never in their lives known to plunder a cargo, knock a sailor on the head, or burn a ship. Oh, no, not they! It was those other fellows, the pirates, you know, who used to come to the island. People read about the pirates, and gradually came to think that all the inhabitants of the island were cut-throat rascals like these, say the modern Block Islanders. But fair and softly, good friends! We cannot dress up all our grim forbears in stoles and albs. This is a wild rough world, and some pretty grisly things have been done on its surface. It won't hurt us to admit it, either.

There has been a little discussion about the authenticity of the thrilling incident told in Whittier's " Pipes at Lucknow ":—

> " Pipes of the misty moorlands,
>   Voice of the glens and hills;
> The droning of the torrents,
>   The treble of the rills!
> Not the braes of broom and heather,
>   Nor the mountains dark with rain,
> Nor maiden bower, nor border tower,
>   Have heard your sweetest strain!

> " Dear to the Lowland reaper,
>   And plaided mountaineer,—
> To the cottage and the castle
>   The Scottish pipes are dear ;—
> Sweet sounds the ancient pibroch
>   O'er mountain, loch, and glade ;
> But the sweetest of all music
>   The pipes at Lucknow played."

The Lucknow incident was enticing to poets, and in Scotland it gave birth to many a ballad and song. But Whittier's in America excelled them all. Late in his life, Tennyson wrote a wretched piece of fustian on the subject. The closing lines are good:—

> " Saved by the valour of Havelock, saved by the blessing of
>   Heaven !
>   ' Hold it for fifteen days ! ' we have held it for eighty-seven !
>   And ever aloft on the palace roof the old banner of England
>   blew."

The city of Lucknow consists chiefly of a long straggling street of houses stretching away from the great compound house called the Residency, which rises from an eminence by the river Goomtee. The garrison building is, or was, in the form of a squarish-built, battlemented structure. For a mile or so in front of it are enormous Versailles-like palaces and court-yards and tombs of princes. Not long after the rebellion broke out, Sir Henry Lawrence had put the Residency into a state of siege. Martial law had been proclaimed; treasure and ammunition buried; houses unroofed or blown up; carriages, mahogany tables, and a splendid Oriental library converted into a barricade; batteries made; stockades formed; and the racket-court thatched and stored with bhoosa for the cattle. The heroic garrison, at the time of the incident of the poem, had held out for nearly three months against the ferocious Sepoys. All hope of rescue had been abandoned; the Residency was riddled with cannon-shot and bullets, and surrender had become only a question of days. It was known that a rescuing force was approaching, but no one knew where it was.

Here, now, comes in the account which gave rise to the poem. It was published in the "Jersey Times" (England) Dec. 10, 1857, with this editorial prefix: "The following is an extract from a letter written by M. de Banneroi, a French physician in the service of Mussur Rajah, and published in "Le Pays" (Paris paper) under the date of Calcutta, Oct. 8."[1]

"I give you the following account of the relief of Lucknow, as described by a lady, one of the rescued party:—

"'On every side, death stared us in the face; no human skill could avert it any longer. We saw the moment approach when we must bid farewell to earth, yet without feeling that unutterable horror which must have been experienced by the unhappy victims of Cawnpore. We were resolved to die rather than yield, and were fully persuaded that in twenty-four hours all would be over. The engineers had said so, and all knew the worst. We women

---

[1] The whole extract is quoted in the Boston "Liberator," Jan. 22, 1858. A poor rewritten copy, with some of the choicest morsels gnawed out, was printed in "Littell's Living Age," Jan. 23, 1858. Whittier's poem "Lucknow" was printed in the "National Era" in the same month.

strove to encourage each other, and to perform the
light duties which had been assigned to us, such as
conveying orders to the batteries, and supplying the
men with provisions, especially cups of coffee, which
we prepared day and night. I had gone out to try
and make myself useful, in company with Jessie
Brown, the wife of a corporal in my husband's regiment. Poor Jessie had been in a state of restless
anxiety all through the siege, and had fallen away
visibly within the last few days. A constant fever
consumed her, and her mind wandered occasionally,
especially that day, when the recollections of home
seemed powerfully present to her. At last, overcome
with fatigue, she lay down on the ground, wrapped
up in her plaid. I sat beside her, promising to
awaken her when, as she said, 'her father should
return from the ploughing.' She fell at length into
a profound slumber, motionless and apparently
breathless, her head resting in my lap. I myself could
no longer resist the inclination to sleep, in spite of
the continued roar of cannon. Suddenly, I was
aroused by a wild, unearthly scream close to my ear;
my companion stood up beside me, her arms raised,
and her head bent forward in the attitude of listening. A look of intense delight broke over her countenance; she grasped my hand, drew me toward her,
and exclaimed, 'Dinna ye hear it? dinna ye hear it?
Ay, I'm no dreamin', it's the slogan o' the Highlanders!
We're saved, we're saved!' Then, flinging herself on
her knees, she thanked God with passionate fervor.

"'I felt utterly bewildered : my English ears heard
only the roar of artillery, and I thought my poor
Jessie was still raving ; but she darted to the batteries,

and I heard her cry incessantly to the men, "Courage !
Courage! Hark to the slogan—to the MacGregor, the
grandest of them a'! Here's help at last!" To
describe the effect of these words upon the soldiers
would be impossible. For a moment they ceased
firing, and every soul listened in intense anxiety.
Gradually, however, there arose a murmur of intense
disappointment, and the wailing of the women who
had flocked to the spot burst out anew as the colonel
shook his head. Our dull lowland ears heard nothing
but the rattle of the musketry. A few moments more
of this death-like suspense, of this agonizing hope,
and Jessie, who had again sunk on the ground [the
best place for detecting a distant sound], sprang to
her feet, and cried in a voice so clear and piercing
that it was heard along the whole line,—" Will ye no
believe it noo ? The slogan has ceased, but the Camp-
bells are comin'! D' ye hear, d' ye hear ?" At that
moment we seemed to hear the voice of God in the
distance, when the pibroch of the Highlanders brought
us tidings of deliverance, for now there was no longer
any doubt of the fact. That shrill, penetrating, cease-
less sound, which rose above all other sounds, could
come neither from the advance of the enemy nor
from the work of the sappers. No, it was indeed the
blast of the Scottish bagpipes, now shrill and harsh,
as threatening vengeance on the foe, then in softer
tones seeming to promise succor to their friends in
need.' "

> " Louder, nearer, fierce as vengeance,
>   Sharp and shrill as swords at strife,
>   Came the wild MacGregor's clan-call,
>   Stinging all the air to life.

> But when the far-off dust-cloud
> To plaided legions grew,
> Full tenderly and blithesomely
> The pipes of rescue blew !"

"'Never surely was there such a scene as that which followed. Not a heart in the Residency of Lucknow but bowed itself before God. All by one simultaneous impulse fell upon their knees, and nothing was heard but bursting sobs and the murmured voice of prayer. Then all arose, and there rang out from a thousand lips a great sound of joy which resounded far and wide, and lent new vigor to that blessed pibroch. To our cheer of "God save the Queen," they replied by the well-known strain that moves every Scot to tears, " Should auld acquaintance be forgot." After that, nothing else made any impression on me. I scarcely remember what followed. Jessie was presented to the General on his entrance into the fort, and at the officers' banquet her health was drunk by all present, while the pipers marched round the table playing once more the familiar air of " Auld Lang Syne." '"

Another lady wrote : " Never shall I forget the moment to the latest day I live. It was most overpowering. We had no idea they were so near, and were breathing air in the portico as usual at that hour, speculating when they might be in, not expecting they could reach us for several days longer, when suddenly, just at dark, we heard a very sharp fire of musketry quite close by, and then a tremendous cheering ; an instant after, the sound of bagpipes, then soldiers running up the road, our compound and veranda filled with our *deliverers*, and all of us shaking hands frantically, and exchanging fervent 'God bless you's' with the gallant men and officers of the 78th Highlanders. Sir James Outram and staff were the next to come in, and the state of joyful confusion and excitement is beyond all description. The big rough-bearded soldiers were seizing the little children out of our arms, kissing them with tears rolling down their cheeks, and thanking God they had come in time to save them from the fate of those at Cawnpore. . . . The faces of utter strangers beamed upon each other like those of dearest friends and brothers." [1]

There was one incident of the rescue that, stupefied and blunted as their feelings were by scenes of carnage, touched the hearts of all. I refer to the bayonetting of several loyal Sepoys by mistake as the infuriated Highlanders rushed in. One of these natives, as he was dying, waved his hand and said : "It is all for the good cause. Welcome, friend !"

The war-cry of the MacGregors, alluded to by Whittier, is " O 'ard choille ! "

No sooner was the story of Jessie Brown and the Highlanders published than the sceptical and critical fry began to open fire on it. Some one in "Notes and Queries" thought the whole story must be apocryphal, because the narrator of it seemed stupidly to confound the slogan, or war-cry, with the pibroch, or music of the bagpipes (but look back, and you will see that it is not so). Mr. Critic thought, further, that the ancient slogans were not likely to

---

[1] A Lady's Diary of the Seige of Lucknow, London, Murray, 1858, p. 119.

have been used by modern Highlanders. Then, the Calcutta correspondent of the "Nonconformist" murmurs, with a rich purr of self-complacency:—

"We have read with some surprise and amusement that wonderful story published in the English papers about Jessie Brown and the slogan of the Highlanders, in Havelock's relief of Lucknow. I have been assured by one of the garrison that it is a pure invention. 1. No letter of the date mentioned could have reached Calcutta when the story is said to have arrived. 2. There was no Jessie Brown in Lucknow. 3. The 78th neither played their pipes nor howled out the slogan as they came in; they had something else to do. 4. They never marched round the dinner-table with their pipes the same evening at all."

"There was no Jessie Brown"; but L. G. R. Rees, one of the surviving defenders, says in his authoritative work on Lucknow that there were at the time eight hundred women and children in the Residency. Pray, how did our Calcutta correspondent know them all? Did he know one of them? Probably not. Did his informer know more than a dozen or more of their names? It was impossible. There were at least two women named Brown there, as appears from Mr. Rees's list of commisioned officers and volunteer helpers and their families. Again, "There was no playing of bagpipes," says our critic, hundreds of miles away from the scene. But every book account we have, written by the besieged, states that the Highlanders *did* play their pipes, not when they were rushing in of course, hard pressed by the enemy, but at some time in the slow march towards the garrison. As for the playing of the pipers around

the dinner-table, we need only recall George MacDon-
ald's "Malcolm," and ask whether the piping was not
almost sure to have occurred.

In the "Diary of the Defence of Lucknow" by a
staff officer, p. 170, it is stated that, some time before the 78th Highlanders (which was fighting its
way slowly up the streets a few miles away) reached
the Residency, several of the besieged thought they
heard musketry in the distance, "and the sound was
listened to with the most intense and painful anxiety by the garrison." Later in the day another
distant cannonade was heard. "This elicited many
and divers opinions, and created the greatest possible excitement." Is it not clear that, on this or
just such another occasion after it, the incident
related of the Scotch woman, with such circum-
stantial detail and verisimilitude, was just the kind
of thing likely to happen? Is there anything in the
lady's narrative (which furnished the text of the
poem) that looks like fiction? Does it not bear the
stamp of artless truth in every word and line? Finally (to finish up the Calcutta fellow), let me prick
the wind out of his assertion that no letter
could have reached Calcutta in the time implied by
the date of the French physician's letter to Paris.
Now, the distance from Lucknow to Calcutta is
given in the gazetteers as less than 564 miles;
the relief of the garrison occurred on September 26;
the date of M. de Banneroi's letter is October 8;
this gives fourteen days for the letter-courier, traveling less than the paltry distance of forty miles a
day, over roads smooth as a floor, to reach Calcutta
Anything impossible in that?

We will close this chapter with some remarks on one other ballad of Whittier's, the accuracy of which has been challenged.

Besse, in his "Sufferings of the Quakers," tells us that the person chiefly instrumental in procuring from Charles II. the letter, styled by Whittier the King's Missive, which prohibited further severe punishment of Quakers in Massachusetts, and required the Governor to send culprits to England for trial, was Edward Burroughs. It is said that Burroughs was had to the King while he was playing tennis out of doors. Seeing that the Quaker kept his hat on, the King gracefully removed his plumed hat and bowed. "Thee need'st not remove thy hat," said Burroughs. "Oh," replied his Majesty, "it is of no consequence, only that when the King and another gentleman are talking together it is usual for one of them to take off his hat." Burroughs told the King that there was "a vein of innocent blood opened in his dominions, which, if it were not stopt, might overrun all." Charles replied, "But I will stop that vein." It was presently arranged, then, that a certain Samuel Shattuck should be the bearer of a letter to America. He sailed with a Friend named Ralph Goldsmith, and arrived in Boston Harbor on a Sunday in the latter part of November, 1661.

"The townsmen," says Besse, "seeing a ship with English colours, soon came on board and asked for the Captain. Ralph Goldsmith told them he was the Commander. They asked whether he had any letters. He answered, 'Yes.' But withal told them he would not deliver them that day. So they returned on shore again, and reported that there were many

Quakers come, and that Samuel Shattuck (who they knew had been banished on pain of death) was among them. But they knew nothing of his errand or authority. Thus all was kept close, and none of the ship's company suffered to go on shore that day. Next morning Ralph Goldsmith, the Commander, with Samuel Shattuck, the King's deputy, went on shore, and, sending the boat back to the ship, they two went directly through the town to the Governour's house, and knockt at the door: he sending a man to know their business, they sent him word that their message was from the King of England, and that they would deliver it to none but himself. Then they were admitted to go in, and the Governour came to them, and commanded Samuel Shattuck's hat to be taken off, and having received the deputation and the mandamus, he laid off his own hat; and ordering Shattuck's hat to be given him again, perused the papers, and then went out to the Deputy-Governour's, bidding the King's deputy and the master of the ship to follow him: being come to the Deputy-Governour, and having consulted him, he returned to the aforesaid two persons and said, 'We shall obey his Majesty's command.' After this the master of the ship gave liberty to his passengers to come on shore, which they did, and had a religious meeting with their friends of the town, where they returned praises to God for his mercy manifested in this wonderful deliverance."

After the appearance of the poem by Mr. Whittier, based on this narrative, in the " Memorial History of Boston," Mr. George E. Ellis attempted, unsuccessfully, to prove that the treatment of the subject by the poet was historically inaccurate. He affirmed that there was no releasing of imprisoned Quakers, since none were held in custody at that time, and that a meeting for praise and thanksgiving would not have been allowed.

Mr. Whittier, in reply, said that it was not easy to be strictly accurate in every detail of a ballad; yet in "The King's Missive" he believed he had preserved with tolerable correctness the spirit, tone, and color of the incident and its time. He quotes from Besse the very order of the Court addressed to William Salter, the jailer, ordering the release of the Quakers. As to the meeting of Friends for jubilation, Mr. Whittier might have referred to the passage in Besse which I have just cited for proof that there was such a meeting, and he does quote from the journal of George Fox the statement that "the passengers in the ship and the Friends in the town met together, and offered up praise and thanksgiving to God, who had so wonderfully delivered them out of the teeth of the devourer," and that, while they were thus met, "in came a poor Friend, who, being sentenced by their bloody law to die, had lain some time in irons, expecting execution."

In view of these facts, Mr. Whittier very justly says that he sees no reason to rub out any of the figures or alter the lines and colors of the poem. He admits that the interview took place at the Governor's residence, and not in the town hall, as the poem has it, but thinks, with Mr. Justin Winsor, that this variation from the facts is a fair poetic license.

The lines,

> "He had shorn with his sword the cross from out
> The flag,"

are the poetical statement of an historical event which is thus dramatically worked out by Hawthorne in his story of "Endicott and the Red Cross":—

"Endicott gazed round at the excited countenances of the people, now full of his own spirit, and then turned suddenly to the standard-bearer, who stood close behind him.

"'Officer, lower your banner!' said he.

"The officer obeyed; and, brandishing his sword, Endicott thrust it through the cloth, and with his left hand rent the red cross completely out of the banner. He then waved the tattered ensign above his head.

"'Sacrilegious wretch!' cried the High Churchman in the pillory, unable longer to restrain himself, 'thou hast rejected the symbol of our holy religion!'

"'Treason, treason!' roared the royalist in the stocks. 'He hath defaced the King's banner!'

"'Before God and man I will avouch the deed,' answered Endicott. 'Beat a flourish, drummer!— shout, soldiers and people!—in honor of the ensign of New England. Neither Pope nor Tyrant hath part in it now!'

"With a cry of triumph, the people gave their sanction to one of the boldest exploits which our history records."

The poet has also wrought into the texture of his rich tapestry a pretty little picture of old Nicholas Upsall. Amid the hootings of the rabble that followed the joyful Quakers about the streets—

> "One brave voice rose above the din.
> Upsall, gray with his length of days,
> Cried from the door of his Red Lion Inn:
> ' Men of Boston, give God the praise!'"

Upsall was at that time an aged and highly respectable citizen of Boston, a member of the Puritan church. For showing kindness to the Quakers—such as having the spot on the Common where the martyred Quakers were buried surrounded by a fence—he was fined, banished, and, on his return, imprisoned for several years, until the hardships he had endured finally broke down his health. Besse says that the old man, when banished, went to Rhode Island in the winter, where he received hospitality from an Indian chief, who said, if he would stay with him, he would build him a warm home. Said the Indian, "What a god have the English who deal so cruelly with one another about their god!"

Upsall's Red Lion Inn stood on what is now the corner of North and Richmond Streets and near the old Red Lion Wharf, North Street being then the shore-line of the city, and corresponding to the modern Atlantic Avenue. Upsall's granddaughter married one of the Wadsworth ancestors of the poet Longfellow. This Wadsworth was a gunsmith, and his sign may still be seen imbedded in a brick wall on the site of Red Lion Inn.

The " much-scourged Wharton " of the " King's Missive " is Edward Wharton of Salem, the same "aged stranger" who was sheltered by Thomas Macey, as described in Whittier's " Exiles."

"Snow Hill " is the Copp's Hill of later times, and

on it stood the principal windmill of the town. "Centry Hill" is now Beacon Hill.

The jail that held the imprisoned Friends stood on the site of the present Old Court House,—the scene of the attempted rescue of Anthony Burns in anti-slavery times. The "Council Chamber" was in the Town House on the site of the present Old State House.

"The Neck" means the long ligature of land by which the city once "hung to the mainland" at Roxbury: it has now been incorporated into a vast area of "made" land.

Readers of New England poets living in other parts of the country need to be reminded that "walnut" in New England means hickory-nut, and not the dumpling-like nut with the black undivided hull which is known as walnut in the West and South.

CHAPTER VI.

WHILE I have attempted to show that there is a sound historical basis for all the ballads discussed in the preceding chapter, I would not be understood as maintaining that Whittier in his rhymed stories has not taken advantage of poetical license in the working out of details. On the contrary, he has oftener than most poets given pictures discrepant with the bare historical facts. As Lowell sings of him,—

> "Let his mind once get head in its favorite direction,
> And the torrent of verse bursts the dams of reflection,
> While, borne with the rush of the metre along,
> The poet may chance to go right or go wrong,
> Content with the whirl and delirium of song."

But it is the privilege of the *raconteur* to embellish his verse with the flowers of imagination, and the strict accuracy of the historian is not always required of the poet or the painter.

Let no one think that, in giving in the succeeding pages the authentic prose source of Whittier's most interesting idyls and ballads, I am actuated by any impertinent desire to make manifest wherein the poet has or has not followed the precise facts of his text. On the contrary, in glancing behind the

268

scenes at the apparatus by which he has produced his tableaux, the object mainly has been to show how genius can glorify the baldest material and by a skillful *mise en scène* turn it into an immortal work of art.

The scene of Whittier's poem "The Cry of a Lost Soul" is laid in the great tropical forest-belt of South America. The traveler's canoe is floating down the Amazon by night; the lamp burns dimly at the prow; vast submerged forests, intertwined with giant lianas and filled with animal life, stretch wide on either hand; and overhead sparkle the brilliant constellations of the tropics. Suddenly a cry, "as of the pained heart of the wood," startles the gliding dreamers, the half-naked Indian at the oar crosses himself and exclaims, "A lost soul! No, Señor, not a bird. I know it well." But the voyager lifts his eyes to the stars, and lo! "the Cross of pardon lights the tropic skies":—

> "'Father of all!' he urges his strong plea,
> 'Thou lovest all: thy erring child may be
> Lost to himself, but never lost to Thee!'"

I have already stated that this poem was a favorite with the late Emperor of Brazil, who translated it into Portuguese. He also sent to the poet some specimens of the bird whose note suggested the poem. The myth was found by the poet in Lieutenant William L. Herndon's Government Report on the Exploration of the Amazon in 1853 (1st ed., Chap. III.). Says Lieutenant Herndon:—

"After we had retired to our mats beneath the shed for the night, I asked the governor if he knew a bird called La Alma Perdida. He did not know it

by that name, and requested a description. I whistled
an imitation of its notes; whereupon an old crone,
stretched on a mat near us, commenced, with animated tones and gestures, a story in the Inca language, which, translated, ran somehow thus:—

"An Indian and his wife went out from the village
to work their chacra, carrying their infant with them.
The woman went to the spring to get water, leaving
the man in charge of the child, with many cautions
to take good care of it. When she arrived at the
spring, she found it dried up, and went farther to
look for another. The husband, alarmed at her long
absence, left the child and went in search. When
they returned, the child was gone; and to their repeated cries, as they wandered through the woods in
search, they could get no response save the wailing
cry of this little bird heard for the first time, whose
notes their anxious and excited imaginations syl-
labled into pa-pa, ma-ma (the present Quichua name
of the bird). I suppose the Spaniards heard this
story, and, with that religious poetic turn of thought
which seems peculiar to this people, called the bird
' The Lost Soul.'

" The circumstances under which the story was
told," continues Lieutenant Herndon,—" the beautiful, still starlight night, the deep dark forest around,
the faint-red glimmering of the fire, flickering upon
the old woman's gray hair and earnest face as she
poured forth the guttural tones of the language of a
people now passed away,—gave it a sufficiently
romantic interest to an imaginative man."

The dense forests of the tropics are full of mysterious sounds. Sometimes in the midst of deep silence

a piercing yell or scream is heard, and at times the sound of an iron bar struck against a hard hollow tree. The natives turn pale and cross themselves when these unaccountable noises are heard. The songs of many of the birds have a pensive mysterious character. For example, the Goatsucker's startling cry of hopeless sorrow—" Ha, ha, ha, ha!" or the Singhalese Devil Bird's magnificent clear shout, ending in "an appalling cry like that of a boy in torture whose screams are being stopped by strangulation"; or the human-like singing of the Realejo, or Organ Bird; or the sweet minute-tolls of the snow-white Campanero, whose pendulous, feather-covered crest, connected with the palate, is a spiral tube capable of being inflated at pleasure. It is said that any of these weird sounds will fill the soul of the traveler with a strange poetic thrill, at once poignant and awesome.

Mr. Whittier's studies in Norse literature have borne fruit in several ballads, the prettiest of which is his free rendering of Christian Winther's " Henrik and Else " under the title " King Volmer and Elsie." He undoubtedly had his attention drawn to the poem by the somewhat close translation of his friends the Howitts, given in the second volume of their " Literature and Romance of Northern Europe." Whittier knows nothing of Danish (nor, indeed, of any other foreign language,—except that he has a school smattering of French and Latin); and we are therefore to regard " King Volmer and Elsie " as a poetical paraphrase of the Howitts' translation. To see what magical work the genius of a true poet can produce,

compare the following prosaic stanzas by the Howitts with Whittier's poem:—

" ' Nay, nay, my noble Lord!   I speak the truth to you :
    She only loves her Henrik, and to him will be true.
    Pure as the slender lily will she, my Else, prove,
    Though she has fired your bosom with such a flame of love.'

" ' My brave good man, to-morrow it is again a day;
    Then will I woo your daughter and win her as I say.'
    Thus spoke the wily Lord and looked upon the ground.
    The other Lords smiled to themselves as they stood listen-
        ing round.

" When sang the summer lark o'er the town of Vording-
        borough,
    And the weathercock shone golden in the fresh dawn of the
        morrow ;
    When the cool and gentle breeze came wafting o'er the corn,
    Were heard amid the leafy wood the sounds of hound and
        horn.

" Sweet Else sate so calmly her father's door beside,
    All busy at her wheel, and round her blossomed wide
    The tulip and the peony, the box and mint so rare ;
    But the maiden was the fairest of all the flowers there.

" Her fair form was attired in a dark blue woolen gown,
    And the sleeves of snow-white linen unto her wrists came
        down ;
    And busily and rapidly her little foot turned round
    The ever-whirling wheel with its cheerful humming sound.

" The humming-bee flew by, the sun shone bright and warm,
    When she raised her head and shaded the sunshine with her
        arm ;
    A troop of gallant hunters came on with thundering speed,
    Over hill and hollow, and right across the mead.

" Each rider was apparelled in all his best array,
  Yet still was he the fairest who rode the charger gray.
  He glittered like the sun amid that splendid train ;
  She stopped her busy wheel and he checked his charger's rein.

" ' 'Mong roses here thou sittest, thyself a rose so fair,
  Sweet Else, I have loved thee, yet all were unaware.'
  Then bowed that modest maiden, and cast to earth her eye,
  For bashfulness and terror she was about to die."

That last line is much more dramatic and truer to
nature than Whittier's,—

" She dropped a lowly courtesy of bashfulness and fear."

Indeed, it must be admitted that the strong simplicity of the Dane's old-ballad style is considerably
weakened by the diffusive paraphrase of the American, in many stanzas, just as the prose of the " Morte
d'Arthur " is weakened by Tennyson.   The gain,
however, in each case, lies in the increased delicacy
of the limning, to say nothing of the melody,—as, for
example, in the two following stanzas by Whittier:—

" In the garden of her father little Elsie sits and spins,
  And, singing with the early birds, her daily task begins.
  Gay tulips bloom and sweet mint curls around her garden-
      bower,
  But she is sweeter than the mint and fairer than the flower.

" About her form her kirtle blue clings lovingly, and, white
  As snow, her loose sleeves only leave her small round wrists
      in sight ;
  Below the modest petticoat can only half conceal
  The motion of the lightest foot that ever turned a wheel."

The Volmer of the poem is King Valdemar IV.,
  18

surnamed Atterdag. It was a frequent saying of his, *Morgen er atter en Dag*,—" To-morrow is again a day." Valdemar suffered from an unfaithful wife, whom he put away. Other stories of him may be found in Thorpe's " Northern Mythology."

Christian Winther was the son of a clergyman, and himself studied theology. He died in Paris. Schweitzer, in his recent " Geschichte der Altskandinavischen Litteratur," says that Winther "is unique in the beauty and melody of his verse and the tenderness and animation of his diction." His special field was Zealand peasant life in its romantic and idyllic aspects. He is spoken of as " der Sänger der dänischen meerbespülten Inselnatur." He once said that creation was with him purely spontaneous : " I have never striven for a direct object. . . . I consider myself as the passive agent of a higher Power, as an instrument that is played upon by the hands of the Unconscious." Schweitzer translates into German a pretty poem of his describing a summer night's storm :—

> " Kanarienvöglein schläft im Bauer,
>   Es piepst ganz sacht der kleine Wicht,
>   Und nur die Uhr dort an der Mauer
>   Ihr unermüdlich Tik-Tak spricht,
>   Ans Fenster Regengüsse schlagen,
>   Durch Baum und Strauch die Windsbraut fliegt ;
>   Die Blume trinkt mit Wohlbehagen,
>   Und leise sich im Grase wiegt."

The story of the building of a church by the aid of a powerful Troll is wide-spread in Scandinavian countries. The essentials of the narrative followed by Mr. Whittier in his " Kallundborg Church " appear in Thorpe's " Northern Mythology," as follows :—

In the Icelandic version the forfeit is the builder's son. The Troll-wife sings,—

> "Soon will thy father come from Reynir,
>   Bringing a little playmate for thee here."

The farmer-builder runs home and says to his workman, "Well done, friend Finnur! how soon you have finished your work!" The Troll lets fall the plank he is holding, and vanishes.

In Whittier's ballad "The Brown Dwarf of Rügen" he has just hit the plain simplicity of style of the genuine folk-ballads. He took only the main idea from Arndt's *Märchen*, and seems to have relied on memory for the rest, there being little correspondence in the details of the poem and the unusually pretty prose folk-tale. This fills sixty small pages in Arndt, under the title of "The Nine Hills of Rambin." The story goes that these hills were formed by a giant spilling earth out of a rent in his apron, as he was going to bridge over the chasm that separates the Isle of Rügen from the mainland of Pomerania. Under the hills now dwell the brown little earth-men, the Trolls. Johann Dietrich (not Deitrich as Whittier has it), the hero of the tale, is an enterprising peasant lad who goes out at midnight to listen for the Trolls, and secures one of their little caps adorned with a tinkling bell. The loss of his cap by a Troll compels him and all his tribe to serve the finder to the utmost of their power. When Dietrich clapped the cap on his own head, it revealed to him the little men who were before only audible, not visible. By warrant of his cap he becomes master of the hill-folk, is drawn down by them to their realm, through a glass door, by chains fastened to a great silver barrel. He lives in great magnificence there ten years, going to school and learning to dance wondrous well and to make little silver flowers and fruits of exquisite designs. He falls in love with a sweet maiden, Lisbeth, who was stolen away by the Trolls from the same village that he lived in. By the law of the *unterirdische* fellows she, with other children they have stolen, is to stay there fifty years as their servant; but Dietrich one day happens to split a crystal in which is a living toad. The dwarfs abhor a toad so unutterably that they are completely at the mercy of him who holds one near them, and are thrown into convulsions before they even see it. In virtue of the toad-find, the lovers and the other youths get away with several wagonloads of gold and silver treasure, besides the library and rich furniture of Dietrich's room.

" They left the dreadful under-land and passed the gate of
    glass ;
  They felt the sunshine's warm caress, they trod the soft
    green grass."

All march down the mountain in the early morning, and enter in procession the village of Rambin, stared at and followed by the wondering peasants. The story ends with the happy marriage of Dietrich and Lisbeth.

" And for his worth ennobled, and rich beyond compare,
  Count Deitrich and his lovely bride dwelt long and happy
    there."

Probably not one reader in twenty thousand of Whittier's has ever seen his early poem "Moll Pitcher." The two copies which I had the luck to dis-

cover had evidently lain undisturbed for fifty-seven
years. The poem is by no means worthless, although
it is not worth reprinting as a whole. It is in part
suffused with a delicate poetical glow which later was
to burst into the fierce flame of the poems of freedom.
The motto is from old Cornelius Agrippa, the German
astrologer : "If the seeker be of an haute and stom-
achful carriage, and maketh merrie of the wisdom of
thine art, thou mayest gain an empery over his orgu-
lous and misbelieving spirit, by some full strange and
terrible misterie, or cunning device, whereat he may
be amort with doleful misgivings." Whittier remarks
in a prefatory note that the poem "is the offspring of
a few weeks of such leisure as is afforded by indisposition, and is given to the world in all its original
negligence." He playfully says that it is not published for poetical reputation nor for money, and
thinks it would puzzle the French cook who made
fifty different dishes out of a parsnip to make meat or
drink out of a poetical reputation. He changed
his mind later in life ; when, for example, Robert
Bonner's Sons sent him a cheque for $1,000 for his
little ballad "The Captain's Well," published in the
"Ledger" in 1890.

The Moll Pitcher of the poem must not be con-
founded with the gunner Moll of Revolutionary fame.
The two were contemporary ; the fortune-teller of
Nahant died in 1813. Whittier's sketch of her is a
piece of pure fancy and bears very little resemblance
to the reality. She was no withered and malignant
hag, but a kind, humane woman, of striking presence
and intellectual features, and of respectable family.
She had married a poor man, and adopted fortune-

telling for the purpose of supporting her son and three daughters, and through her exertions they were enabled to make good marriages. Among her descendants are some of the handsomest women in Lynn. Her fame as a fortune-teller spread all over the globe wherever an American ship sailed. The well-worn path up the rocks to her cottage was trod by the feet of sailors, merchants, lovers, adventurers of every sort, and people in search of lost or stolen goods. Upham, in his Lectures on Witchcraft, says that she was " the most celebrated fortune-teller, perhaps, that ever lived," and it is thought that her predictions influenced the destinies of thousands of persons. In her day many a vessel was known to lie idly at the wharf for weeks, deserted of its superstitious crew in consequence of her adverse predictions. "An air of romance is breathed around the scenes where she practised her mystic art, the charm of which will increase as the lapse of time removes her history back toward the dimness of the distant past. Her name has everywhere become the generic title of fortune-tellers, and occupies a conspicuous place in the legends and ballads of popular superstition."

Mary Pitcher's maiden name was Dimond. Her father was captain of a small sailing-vessel of Marblehead. She inherited her gifts of clairvoyance and fortune-telling from her grandfather, who, the legend goes, used to pace up and down in the churchyard during violent storms and direct the course of ships attempting to make the harbor. His voice was always audible to the crew, no matter how far off they might be.[1]

---

[1] Hobbs's " Lynn and its Surroundings," 1886.

For fifty years the " witch of Nahant " (so called) dwelt in her little cottage under the shadow of High Rock, on what was then a lonely road, but is now Pearl Street in a thickly inhabited part of the city. The house still stands, the prospect is a fine one, embracing a view of rocky Marblehead, the beaches of Chelsea and Nahant, and " the islands sleeping like green-winged sea-birds in the distant bay of Boston." Over the gateway of the house opposite hers, in her lifetime, were the jaw-bones of a whale, forming a Gothic arch, and sea-faring strangers who wished to consult her were often heard furtively inquiring the way to the big whalebones.

Whittier's portrait of Moll Pitcher was painted in the land of dream :—

> " She stood upon a bare, tall crag
>   Which overlooked her rugged cot—
>   A wasted, gray and meagre hag,
>   In features evil as her lot.
>   She had the crooked nose of a witch,
>   And a crooked back and chin ;
>   And in her gait she had a hitch,
>   And in her hand she carried a switch
>   To aid her work of sin,—
>   A twig of wizard hazel, which
>   Had grown beside a haunted ditch."

The notes to his poem show that he had only read Upham's two pages about the fortune-teller. The true portrait lay ready to his hand in Lewis's History of Lynn (1817), and would have furnished a richer material to the flame of that ardent young fancy of his. Moll Pitcher was of medium height (says Lewis, who knew her), good form, and agreeable manners, her forehead broad and full, hair dark brown, nose inclining to long, face pale and thin and rather intellectual. "She had that contour of face and expression which, without being positively beautiful, is nevertheless decidedly interesting,— a thoughtful, pensive, and sometimes downcast look, almost approaching to melancholy—an eye, when it looked at you, of calm and keen penetration—and an expression of intelligent discernment, half mingled with a glance of shrewdness." Mrs. Pitcher was of a benevolent disposition, as I have said, and she was once known to rise before day and walk two miles to a mill to get a destitute woman meal for her breakfast.

As to the source of her power, it clearly lay in her canny native shrewdness in reading character and in that indescribable mind-reading or soul-piercing faculty called genius which she possessed. She would usually, or always, enter into conversation with her visitors, and, having got her clew, make her prediction. Her visible apparatus of divination—a cup into which she poured tea or coffee, for the purpose of seeing how the dregs arranged themselves— was of course only a simulated assistance, a sop to the credulous.

The legend of Whittier's poem is of a maiden whose sailor lover had gone on a long voyage in order to get rich and come back and marry her. In his absence her mind becomes filled with gloomy forebodings, and she goes up the rocky path to the witch's cottage to consult her. Now the hag cherishes a secret enmity against her, and determines to have her revenge. The poem opens in a curious way:—

" Ha, ha—ha, ha—ha, ha !—
  The old witch laughed outright—
Ha, ha—ha, ha—ha, ha !—
  That cold and dismal night
The wind was blowing from the sea
As raw and chill as wind might be,—
Driving the waves, as if their master,
Towards the black shore, fast and faster,—
Tossing their foam against the rocks
  Which scowl along yon island's verge,
And shake their gray and mossy locks
  Secure above the warring surge.

" Keen blew the wind, and cold,
  The moon shone dim and faintly forth.

 * * * * * *

And now and then a wan star burned,
Where'er its cloudy veil was rended—
A moment's light, but seen and ended,
As if some angel from on high
Had fixed on earth his brilliant eye,
And back to heaven his glances turned! "

The maiden meets the fortune-teller on the path to
her house.

" The twain passed in—a low dark room,
  With here and there a crazy chair,
A broken glass—a dusty loom—
A spinning-wheel, a birchen broom,
  The witch's courier of the air,
As potent as that steed of wings
  On which the Meccan prophet rode
Above the wreck of meaner things
  Unto the Houris' bright abode.
A low dull fire by flashes shone
Across the gray and cold hearthstone,

Flinging at times a trembling glare
On the low roof and timbers bare.

* * * * *

    " In contrast strange,
Within the fire-light's fading range
The stranger stands in maiden pride,
By that mysterious woman's side.
The cloak hath fallen from her shoulder,
  Revealing such a form as steals
Away the heart of the beholder
  As, all unconsciously, it kneels
Before the beauty which had shone
Ere this upon its dreams alone.
If you have seen a summer star,
Liquidly soft and faintly far,
Beaming a smiling glance on earth
As if it watched the flowret's birth,
Then have you seen a light less fair
Than that young maiden's glances were.
Dark fell her tresses. You have seen
  A rent cloud tossing in the air,
And showing the pure sky between
  Its floating fragments here and there:
Then may you fancy faintly how
The falling tress, the ringlike curl,
Disclosed or shadowed o'er the brow
  And neck of that fair girl.
Her cheek was delicately thin,
  And through its pure transparent white
The rose-hue wandered out and in,
  As you have seen th' inconstant light
  Flush o'er the Northern sky of night.
Her playful lip was gently full,
  Soft curving to the graceful chin,
And colored like the fruit which glows
Upon the sunned pomegranate boughs;

And, oh, her soft-low voice might lull
　　The spirit to a dream of bliss,
As if the voices sweet and bland
Which murmur in the seraph-land
　　Were warbling in a world like this!

" Out spoke the witch : ' I know full well
　　Why thou hast sought my humble cot.
Come, sit thee down : the tale I tell
　　May not be soon forgot.'
She threw her pale blue cloak aside,
　　And stirred the whitening embers up,
And long and curiously she eyed
　　The figures of her mystic cup ;
And low she muttered, while the light
Gave to her lips a ghastlier white,
And her sunk eye's unearthly glaring
Seemed like the taper's latest flaring :
' Dark hair—eyes black—a goodly form—
　　A maiden weeping—wild dark sea—
A tall ship tossing in the storm—
　　A black wreck floating—*where is he?*
Give me thy hand : how soft and warm
　　And fair its tapering fingers seem !
　　And who that sees it now would dream
That winter's snow would seem less chill
Erelong than these soft fingers will ?
A lovely palm, how delicate
　　Its veined and wandering lines are drawn !
Yet each are prophets of thy fate,—
　　Ha ! this is sure a fearful one !
That sudden cross—that blank beneath,—
　　What may these evil signs betoken ?
Passion and sorrow, fear and death,—
　　A human spirit crushed and broken !
Oh, thine hath been a pleasant dream,
But darker shall its waking seem ! ' "

The words of the fortune-teller were like the icy hand of death upon the maiden's heart:—

> "Like the mimosa shrinking from
>   The blight of some familiar finger—
> Like flowers which but in secret bloom,
>   Where aye the sheltering shadows linger,
> And which beneath the hot noon ray
> Would fold their leaves and fade away,—
> The flowers of Love, in secret cherished,
> In loneliness and silence nourished,
>   Shrink backward from the searching eye,
> Until the stem whereon they flourished,
> Their shrine, the human heart, has perished,
> Although themselves may never die."

The girl becomes mildly insane, and is always standing on the rocky headland of Nahant watching for the ship of her lover. One day it comes sailing into the bay, with the beloved one aboard. At first she does not recognize him, but gradually her reason returns. After many years the witch dies miserably in her hut, attended in her last illness by the daughter of the woman she once so deeply wronged.

The opening lines of Part Two are certainly finer than many a poem which the poet has retained in his works:—

> "Nahant, thy beach is beautiful!—
>   A dim line through the tossing waves,
> Along whose verge the spectre gull
>   Her thin and snowy plumage laves,
> What time the summer's greenness lingers
>   Within thy sunned and sheltered nooks,
> And the green vine with twining fingers
>   Creeps up and down thy hanging rocks.

.

<blockquote>
Around, the blue and level main;
　Above, a sunshine rich as fell
Brightening of old with golden rain
　The isle Apollo loved so well;—
And far off, dim and beautiful,
The snow-white sail and graceful hull,
　Slow dipping to the billow's swell.
Bright spot! the Isles of Greece may share
A flowery earth, a gentle air;
The orange-bough may blossom well
In warm Bermuda's sunniest dell;
But fairer shores and brighter waters,
Gazed on by purer, lovelier daughters,
　Beneath the light of kindlier skies,
The wanderer to the farthest bound
Of peopled earth hath never found
　Than thine,—New England's Paradise!
Land of the forest and the rock,—
　Of dark blue lake and mighty river,—
'Of mountains reared aloft to mock
The storm's career, the lightning's shock,—
　My own green land forever!"
</blockquote>

Of the sailor it is said in Part Three,—

<blockquote>
"Oh, he hath been a wanderer
　Beneath Magellan's moveless cloud,
　And where in murmurs hoarse and loud
The Demon of the Cape was heard;
And where the tropic sunset came
O'er the rich bowers of Indostan,
And many a strange and brilliant bird
　Shone brighter in the western flame."
</blockquote>

The last lines recall Tennyson's sumptuous imagery
in the apostrophe to Milton, which everyone ought to
have by heart :—

> " Me rather all that bowery loneliness,
>   The brooks of Eden mazily murmuring,
>   And bloom profuse and cedar arches
>   Charm, as a wanderer out in ocean,
>   Where some refulgent sunset of India
>   Streams o'er a rich ambrosial ocean isle,
>   And crimson-hued the stately palm-woods
>   Whisper in odorous heights of even."

The idea of Whittier's "Cassandra Southwick" is worked out also by Longfellow in his "New England Tragedies," his Edith Christison corresponding to Whittier's heroine.

Whittier, as usual, has availed himself of poetic license. His imprisoned Quaker maiden sees the sunset melt through the prison bars, and across the floor of her cell falls the quiet light of the stars. Sleepless she watches, thinking of her schoolmates, sitting by the warm bright hearth of home,—

> " How the crimson shadows tremble on foreheads white and
>   fair,
>   On eyes of merry girlhood half hid in golden hair."

With the breaking of the morn, the heavy bolts fall back, and the sheriff comes and leads her down to the wharves, where dark and haughty Endicott, and Rawson, his cruel clerk, ask the sea-captains who of them will take her away to sell. Grim silence from the bronzed seamen; she feels the hard hand of one of them press her own; and a word of encouragement is whispered in her ear.

> " And when again the sheriff spoke, that voice, so kind to me,
>   Growled back its stormy answer like the roaring of the sea,—

"'Pile my ship with bars of silver, pack with coins of Span-
    ish gold,
From keel-piece up to deck-plank the roomage of her hold,—
By the living God who made me, I would sooner in your bay
Sink ship and crew and cargo than bear this child away!'

    *   *   *   *   *   *

"I looked on haughty Endicott, with weapon half-way drawn;
Swept round the throng his lion glare of bitter hate and
    scorn;
Fiercely he drew his bridle-rein, and turned in silence back,
And sneering priest and baffled clerk rode murmuring in his
    track."

Whittier found the quarry for his poem in the books
of George Bishop and Joseph Besse. Bishop's book,
having been published fifty years earlier than Besse's,
may be considered the more trustworthy. With a
poet's true instinct Whittier has chosen the musical
name of Cassandra for his heroine. But in reality it
was Cassandra Southwick's daughter "Provided"
and her son Daniel who were offered for sale. She
herself, with her husband Lawrence, had already
been banished to Shelter Island, and another son
exiled to Europe. Lawrence and Cassandra, "an
aged grave couple" of Salem, cultivators of the soil,
had previously been imprisoned for entertaining two
Quaker preachers. The husband, wife, and son were
stripped in the coldest season of the year and whipped
with a knotted thong of three cords that cruelly cut
their flesh, "the executioner measuring his ground,
and fetching his strokes with all his strength." At
another time they were imprisoned in a dark un-
ventilated room during all of harvest time, when their
crops were suffering.

"And now," says Bishop, "I shall declare the execution of your warrant on the said Daniel Southwick and Provided, whom Edmund Batter (a cruel wicked man, one fit for your purpose) sent your marshall for, who fetch'd them accordingly, and sought out for passage to Barbadoes, to send them there for sale, as men sell goods, to fill his purse, who was your treasurer ; but the man to whom he spake would not carry them on that account (a thing so horrible !), and one of them, to try Batter, said 'that they would spoil all the vessel's company,' laying that as an argument why he should not carry them. 'Oh, no,' said Batter, 'you need not fear that, for they are poor harmless creatures, and will not hurt anybody' (or words to this purpose). 'Will they not so ?' said the ship-master. 'And will ye offer to make slaves of so harmless creatures?' So Batter sent them home again . . . till he could get a convenient opportunity to send them away."

Another of Mr. Whittier's ballads on Quaker subjects is "The Exiles." It is very interesting to see how, out of a mere word of history and a bit of manuscript, he has built up so long and capital a poem. Thomas Macey was far from being the brave man he is represented to be in the verses, as the following from his humble and deprecatory letter to the General Court proves:—

"On a rainy morning there came to my house Edward Wharton and three men more. The said Wharton spoke to me, saying that they were traveling eastward, and desired me to direct them in the way to Hampton, and asked me how far it was to Casco

Bay. I never saw any of ye men afore except Wharton, neither did I require their names, or who they were, but by their carriage I thought they might be Quakers, and told them so, and therefore desired them to passe on their way, saying to them I might possibly give offence in entertaining them; and as soone as the violence of the rain ceased (for it rained very hard) they went away, and I never saw them since. The time that they stayed in the house was about three-quarters of an hour, but I can safely affirme it was not an hour. They spake not many words in the time, neither was I at leisure to talke with them, for I came home wet to the skin immediately afore they came to the house, and I found my wife sick in bed."

Two of the friends harbored by Macey that day were Robinson and Stevenson, afterwards hanged on Boston Common. The antiquaries all say that Macey did not fly from direct persecution. The records of Salisbury and of the State only show that he sailed to Nantucket in an open boat, with his family and two friends, not to escape the paltry fine of thirty shillings and his admonishment, but at his leisure, in disgust at the intolerance of the Puritan leaders. Whittier, in a note to his "Exiles" in the "North Star" anthology, says that "a quaint description of Macey's singular and perilous voyage, in his own handwriting, is still preserved." It is said that during the voyage a storm arose, and Macey said to his terrified wife, "Woman, I fear not the witches on earth, nor the devils in hell." His place of refuge was Nantucket Island, nurse of great women and brave men, the birthplace of Lucretia Mott, Maria Mitchell, and the mother of Benjamin Franklin. The island had been bought as a place of refuge in 1659 by ten men, among whom were Whittier's remote kinsmen, Christopher Hussey and Stephen "Greenleafe." There were no other white men on the island when they came.[1]

"She came and stood in the Old South Church,
    A wonder and a sign,
With a look the old-time sibyls wore,
    Half-crazed and half-divine.

Save the mournful sackcloth about her wound,
    Unclothed as the primal mother,
With limbs that trembled and eyes that burned
    With a fire she dared not smother."

In the poem of which the foregoing are the two opening stanzas, Mr. Whittier has, with the freedom permitted to a poet, wrenched the actual facts for a dramatic end. He makes it appear that the cause of his heroine's appearing in the Old South Church clothed in sackcloth was to exhort preacher and people to religious toleration. But the original accounts in Besse, including the warrant for her arrest and the verbatim report of the trial, prove that her object on that occasion was simply to warn the people of the coming of the black-pox. But as she had addressed a petition to the Governor that he would not put in force the "cruel laws" that required oath-taking

---

[1] Mr. Whittier refers his readers to James S. Pike's book on this incident of Macey. But Pike is only a borrower, and is not so good as S. J. Macy in his "Genealogy of the Macy Family," 1868, and Hough, "Nantucket Papers" (Albany, 1856).

even from Quakers, and since during her trial she incidentally besought him not to persecute the Friends for meeting together to worship God after their own way, the poet was justified in slightly changing the facts for artistic ends, so as to make the central idea that of a plea for religious toleration. The name of the woman was Margaret Brewster. She had come to Boston from the Barbadoes, perhaps to collect money due her,—and hence her trouble of mind about the oath-taking. Her appearance so amazed and frightened the congregation that it was said several women were in danger of miscarrying. She was kept in prison for a month, and then stripped to the middle, tied to a cart's tail, and whipped up and down the town, all of which she endured with a fortitude worthy of a better cause. Her fanatical folly was, however, well matched by the unmanly cruelty of the Governor's sentence.

Old Judge Sewall in his Diary (i. 43) makes a minute of the scene in the church :—

"July 8, 1677. New Meeting House [not the present Old South, but its predecessor] *Mane :* In Sermon time there came in a female Quaker, in a Canvass Frock, her hair disshevelled and loose like a Periwigg, her face as black as ink, led by two other Quakers, and two other followed. It occasioned the greatest and most amazing uproar that I ever saw. Isaiah i. 12, 14."

The venerable ex-magistrate William Coddington wrote to a friend in the Barbadoes as follows :—

RALPH FRETWELL!

Friend,

I have written to thee already concerning the apprehending

of Margaret Brewster, and committing her to prison, upon her going into Thatcher's meeting in sackcloth, with ashes upon her head, and barefoot, and her face blacked. With her was Lydia Wright of Long Island, and Sarah Miles and Elizabeth Bowers, jun., and John Easton, jun., who took her riding-clothes and shoes when she went into the house.

At the trial the Governor says,—

"Are you the woman that came into Mr. Thatcher's meeting-house with your hair fruzled, and dressed in the shape of a devil?"

She replies,—

" I am the woman that came into priest Thatcher's house of worship with my hair about my shoulders, ashes upon my head, my face colored black, and sackcloth upon my upper garments."

Another poem commemorating a brave fight for religious freedom is "Calef in Boston: 1692." Robert Calef, merchant of Boston, was the author of "More Wonders of the Invisible World," published to counter-act the influence of Cotton Mather's "Wonders of the Invisible World," and especially his "Brand Pluckt from the Burning." The incident that brought the two men to a clash of arms was the case of Margaret Rule, a young girl supposed to have been bewitched, whose experiences are detailed in Mather's "Brand Pluckt from the Burning." That credulous old prodigy of learning says in this booklet that "the devils have with most horrendous operations broke in upon our neighborhood." Margaret he affirms to have been "most prodigiously handled by the evil angels." The enchantments she endured were such as being stuck with invisible pins, pinched black and blue, made to swallow brimstone by the devils, and

drawn up by them to the garret ceiling with such
violence that she could scarcely be drawn down
again by a strong man. She described herself as
being haunted by eight demons led on by a black
Master. Whittier's words, " Your spectral puppet-
play," refer to the pranks of these demons, who would
stand at one side of the room and stick pins into
puppets, or dolls, that she might feel the pain in her
own flesh. And when they were not able to stick the
pins into the " Poppets " she would deride them, whereupon their black Master, in a rage, would strike them
and kick them, " like an overseer of so many negro's,
to make them to do their work."[1] The superstition
that persons could be made to suffer by proxy is an
old one. In his " Wonders," Mather tells of the con-
sternation of some workmen when they discovered,
in holes in the cellar wall of a house belonging to a
reputed witch, certain " poppets " made up of rags
and hogs' bristles, with headless pins in them, the
points being outward. The delusion is common
among our Southern negroes at the present day.
They make a waxen or dough image of their enemy,
and then pierce it with pins or burn it. To find on
his door-sill, says Cable, a little box containing a
wax heart stuck full of pins, will strike terror to the
heart of a Louisiana negro.

Calef was a man much in advance of his time,—
brave, clear-headed, and liberal. A fac-simile of his
vigorous signature is given in Drake's History of
Boston, p. 568. He was one of those who were bold

---

[1] Calef's work, original ed., 1700, p. 9. Other editions, as Mr.
Deane has shown, are very inaccurate.

enough to brave public opinion by having his children inoculated for the small-pox. He pressed the Mathers hard, arraigned their methods of extracting information from Margaret Rule, and was even arrested for libel by them ; but no prosecutor appeared, and he was released. His book was burned in the college yard at Cambridge by President Increase Mather.

It appears from Cotton Mather's "Brand" that Calef was not the only incredulous person in Boston. "The learned witlings of the coffee-houses" are sarcastically described by Mather, who says that, if anyone would but read one or two little books he names, he or she could "give a far more intelligible account of these appearances than most of these blades can give why and how their tobacco makes 'em spit ; or which way the flame of their candle becomes illuminating."

It seems to be an indispensable condition of poetical inspiration with Whittier, in writing a ballad, that his legend, or story, shall first have been read or heard by him, and then laid away in his mind. When it lies dim and somewhat vague in his memory, it assumes the hues of romance ; and at some happy moment, perhaps after the lapse of years, the finished poem is detached, like a ripened pear from its bough. It may be historically accurate or it may not: as it comes, so it must be; he is only the scribe to write down what his genius dictates.

Yet it must not be thought that all, or perhaps any, of the poems of the Essex minstrel have been at once transferred from the mind to the paper in their final shape. Many of his poems were first conceived in the open air, and jotted down in rough state on such paper as he might have in his pocket-book. Mr. Charles E. Hurd, assistant editor of the Boston "Transcript," has the original MS. of Whittier's "My Playmate." It is written, with many erasures and interlineations, on three sides of an old letter.

Whittier's portrait of the Puritan Indian fighter, John Underhill, in the poem of that name, is considerably idealized. The real man bears more resemblance to Captain Dalgetty, in the "Legend of Montrose," than to the frail soldier-saint pictured by our poet. Underhill was banished from the Massachusetts Colony for making slighting remarks about the authorities. Some two years before this sentence of banishment, he had been publicly questioned and admonished on suspicion of incontinency with a neighbor's wife.

Underhill retired to the Cocheco settlement in Maine, where he was made governor. After his departure from Boston, proof of his adultery was discovered, and he was summoned to appear and stand his trial. He parleyed and quibbled and hesitated a long time, but finally appeared one day in 1640, and after sermon, upon the lecture day, the pastor of the church gave him leave to speak. The scene that followed is both amusing and dramatic. It was a spectacle that caused many weeping eyes. His penitence seemed to be sincere; but the piercing eye of Winthrop detected its superficial nature, notwithstanding his "blubbering" and sobbing.

"He came," says Winthrop, "in his worst clothes (being accustomed to take great pride in his bravery and neatness), without a band, in a foul linen cap pulled close to his eyes; and, standing upon a form, he did with many deep sighs and abundance of tears lay open his wicked course." [1]

This scene of repentance is by Whittier laid at Cocheco. Underhill afterwards took service with the Dutch. The Mantinenoc Indians gave him a hundred and fifty acres of land on Long Island, which is still in the possession of his descendants.

Out of the following bit of bare prose in Mather's "Magnalia Christi" Whittier has constructed his ballad, so rich in picturesque incident, "The Garrison of Cape Ann" :—

"Now, in the time of that matchless war [made by "the spirits of the invisible world upon the people of New England "] there fell out a thing at Gloucester which falls in here most properly to be related.

"Ebenezer Bapson, about midsummer, in the year 1692, with the rest of his family, almost every night heard a noise as if persons were going and running about his house. But one night being abroad late, at his return home he saw two men come out of his door, and run from the end of the house into the corn. But those of the family told him, there had been no person at all there ; whereupon he got his gun, and went out in pursuit after them, and coming a little distance from the house, he saw the two men start up from behind a log, and run into a little swamp, saying to each other, *The man of the house is come now, else we might have taken the house.* So he heard nor saw no more of them.

---

[1] Winthrop's History of Massachusetts, ii. 13.

"Upon this the whole family got up, and went with all speed to a garrison near by ; and being just got into the garrison, they heard men stamping round the garrison. Whereupon Bapson took a gun and ran out and saw two men again running down a hill into a swamp. The next night, but one, the said Bapson, going toward a fresh meadow, saw two men which looked like Frenchmen, one of them having a bright gun upon his back, and both running a great pace towards him, which caused him to make the best of his way to the garrison, where being come, several heard a noise as if men were stamping and running not far from the garrison." [1]

After a great deal of shooting, and running, and missing fire, both on the part of the beleaguered and the besiegers, the men of the garrison-house, "concluding they were but spectres," took little further notice of them.

The story of "The Swan Song of Parson Avery," as related by Whittier with his usual latitude, is told by the Rev. Anthony Thacher in a letter given in Increase Mather's "Essay for the Recording of Illustrious Providences." The persons shipwrecked were in all twenty-three souls,—the two families of the ministers, a passenger, and four sailors. The island upon which their pinnace went to pieces is off Cape Ann and the town of Rockport. It is now a United States lighthouse station, containing about eighty acres of rocky soil. It is a pretty trip to visit the lighthouses, as the writer did recently. You hoist a signal on the

---

[1] First edition, 1702, p. 82.

mainland, and one of the keepers will sail or row over from the island and take you across. The view is magnificent. The storm in which the ship was wrecked was of terrible force, overturning houses, tearing up and twisting off thousands of trees, and nearly ruining the harvest.

There was in reality no dying song by Parson Avery, but a deal of praying and pious discourse back and forth betwixt the poor man and his cousin.

The letter of Thacher is a classic in its kind, and a few extracts will be appreciated. The style is pure Greek, and is worthy of Defoe.

" I must turn my drowned pen and shaking hand," says he, " to indite the story of such sad news as never before this happened in New England. There was a league of perpetual friendship between my cousin Avery [" note," says Mather, " that this Mr. Avery was a precious holy minister, who came out of England with Mr. Anthony Thacher "] and myself never to forsake each other to the death, but to be partakers of each other's misery or welfare, as also of habitation in the same place." They were solicited to go to Marblehead to become the pastors of the place, and accordingly set sail from Ipswich, with their families and substance, in a pinnace. They had rough weather and were two days in getting around Cape Ann, when suddenly in a fresh gale their sails, " being old and done," were split. The anchor slipped, the storm burst upon them, the ship was beaten to pieces, and about daylight all were drowned except Thacher and his wife, who were washed ashore. The good man, after narrating all these woes, continues: " I and my wife were almost naked, both of us, and wet and cold, even unto death. I found a knapsack cast on the shore, in which I had a steel and flint and powder-horn. Going further I found a drowned goat, then I found a hat, and my son William's coat, both which I put on. My wife found one of her petticoats, which she put on. I found also two cheeses and some butter, driven ashore. Thus the Lord sent us some clothes to put on, and food to sustain our new lives which he had lately given unto us; and means also to make fire, for in an horn I had some gunpowder, which to my own (and since to other men's) admiration was dry; so taking a piece of my wife's neckcloth, which I dried in the sun, I struck fire, and so dried and warmed our wet bodies, and then skinned the goat; and having found a small brass pot, we boiled some of her. Our drink was brackish water; bread we had none. There we remained until the Monday following [three days in all]. When about three of the clock, in the afternoon, in a boat that came that way, we went off that desolate island, which I named after my name, Thacher's Woe; and the rock [on which the vessel split] Avery his Fall: to the end that their fall and loss and mine own might be had in perpetual remembrance. In the isle lieth buried the body of my cousin's eldest daughter, whom I found dead on the shore."

Winthrop in his Journal says, "The general court gave Mr. Thatcher £26: 13: 4: towards his losses, and divers good people gave him besides. The man was cast on shore when he had been (as he supposed) a quarter of an hour beaten up and down by the waves, not being able to swim one stroke, and his wife sitting in the scuttle of the bark, the deck was broke off and brought on shore as she stuck in it."

In reading for the sources of this poem, I discovered that Whittier got its title out of Cotton Mather's "Magnalia Christi" (I. ii. 3). Speaking of Avery's prayer, Mather quotes a line—

"Carmina jam Moriens, Canit exequialia Cygnus"—

which had been found in the chair of a Dr. Hottinger eight days before he was drowned (in Lake Leman, Switzerland). This Latin line about the song of the dying swan Mather applies to Avery : " Never forget the memorable *swan-song* which *Avery*, not *eight days*, but scarce eight seconds of a minute, before his expiration, sang in the ears of heaven."

On July 6, 1724, Rev Christopher Tappan, of Newbury, wrote to Cotton Mather the account of a double-headed snake, or Amphisbæna, from which, as given in Joshua Coffin's History of Newbury, Whittier got the materials for his ballad "The Double-headed Snake of Newbury." Coffin copied it from the original now in the library of the American Antiquarian Society at Worcester, and it is found nowhere else in the literature of the time:—

" Concerning the amphisbæna, as soon as I received your commands I made diligent enquiry of several persons, who saw it after it was dead, but they could give me no assurance of its having two heads, as they did not strictly examine it, not calling it the least in question because it seemed as really to have two heads as one. They directed me for further information to the person I before spoke of, who was out of town, and to the persons who saw it alive and killed it, which were two or three lads, about twelve or fourteen, one of which a pert sensible youngster told me yt one of his mates running towards him cryed out there was a shake with two heads running after him, upon which he run to him, and the snake, getting into a puddle of water, he with a stick pulled him out, after which it came towards him, and as he went backwards or forward, soe the snake would doe likewise. After a little time, the snake, upon his striking at him, gathered up his whole body into sort of a quoil, except *both heads*, which kept towards him, and he distinctly saw *two mouths* and two *stings* (as they are vulgarly called), which stings or tongues it kept putting forth after the usual manner of snakes, till he killed it. Thus far the lad. This day, understanding the person mentioned before was returned, I went to him, and asked him about the premises. He told me he narrowly examined the snake, being brought to him by the lads after it was dead, and he found two distinct heads, *one at each end*, opening each with a little stick, in each of which he saw a sting or tongue, and that each head had two eyes. Throwing it down and going away, upon second thoughts he began to mistrust his own eyes, as to what he had seen, and therefore returned a second time to examine it, if possible, more strictly, but still found it as before. This person is so credible that I can as much believe him as if I had seen him myself. He tells me of another man yt examined it as he did, but I cannot yet meet with him.

"*Postscript.* Before ensealing I spoke with the

other man, who examined the amphisbæna (and he is also a man of credit), and he assures me yt it had really two heads, one at each end, two mouths, two stings or tongues, and so forth."

> " Far and wide the tale was told,
> Like a snowball growing while it rolled.
> The nurse hushed with it the baby's cry;
> And it served, in the worthy minister's eye,
> To paint the primitive serpent by.
> Cotton Mather came galloping down
> All the way to Newbury town,
> With his eyes agog and his ears set wide,
> And his marvellous inkhorn at his side;
> Stirring the while in the shallow pool
> Of his brains for the lore he learned at school,
> To garnish the story, with here a streak
> Of Latin, and there another of Greek:
> And the tales he heard and the notes he took,
> Behold! are they not in his Wonder-Book?"

The last two lines seem to imply that the story of the snake can be found in the Wonder-Book. But you will search in vain for it there. There is no galloping down to Newbury in that book; but there are rich "tales,"—such as that of the black creature with the body of a monkey, the feet of a cock, and the face of a man, which was going to fly at a certain man, and when he cried out, "The whole armour of God be between me and you," it "sprang back, and flew over the apple-tree; shaking many apples off the tree in its flying over. At its leap, it flung dirt with its feet against the stomach of the man."

There is a snake (really a lizard) which is called the Amphisbæna, but is found only in tropical America. It actually has the habit of moving backward or forward at pleasure. The tail is thick and short, and the eyes of the head so small (it lives mostly under ground) that it is almost impossible to tell head from tail. The story of the Newbury Amphisbæna is as well attested as anything can be, and we may suppose the creature to have been a monstrosity of the true snake species, like the two-headed chickens, calves, etc., which occasionally occur.

In the "Tent on the Beach" the locality is the mouth of Hampton River at the northern extremity of Salisbury Sands. The scene of two of the ballads sung in the tent of the three friends is also here ; namely, "The Changeling" and "The Wreck of Rivermouth." In the latter poem, "the grisly head of the Boar," "the green bluff" breaking the chain of sand-hills northward, refers to the wind-swept and treeless headland known as the Boar's Head. It is a heap of gravel-drift with bowlders sticking in the sides. "A low reef, stretching out towards the southeast, resembling the broken vertebræ of some fabled sea-monster," says Drake, "shows in what direction the grand old headland has most suffered from the unremitting work of demolition carried on by the waves, which pour and break like an avalanche over the blackened bowlders, and fly hissing into the air like the dust rising from its ruins."

> "And Agamenticus lifts its blue
> Disk of a cloud the woodlands o'er."

Mount Agamenticus is a bold landmark for sixty

miles or more up and down the Atlantic coast. The mountain rears its huge form almost at the edge of the sea in Maine. On its summit is said to be buried Saint Aspenquid, a converted Indian, who, according to tradition, had wandered all over the continent preaching the gospel of Christ. Lowell paints Agamenticus in his " Pictures from Appledore ":—

> " He glowers there to the north of us,
> Wrapt in his mantle of blue haze,
>
> *   *   *   *   *
>
> Him first on shore the coaster divines
> Through the early gray, and sees him shake
> The morning mist from his scalp-lock of pines."

The wedge of the Boar's Head, as I saw it in 1890, was a superb earth-poem, its level surface covered with grass and flowers, the green lines of the sod merging into the blue of the sky,—not a discord anywhere. To the south, a mile away, are always seen the Rivermouth Rocks, black and grisly in their garments of sea-weed.

The Goody Cole who figures in " The Changeling " and in " The Wreck of Rivermouth " was Eunice Cole of Hampton, New Hampshire, who lived alone in a little hovel near where the Hampton Academy now stands. Once when she was imprisoned the Court ordered a padlocked chain to be attached to her leg. She died alone in her cottage, and it was some days before her death was known; whereupon she was hastily buried, and a stake driven through her poor body to exorcise the evil spirit. She was as much feared as was old Susanna Martin, alluded to in " The Witch's Daughter." Goody Martin lived

20

near the Old Ferry in Pleasant Valley on the Merrimack.

Goody Cole was first prosecuted in 1656; in 1657 occurred the catastrophe described in "The Wreck of Rivermouth." Whittier puts the two things together, imagines the shipwreck to have been attributed to the witch, and makes a ballad which for choice English, perfect melody, and native savor can scarcely be surpassed. The prose text of the story is merely this dry paragraph, referred to by the poet in the "Atlantic Monthly," where the poem first appeared:—

"A boate going out of Hampton River was cast away and the psons all drowned who were in number eight: Em. Hilliar, Jon. Philbrick and An Philbrick his wife; Sarah Philbrick there daughter; Alice the wyfe of Moses Cox, and John Cox his sonne, Robert Read; who all perished in ye sea ye 20th of the 8 mo. 1657."[1]

The convent song of sister Maria in Whittier's "Hymn of the Dunkers"—

"Wake, sisters, wake! the day-star shines;
  Above Ephrata's eastern pines
  The dawn is breaking, cool and calm.
  Wake, sisters, wake to prayer and psalm!"—

somehow recalls that little snow-tinted poem, Tennyson's "St. Agnes,"—

---

[1] From the "Norfolk County Records," quoted in vol. i., No. 2, of the "New England Historical and Genealogical Register" (not vol. ii., as the printers got it in the "Atlantic").

> " Deep on the convent roofs the snows
> Are sparkling to the moon,"—

a poem of the quality of a diamond or a lily, in which the sentiment of vestal purity and mediæval Christianity is embodied in flawless music.

About a hundred years ago there were occasionally to be seen in the streets of Philadelphia certain strange foreign-looking persons offering country produce for sale. The men wore no hats, which were supplanted by the Capuchin hoods of the long white woolen gowns they wore (belted at the waist). The women concealed their faces when they walked. The visages of the men were pale, their beards long and shaggy, and their hair short. In summer the woolen dress described was exchanged for one of linen.

These people were Dunkers (or Tunkers, *Taeuffer*, i. e. Baptists) from Ephrata in Lancaster County, Pennsylvania, eleven miles out from Lancaster town. Their land lay in a beautiful vale between two wood-crowned hills, a stream flowing through the vale. The town of Ephrata lay on the southeastern slope of a little hill. At first the members of the community dwelt alone, each in a little cottage, that one might not interrupt the devotions of another. They were celibates, and of course the women dwelt apart. If any one married, he or she left the order, but settled in the neighborhood. They touched no animal food, had worship four times a day, and slept at night upon benches with little wooden blocks for pillows (reminds one of the Japanese and Chinese head-rests). The sisters drew beautiful ornamental texts in Gothic characters (the members of the order spoke German) to adorn the church walls.

The Dunkers had their origin in Schartzenau, Germany. Being frowned upon and shunned there, they separated from their Pietist brethren and came to Pennsylvania about 1719. The founder of the fraternity at Ephrata was Conrad Beissel, whose self-chosen fraternity name was Friedsam Gottrecht.

About 1738 (the date prefixed to Mr. Whittier's poem) their life became conventual, and the church building was converted into a nunnery called Kloster Kedar,[1] another building being erected for the men. It was now that monastic rules were adopted, and the Capuchin dress chosen.

The Dunkers denied original sin, reprobated war and all kinds of violence, and denied eternal punishment. Affection was their bond of union. A part of the title of one of their hymn-books reads, "The songs of the solitary and forsaken turtle-dove, that is, the Christian Church, . . . brought into spiritual rhymes, by a *Peaceable* pilgrim wandering to silent eternity." It is by Friedsam Gottrecht, who puns upon his Christian name in the italicized word. The Dunkers, it will be seen, spoke and wrote in a highly metaphorical, mystical style. These ascetics, in their ecstatic reveries and fasts, created an imaginary world, or heaven, wherein their imaginations ran riot. They believed in a mystical union with the Redeemer: "He was the little infant they carried *under their hearts*, the dear little lamb they dandled on their laps."[2]

---

[1] **Name** chosen in allusion to their agricultural, or pastoral, life, Kedar being the name of a pastoral tribe descended from Ishmael, —"the glory of Kedar," "the tents of Kedar," "the flocks of Kedar."

[2] Memoirs of the Historical Society of Pennsylvania for 1827,

A Pennsylvania critic of Mr. Whittier affirms that his sketch of Meister Eckhart, in "The Vision of Echard," and his "Hymn of the Dunkers," are both failures as historical studies, the lyrical element overpowering the historical. He thinks a Dunker mystic would not have singled out Rome and Geneva as the embodiment of the ecclesiasticism against which he protested, and says very truly that the sect "founded by Alexander Mack" never suffered from the "prison" and "the stake." Whittier catches the Adventist doctrine of the sect, but misses the mystic theosophical character of the doctrine as held by them.

One of the "Tent" poems is a blank-verse piece on "Abraham Davenport," the text for which was taken from old Dr. Dwight, of New Haven. "The 19th day of May, 1780," says he, "was a remarkable dark day. Candles were lighted in many houses; the birds were silent and disappeared, and the fowls retired to roost. The legislature of Connecticut was then in session at Hartford. A very general opinion prevailed that the day of judgment was at hand. The House of Representatives, being unable to transact their business, adjourned. A proposal to adjourn the Council was under consideration. When the opinion of Colonel Davenport was asked, he answered, 'I am against an adjournment. The day of judgment is either approaching or it is not. If it is not, there is no cause for an adjournment; if it is, I

---

ii. 130 ff. This seems to be the sole printed account of this curious order.

choose to be found doing my duty. I wish therefore that candles may be brought.'"[1]

> "And there he stands in memory to this day,
>   Erect, self-poised, a rugged face, half seen
>   Against the background of unnatural dark,
>   A witness to the ages as they pass
>   That simple duty hath no place for fear."

Abraham Davenport's grandfather was one of the founders of New Haven, a friend of the Regicides, Goffe and Whalley, and first suggested the establishment of the college now called Yale : he was known by the Indians as "so big study man."

When Abraham Davenport was well stricken in years, and, as Chief Justice of the Court of Common Pleas, was hearing a case at Danbury, the summoning hand of death was suddenly laid upon him. But, firm and unflinching to the last, he refused to leave the Court until he had given the charge to the jury, and called their attention to an article in the testimony that had escaped the notice of the counsel on both sides ; he then retired to his home, and was soon afterward found dead in his bed.

Whittier got the nucleus of his "Bridal of Pennacook" from Book I., Chapter XI., of that dry old chronicle of border wars and Indian history, the "New English Caanan," written by that dissolute and jolly Roger Wildrake, Thomas Morton. In this book Morton gives an account of the May Pole of his Merry Mount, and the far from innocent festivities connected with it. For the writing of this book he

---

[1] Quoted in Barber's Connecticut Historical Collections, p. 403.

was imprisoned for a year by the Puritan authorities, and fined.

In his "Prophecy of Samuel Sewall" Whittier speaks of Newbury as Sewall's "native town," but, says Tyler, Sewall was born at Horton, England. He also describes Sewall as an "old man," propped on his staff of age, when he made his famous prophecy; but Sewall was then forty-five years old. Samuel Sewall was one of the witchcraft judges, and the author of the quaint diary recently published. It was said that his wife—Hannah Hull, daughter of a goldsmith in Boston—received her own weight in silver pine-tree shillings as a wedding portion.

"The Golden Wedding of Longwood" was celebrated in the rich old rural town of Kennett, Chester County, near Philadelphia :—

" Again before me, with your names, fair Chester's landscape
        comes,
    Its meadows, woods, and ample barns, and quaint, stone-
        builded homes.

    The smooth-shorn vales, the wheaten slopes, the boscage
        green and soft,
    Of which their poet sings so well from towered Cedarcroft."

The poem was written for the fiftieth anniversary of the marriage of John and Hannah Cox, Quakers. Whittier, with Bayard Taylor who lived near by, often visited at the house of these Friends. Lowell, too, speaks of the "Arcadia of Friends in Chester County," and of the beautiful homes to which he was welcomed there.

" Conductor Bradley, (always may his name
   Be said with reverence !) as the swift doom came,
   Smitten to death, a crushed and mangled frame,

" Sank with the brake he grasped just where he stood
   To do the utmost that a brave man could.

   *   *   *   *   *   *   *

      " Lo ! the ghastly lips of pain,
   Dead to all thought save duty's, moved again:
   ' Put out the signals for the other train ! ' "

Following the date-clew given by the poet, I look up an old file of newspapers and find in the New York " Times," May 9, 1873, an obscure item, such as we see dozens of every year,—how two cars of a freight-train were thrown from the track at Tolles Station on the Hartford, Providence, and Fishkill Railroad, and Conductor George F. Bradley mortally injured. Heroic Conductor Bradley found his poet, and a hundred, a thousand, others just as heroic did not : that is all the difference. It is the privilege of genius to touch with immortal lustre what is ordinarily regarded as a dry prosaic idea.

APPENDIX.

I.

REFERENCE TABLE FOR DATES.

1807. Whittier born, December 17.

1821. Reads Burns for the first time.

1824. Writes poem on William Penn.
Uncle Moses dies.

1826. Poem, " The Deity," published.

1827. Attends Haverhill Academy six months.
Teaches school at West Amesbury.

1828. Another six months' term at Haverhill Academy.
Editor of the " American Manufacturer " in Boston.
In April, Garrison invites subscriptions for the purpose
of publishing a volume of Whittier's poems, to enable
him to pursue his studies longer. Project not realized.

1829. June, 1829, to July, 1830, at home.

1830-31. Edits the " New England Weekly Review " at Hart-
ford, Connecticut.
First book published at Hartford,—the little
" Legends of New England."

1831. Visits his father in his last sickness at the Haverhill
farm. Father dies in June.

1832. Gives up editorship of " New England Weekly Review."
From 1832 to 1837 manages the farm in Haverhill.
Writes for " Buckingham's New England Magazine."
In 1832 publishes " Moll Pitcher," and edits the " Lit-
erary Remains of J. G. C. Brainard."

1833. Publishes " Justice and Expediency."
Delegate to the National Anti-slavery Convention at
Philadelphia.

1834. Corresponding Secretary of the Haverhill Anti-slavery
Society.

1835. Mobbed at Concord, New Hampshire.

Chosen member of the Massachusetts State Legislature.

1836. Publishes "Mogg Megone."

Editor of Haverhill "Gazette."

1837. In New York as Secretary of the National Anti-slavery Society. Visits John Quincy Adams, and edits that statesman's Letters to his Constituents; also edits Miss Harriet Martineau's "Views of Slavery." First collection of his poems issued by Isaac Knapp.

1838. Joseph Healey, of Philadelphia, publishes a collection of his poems. From 1838 to 1840 Whittier is in Philadelphia, editing the "Pennsylvania Freeman." Burning of Pennsylvania Hall in 1838.

1839. In December, 1839, still in Philadelphia (see Preface to "The North Star").

1840. Edits a booklet of poems called "The North Star."

Farm sold; family removes to Amesbury.

1841. Helps edit the "American and Foreign Anti-slavery Reporter" (a monthly) in New York City.

1842. Temporary editor of the "Emancipator" in Boston (during December, 1841, and January, 1842).

1843. "Lays of my Home" published.

1844. In Lowell, editing the "Middlesex Standard." First English edition of his poems published in London; introduction by Elizur Wright.

1845. Publishes "The Stranger in Lowell."

1846. Aunt Mercy Hussey dies. "Voices of Freedom" published in Philadelphia by Thomas S. Cavender.

1847. "Supernaturalism in New England." 1847-1850, associate, or corresponding, editor of the "National Era."

1849. "Voices of Freedom" (Philadelphia); Mussey's complete edition of his poems published in Boston; "Leaves from Margaret Smith's Journal."

When Esbern Snare was building Kallundborg church, the work did not go forward as fast as he wished. So he accepted the offer of a Troll to help him :—

> " ' Build, O Troll, a church for me
> At Kallundborg by the mighty sea ;
> Build it stately, and build it fair,
> Build it quickly,' said Esbern Snare."

The Troll agreed, on condition that he should tell him his name when he was through, or forfeit his heart and eyes. Esbern accepted the terms, and the work went bravely on. One day, when all was finished except one pillar, Esbern Snare was wandering disconsolate in the fields, and, chancing to lie down on Ulshöi Banke to rest, he heard a Troll-wife within the earth say, " Be still, my child ; to-morrow Fin thy father will come and give thee Esbern Snare's eyes and heart to play with." (This is the English of the motto prefixed to Whittier's poem.) Esbern returned home overjoyed, and saluted the Troll by name, which so enraged him that in spite he immediately vanished with the remaining half-pillar in his arms.

Trolls always lose their power when a Christian man calls them by name. The above legend is told of St. Olaf and his building the first church in Norway, and of the building of the cathedral of Lund, opposite Copenhagen, by St. Lawrence. Kallundborg church still stands in the town of that name on the west coast of Seeland, its five towers rendering it a conspicuous mark for miles around. The legend appears also in Jón Arnason's collections of Icelandic folk-tales under the title, " Who built Reynir Church ? "

1850. "Songs of Labor"; "Old Portraits and Modern Sketches"; "Little Eva"; collected poems published in London.

1853. "The Chapel of the Hermits," "A Sabbath Scene."

1854. "Literary Recreations," "Maud Muller."

1856. "The Panorama."

1857. Mother died; Ticknor's blue and gold edition of poems; "Skipper Ireson."

1860. Chosen Member of Electoral College; publishes "Home Ballads, and Other Poems."

1861. Death of his sister, Mary Whittier Cartland.

1863. "In War Time, and Other Poems"; "Barbara Frietchie" published in October in "Atlantic Monthly"; complete edition of his works.

1864. Again member of the Electoral College; death of Elizabeth Whittier, September 3.

1866. "Snow-Bound"; Prose Works, 2 Vol. edition; "National Lyrics" published.

1867. "The Tent on the Beach."

1868. "Among the Hills." Also an illustrated edition of his poems. "Whittier College" founded at Salem, Iowa.

1869. Illustrated edition of "Ballads of New England."

1870. "Miriam, and Other Poems."

1871. "Child-Life : A Collection of Poems."

1872. "The Pennsylvania Pilgrim."

1873. "Child-Life in Prose"; Journal of John Woolman edited.

1874. "Mabel Martin."

1875. "Songs of Three Centuries"; "Hazel Blossoms."

1876. "Centennial Hymn" published.

1877. Seventieth birthday celebrated in Boston ; founding of a Whittier Club in Haverhill.

1878. " The Vision of Echard."

1881. "The King's Missive."

1882. Letters of Lydia Maria Child edited; " Bay of Seven Islands " published.

1883. Death of Matthew Franklin Whittier, January 7.

1884. Portrait of Whittier unveiled in Friends' School in Providence, Rhode Island.

1885. September 10, Reunion of Haverhill Academy graduates. " Poems of Nature " published.

1886. "St. Gregory's Guest, and Recent Poems," published; dedicated to General S. C. Armstrong.

1887. Birthday celebrated by school children throughout the country; Boston " Advertiser's " Whittier Memorial issue; social greetings and gifts of friends at Oak Knoll.

1890. Birthday again celebrated at Oak Knoll. For his ballad " The Captain's Well " receives $1,000 from " New York Ledger."

1891. Eighty-fourth birthday celebrated at home of Joseph Cartland in Newburyport, Mr. Whittier being present.

1892. Death of Whittier at Hampton Falls, N. H., September 7. Publication of his posthumous volume, " At Sundown," dedicated to E. C. Stedman.

II.

BIBLIOGRAPHY.

Notes on Rare and Early Editions.[1]

COLLECTED WORKS.

New England Legends in Prose and Verse.
Hartford : Hanmer & Phelps, 1831.

A slender volumet issued in February by the publishers of the " New England Weekly Review," which Whittier had been editing. It is his first book, and is now suppressed. A copy was sold in Boston for $14. The poems are juvenile in character. Titles of some of the sensational prose tales are " The Midnight Attack," " The Rattlesnake Hunter," " The Human Sacrifice," and " The Unquiet Sleeper." " The Spectre Ship " is a tale in verse.

Poems written during the Progress of the Abolition Question in the United States, between the years 1830 and 1838. Boston:
Isaac Knapp, 25 Cornhill, 1837.

Very rare, and quite a pretty booklet ; the first separate collection of his poems. Price 37½ cts. " Issued in compliance with the urgent request of a large number of the admirers of Whittier " (p. 97). Garrison is thought to have been the

---

[1] All the information imparted here has been derived at first-hand from the original copies and first editions.

editor. Underwood says published in '38; so perhaps there were other editions. Most of the poems were republished in the " Emancipator " of 1839 and 1840. The frontispiece is a fine copper-plate engraving, " just received from London "; it shows Britannia rebuking a planter who is whipping a slave, and illustrates a stanza in Cowper's " Morning Dream,"—a poem which is prefixed to the text. Facing each other on fly-leaves are two medallions of slaves in chains, one a man and the other a woman. Each poem is followed by a pretty tail-piece,—a branch of a tree with fruit, or a sheaf of grain, etc., emblems of peace. The weak poem " To George Bancroft, Esq., Author of the Worcester Democratic Address," not afterwards reprinted; nor the fine verses on " Governor McDuffie "; nor a poem by Elizabeth Whittier, " Our Countrymen."

Ballads, Anti-slavery, etc. Joseph Healey: Philadelphia, 1838. 180 pp.

Issued November 1, Whittier being then editor of the " Freeman " in Philadelphia. Healey was the financial agent of the National Anti-slavery Society. The motto is from Coleridge: " I concluded this was *not* the time to keep silence; for Truth should be spoken at all times, but more especially at those times when to speak Truth is dangerous."

Lays of my Home, and Other Poems. Wm. D. Ticknor. Boston, 1843.

Issued in May; the dedication, " To John Pierpont," is included in the recent complete poetical works. Twenty-three poems, chiefly non-slavery.

Voices of Freedom. Philadelphia: Thos. S. Cavender; Boston: Waite, Pierce & Co.; New York: Wm. Harned. 5th ed., 1846, 192 pp.

" Several years having elapsed since the first edition," the preface states. Underwood describes an ed. with the title " Voices of Freedom. From 1833 to 1848," published by Lindsay & Blakiston: Philad., 1849.

Poems by John G. Whittier. Boston : Benjamin B. Mussey & Co., 1849.

This is, on the whole, the most beautiful ed. of the poems ; a second ed. appeared in 1850; copyrighted 1848 ; an ed. from same plates appeared in 1856 (new title-page) by Sanborn, Carter, & Bazin of Boston. The exquisite steel plates (by H. Billings), the heavy paper, and large type are explained by the fact that Mussey was a Free-Soiler, and took a pride in seeing the laureate's verses in rich dress; he died in 1857. The plates were bought by Ticknor & Fields. Mussey was a pill-seller as well as a publisher. Whittier was overcome with amazement, and thought the man was demented, when, one day, as they were walking in Cornhill, Mussey offered him $500 for the copyright of his poems and a percentage on the sales. However, he closed with his offer, and was still more astonished at the large sales of the hitherto ill-dressed and somewhat obscure children of his brain.

Other noteworthy collections are the little 2-vol. blue and gold ed. of Ticknor & Fields, 1857, and the 4-vol. ed. of 1888 by Houghton, Mifflin & Co. The latter forms part of a superb 7-vol. ed. of Whittier's complete works, with four admirable portraits, hundreds of new illustrative notes by Whittier, as well as new prefaces, entirely new arrangement, or grouping, of the poems, table of first lines, inclusion of many early poems which had been dropped out or forgotten, and a collection of fugitive prose pieces. This ed. is worth all the others put together, for the scholar. The present volume, however, contains a half-dozen of Mr. Whittier's most interesting poems that are not included in this Boston edition of the poems, besides many valuable letters and prose articles not included in the volumes of prose in said edition.

SINGLE POEMS.

Moll Pitcher. Boston : Carter & Hendee, 1832.

The two copies I have seen are in pamphlet form, and probably the whole ed. was of that character. The brochure is printed by Joseph H. Buckingham of Newburyport; no author's name anywhere given ; 28 pp. in all, including a page of notes. Poem dedicated to Eli Todd of Hartford; motto from Cornelius Agrippa; prefatory note by Whittier. Nearly a column quotation was made from the poem by Garrison in his "Liberator," May 8, 1840, eight years after its publication.

There is a poor dramatic poem, "Moll Pitcher," by a certain J. S. Jones. It was put on the boards at the original National Theatre in Boston in 1839, the part of Moll being played by Mrs. William Pelby. The play was given in every State in the Union which then permitted dramatic performances. The plot is entirely different from Whittier's, though the heroine appears as the conventional witch, with red cloak, spectacles, crutch, and black cat, much as in Whittier's poem.

Mogg Megone. Boston : Light & Stearns, No. 1 Cornhill. 1836.

A tiny 32mo of 69 pp.

Little Eva ; Uncle Tom's Guardian Angel. Boston and Cleveland, 1852. 4to, 4 pp.

Music by Emilio Manuel ; present title " Eva."

A Sabbath Scene. Boston : Ticknor, Reed, & Fields, 1853.

A thin volume, illustrated by Baker, Smith, and Andrew, in quaint Sunday-school style.

Snow-Bound is translated in Karl Knortz's "Zwei Amerikanische Idyllen," with the title " Eingeschneit," " Snowed In."

THE NORTH STAR.

The North Star: The Poetry of Freedom by her Friends. Philadelphia: Printed by Merrihew & Thompson, No. 7 Carter's Alley, 1840.

Cream-colored covers; motto from William Penn; preface dated "Philadelphia, 12th mo., 1839." That it was edited by Whittier is certain. In looking over an old bundle of " Emancipators" I lighted on a notice of the book by the editor, Joshua Leavitt, in his issue of Jan. 9, 1840. This was the very time when Whittier was his contributor and editorial assistant. Says Mr. Leavitt: " That it is edited in the best taste, and by one whose real worth does not need to sound its own praises, may be certainly known from the exclusion of the following lines, which, we happen to know, were written expressly for the work, but excluded by the editor." The lines contain a prophecy that has long since been fulfilled :—

TO JOHN G. WHITTIER.

BY JONATHAN BLANCHARD.

Thy soul is gentle, WHITTIER—yet thy mind
Was made to startle and instruct mankind :
And tyrants dread thee, gentle though thou art—
A lamb in temper with a lion's heart !
Yet so averse to scourge the sins of men,
That others' sufferings only move thy pen.
If thou alone hadst felt the oppressor's wrong,
The world had lost the lightning of thy song.
God, in thy genius, crowned thee with the art
To pour thyself upon the human heart—
Bid thine own soul to thrill along thy line,
An inbreathed fervor only not divine.
New England yet shall hail her gifted son,
When Freedom's work (*and Slavery's*) is done ;
And own thy fire, caught from her pilgrim-graves

Hath taught the world that *poets are no slaves!*
The slave shall hail thee, when his sorrows end,
In nature, as by name and birth, a FRIEND.

In a long notice of the book in the " Liberator," Garrison says : " Right glad are we to find that the anti-slavery women of Philadelphia, at their recent fair, have procured the publication of a beautiful little volume, all glittering with light, called ' The North Star : The Poetry of Freedom by her Friends.' We are indebted for a copy of it, superbly bound, to our esteemed friend Lucretia Mott, and have perused its contents with a keen relish and perfect satisfaction."

The preface is in Whittier's style exactly, and is dated Quaker fashion. So is the longest poem in the book, " Ægypt : a Fragment from an Unpublished Poem " (" Philadelphia, Eleventh mo., 1839 "). I had attributed this to Whittier, from internal evidence of italicizing, etc., before I read Garrison's notice in which he also says he ventures to attribute it to him. The only poem accredited to Whittier in the contents is " The World's Convention " ; out his " Exiles " ballad here appears for the first time. Among the contributors are Lucy Hooper (the Brooklyn, Long Island, young lady on whose subsequent untimely death Whittier has a poem), Elizabeth Whittier, James T. Fields, and W. L. J. Kiderlen, who has a poem in German,—" Der Sterbende Sclave."

Those who have examined the old files know that very many of Whittier's poems appeared anonymously at first, and it would have been inconsistent with his habits to acknowledge the editing of an anthology which contained three or four poems of his own. And, then, the printing of that " Ægypt " poem probably gave him qualms afterwards.

Justice and Expediency.—Whittier published his pamphlet " Justice and Expediency " in June, 1833 (500 copies). In September it appeared as No. 4 of Vol. I. of the " Anti-slavery Reporter " (monthly), the organ of the American Anti-slavery Society, and is advertised as for sale by the single copy or by the thousand. This is evidently the Tappan issue of 5,000 copies. The " Anti-slavery Reporter " was merged with an " American Anti-slavery Reporter," and the name was afterwards revived by Lewis Tappan in the " American and Foreign Anti-slavery Reporter," which Whittier helped edit in 1840.

Notes.—In 1856, C. H. Brainard, of Boston, published on one sheet the portraits of Whittier, Seward, Sumner, John P. Hale, H. W. Beecher, Salmon P. Chase, and Horace Greeley, styling them the "Seven Champions of Freedom. Rather an ill-assorted group ! Whittier's portrait occupies the place of honor, in the centre.

Poems of Whittier especially autobiographic are " Burns," " To J. T. F.," " My Birthday," " My Namesake," " My Triumph," " My Playmate," and " Benedicite."

The first volume of that mild and dainty annual, the " Liberty Bell," contains five stanzas by Whittier, which, like a number of his early poems, he has wisely dropped. The last remark applies to " Reflections of a Belle," in " Liberator," Sept. 10, 1831 (quoted from " New England Weekly Review "), to several pieces in " The Yankee," and early verses in his " Legends of New England." The " Liberator," Sept. 2, '64, has a letter by Whittier in defence of General Fremont, who was nominated for the Presidency at same time with Lincoln. Whittier cherishes the kindliest feelings for the old standard-bearer of freedom in '56.

In 1846 Whittier published a poem on the Mexican War. The entire piece is given in the " Literary World " of Boston, March 22, '84. The following stanza is the only one of any particular merit :—

> " Ghostly hands in Tenochitlan
> Strike the old Aztec battle-drum ;
> Sharp of beak and strong of talon,
> Lo ! Mexitli's eagles come !"

The writer was told in Amesbury by a friend of Mr. Whittier's that his nephew, Mr. Pickard, was one day passing the ash-barrel in the yard, when he noticed a roll of wet crumpled manuscript.   Smoothing it carefully out, he discovered to his joy that it was the original draft of " Snow-Bound," written on fragments of paper pasted together.   He spread it out in the orchard to dry, but on returning after an hour's absence found his treasure gone! The poet himself had found it, and destroyed it.

For an inscription to be engraved below the cliff-carved Indian of Preston Powers in Colorado, Mr. Whittier wrote in 1891 these strong lines :—

> " The eagle stooping from yon snow-blown peaks,
>   For the wild hunter and the bison seeks
>   In the changed world below, and finds alone
>   Their graven semblance in the eternal stone."

INDEX.

www.ingramcontent.com/pod-product-compliance
Lightning Source LLC
Chambersburg PA
CBHW021808110726
47902CB00006B/1696

www.ingramcontent.com/pod-product-compliance
Lightning Source LLC
Chambersburg PA
CBHW021808110726
47902CB00006B/1696